The Twenty-Third Psalm

Surviving the Rwandan Genocide,
And Everything Before, And Everything After

A Novel

Philip J. Keough

For information, please contact:
Philip J. Keough at
philipjkeough@gmail.com

ISBN: 979-8-218-57067-5

Cover photo ©2024
Cover design by Nick Kent

This is a work of fiction: Unless otherwise stated, all characters, names, places, businesses, events, and incidents in this book are either the product of the author's imagination or used in a fictitious manner. Any resemblance to actual people, living or dead, or actual events is purely coincidental.

Table of Contents

Chapter One: The Nightmare

I am running down back alleys, between walled compounds and hibiscus bushes, in Biryogo, my neighborhood. Biryogo is the center of Hutu Power, the group that collected the names and addresses of all the Tutsis in Rwanda, the execution lists. My name is on one of those lists, and I am running from a Hutu mob. I am just a teenage girl, but they don't care.

On a bullhorn, in the distance, I can hear a man commanding, "*KORA AKAZI KAWE*!" (Kinyarwanda for DO YOUR WORK!)

By "work" he means killing Tutsis, Tutsis like me. For months on RTLM, the radio station Hutu Power has been using to incite and organize the genocide, they have been calling us "*inyenzi*" (cockroaches) and saying that we must be stamped out.

I'm running ahead of the mob. I turn down an alley I think I know.

I'm running as fast as I can, but they are so many. There are high brick walls on either side of me, too high to climb. And even if I did, I know they all have sharp, jagged, broken glass set into the concrete along the top.

I realize that I've gotten lost. My heart is pounding, and in my panic, I stumble over a tree root. I try to maintain my stride, but I lose my balance and scrape my arm on the rough bricks. I cry out in pain and then slap my hands over my mouth as soon as I do. Did I give myself away? I look back.

"Over here!" one of the Hutus yells. I can see him at the end of the alley behind me, motioning to the others. I'm still running away from them, but now I can see that there's another Hutu mob in front of me.

Oh no, I am thinking. *This is it. I am going to die!*

But then, off to my left, I can see that there's another alley! When I get to the point where I can see down it, I see that it leads to a road. *That's the road that runs in front of our church!* I recognize, as I sprint up the empty alley.

When I reach the road, I see the gate to our church compound. And, by some miracle, it's been left it open a crack. So, I sprint across the road, squeeze myself through the open gate, and run inside the compound.

I know the church is locked, so, even if there was someone inside, I'd have to pound on one of the doors so they could let me in, and that noise could attract the mob. *So that's not an option,* I think, as I'm searching for someplace else to hide.

And then I see it, off to my right. *Oh God, no!* I think. It's a raised rectangle of grass with a knee-high cement wall around its base and a stone at one end. It fills me with terror, but it's the only place to hide.

Just then I hear the crash of the gate being ripped open. I turn to see the mob rushing into the compound behind me.

They are unwashed and bloody. Their clothes are ratty, but they are each wearing their own version of a uniform: at least one of the colors of the old Rwandan flag: red, yellow, and green. Most have machetes in their hands, but a few have made their own *massues* (maces) by pounding nails through clubs. Some of them are blowing whistles over and over again like this is some kind of insane party.

Even though I know they've been trained by the Rwandan Army (I've seen it) they don't move like soldiers. They move like hyenas, crafty and slow, focused, and inching closer. They smile like they know they're getting away with something. I'm backing away from them. Then the ones closest to me rush in, drawing their weapons over their heads, ready to hack at me.

The one who gets to me first shoves me down onto the rectangle of grass and jumps on top of me. I can smell his rank sweat and the sour rotten alcohol smell of *urwagwa* (home-made banana beer) on his breath. He puts the edge of his machete to my throat. I know he is going to rape me, and then he's going kill me!

Then I hear Mama's voice calling to me. "Elise…" she says.

I am screaming, "No! NO!!"

In the distance, I hear Imani screaming, "Mommy, Mommy!"

I opened my eyes to find I was in my bed, and Imani, my six-year-old, standing next to me, crying, "Mommy! What's wrong?" in frightened sobs.

Paul, my eleven-year-old, was standing next to her. He had that horrible look he gets on his face when he's really scared.

"*Mana we!* (Oh, my God!) My sweethearts!" I said, rushing out of bed, kneeling down in front of them, and pulling them close.

"We heard you screaming!" Imani managed to get out between squeaking, uneven breaths, with tears streaming down her cheeks.

"Are you okay, Mom?" Paul asked.

I drew back a little, with a hand on each of their faces. I looked into their eyes. I could tell they were waiting for an explanation, again.

Then I found myself putting on that same smile, like a mask, and saying, "Everything's fine. Your Mama just had a bad dream. I'm sorry I woke you up." I hugged them again. "Go back to sleep," I told them. "It's okay. It's nothing. Everything's fine."

I gave them each a kiss.

I wanted them to feel soothed, but they didn't look soothed. They looked confused, like they wanted to ask more questions. Even so, they both turned and started walking down the carpeted hall, back to their rooms.

I closed the door behind them and let out a long sigh. I felt drained. I realized that I was crying. I wiped away my tears with the palms of my hands as I walked, heavily, back to my bed and dropped down onto it.

I just lied to my children, I thought. *Again. It wasn't "just a dream," and it certainly wasn't "nothing." It was another nightmare about the genocide!*

And even though it happened so many years ago, it's still controlling my life. It's my monster in the dark that I'm always trying so hard to not think about. It keeps invading my dreams. Trying to avoid it is keeping me from telling my children about my past, making me lie to them over and over again. And right now, it's keeping me from getting back to sleep.

I wished that Sam, my husband, was home. Usually, when my nightmares woke me up like this, he was there to talk to me, to hold me, and comfort me. But now I was alone. It was just me and my thoughts.

I sat there for a long time.

I just can't see any way forward like this, I thought. *I can't keep doing what I'm doing. I can't keep avoiding my past. It isn't working. There's only one way left to go. I have to go back. I have to remember.*

I remembered being happy as a very, very young girl. I remembered feeling safe and feeling loved by Mama and Papa, my older brother, Robert, and my older sister, Claudine. I remembered the warmth of sunlight falling on my skin, as I played one of my favorite games: running between the rows of corn in our yard, with Robert chasing after me, calling playfully, "I'm gonna get you!" I would run away from him, shrieking with laughter.

Our house was on a big piece of land, high up on the side of a hill, where Mama and Papa grew all sorts of things: corn, beans, sweet potatoes, cabbage, cassava, and one of my favorites: *matoke* (green plantains).

Sometimes, as I was running through the garden, I would look up and be dazzled by the view: steep, terraced, green hills, with hills beyond them, and hills beyond them, for as far as the eye could see. This was before everyone put up high walls around their property, back when everything seemed so open, and big, and wonderful. Back then, from our piece of land, high up on the side of our hill in Biryogo, it felt like I was looking out over the whole world.

It was a world of greens. There were dark greens of pine and acacia trees, and light greens of corn and the grasses that grew everywhere. There were the blue greens of eucalyptus trees, and yellow greens of the giant leaves on the banana and plantain trees. There were the brown greens of sorghum and wheat fields, and red greens of the flowering plants. Everywhere you looked there were plants and trees thriving in the warm sunshine and the moist, clear, mountain air. Every slope, terraced hillside, and valley was thick with crops, or forests, or high grasses. From our compound, I could see the houses and farms on the hills across from us, with their dark brown rusted tin roofs. And sometimes I would see the people who lived there, working in their fields. I would wave to them, and they would smile and wave back.

And above all of these beautiful green hills, there were deep, deep blue skies with puffy white clouds that looked like giant mountains. This was the Rwanda I knew then: warm, beautiful, and safe.

But all of that changed one night when I was five years old.

*   *   *

"Elise! Claudine! Wake up! Come with me! Quickly!"

Mama, who was usually so calm, sounded frantic. I had never seen her so upset. It made me feel cold and sick to my stomach.

"What is it, Mama?" I asked, feeling my heart beat fast in my chest.

"We have to go get your father! Come with me! Outside! Now!"

In Rwanda, when something bad is happening in your village or your neighborhood, you make a high-pitched noise and tap your lips with your flat hand to alarm everyone. It's called the *induru*. When someone in the neighborhood starts it, everyone immediately drops whatever they are doing, joins the chorus, and rushes to see what is the matter. I could hear the induru echoing across the hillside, ghostly and terrifying. I could hear men yelling in the distance and Papa yelling back.

Claudine was already putting on her shoes and saying, "Elise! We've got to go! Right now!"

I had to run as fast as my little legs would carry me to keep up with Mama, Claudine, and Robert, as we rushed up the rise between our front door and the road, toward where all of the yelling was coming from. By the light of the moon and a few dim lanterns and flashlights, with each step I was seeing more and more of what was going on, and the more I saw, the more I wanted to turn away. But I couldn't.

There were three men, men I thought were Papa's friends, men he had invited over to the house many times for parties, men who were his tenants. Papa owned the land they farmed. But now they were standing over him, yelling at him, holding machetes, kicking him! All around them was a crowd of maybe fifty. Some were still making the induru, and others were just watching, not sure what to do.

Even though he was lying on the ground, bloodied, his face swollen so much that it made him sound strange, Papa was yelling back at the three men, "Back off before I give you a beating you won't soon forget!"

"Jean-Michel!" Mama yelled at one of the men with the machetes.

He stopped and looked at Mama.

"You know that I am good friends with your Mama! **I SEE YOU!** What would she say if she knew that you were out here drunk, fighting, and out of control like this?"

"She would say that I should kill this Tutsi cockroach for trying to bleed money out of me I don't have!" Jean-Michel yelled, slurring his words.

"Sonia!" Papa cried out, blood dripping from his mouth. We were closer now. I could see how swollen Papa's face was. He tried and failed to get to his feet. "Help me up!" he commanded from the dirt.

"You get away from my husband! All of you!" Mama yelled. "Go home and sleep it off, and we will work this out later, when you aren't so drunk! Children, help me get your father home. Come on, come on!"

The four of us got under Papa's long arms, Mama and Claudine on one side, Robert and me on the other, and we got Papa up on his feet. He could barely walk, but we got him back inside the house and locked the door. Then we got him into bed.

Following Mama's directions, we gathered towels and a basin of water from the faucet behind the house. Mama washed and dressed Papa's many wounds in silence, and we all helped.

When we'd finished, Mama brought us out into the hall and told us to go back to bed. "You have church in the morning and then school," she said. She seemed so calm. "Try to get some sleep."

"Mama…" I began.

"Yes, *kobwa*?" (a Kinyarwanda term of endearment for daughter) she said, looking into my eyes.

I didn't understand anything I'd just seen. *Why did that man call Papa a Tutsi cockroach?* I wondered. *Why were those men all holding machetes? Weren't they Papa's friends?* "What happened, Mama? Why were those men beating Papa?"

"Oh, Sweetheart," Mama said. "Don't worry. Everything's fine. Sometimes when men drink, they have these little fights."

"But Mama, Papa's face!"

"He'll be fine, kobwa. Don't worry. Good night, my love," she said, and kissed me on the forehead.

I was feeling something then that I had never felt before.

Whenever Mama had used these words and kissed me on the forehead before, I had felt soothed. But this was so confusing. I didn't feel soothed at all. I felt like I was being put away, like a plate on a shelf, or a shirt in a drawer. But I didn't know what else to do. So, I said, "Goodnight, Mama," and went back to my room.

Once I had gotten back into bed, I whispered, "Claudine? Claudine!"

"Go to sleep, Elise," she said. "We have to get up for church in a couple of hours! No more talking!"

I lay there looking into the darkness. I turned my head and looked out our bedroom window. Before that night, I had always wondered why it had bars on it. But it was starting to make sense. I nodded slowly as I thought about the heavy steel mesh outer doors on the front and back of the house.

Even though she was trying not to make any noise, I could tell that Claudine was crying. From across the hall, I could hear Mama too, sniffling and taking short, sharp breaths in between sobs she was trying to keep quiet. I couldn't stop wondering why everyone was trying to act like nothing was wrong, when clearly, we were all upset, as I drifted off into a short, nervous sleep.

Chapter Two: Everything's Fine

We had only slept for a few hours when the church bells woke us up the next morning. We washed and dressed, but Papa, who was usually washing and shaving right next to us, and getting ready to go to work at his delivery van business, wasn't there.

When we were all ready, Mama came to the door to meet us. Usually, she would be all dressed up, ready to take us to church, but that morning she was still in her robe.

"Aren't you coming with us?" I asked.

"Papa's not feeling well," she said. "He's staying in bed today, and I'm going to be looking after him. Robert and Claudine will take you to church. Go on," she said, waving her hands toward the front door.

I remember feeling confused and cold. It was clear that there wasn't going to be any discussion of what had happened the night before. I looked around. The sun was shining. Everyone was acting as though it was a normal morning, as though we hadn't saved Papa from being beaten to death just a few hours before.

As we walked to church, I tried to ask questions. "Claudine? Claudine?" I tried to get her attention, but she just hiked Gabriel, my three-year-old brother higher on her hip, walked faster, and quickly got ahead of me.

I watched our neighbors walk by us on the street. I thought about how everyone was always smiling and acting so "nice" to each other, how Mama and Papa were always helping out our neighbors when they needed it by giving them food from our small farm, how I had seen Papa lending money to other men from the neighborhood and saying, "Pay it back when you can."

But some of those same people had almost beaten Papa to death. They were men that he drank with at the bar. I once saw one of them with his arm around Papa's neck, smiling, and talking about how great Papa was for charging such low rent to farm a piece of his land.

"Robert?" I said, but he had sped up too. All I could see of him and Claudine were their backs.

Without even turning his head to look back at me, Robert said, "Everything's fine, Elise." Well, I knew that wasn't true. And this was coming from Robert, the one I always thought I could rely on to be straight with me.

It felt like the earth was coming apart under my feet. With all of the lies I could suddenly see all around me, what could I hold on to as true? I felt sick to my stomach. I stopped walking and started to cry.

Robert stopped and turned around. "Elise…" he said, kneeling down in front of me. "Don't cry." He was trying to smile. He took a handkerchief out of his pocket and wiped away my tears. Then he hugged me, picked me up, and carried me the rest of the way to church. I was still confused, but I no longer felt so completely alone.

We didn't really see Papa for the next two weeks. Whenever I asked about him, Mama would say, "He's resting."

The more questions I would ask, the more Claudine would glare at me, even though I knew she had just as many questions as I did. But she was trying to get her answers from Robert instead of Mama. They always seemed to be having whispered arguments as they walked ahead of me each morning on the way to church. I could never quite hear what they were saying. But every once in a while, I would catch a word or a phrase, words like "Hutu" and "Tutsi" and phrases like, "…more dangerous for us now."

Sometimes I caught pieces of whispered conversations coming from Mama and Papa's room, too. The only way I could get any information about what was really going on was by secretly listening in the hall, outside their door. I could hear Mama washing Papa's wounds and saying things to him. It often sounded like they were yelling at each other, but all in whispers.

I got into the habit of walking through the house silently.

One night, as I was on my way to the outhouse, I could hear that Mama and Papa were talking. I sopped outside their door and strained to listen. I could only make out some of the words.

"I know … … didn't want to talk … … … …, … … … respected your wishes, … … need to know now. Please … …, …. happened that …?"

"I … … … the bar … … drink after work." Papa sounded odd. I guessed that it was because his face was still so swollen.

I crept a bit closer to their door so that I could hear better.

"… … hadn't paid me rent on the land in three months."

"Why not?"

"Sonia, they're Hutu. We're Tutsi. If they don't pay, who's going to do anything about it? The Hutu police? The Hutu government? Our 'glorious' Hutu President Habyarimana, who only paves the one road in our neighborhood that takes him to his party house at the top of the hill? No! No one will act to help a Tutsi. So, I knew it was up to me to get the rent money. I was having a few beers with them after work. I started joking about it."

"But you know better than that, Joseph."

"I thought they were joking right along with me until Jean-Michel wanted to start an argument. You know me. I would never start a fight."

"But you'll finish it!"

"I am a strong man, Sonia."

"Well, yes. But, I've…I've never seen you lose. I've seen you beat three men before. This isn't the first time I've cleaned you up after a fight, but…they almost killed you this time, Joseph!"

"I think they had it planned. All three of them were on me in seconds. And they must have had their machetes behind the bar. I threw them off and tried to run home, but they caught me."

"And that's where I found you in the dirt."

"… Yes."

"They were willing to kill you just to avoid paying the rent?"

"They're Hutus. They're poor. And with the way things have been going lately, with the economy? It's been even harder for them. Besides, you've heard the radio-"

"I don't listen to that!"

"Our neighbors have it on. It's on in the market, Sonia. It's everywhere! If they had killed me, what would have happened to them? Nothing. The police might have even thanked them."

Just then, I heard Claudine getting out of bed. I silently hurried past Mama and Papa's door and continued on my way to the outhouse.

A few days later, as I was passing Mama and Papa's door on my way outside, I heard them whispering again:

"Sonia, my love, if we're going to live, we're going to live. If we're going to die, we're going to die. We're not going to live our lives in fear, right? Remember? That's what we decided when we came back from Burundi? That we wanted the rest of our children to be born and to grow up in Rwanda?"

"That's what *you* decided!"

"We had nothing there, Sonia! Here we have a business! We have land!"

"That your Hutu 'friends' would rather kill you for than pay rent on!"

"What do you want, Sonia? To go back to Burundi? To let ourselves be chased out of our own country? Again? Rwanda is our country, too!"

There was a pause. I was afraid that they had sensed that someone was listening. I was just about to rush away as silently as I could. But instead, I stayed still and kept listening. I didn't hear Mama coming toward the door.

Then I knew what it was. I had seen them do it before. They must have been looking at each other, and then Papa must have smiled in that way he had, that could melt any hard feelings. "We haven't died yet, Sonia," I heard him say. "I think God must be looking out for us."

"*I'm* the one who picked you up out of that ditch, Joseph, not God!"

"Well, see? Between God, and you, and the kids…"

I could hear Mama laughing. "I'd kiss you…" I heard her say.

"I know," Papa said. "You can hardly resist. Easy, Ow! Easy!"

"Oh, Joseph, look what they've done to your beautiful face."

"I thought women found scars sexy. Besides, I'm still the tallest man in Biryogo. It will be alright. Everything's going to be fine. Now, my head is killing me. Could you please go and get me some Panadol?"

"Of course," Mama said.

I rushed out of the hall as quickly and quietly as I could and went back outside to help Claudine and Robert pick beans.

"Elise!" Claudine said. "Where have you been? Are you okay?"

"Uh...I'm...fine," I said. "Everything's... fine."

Claudine smiled. For the first time in weeks, it didn't feel like she was mad at me. It seemed like I had finally chosen the right thing to say.

I picked beans in silence, going over this new information in my head. I felt like I was about to burst with questions, but I knew by then that bringing them up with Claudine or Robert was a waste of time.

Soon Mama came outside with Gabriel wrapped in a blanket, holding him against her back. She began picking beans next to me. I felt like maybe, if I asked just the right question, in just the right way, if I made it easy for her, then Mama might tell me the truth, or at least some small part of it. I thought as hard as my five-year-old brain could think. Finally, I came out with:

"Mama?"

"Yes, kobwa?"

"Is it...bad to be a Tutsi?"

"No, of course not."

"Is...is Papa... in ... trouble for being a Tutsi?" I looked into Mama's eyes. I thought that I could see a flash of something. Maybe I would finally get a real answer!

But then she smiled that same smile, that mask, and said exactly what she always did: "No-no, kobwa. Everything's fine."

And then, one morning, as I was going out to the wash area behind the house to brush my teeth, there was Papa, shaving, just like it was any other morning, not as though the last time I had seen him, two weeks ago, we had saved him from being beaten to death!

I just stood there, unable to move, part of me wanting to rush over to him and hug him, and part of me just furious with him for putting on this act that everything was normal, even though I could tell he was stifling the urge to wince each time he drew the razor along the edge of his still badly bruised jaw.

He looked over at me and smiled. "Good morning, sweetheart," he said.

I kept staring at him for a moment, not sure what to do or say. I wanted to ask him so many questions.

"Elise!" Claudine called from inside the house.

Papa smiled again and said, "If you keep standing there, staring at me like that, you're going to be late for church."

I turned and ran through the house. It was clear to me that with Papa back on his feet, the beating was another one of those things that no one was going to talk about. Just like everybody else, Papa was just going to pretend that nothing had happened.

It wasn't long before Papa started having the men who had beaten him over to the house again. They all acted like they were still friends, as if the beating had never happened. They laughed, and joked, and drank together, just like they always had. Mama joined in. Everyone was pretending everything was fine.

So, on the outside, I played along. But inside I wondered, *Is this what you're supposed to do when something horrible happens? Do you just ignore it and move on?*

But there was no one I could ask that question to, not Claudine, not Mama, not Papa, not even Robert. The only thing I could do was ask myself. I did, and the answer came back: *What else can you do?*

Chapter Three: School

I had spent almost all of my early life inside our family compound or at church. But the fall after Papa's beating, I was old enough to start school. I was very excited. I was finally going to experience the outside world!

On the first day, Claudine and Robert walked me to school. Robert was holding my hand.

"Elise, stop walking so fast!" Claudine called from behind us. "I don't know what you're so excited about."

"It's her first day of school, Claudine," Robert said.

"You know what's going to happen, Robert," she said.

"What's going to happen?" I asked. "Robert?"

"Come on," he said, squeezing my hand. "We don't want you to be late."

We entered the front gates of my school together. As we walked down the dirt paths between the buildings with their rough brick walls and rusted tin roofs, I felt a little scared. Compared to our house, and our church, the school looked a bit thrown-together and uncared for.

Robert and Claudine dropped me off at my classroom.

Claudine went to her classroom in another building.

"Claudine will be here to pick you up when it's time to walk home for lunch," Robert said. Then he left to go to his school, a few blocks away. As soon as I looked in the doorway to my room, my heart swelled. There was a whole classroom filled with children who were my age!

Feeling a little shy, but excited but at the same time, I walked up to one of the other girls and said, "Hi. My name's Elise."

"I'm Claudette," the girl said. "You're tall."

I looked around the room. It was true. I was the tallest child there. "Uh, thanks," I said. The two of us started talking, and Claudette introduced me to several other girls she knew from the neighborhood. We all started talking and getting to know each other. Things seemed to be going well.

Then the teacher, who had been working at her desk, stood up and told us to take a seat. We did. Each student desk had a bench built into it that held two people. I ended up sitting next to Claudette.

"My name is Madame Gautama," the teacher said. "Attendance. All of the Hutus, stand up."

Most of the children, including Claudette, stood up. "Move to the front of the room," Madame Gautama said. They did.

"Now, all of the Tutsis," she said, "stand up."

I looked around and saw just two boys and a girl left standing at their desks.

"All Tutsis, move to the back of the room, and stand along the wall there. Now, all of the Hutus find a seat as close to the front of the room as you can." The teacher took out her roll book and a pencil. "When I call your name, say, 'Here'," she said.

She started calling off names. As each child said, "Here," she
looked up at him or her, and then wrote something in her book. The
whole time that she was taking attendance, we Tutsis were still
standing along the back wall, waiting to be told where to sit. The other
Tutsi girl raised her hand, but Madame Gautama ignored her and
continued taking attendance. Eventually the girl started jumping up and
down.

The teacher sighed and said, "Yes?"

"Teacher?"

"I said 'yes.'"

"Can…can we sit down?" the girl asked.

Madame Gautama stared at the girl for a moment. Then she said,
"No," and went back to taking attendance.

After calling on a bunch of Hutus, and one of the Tutsi boys, she
called my name. "Here," I said.

Madame Gautama looked me up and down, scoffed, and shook her
head while she wrote something down next to my name. As she worked
her way through the rest of the names, she eventually got to the other
Tutsi girl, the one who had asked if we could sit down, and then the
other Tutsi boy.

When she was done, Madame Gautama said, "Tutsis must stay in
the back of the room. That is where you belong. Every day you must let
the Hutus sit down first. And then, if there is room, as there is today,
you may sit, but only in the back row."

The two boys, the other Tutsi girl, and I sat down. One of the boys
and the other girl were tall, but not as tall as me. The other boy was

more the height of the Hutu children. The four of us all sat, hunched over, in the back row.

This same thing happened the next day, and the next, and the next. I wondered what was going on. Why did Madame Gautama need to count the Hutus and then the Tutsis every single day? I wasn't going to risk the heartbreak of asking Mama or Papa about it and then having them act like it wasn't odd or change the subject. I knew that Claudine would roll her eyes and tell me to stop asking stupid questions. *Maybe Robert…* I thought.

So, the next day, as Robert and Claudine were walking me home from school, I slowed down.

"Hurry up!" Claudine demanded.

"I'm tired," I said.

"Go ahead, Claudine," Robert said, "I'll walk with Elise."

I smiled a little to myself.

"Fine," Claudine answered, and walked on ahead.

"No sleep last night, Elise?" Robert asked.

"I just keep thinking," I said.

"About what?"

"I can't understand why the teacher keeps counting the Hutus and the Tutsis every single day."

Robert smiled. "Oh that," he said. "I think that's something the government makes them do."

"Why?"

"Something about making sure they have the right number of Hutus and the right number of Tutsis."

"What?" I asked.

"I don't know," he said. "Don't worry about it, Elise. Just try to talk as little as you can in class, and if the teacher asks you a question, just tell them what they want to hear."

"What do they want to hear?"

"Oh, each one's a little different. You'll figure it out. Watch what they say, and who they say it to, and how they say it. It's not hard. Just don't argue. And don't fight. Unless…"

"Unless what?"

Robert looked at me for a moment. Then he smiled and said, "Ask me again when you're older. But for now, like I said, try not to worry about things. Just… when something unpleasant happens to you, just… do your best to move on."

I tried to follow Robert's advice. I tried not to worry, but it never seemed to work. And the questions in my head never got answered, and they never went away. *Why are things like this? Why are the teachers so concerned with counting the Hutus and the Tutsis during attendance?* Every single day it was, "Hutus stand up. How many Hutus in the class? Hutus, take a seat. Tutsis stand up. How many Tutsis in the class?" It all just seemed so strange.

Most days, we Tutsis were left standing in the back of the room unless, eventually, one of us would ask if we could sit down. That was always

a risk for the person who asked, though. As the trimesters went by, I
was that person more often than anyone else.

The first time I did it, just a few days into that school year, the teacher
said, "On your knees."

I was so taken by surprise I said, "What?"

The teacher glared at me and said, "I'm not going to repeat
myself!"

I got down on my knees.

"You see, class?" she said. "That's where Tutsis should be: on
their knees."

The Hutus all laughed.

The Tutsis all looked down.

"Now," the teacher said to me. "Stay there."

I did, which was fine, at first. But the floor was concrete. It may
not seem like kneeling is much of a punishment, but if you ever try it
for any length of time, you'll find that after just a few minutes kneeling
becomes uncomfortable. After ten minutes, it gets painful. And when
you are forced to do it for an hour or several hours, it becomes
unbearable.

But I had to bear it. There was nothing else I could do. The teacher
made me kneel for the whole rest of that day. She didn't seem to care
that my legs were shaking and that tears were streaming down my face.

As soon as school was over that day I said, "Thank you, God!" under
my breath. But when I tried to stand up, my legs were so cramped and

sore and asleep, I could barely pull myself up to sitting at an empty desk. My knees had little spots of wet blood on them.

I looked at the teacher, hoping for at least some small sign of sympathy. But she didn't even look up from her desk. She was writing something on a piece of paper. "Elise," she said. "Come here."

I did, the best I could.

"Stand here," she said, still not looking up, pointing to a spot on the floor. She took out an envelope, folded the piece of paper, and put it inside. "Take this letter home, and give it to your mama," she said.

Then she put her things in her bag and left me standing there, thinking, *I wonder what I did wrong.*

When Claudine and Robert came to pick me up, they saw my bloody knees. They didn't even ask what had happened. They seemed to know.

"You see, Robert?" Claudine said. "I told you!"

"In first grade?" Robert said, shaking his head.

"I knew it! I knew you shouldn't have let her get her hopes up!" Claudine said. She shook her head, folded her arms, and walked a few steps ahead of us. Then she stopped with her back to us.

Robert and I stopped too and looked at her back. I could feel tears welling up inside me. I fought to hold them back. I was in public, and I certainly didn't want anyone from school to see me doing any more crying.

But then Claudine, who still had her back to us, put out her left hand. I did my best to run toward her, with my still-sore knees and legs, and took her hand. Robert walked up on the other side of me and put out his hand.

I held up the envelope. "It's for Mama, from my teacher," I said.

Robert took the envelope and put it in his pocket. "I'll give it back to you when we get home," he said. "And then you can give it to Mama." He took my hand.

We walked home like that, with Claudine holding one hand and Robert holding the other. They didn't rush me. They even played a game with me, where they would pick me up in the air between the two of them, like I was jumping very, very high. Neither of them said a word. I thought that they both must have known what the letter said.

When we got home, I showed the letter to Mama. I stood there shaking, with tears running down my face as she read it.

"Elise," she started quietly. "I just can't believe this. Do you know how much money it costs to send you to school? Do you know how hard it is to get them to take a Tutsi? I had to beg them, Elise! I had to beg them to take one more of my Tutsi children! And then I get this letter saying you've been talking in class?!" She was yelling now. "Come here!" She bent me over her lap and spanked me, hard, again and again.

I was shrieking as Mama continued to spank me. "And now I have to go in there and have a meeting with your teacher? And have her tell me how horrible my child is?" she yelled, "and how bad of a mother I am? And how Tutsis don't… don't even *belong* in the school?"

When she had finished, she stood me back up and said, "Now, go to your room and think about what you've done!" Between being made to kneel on the concrete floor all day and the spanking Mama had just given me, it was hard to walk. Everything hurt so much, I barely made it into my room. I threw myself on my bed and sobbed into my pillow. I felt like it would never stop. I still didn't know what I had done wrong, and, even worse, I was afraid that no one was ever going to explain it to me.

Mama met with Madame Gautama the next day after school, while I waited outside the classroom. I couldn't hear well enough to understand what they were saying. Mainly I just watched their silhouettes through the open door. Mama said almost nothing, except, when she stood up, she shook the teacher's hand and said, "I'm very sorry, Madame Gautama. I'll do my best to make sure that it never happens again."

"See that you do," Madame Gautama said. "You know, a lot of people tell me that Tutsis can't help being badly behaved, that it's just in their nature, but I just don't believe that. You just have to be firm with her. You have to beat her more at home."

"Well," Mama said. "Thank you for the advice, and for taking the time. And again, I'm very sorry."

Mama *did* spank me when we got home, and I ran to my room and cried.

I should explain here that when I was growing up in Rwanda, even the most loving parents would hit their children, not to injure them, just to discipline them. I've certainly run into the idea since that beating your children is abuse. I think if you asked anyone in my parents' generation about it, they'd probably tell you that *not* beating your children would make you a negligent parent.

That night, after everyone had gone to bed, I was walking down the hall, past Mama and Papa's room to go to the toilet, when I heard my name mentioned. I couldn't keep myself from stopping to listen.

"A letter from Elise's teacher!" Papa was saying, in a quiet voice. "Do you really think Elise is talking in class?"

"Of course I don't think she's talking in class!" Mama said.

"Elise's a good girl."

"I know, Joseph. I know. That's just how they harass the Tutsi kids."

"They didn't start this early with Claudine. They certainly didn't start this early with Robert."

"Well, things are getting worse. You know that."

"And you still beat her when the two of you got home?"

"What else can I do, Joseph? She has to go to school. An education is the only chance she has. We had a hard enough time getting that school to take our kids in the first place. It's not just Elise. They all get 'punished', all the time. You know, I think the only reason they take Tutsis into that school is to use them for free labor?"

Papa laughed, "No, it's because President Habyarimana says that they have to have eight percent Tutsis in the school, just so no one can accuse his government of discriminating against us, not because they care about the education of our children!"

"Well, we do. So, we have to play along. I can't tell the teacher that I agree with her and then tell Elise I know that the teacher is lying! What if she blurted that out in school one day? What would happen to her? What would happen to us? It breaks my heart, but what else can we do? It's not like I can complain to the headmaster. I'm sure he tells the teachers to do everything they can to harass the Tutsi kids. And you know what happens to a Tutsi who tries to complain to anyone in the government."

"Mmm," Papa said. "Sometimes they don't come home."

I kept getting letters from my teacher for Mama, and every time, Mama would beat me. But having overheard the truth about the situation, knowing that Mama was "playing along" made it all easier to bear.

But the counting! That was like a torture all by itself! Day after day, week after week, it continued. Even though it was the same four Tutsis in our class, every day would start with the teacher saying, "How many Hutus? Raise your hands." Then the teacher would count them and write down the number in her book. And then the teacher would say, "How many Tutsis? Stand up." Then the teacher would count us and write down the number in her book. But she would never tell the Tutsis to sit back down.

Sometimes we would sit down quietly, subtly, one at a time, and the teacher would let it pass. But other times, once we were sitting, the teacher would notice, and say something like, "Who told you you had the right to sit down?" and all the Tutsis in the class would have to stand or kneel for the rest of the day.

One day Madame Gautama asked, "Class, who can tell me: How can you tell a Hutu from a Tutsi?"

All of the Hutu students' hands went up. Even one of the Tutsi boys raised his hand.

"Gerard?" Madame Gautama called on one of the Hutu boys.

"They're very tall," Gerard said.

Some of the other children laughed.

"They are very tall," Madame Gautama confirmed. "Very good. What else? Who can tell me? Daniel?" He was the tall Tutsi boy, the one who wasn't raising his hand. "Stand up," Madame Gautama said.

Daniel stood.

"What are you?" she asked him.

"I'm a Tutsi," Daniel said.

The Hutu students laughed.

"He's a Tutsi. See class? Are you tall?"

"Yes," Daniel mumbled. "I am tall."

"Speak up!" Madame Gautama demanded.

"Yes, Teacher," he said in a full voice. "I am tall."

"What else makes you look like a Tutsi?"

"… I, I don't know, teacher."

"Stupid Tutsi. Who can help him?"

The students' hands went back up.

"Rene?"

"He has a skinny nose."

"Very good, Rene. Tutsis have skinny noses. Daniel, do you have a skinny nose? No mumbling this time! Speak up!"

"Yes, Teacher," he said, "I have a thin nose."

"And big eyes!" another student called out.

"And lighter skin," called another.

"And straighter hair!"

"Like a *muzungu*!" (white person) yelled another. The class was getting a little bit wild. The Hutus were laughing and talking to one another.

"Now, now, children, listen," Madame Gautama said, "because this is a very important point: 'Like a muzungu.' You see, because the Tutsis have features that make them look more like a muzungu, with the thinner nose and higher cheek bones and the lighter skin." (Not all Tutsis actually look like this, but Daniel had all of these features. In that moment, I felt so sorry for him.) "They think that they are better than Hutus. Isn't that right?" she yelled, eyeing all of us in the back row.

"I... I..." I could tell Daniel didn't know what to say.

"And like all other Tutsis," Madame Gautama continued, "they are the cause of so many of our problems. They are weak, especially when confronted with the truth," she said, waving a hand toward Daniel as though she was trying to negotiate down the price of a cow. "But watch out for them! Like a snake, a Tutsi is sneaky. But we all know what we do to snakes, don't we class?"

The class all said "Uh-huh" and "Yes" together. What you do in Rwanda with snakes is you kill them.

There were "punishments" for Tutsis in school almost every day. And no matter how many of them happened to you, or how many you had to watch happening to another Tutsi, they never got easier to take.

One day in fifth grade we were doing math problems, and Nicole, the other Tutsi in our class, scratched her head. The custom in Rwanda back then, for all boys and girls, was to keep your hair very, very short. Nicole's hair had gotten a little long, maybe an inch or so. She scratched her head again, and suddenly the teacher said, "Nicole!"

"Yes, Teacher?"

"Come here!"

She did.

"Dirty Tutsi! You think you don't have to follow the rules? You think you're above them because you're a Tutsi?"

"No, Teacher! I-"

"Shut up!" the teacher said. "And now you're threatening everyone's health. You've got lice! Well, we can't have you infecting the whole class, can we? So, get down on your knees."

Another custom in Rwanda is doing what you're told. Nicole got down on her knees. The teacher took a straight razor out of her desk.

"Don't move," the teacher said, opening the razor. I could see the blade shining. With all of the crazy things that I had seen and heard about, I didn't know what the teacher was going to do next. I wanted to scream, but I was frozen with fear.

Nicole whimpered as the teacher grabbed a handful of her hair.

"Quiet!" the teacher commanded, giving the handful of hair a yank. "You'll just make this worse!"

The teacher had to pull hard on the dull blade, and as she put more pressure on the razor, she was also pulling harder and harder on Nicole's hair. I could see the pain building on Nicole's face until she cried out.

"I thought I told you to be quiet!" the teacher said, yanking Nicole's hair again, like she was a dog on a leash. Frustrated, the teacher started sawing back and forth at Nicole's hair. But that didn't seem to be working either, so the teacher just started grabbing handfuls of hair and hacking at each clump until it came free in her hand.

Once she had cut off all of Nicole's hair, the teacher began to scrape the razor across Nicole's scalp, not carefully, the way a barber or a parent would. Instead, she was just raking it over her scalp, fast and dry. The rest of the class looked on and laughed. Nicole cried and bled.

"Quiet!" the teacher ordered.

Tears were streaming down Nicole's face.

Then the teacher yelled, "Elise!"

I froze. Was I next?

"Clean this, this … lice farm up! Then take this dirty Tutsi to her house, and you tell her mama to keep Nicole's hair short and her head clean, and that if I have to do this again, we may have to kick her out of the school! Do you understand?"

I was so shocked, and afraid that I might be next, it was hard to speak, but I managed to get out, "Yes, teacher." I steadied Nicole as she stood up, and I helped her back to her seat.

As I started out the door to get a dustpan and a broom, the teacher, in a very annoyed voice said, "Elise! What are you doing?"

"I'm going to get a dustpan and broom, teacher."

"Too good to get on your knees and use your hands? Too good for honest work?"

I had the urge to defend myself, but I remembered the things Claudine and Robert had told me. So, trying to be as polite and submissive as I could, and to say as little as possible, I simply said, "No, Teacher." Then I walked to the front of the room, got down on my hands and knees, and picked up all of Nicole's hair with my fingers. There were no lice.

School ran on trimesters, and every trimester brought a lot of change. For one thing, almost every trimester we got a new teacher. I was never sure why.

There was a lot of turnover with the students, too. A lot of people in Rwanda, especially Hutus, were very poor then, and not everyone could afford to send all of their kids to school at the same time. So, often, in a new class, there would be some kids that you recognized and some kids you had never seen before.

The number of kids in each grade changed a lot, too, from trimester to trimester. Sometimes there would be one room of your grade; sometimes there would be three. It made making friends hard; that and the fact that all the lessons about how evil the Tutsis were seemed to have sunk in. None of the Hutu kids would go near the Tutsi kids, and the Tutsi kids mainly just kept their heads down, trying to keep from being noticed and "punished."

A lot of the Hutu kids liked that we got a new teacher every trimester. They liked that everything changed, but I hated it. Term after term, it was always the same thing. Teachers would look for, or even make up, reasons to "punish" any Tutsis, but as I was usually the tallest kid in class, and the most obviously Tutsi-looking, I got "punished" the most.

It was never long before a new teacher would say something like, "You, in the back," pointing at me. "Stand up."

I would stand up.

Everyone would look at me, and the teacher would say something like, "What is your name, Tutsi?"

I knew I couldn't stay silent, so I would answer, "Elise."

Then the teacher would say something like, "Stupid, stupid Tutsi! You know you're not allowed to talk out of turn!"

All the Hutus would laugh, and the teacher would tell me, "Keep standing for the rest of the day, and see me after class." Sometimes it was kneeling for the whole day.

That meant he or she was going to send another letter home, saying that I had been talking in class, and that meant another beating from Mama.

On the first day of sixth grade, I decided to try something new. I snuck from the back of the room, into the next to last row and sat down, hunched over to try to hide my height. When the new teacher asked, "How many Hutus? Raise your hands," I raised my hand too.

"Keep them up," the teacher said, counting. All of the students were looking around the room to see who was in their class this term. Linda, one of the Hutu girls I had been in class with the year before, saw that I was raising my hand. I saw her look at the board, struggling to read the teacher's name. Linda wasn't very bright.

"Excuse me? Teacher?" Linda said, interrupting the count.

"Yes?" Madame Kalimba answered.

"That girl, back there, with her hand up, the tall one? Her name's Elise, and she's not a Hutu. She's a Tutsi!"

"Is she?" Madame Kalimba said. "Elise, stand up."

I did.

"Oh yes," she said, looking me up and down. "You *are* a Tutsi, yes? Trying to pass yourself off as a Hutu? Admit it!"

I nodded.

"I didn't say nod. I said admit it!"

"I … am a Tutsi," I said.

"You see class?" she said. "Just like a snake, dishonest. Just like a Tutsi. Come here."

I was frightened. I started walking toward her desk slowly.

"Come on, quickly!" Madame Kalimba demanded. "You see, class, also slow and lazy, just like a Tutsi. Bend over my desk," she said.

I did. And then WHACK! There was a sharp stinging, burning pain across my backside. WHACK! Another! And another, and another! Madame Kalimba was beating me with a stick! I thought the beatings from Mama were bad, but I could tell that Madame Kalimba was actually trying to cause me as much pain as she could! The Hutus all laughed as though they were watching a show. They cheered with every strike.

When she had finished, Madame Kalimba said, "Now go sit down." I think she knew that this would be more painful than standing up. I was in agony as my bruised backside pressed against the hard wooden bench. She had even bruised my private parts.

"Well," the teacher said, looking at Linda with a smile on her face, "What is your name, Dear?"

"Linda."

"Well, everybody, I think we have found our class chief! Linda will be in charge whenever I'm out of the room, or whenever I need her to be. Congratulations, Linda!" she said, and everyone started clapping, even me. I didn't want any more trouble that day.

When Claudine saw that I was walking funny on the way back home, she pulled me aside. "Keep walking," she told Robert. "We'll catch up." Then, to me, she said, "The next time the teacher whips your backside, keep your hands at your sides, and pull your skirt as tight as you can across the back. That way they won't be able to hurt your private parts so badly." Then she put out her hand. "Come on," she said. I took her hand, and we walked home, in silence, again.

Several days later, during class the teacher said, "Linda, will you come here please? Class, I have to leave the room for a few minutes. While I'm gone, Linda will be in charge. I've put a reading assignment here on the board. Everyone is to read silently at their desks. If anyone does anything wrong, Linda, I want you to write down their name on this piece of paper here on my desk. Okay?"

"Okay," Linda said, smiling and looking at me. "Can I sit at your desk while you're gone?"

"Of course you can," the teacher said. Then she left the room.

We all started reading in silence. But after a few minutes, I noticed that the Hutu boy in front of me was holding a piece of paper out, behind his back. I ignored it and went back to my work. But then he started shaking the piece of paper. I still ignored it. Then he pretended he was stretching and dropped the piece of paper on my desk. As secretly as I could, I took it and flattened it out inside my book. It said:

Hello Elise,
My name is Albert.
I like you.

I kept looking down, pretending I was doing my work, but I couldn't keep myself from smiling. When I looked up to see if anyone had noticed, there was Linda, looking right at me. She smiled and wrote my name on the piece of paper that the teacher had given her.

Mana we! I thought.

When the teacher returned a few minutes later, Linda gave her the sheet of paper.

"Thank you, Linda," the teacher said. "Oh, of course. Only Tutsis on the list. Elise, Colette, stand up."

We stood up.

"Linda, please take these two to the office. Tell the headmaster's secretary that these Tutsis are being punished. I believe she'll have some work for them to do. Oh, and you may oversee them while they work."

Linda smiled.

Colette and I looked at each other, but we didn't say anything. By that point we were all learning that innocence was no defense, if you were a Tutsi.

Linda took us to the office. The secretary there sent us to the groundskeeper. He gave us shovels and brought us to a patch of hard dirt behind the school.

"You have to turn over this soil so that we can plant things here," he said. "Now, dig," he commanded, smiling.

"You heard him," Linda said. "Dig!"

We did.

And Linda made us keep digging, all day long.

This sort of "punishment" happened to all the Tutsis at school. As you walked around the campus, you would see Tutsi students cleaning, and painting, and digging in the dirt. In fact, we spent so much time out of the classroom it was hard to learn much of anything.

Not that the Hutus who got to stay in class all the time were getting a great education. Aside from reading, writing and some basic mathematics, the lessons were mainly about how there were too many people in Rwanda, and how if the population was reduced, there would be enough land, and the Hutus wouldn't all be so poor. That never quite made any sense to me, but I remembered what Robert had told me. So, I didn't say anything about it.

All of our lessons were taught in Kinyarwanda. Everyone in Rwanda knew that the good schools where the few rich Hutus went, the ones called *École Belge* (The Belgian School), and the *École Française* (the French School), taught their lessons in French. I had never seen the inside of an École Belge, but when I imagined one, everything there was bright, well painted, and clean, the opposite of my school.

All of the jobs they made the Tutsi students do at our school were awful, difficult, and dirty. But there was one job that was the worst of all. The first time I was made to do it wasn't long after Linda had been made class chief. The teacher had left the room, leaving Linda in charge, again. I tried to sink down in my seat so I wouldn't look so tall and noticeable. But as soon as I looked up, there was Linda, staring right at me. By that point the teacher had her writing the names of the students who would be "punished" on the board for everyone to see. There were two Hutu boys in the row in front of me who were talking. Linda looked at them and then at me.

And then, with a smile, she said, "Elise!" and clicked her tongue. "I would think that you would have learned not to talk in class by now."

The whole class laughed, even the Tutsis. I guess they were trying not to draw attention to themselves. I narrowed my eyes at Linda.

"Oh, that's two," she said. Then she turned and wrote my name on the board. Next to it she wrote a "2."

When the teacher came back, she looked at the board, and with a smile said, "Elise, you just don't learn. Thick-headed Tutsi," she said to the class, like she was putting on a show.

They all laughed.

"And twice. Twice? I was only gone for a few minutes. It's as though you *want* to be punished. Well, all right. If that's what you want. Linda, you know what to do. Only this time, tell them that Elise should clean our school's newest building."

I didn't know what she was talking about. As far as I knew, the school didn't have any new buildings. There certainly weren't any that looked new. Linda took me to the office, and when the groundskeeper came out, she repeated what the teacher had told her to say.

"Ah-ha-ha, yes. Good. It could use it," he said. "This way."

"Come on," Linda said. "Let's go."

We followed the groundskeeper away from the administration building, past the classroom buildings, and down to the football (that's what we call soccer) fields.

"There aren't any new buildings down here," I said. "The only thing down here is the…" I trailed off.

"The rest of the buildings were built thirty years ago," the groundskeeper said. "But the toilets were built five years later. They are our newest building."

Linda started laughing.

"Now, I want them nice and clean," the groundskeeper said.

"What am I supposed to clean them with?" I asked.

"Uppity Tutsi," the groundskeeper said and nodded to Linda.

She slapped me across the cheek and then held her finger right in front of my face.

"There's a bucket over there, by the faucet," the groundskeeper said. "But I want them clean, not just rinsed."

My face was still stinging, but I couldn't keep from asking, "What else am I supposed to use?"

"Typical stupid Tutsi," the groundskeeper said. "Isn't it obvious? Use your hands!" Then he walked away, laughing.

Linda looked at me. "Well?" she said. "You've only got until three o'clock." It was ten in the morning.

Now, to call these things toilets was giving them much more credit than they deserved. The building was a long latrine. There were thirty stalls, each with a hole in a creaky wooden floor, all built over a long, stinking trench filled with reeking sewage, and thick with flies. They were beyond disgusting. I tried to use them as little as possible.

You had to bring your own paper to wipe with, usually used notebooks. There was nothing to sit on. You had to squat over the hole, and very often people missed, with everything.

I went to the first stall and opened the door. There was cloud of flies and stomach-churning stench that hit me in the face like a fist. It was so vile, I had to put my hand over my mouth and nose to keep from vomiting. The groundskeeper was right. These "toilets" clearly hadn't been cleaned in a very long time, if ever.

"Well, go ahead," Linda said, standing far enough away from the latrines that the stench didn't make her sick.

"Can I get a shovel?" I asked.

"We don't want to get poo-poo all over the shovel," she said. "We use those for the garden. Remember? What's the matter, Tutsi girl? Too good to get your hands dirty?"

No, I thought. *I'm just disgusted by the thought of putting my hands in feces. Aren't you?* But I didn't say it out loud. I wasn't going to give Linda the satisfaction. I just gave her a hard look and got to work. *Who does she think I am?* I thought, *some sort of Tutsi princess, who's never cleaned a toilet before? This is no big deal. I've cleaned the squat toilet at home plenty of times with Mama. I know what to do.*

I grabbed the bucket, walked up the hill, filled it, and brought it back down to the toilets. Linda was following me the whole time. I opened the door to the first stall and held it open with my left foot. *All I need to do is slosh the water against the back wall and it will wash everything down the hole,* I thought. *This will be easy!* I doused the back wall, but as I watched the water drain down the hole, I realized there was so much build-up that had been there for so long, the water was having almost no effect. *Mana we,* I thought. *I do have to use my hands!*

I did get my hands dirty. Very, very dirty. It was absolutely the most disgusting thing I had ever experienced in my life. The smell, the feel. I vomited over and over, and every time I did, Linda would click her tongue and say, "Well, I guess that's just more you'll have to clean up."

Oh, the things I wanted to say to her! But I stuck to my decision not to give her the satisfaction, and just kept working.

When I had finished pushing all of the filth into all of the holes, I felt a huge sense of relief. I was finally done with that awful job. I was just about to climb the hill to wash my hands at the faucet when the groundskeeper came by.

"Well," he said, "maybe Tutsis are good for something. That's a good start."

"What … do you mean?" I asked.

"You got everything into the holes," he said. "But now, you need to get every stall clean! Why do you think I gave you the bucket?"

I wanted to cry, but I didn't. I didn't even stop. I just picked up the bucket, walked up the hill, filled the bucket at the faucet, brought it back down, and got to work. I rubbed and rubbed the rough brick walls and the coarse wooden floors that were soaked with what must have been years of urine, with just the water and my bare hands, for hours and hours.

When I had finally finished cleaning the last "toilet", I walked up the hill to clean myself. There was no soap, so I had to use my fingernails to scrub, and scrub, and scrub. As hard as I tried, though, I still could not get myself completely clean. I still smelled horrible. There was filth left underneath my fingernails. The powder blue button-down shirt and the navy-blue skirt that Mama always took such pains to keep looking clean and well ironed now both had brown spots and streaks on them that I hadn't been able to scrub out.

As I stood up from the faucet, there was Linda, holding an envelope. "For your Mama," Linda said, smiling as she handed it to me.

I grabbed the envelope and started walking toward the front gate of the school.

Linda was following right behind me. "You still stink, dirty Tutsi!" she said. "And no matter how much you wash, you always will. And do you know why? Because the stink comes from the inside!"

I spun around so quickly that Linda almost ran into me. She had to take a step back. I glared at her. She tried to glare back, but she had to hold her neck at an odd angle because I was much taller than she was.

"Elise!" I turned my head to see Claudine calling to me from the front gate. "Come on!" she said. "It's late!" I turned back to Linda and held up my pointer finger in front of her face.

"Elise!" Claudine called again. "Right now!"

I turned and walked quickly up the hill to join her.

"Mana we!" she said as I got closer to her, "What happened to you? You look-" Then she caught a whiff of me. "Elise! You smell like poo-poo! 'Punishment'?" she asked, looking at me.

I nodded.

"Come on," she said.

As we started walking home, Claudine said, "What was going on between you and that girl?"

"Linda?" I said. "The teacher made her class chief. And for some reason she puts me on her 'list' every day."

"You looked like you were about to have a fight with her."

"Claudine, you know I would never start a fight-"

"But you'd finish it," she said, cutting me off. "Just like Papa. You need to learn how to just..."

"Just what?" I said.

"Keep your damned mouth shut sometimes!"

"I don't talk in class, Claudine! The teacher and Linda just...hate me for some reason!"

"It's not for 'some' reason, Elise. It's for *one* reason. It's because you're a Tutsi! And she's a Hutu!"

"That's two reasons," I said.

"What?"

"You said there's one reason. That's two reasons."

"Oh Yezu Christ, Elise!" she said, smacking me hard on the shoulder. "That's what I'm talking about! You just have this way of ...

making people so angry when you talk like that! And you've got to stop doing that, especially with Linda."

"But she always puts me on her list, so much more than any of the other Tutsis! And I never do anything to deserve it!"

"Oh really?"

"I swear, Claudine!"

"Well, you need to do something to fix that. You don't want her angry at you."

"Fix it how, Claudine? It seems like most of the time a Hutu doesn't need a reason to get mad at you if you're a Tutsi. They just seem to be mad at us all the time."

"Yeah, but Linda's not just any Hutu, Elise!"

"What do you mean?"

"Do you know who she is?"

"She's Linda, who lives down the street from us."

"Her parents are Estelle and Laurent Safari!"

"Does that mean something?"

"Don't you know who they are?"

"They're Linda's parents?" I said.

"Yes, and they're big people in Hutu Power!"

"In what?"

"Hutu Power!"

"What's Hutu Power?"

"Mana we, Elise! Mama and Papa really do keep you sheltered! Don't you listen to the radio? Don't you see it everywhere? Who do you think organizes those Hutu rallies on our street?"

"Hutu Power?" I guessed.

"And you know when you hear on the radio that all Tutsis are 'inyenzi,' and that we need to be 'stamped out?'"

"Yes," I said.

"Well, who do you think is saying that?"

"Hutu Power?" I guessed again.

"That's right," she said. "Hutu Power!"

"But what is it?"

"Elise!" she said rubbing her forehead in frustration.

"Please, Claudine. It's not like Mama or Papa are going to tell me. You know I've been asking questions for years, but… one will tell me what's going on! No one will tell me anything."

"Okay," she sighed. "Hutu Power is...it's a group. It's... I guess it's a political party. They run all the neighborhoods in Rwanda. They basically run the government, and they hate Tutsis. You know that Tutsi man that got killed last week in Murama?"

"Yeah …"

"And you know how we've been hearing about that kind of thing happening more and more often these days?"

"Yes…"

"Well, some people are saying that Hutu Power is behind those killings."

"Who's saying that?"

Claudine was silent.

"Who, Claudine?"

"You can't tell anyone," she said.

"I won't."

"You've got to swear."

"I swear."

"Okay," she said and looked around to see if anyone could hear us. Then she came in close to me and said, "You know my friend, Rose?"

"Yes."

"Well, her for one."

"How does *she* know?"

"Her father's the neighborhood chief."

"I know. So?"

"No, he's not just part of the city government. He's also the neighborhood chief for Hutu Power!"

I thought for a moment. "Are there a lot of people who are part of Hutu Power in our neighborhood?" I asked.

"Elise, Biryogo is the center of Hutu Power!"

"Mana we!" I said.

"And that's why little Miss Elise has got to stop making the Hutu children so angry!"

"How am I supposed to do that?"

"I don't know. When they make you stand in the back of the room, do you try to sit down?"

"Of course. I mean, I usually ask first."

"Well, first of all, make sure you're never the one who asks. Let one of the other Tutsi kids do that. Do anything you can think of to just… get along."

I thought about that for a minute. I wasn't sure I could always do that.

"That's what *I* do," Claudine continued.

"Like what?"

"For you? Well, you're even taller than I was at your age. So, slouch down in your seat."

"I've tried that! And besides..."

"What?" she said.

"Well, you're a Tutsi too. How often do *you* get to sit down in class?"

That stopped her. She looked at me and said, "I know…" She looked down at the ground.

But then she looked back at me, smiling, and shoved me, playfully. "I'm sure a lot more than you do! I don't know, Elise, just… try not to make people angry, especially Hutus."

"Oh, thank you so much, Claudine. That's sooooo helpful!"

"I'm just looking out for my little sister. And, speaking of that, you've got to stop getting so many of these!" she said, grabbing the envelope Linda had given me. "Mana we, Elise!" she said laughing. "Mama is going to beat you so hard when you get home!"

"I know," I said. "Let's go get it over with."

"And then I'll boil some water so you can take a hot bath and clean those clothes!"

"I can take a cold bath, just like everybody else. I like it better. It wakes you up."

"Oh, I know, Elise. But this bath won't be to wake you up. It'll be to get you clean. You smell like poo-poo!" she said, laughing and shoving me.

"I know," I said, laughing and shoving her back. "I'm a mess."

"Eww!" she said. "Don't get it on me!"

"You'd better run!" I said, putting my hands out in front of me. "Or I'll get you with my poo-poo hands!"

She ran ahead of me, squealing.

I chased her, calling, "Poo-poo hands! Poo-poo hands!"

She tried to avoid me by running up one of the steepest roads in Biryogo. It's so steep that when it rains, the water cuts a deep trench into it. The hard-packed cinnamon-colored earth turns blood red and the trench flows like a small rushing river. It wasn't raining that day, but the trench was still there. Every time I got almost close enough to Claudine to tag her, she would jump across the trench. When I jumped after her, she would jump back. We did that all the way to the top of the hill. When we got to the one paved road in all of Biryogo, Claudine ran down it, dodging me, like a football player who has the ball, the rest of the way home.

Chapter Four: Papa

The things that happened to me at school were awful, but not having anybody I could talk to about them was even worse. It felt like the hurt just kept building up inside me, and I had to just keep on taking it, day after day, and pretending that "everything" was "fine".

But then, one night, as I was on my way back from the outhouse in our back yard, I ran into Papa, who was headed toward it. When he saw me, I could see his whole face light up, even in the dark, almost moonless night. I could tell from the look of him, and the way he was walking, that he had been drinking. He spread his long arms wide and said, "How is my little girl?" as he got down on one knee and hugged me.

"I'm fine, Papa," I said, hugging him back, but not with much enthusiasm.

"You don't seem fine," he said. "You're not hugging me like you're fine." He pulled his head back a little and looked at me. "What is it, Sweetheart?" he asked.

I wanted to tell him about all of the horrible things that I had to put up with in school, but I was afraid that would just make things worse, that Papa might try to make a joke or say something like, "It's not so bad," because he wanted that to be true for me.

So, I said, "I'm just tired, Papa,"

"Of what?"

"Of school," I said. Tears had started to leak out of me.

He hugged me again. "Elise, Elise, Elise," he said. "I know. I know. School is hard."

"It's awful, Papa!" I sobbed. I couldn't help myself.

"I know, Sweetheart. I know," he said, still hugging me.

The sobs kept coming, and with them came questions that I normally never would have asked, but in that moment of tenderness from Papa my sadness and my need for answers was so much stronger than my fear of another false answer. "Why do we have to go, Papa?" I asked through my sobs. "They don't teach us anything! All they do there is make us clean, or dig, or they beat us! And we never do anything wrong!"

"I know, Sweetheart," he said. "I know. But even if school's not so good-"

"It's horrible, Papa!"

"Even if school is *horrible*, it's what we call a necessary evil, Elise. Even a bad education makes you…bigger, stronger, able to do things, able to control your life so much more! You see all of those *mayibobo* (homeless kids) on the street every day? They're lost."

"They've got nothing, and they probably never will. That's what happens when you don't have an education! You'll see when you get older. Now," he stumbled back to his feet. "Papa needs to go use the toilet." He pointed me to the faucet on the other side of the yard. "And my little princess needs to go wash her face with cool water, so Mama doesn't see it like this. And then, my love, back to bed. Okay?"

"Okay, Papa," I said.

I don't know why Papa was honest with me that night. Maybe the fact that he had been drinking allowed his love to overcome his concerns for just a moment. But I do know that that moment stayed with me. It gave me strength. It made me know that I wasn't crazy, as I watched what was happening around me and felt Rwanda changing, getting darker and more menacing.

It seemed like everyone had become scared and suspicious of everyone else. On the streets people still smiled as they passed each other, but now I was always left wondering what people were really thinking, behind their smiles.

Everyone started building brick walls around their property, us included. Every time a neighbor built their walls higher, everyone else did the same. And it went on like this until you couldn't see over the walls anymore, and you needed a big metal gate at the front of your compound to get in.

Eventually it got to the point where, except for school, church, and going to the market, we spent almost all of our time inside our compound. With the world outside becoming scarier by the day, it was the only place we really felt safe. It sort of became our own little word. It was where almost all of my good memories from that time happened: spending time with Robert, Claudine, and my younger brothers, Gabriel, and Patrick, and my baby sister Alice, helping Mama plant and harvest our fields, cooking with her, learning her recipes.

Mama taught me how to make things like matoke, plantains, and *isombe*, a stew made with cassava leaves and eggplant. Cooking with her was like magic.

I helped Mama cook for a party we threw to celebrate Robert and Claudine's confirmations. It was the spring I was twelve. That night is my favorite memory from that time.

The evening started with dinner, a whole goat that we cooked outside on a spit. We served it in a brown curry sauce with rice, corn, potatoes, and sweet potatoes from our garden. We also had beans and matoke, and *ugali*, a dish made from cassava flour and water. It's squishy, like bread dough. You dip it in a *pilipili* (spicy) sauce, or use it to mop up the goat gravy, and then pop it in your mouth. Mmmmm, delicious!

There were so many people at the party that we had to put our dining room table, another table from a neighbor, and a card table all together to make sure there was room for everyone.

Everybody was talking and joking and laughing. Then, after dinner, came the best part of all, for the children.

Sugar, or anything made with it, was very expensive back then, so Mama only let us have it on special occasions. And because this was a very special occasion, we had cake, and candy. And because we almost never ate sugar, we all suddenly found ourselves with more energy than we knew what to do with.

So, while the adults stayed inside, around the table, drinking and laughing and telling jokes and stories, the children were all sent outside, where we ran and laughed and played like we had never played before. We ran up and down the rows of corn behind the house playing hide-and-seek. We chased each other around the fruit and avocado trees. The boys tackled one another and wrestled on the grass, while the girls played tag.

Then it started to rain. I should explain something here about rain and Rwanda. In some other places, like America, people act like the rain is dangerous. They run to get out of it. They cover themselves up with raincoats. They hide from the rain under umbrellas.

In Rwanda, it's the complete opposite. We love the rain. We walk around in it. We enjoy it. Since it's always warm, the rain doesn't make you cold, and it's never long before the sun comes out and dries you off.

So, when it started to rain that evening, it just added to the sugar-fueled energy and the fun. You could hear the rain being blown through the leaves in the tall eucalyptus trees. We all stopped and listened to the drops hitting the tin roof of our house. First it was just a few, here and there, then more and more until it became loud, like the sound of a giant waterfall.

We danced in the rain, twirling around with our hands out and our eyes closed, feeling the drops hit our skin. As the cinnamon-colored ground got soaked, it turned a deep, deep red. It looked like blood.

Soon puddles started to form, and it wasn't long before Robert ran his foot through a puddle and flung a wave of muddy water at me. My eyes snapped wide in shock to see him looking at me and smiling at his mischievous deed.

"Oh, Robert!" I said, "You're going to get it!" I ran my foot through the other end of the puddle, splashing red, muddy water all over his confirmation suit.

"What are you doing?" Claudine yelled. "Mama will beat you for getting your church clothes muddy!"

Robert and I were standing at opposite ends of the puddle and looking at each other. Claudine was standing in between us. She was right, but I could tell by the crazed look in Robert's eyes and the smile I could feel on my own face that we both had the same idea, and that we were both way past caring. We looked at Claudine, then back at each other. We knew what we had to do. Then Claudine figured it out.

"Guys, no. No!" she yelled, holding up her hands to shield herself. But there was a smile on her face too, as Robert and I each kicked a big wave of muddy water onto Claudine, soaking her and turning her best clothes a reddish brown. Well, that was it. She ran into the puddle and began kicking water at us. Everyone started laughing, and decided to join in. The bigger kids were copying us.

The toddlers rushed into the puddle and started splashing everywhere with their hands. Alice, my baby sister, just sat down in the puddle and threw muddy water on herself. But by this point Claudine had found the next new game.

Trying to escape the muddy water fight, she ran away across the lawn. Robert and I chased her, and, as she tried to make a sharp turn in her leather-bottomed shoes, she slid on the grass. She stopped, holding up a hand as if to say, "Wait." Then she backed up, got a running start, and slid on the soaking wet grass for two meters. Obviously, we all had to try this, taking turns. And soon we had worn a slick, muddy track into the grass.

"Joseph!" we all heard Mama call to Papa from the back porch. "You really need to see this!"

We were all frozen with fear.

Papa came out onto the back porch. He looked at all of us soaked through to the skin and dripping with mud. He leaned on a chair, and slowly shook his head. We all watched Papa to see what our fate would be. He started shaking. Was he crying? Was he angry? Had we disappointed him that much? Then he lifted up his head and we could see that he was laughing so hard he wasn't making any noise. This made Mama start to laugh. Then all of the children started laughing, too. I can't speak for anyone else, but I was laughing mostly out of relief.

"All right, all right. All you children, come with me," Mama said. She led us around the main house to the wash area. "Stand over there," she told us. "No, no, leave your clothes on."

We all looked at her, puzzled.

"Well," she said, smiling, "You're not going to get any wetter. We just need to get as much of that mud off you as we can," she said as she doused us with bucket after bucket of water. I guess we shouldn't have been surprised. Mama always seemed to do the most sensible thing.

Mama hung our clothes on the line to dry as we finished washing ourselves. Then she helped us towel ourselves off and put us all to bed with a kiss. Now we were all clean and dry and packed in with the guest children, two to a bed. We had all finally worn ourselves out.

Every year my brothers and sisters and I looked forward to the rainy season, when we could play in the rain every day. That April, when I was twelve, it seemed like almost every afternoon it rained longer and harder than it ever had before.

That year, it felt like that's what we needed. As the world outside our compound was getting scarier and more threatening, inside our compound, for an hour or two every afternoon, we could forget all of that and just surrender to the falling rain. Sometimes we would dance in it, or sometimes we would just stand there, feeling the drops hitting our skin, bathing us. I loved to close my eyes and listen to the rain hitting the leaves in the trees and the tin roofs of our house and the houses all around us. I've always thought that was the most calming sound in the world.

On one of those April days, as we were out playing in the rain, several of Mama's friends from the neighborhood came through our front gate and walked right past us, into the house, without saying a word.

"Claudine," I said. "Why do you think Mama's friends aren't saying hello to us?"

"I don't know," Claudine said. "That's strange. Let's go see what's happening."

We went inside the house, but we couldn't find Mama and her friends. We went to Mama and Papa's room. The door was closed. I knocked. "Mama?" I called, opening the door. There was no one inside. We went to the living room and then through the dining room, calling, "Mama?"

We heard voices coming from outside. We walked out to find Mama and her friends standing in the kitchen. It looked like they were packing Papa's lunch pail, and it looked like Mama was crying.

"Mama?" Claudine called.

Mama and her friends stopped talking. Mama turned away from us.

"What's wrong?" I asked.

I could see Mama was wiping her cheeks as she said, "No, no. You children go back out to the front yard. Keep playing with your brothers and sisters. I'm just going to take this to your father in the hospital."

"What?" I said.

"Why is Papa in the hospital?" Claudine asked.

"Don't argue with me!" Mama said. "Just go. Go out in the front yard and play. Go!"

We did as we were told, but as we were going out to the front yard, I kept flashing back to the night Papa was almost beaten to death. I wanted to ask Claudine if she had any idea what was going on, but just then she slapped me hard on the shoulder. With wide eyes and a scared smile, she yelled, "TAG! You're it!" and sped off faster than I'd ever seen her run before.

I sprinted after her, caught up to her, and smacked her hard on the back, right in between her shoulder blades, saying, "Tag! You're it!" and rocketed away from her.

We played hard like this, like we were professional athletes.

Every time Claudine was just about to tag me, I would spin and change direction, two or three times in a row, avoiding her until she would slip and fall in the mud. Then, when she would finally tag me, after ten or fifteen minutes of sprinting, and hard breathing, and sweat mixed with pelting rain, she would dodge me, over and over again, the same way I had dodged her. We went on and on like that, all afternoon, neither of us wanting to stop, because, as long as we played, we didn't have to think about anything else.

Mama came home later that night with several friends surrounding her, but every time we tried to get near her, one of her friends would get in the way. They would get us something to eat, or take us outside to wash, or talk with us about anything that didn't have to do with Papa being in the hospital.

We could see that Mama was crying at the dining room table, but every time we asked what was going on, we were told something like: "Don't worry. Everything's fine."

"I wish Robert would come home," I said to Claudine.

"He can't always be here," she said with a scowl on her face. "He's doing important… He's, he's… making money. He'll come home at some point."

Robert had started working as a driver for some very important Hutus. Sometimes it kept him away from home for days at a time. "In the meantime," Claudine continued, "just… don't be so…" she trailed off and walked quickly to our room.

The next morning, another one of Mama's friends came pounding on the front gate.

"What is it? What's wrong?" I asked as I let her in.

"Oh, nothing," she said. "I just need to speak with your Mama. Alone. Why don't you take your brothers and sisters outside to play?"

Claudine and I took Alice, Gabriel, and Patrick, into the back yard, but the whole time we were out there, we could hear Mama wailing inside the house. I looked at Claudine. She looked back at me with a stern expression and shook her head slowly.

Then she made herself smile, opened her eyes wide, looked down at Alice, and said, "I am gonna get you!"

Alice squealed and ran off ahead of her. I suddenly wondered what Claudine and Robert might have been trying to keep from me when I was Alice's age, and they had played the same game with me.

I looked down to see little Patrick at my feet. Mama's wails had become even louder, and they were starting to catch Patrick's attention. Alice was still running and squealing. She was happy, and completely unaware that anything was wrong. But Patrick was turning his head toward the house, and I could tell that he was about to start crying.

It was suddenly clear to me what I had to do. "Patrick?" I said, putting a smile on my face, opening my eyes wide, and I turning my hands into playful claws.

Patrick turned his head, and looked at me, and smiled.

I had his attention. Now I had to keep it. "I'm gonna get you!" I said.

He giggled and ran away from me as fast as his little legs could carry him.

Claudine and I spent the whole day doing this, keeping the little kids distracted, as more and more of Mama and Papa's friends kept coming by.

Some women started cooking. Some men who I had only met once or twice started building a fire in the backyard.

All day, people kept coming. The fire in the backyard became massive. People brought chairs and made makeshift benches to sit around it. They brought food and all kinds of alcohol: urwagwa, *ikigjye* (homemade sorghum beer), whiskey, palm wine, Primus Beer, and gin. Men, and some women, were sitting around the fire, passing bottles, eating, and telling stories about Papa.

One of the women sitting by the fire said, "Joseph took me and my whole family in one night when we were starving, I mean really starving. He had us over for breakfast, lunch, and dinner for two weeks. And then he and Sonia would always give us extra food to take home."

Several others who were sitting around the fire said, "*Eeeyyyyyy,*" like a chant. That's what we do in Rwanda when someone has said something that we really agree with.

"Whenever we couldn't make the rent, Joseph was always willing to lend us a little money to help out," a man said.

"Eeeeeeeyyyy," others said, and then they drank.

It went on like that, with everyone telling stories about Papa's charity, and what a good man he was, and how much they loved him. But no one was talking about why he was in the hospital, or what was happening!

Finally, Robert arrived, and I rushed toward him, calling his name.

"Elise!" he called back. He waved to me with a sad smile on his face. But even that faded as he was instantly surrounded by people, mostly men, shaking his hand, and patting him on the shoulder, and saying what a great man Papa was. It was like Robert was the star of some crazy movie.

"Robert!" I called to him again, but I was also surrounded, by neighbors and family friends, all women, ushering me away, saying things like, "Come on, Elise. Let's get you something to eat."

"Will someone please tell me what has happened to my Papa!" I yelled.

Everyone stopped. They were all looking at me, especially Claudine, who had an icy expression on her face, like I had just done the worst thing in the world.

Then one of the women smiled and said, "Look what I've got!" She was holding up a piece of candy. "Sweets!"

Day after day, the fire in our back yard kept getting fed, and more food and alcohol kept appearing, along with more and more people. There were neighbors and friends, even some people who were high up in Hutu Power. There were always women taking care of us, feeding us, dressing us, sitting with us, and talking about what a good man Papa was, how generous, and kind he was. They talked about every part of Papa's life, every part except what had happened to him, and why Mama couldn't stop crying.

Then one day, some of the women who were taking care of us brought us into the living room to see Mama. Up to this point she'd been surrounded by her friends all the time. They sat with her while she cried. They fed her when she was hungry. They even stayed with her when she went to use the toilet or bathe. Until that day we hadn't been able to get close to her.

Now there was a man with her who I had only seen a few times before, when Papa had had him over to the house for dinner. I was pretty sure he was a friend of Papa's. I could see that Mama had been drinking and crying. She was staring off into space. She looked numb.

"Children," the man said, "we have to tell you something. Your Papa was in an accident. He was coming back from Kabuye in his delivery van. There was another van, with a priest and two nuns in it, that… ran into your father's van. When the police and ambulance came, your papa told them to see to the priest and the nuns first. They were very badly injured."

"When your mama heard about the accident, she went to the hospital to see your papa. He seemed fine, just a little dizzy. What no one knew at the time was that your papa was bleeding on the inside. That night, after your mama went home, your papa died in the hospital. All of these people have been coming to your house for the *icyunamo*" (mourning period) "to be with your mama, to take care of you, and to pay their respects to your papa."

Now *I* was numb. This was so much to take in. The whole world had changed. I just sat there and stared at Papa's friend. We all did, for a long time.

Then Alice said, "But when is Papa coming home? I miss him!"

"There is no Papa anymore!" Mama burst out. "You just have to get used to it!"

Alice started wailing, which made Patrick do the same. Mama's friends ushered her into her bedroom and put her to bed. Gabriel, Claudine, and I had all started crying. I cried so hard I felt like I was vomiting, like I couldn't stop, like my body had to squeeze the hurt out of me.

"Your mama has had too much to drink," Papa's friend said. "She doesn't mean to be so… harsh."

Chapter Five: Growing Up

I had always felt certain, deeply certain, that no matter how dangerous the outside world became, Papa and the compound walls he built would protect us and keep us safe.

But it turned out I was wrong. It turned out that Papa hadn't had any special power to protect anybody, not even himself. Our compound walls hadn't protected him. The world outside had killed him, without even trying.

He hadn't been beaten to death by a Hutu gang. How good, or how big, or how strong, or how smart he had been didn't matter. He had been killed. By accident. I spent hours sitting in the back yard, looking out at the beautiful hills, thinking about all of this and crying.

I remembered one time, when I was little, when we had driven out to where our cows were kept. In Rwanda you don't put your money in a bank. You buy cows. We had fifty of them. Standing on the middle rung of a fence that penned them in, looking out at our cows, I asked, "Papa, are we rich?"

He smiled and said, "We're doing okay."

As I was growing up, I was aware that Papa owned land that people paid him rent to farm, and that he had a delivery van business that had grown over the years. So, I always felt like financially, we *were* okay.

But one night, not long after Papa died, I overheard Mama talking to a friend of hers "…And these are tenants that Joseph has had for years, tenants that he would give extra time to if they couldn't make the rent one month, sometimes for two or three months! Now they won't pay. None of them! And what can I do? A Tutsi woman? I can't beat them when they don't pay. I certainly can't go to the police! And Joseph's delivery van? Destroyed. And his drivers? Disappeared, with the rest of Joseph's vans!"

"What will you do, Sonia?" Mama's friend asked.

"I'm going to go talk to Gael."

"You can't rely on hand-outs, Sonia. Nothing comes for free."

"I'm not going to ask him for a hand-out! I'm going to ask him for a job! He's not just a rich man who owns a soap factory. He's been one of Joseph's best friends for… well, forever. And he's been my friend, too. And our families have always had an agreement that if anything were to ever happen to either of them, then the one who's left alive will help to take care of the other's family."

Papa's friend kept his word. When Mama went to him, he gave her a job in his factory. Even so, we had to move.

We had always been renters. Almost everyone in Rwanda was back then. But a few months before his accident, Papa had decided to change that. We must have been doing really well right before he died, because he had bought a piece of land, and started building us a home of our own.

We didn't find out until one Saturday morning when Mama started wrapping our things in sheets and blankets and towels and handing them to a bunch of boys she had gathered from the neighborhood.

"What's happening, Mama?" Claudine asked.

"Now that Papa is gone, we can't afford to keep renting this house anymore," Mama said. "We have to move into the new house that Papa was building for us. Now, Elise, help me with wrapping these things, and Claudine, take this," Mama gave her a lamp wrapped in a blanket, "and bring these boys to the house across the street and stay there. We're moving."

"I don't understand why Mama isn't at least a little bit excited about this," I said to Claudine. "We've never lived in our own house before!"

Claudine scoffed. "You're so… *innocent*," she said.

Mama took me over to the new house. In a lot of ways, it was just like our old house. It had the same high compound walls. It had a similar gate made out of corrugated tin. There was a little more land inside than our old compound had. Out back, just like the old house, the shower and toilet were in one building and the kitchen and wash area were in another. There was room to grow crops, too, just like there had been at our old house.

But I realized that some things were missing. The walls were all there, but there was a tarpaulin over part of the roof. Nothing was painted. Everywhere you looked, there was an empty hole in the wall where a window and bars were supposed to be.

It took months, but little by little, the house got finished, and new crops got planted.

We had a lot less money than when Papa was alive. But Mama had other ways of getting things. She was very popular in the neighborhood. It was no wonder, with the way she was always giving away food to people when they needed it, and with the way she could talk to people and just put them at ease. People would even come to her to settle disputes. So, as word got around that Mama needed help finishing our new house, here and there, people showed up to help.

It wasn't all at once. First it was the roof. One day, two men showed up with sheets of corrugated tin and a ladder. They finished the roof in a few hours. Mama made them tea and gave them some corn and other vegetables from our garden. The windows were next, about a week later. It was the same sort of thing as the roof.

Finally, there were the bars on the windows and the house got painted. We all helped out with that.

But after Papa's death money was always tight. Sometimes there wasn't enough money to pay for all of us to go to school at the same time, even with Mama working full-time at the soap factory.

We weren't the only ones having money troubles then. A lot of families in Rwanda were. Times were hard. Usually, though, if Hutu parents couldn't afford to pay, their children could still go to school, and the parents were usually allowed a grace period to pay what they owed. But we were Tutsis. So, if we were late with the tuition by even one day, they would send us home, where we'd have to stay until we could pay.

There were four of us in school by then: Robert, Claudine, Gabriel, and me. So, some years each of us would not go to school for a trimester. Sometimes it had to be two of us. The result was each of us ended up missing a lot of school.

Even so, I kept doing really well on all of my exams. Whenever grades were posted, I usually got the highest, or the second, or third highest score. That really seemed to annoy everybody at school, the students, and the teachers, which wasn't great. But it meant that I never got left back.

So, every year I ended up in the same class with a lot of the same people and a lot of the same problems.

Albert kept sending me love notes, which I never responded to, and Linda kept being made class chief. That allowed her to keep putting me on her list for the teacher, and it allowed her to keep overseeing my "punishments."

Not responding to Albert's notes for all those years wasn't easy. He was cute, very cute. He'd always been the cutest boy in school. All the girls thought so. But he was a Hutu, and I was a Tutsi. And my life at school was complicated enough.

One day, in ninth grade, as we were walking home for lunch, I saw Albert kneeling down on the side of the road, tying his shoe.

Linda was standing next to him, trying to talk to him, but he kept looking at me as I was walking toward them. When he smiled at me, I felt like there were butterflies inside my stomach. I looked away as I passed him, but Albert quickly rose to his feet and caught up with me, leaving Linda standing there by herself.

This was very, very uncomfortable for me. Here was this handsome, tall boy, taller than I was, even though he was a Hutu, with the warmest smile I had ever seen, trying to walk with me.

Meanwhile Linda went clomping by us, very quickly, almost running. She looked like she was about to cry.

"Elise," Albert said.

I kept walking, not looking at him.

"Elise? You know, we take the same way to and from school every day?"

"Yes," I said. "I suppose we do."

"Maybe…we should walk together," he said.

I wanted to. I wanted to so badly. In a flash, I saw us walking together, holding hands. First love. First kiss. First boyfriend. But then I saw Linda with a couple of Hutu boys pulling us into an alley, beating us. Albert's beautiful face beaten, bloody, and swollen like Papa's face the night we had saved him. So, I said, "I don't think that would be a very good idea."

"Why not?" he said.

I wanted to keep things as simple and straight forward as I could. So, I said, "Because you have been the cause of a lot of my 'punishments,' Albert!"

"I have?"

"Haven't you noticed that every time you've sent me a note, Linda's put me on her list, and then I got sent out to clean the toilets?"

"They make you do that?"

"You never noticed how dirty or smelly I was walking home on those days?" I said, rolling my eyes.

"My goodness, Elise! I'm so sorry!"

"And did you ever notice that I never sent you a note back?"

"I thought you were just, you know, playing hard to get."

"For five years?"

"Well…"

"Look. You need to stop sending me notes in class. Okay? I don't want to give the teacher or Linda any more excuses for 'punishing' me."

"I'm sorry, Elise," he said. "I really am." He did look sorry.

"I don't want to be mean," I said. "But I don't want to be made to clean toilets with my bare hands any more than… well…at all, if I can help it."

"No, you're right. Of course," Albert said. "I'm so sorry, Elise. I'll stop sending you notes. I promise."

"Thank you," I said, heartbroken.

When we got back to school after lunch, we all took our seats, and the teacher started the lesson. Linda raised her hand. The teacher called on her.

"Elise was talking!" Linda said.

"Elise. Again?" the teacher said.

"That's not true!" I blurted out. I don't know why, but I for some reason I just couldn't take it that day. "Teacher," I insisted. "I was *not* talking, and everyone knows it!"

"You dirty, lying Tutsi!" Linda said, jumping out of her seat and running over to my desk. "You **were** talking, and you need to be punished!" She was standing over me, shoving her finger in my face.

I stood up. I was about six inches taller than she was. I looked down at her, into her eyes. "I'm not afraid of you," I said.

"Well, you should be, you skinny Tutsi inzoka (snake)!" she said, shoving me with both hands. I grabbed her wrists, but she pulled them free and shoved me again. I shoved her back, and she punched me right in the face! This drew gasps and a few cheers from the other students. I had been beaten before by Mama, even slapped across the face, hard. But I had never been punched in the face before. Linda was shorter than I was, but she was wide and strong. Her punch really hurt. It also made me really, really mad. All of the anger towards her that I had been stuffing down for all of those years came up, and I punched her back, as hard as I could, right in the face.

"Everybody outside! Right now!" the teacher commanded, "…except Linda and Elise."

All of the children rushed out of the room. I thought the teacher was going to gather all of them in the courtyard, and then come back in to break up the fight, but she didn't. Linda and I watched as she directed the students to gather around the outside of the room so that they could watch us through the windows. They looked excited. They were smiling. Finally, there they were, each in their spot, waiting for the show to start. The teacher was leaning against the doorway, looking annoyed that Linda and I were just standing there.

"Well…" the teacher said.

The students all started chanting: "Lin-da! Lin-da! Lin-da!" and she lunged at me, howling, with her hands stretched out, ready to choke me. I grabbed her hands and used them to throw her against the blackboard. A plume of chalk dust went up, and Linda grunted.

I crouched down as she came back at me. She managed to get in a punch to one side of my nose, as I punched her in the stomach, a mass of fat and muscle. I felt something warm trickling down my top lip. I wiped it and looked at my hand. It was smeared with blood. I punched her twice in the face. She kicked me in the shin. I fell to my knees, scraping them on the hard concrete floor. She grabbed at my throat. I threw her off.

I kept thinking that someone was going to come in to break this up, but it just went on and on. The crowd was going wild.

Students had come from all over the school. Other teachers had brought their classes over to watch! Everyone was cheering, and pushing, and shoving each other, trying to get a better spot to see the fight. The crowd cheered every move of Linda's and booed every one of mine. They screamed. They laughed.

Linda and I kept trading punches and kicks. We shoved each other, and rolled around on the floor, struggling. Then Linda tried to choke me again, and this time it seemed like she was really trying to kill me. I realized that she wasn't going to stop, and that no one else was going to stop her, so I had to, and I knew I couldn't hold back.

I punched Linda in the stomach as hard as I could. She doubled over. The second she took one hand off my neck, I grabbed the other and rolled over on top of her. I punched her in the face. She spat in mine. I punched her in the face again as she managed to get on top of me. Then she hit me again and again and again. And finally, two teachers rushed in and pulled us apart.

One of the teachers took me to the headmaster's office. They called Mama at work. I waited in the hall, bleeding, as I watched Mama come in to meet with the headmaster, a big, scary Hutu man. They were in his office for a long time. I was so nervous I felt sick to my stomach. I was sure that I was going to get kicked out of school. Finally, I was called in. I stood next to Mama.

"Elise," the headmaster said. "We can't have you fighting here at our school. No more fighting! Do you understand?"

"...Yes," I said.

"All right," he said.

Then Mama stood up. "Come on," she said.

That's it? I thought. *I'm not even suspended?* But I was far too scared to ask Mama any questions or to say anything.

We walked home in silence. When we got there, Mama beat me and sent me to bed without supper. As I lay there, feeling my bruises, I wondered what would happen next.

The next day I got up, with the rest of my family, got ready, went to church, had breakfast, changed into my uniform, and then went to school. No one talked about what had happened.

When I got to school, I walked into my classroom, just like I did every day, and took my seat in the back row, with the rest of the Tutsis. I looked around, cautiously. All day I waited for something to happen to me, but nothing did. No one mentioned the bruises on my face, or my neck, or the fact that Linda wasn't there.

It took a few days, but eventually Linda came back. Her face looked horrible, much worse than mine, a little bit like Papa's face after his fight with his tenant "friends." It wasn't more than five minutes before I could see Linda writing my name down on her list of students that needed to be "punished." It seemed that nothing had changed, that everything was back to normal. Except that, for the first time, in the outside world, I had stood up for myself.

I never found out why those teachers stopped the fight, or why I didn't get kicked out of school or even suspended. Maybe everybody at the school just wanted to bury what had happened. Maybe they would have gotten in trouble for letting a murder happen in front of so many witnesses, even if it was the murder of a Tutsi girl.

With Mama keeping me inside our compound all the time that I wasn't in church or school, I didn't really ever make any friends.

School was no help. Albert was the only Hutu kid there who ever tried to be friendly to me, and we Tutsis almost never talked to each other because we were trying not to give anyone an excuse to "punish" us.

Claudine was different. She always seemed to have friends, or at least acquaintances. She was certainly better than I was at not making enemies. There was one girl named Rose, a Hutu girl. She was Claudine's age. They were friends, sort of. They had been for some time.

Rose would try to joke around with Claudine, but Claudine almost never picked up the joke and made more of it. I could never understand that. I thought, *Maybe Claudine just doesn't like Rose, or maybe she's afraid of her because she was a Hutu, or because of who her father is.*

I didn't ask Claudine about it. Mostly by that point I had stopped asking her about anything. I didn't like how she always acted as though I was stupid for asking. It hurt my feelings.

I did like Rose, though. Sometimes I would sit with her and Claudine. And sometimes, when Claudine would just let a joke die, I would pick it up, and Rose and I would run with it. Claudine would sit with us a while, looking a little uncomfortable. Then she would get up and walk away, and Rose and I would keep laughing, and joking, and talking. And over time, Rose and I kind of gradually realized that we were friends and started spending time together without Claudine.

One day, as we were walking together, I asked Rose, "Have you heard about the disco downtown that's just for teenagers?"

"Oh, The Boom?" she said. "Sure. I go there all the time!"

"…What's it like?"

"Oh, it's boring," she said. "It's really, really boring."

"Oh," I said. "Really?"

"No!" Rose said. "Of course not! It's fantastic! I'm going there today, and so are you."

"What?"

"You're coming with me," she said.

"I am?"

"Of course, you are!" she said. "Why not?"

"Well, I'm a Tutsi. And I'm only fourteen."

"Yes. But you're with me!"

"What will I tell Mama, though?" I asked.

"Tell her I'm tutoring you. I'll back you up."

I wasn't sure whether or not to say anything about Rose's father. I decided to take a chance. "So, you're, what, Miss Big Hutu?" I asked.

"Well," she said. "Kind of, yeah."

"So, I suppose we're going to go in your private limousine?"

"Don't be ridiculous," she said. "Then Papa would know what I was doing. We'll take the bus."

I had never been into downtown Kigali without Mama or Claudine or Robert. I was so excited. I tried to pay as we were getting on the bus, but Rose wouldn't let me. She paid for both of us.

When we got to the club, I could hear the music thumping from inside. A big, scary-looking Hutu man with a shaved head stopped us at the door, demanding: "*Cartes d'identité!*" without even looking at us. These were the cards the law said you had to carry with you at all times.

Rose gave him her card.

"Hutu. Sixteen," he read. Then he looked up at Rose with a smile. "Ah, Mademoiselle Kayihura! Please, come right in."

As she headed in, I tried to follow her, but the Hutu man swung in front of me like a big, scary door.

"Carte!" he demanded.

"She's with me," Rose was trying to say from inside, but either the man couldn't hear her, or he didn't want to.

I gave the man my carte.

"Tutsi?" he read. "Fourteen? No-no-no-no-no," he said with a sour expression. "Next!"

"Pardon, pardon, Monsieur?" Rose said as she came back outside. "Monsieur, she's with me."

"I am sorry, Mademoiselle Kayihura. Fifteen is the minimum age. Those are the rules."

"Pleeeeease?" Rose said, motioning for me to do the same.

"Pleeeeease?" we said together. "Pleeeeeeeeeease?"

"But she's a Tutsi!" the man said.

"A beautiful Tutsi!" Rose said, holding up my face. "A-and," she kind of sang, smiling a devilish smile, and holding up a folded twenty-franc note, "I could make it worth your while. And I could certainly tell Papa what a good job you're doing, helping to provide a safe place where all of the Hutu teens can go and have fun. Come on," she said, motioning to me again.

And together we both said, again, "Pleeeeeeeeeeease?"

At last, the man broke into a smile. "Okay, okay," he said, taking the twenty francs.

We jumped up and down with excitement and headed inside.

We danced, and drank soda, and had lots and lots of fun. We talked with boys, kind of.

"I've never heard music this loud before!" I yelled in one boy's ear as I danced with him. We were all doing some very weird, fast, exaggerated version of a traditional Rwandan dance that we had learned as children, mixed with whatever other moves we could come up with to "Whoop, There It Is!"

"What?" the boy yelled back.

"I said I've…" then I couldn't stop laughing. I was talking about how loud the music was, and the boy couldn't hear me because the music was so loud. And I was nervous, and excited, and a little out of breath.

When Rose and I got back to my house, it was late. Rose told Mama that she had been tutoring me. Mama thanked her, but as soon as Rose left, Mama had me bend over the dining room table.

"I can't believe you, Elise!" Mama yelled as she beat me. "Do you know what can happen to you out there, when you're not in school, or here at home? Why do you think I tell you that you have to be home at six o'clock every day? You could get robbed! You could get killed! You could get raped!" She was crying by that point.

"Tutsis get robbed and killed, and Tutsi girls get raped all the time now!" She was sobbing so hard that, for a moment, she couldn't go on. "Now, go to your room and think about what you've done!" She sobbed some more. "How could you do this to me, Elise?"

I didn't really know what rape was then. I knew it was bad. I had heard the word before, but I had never heard Mama use it. It definitely wasn't a good time to ask her about it. I didn't want Mama to feel angry or scared for me. All I could think to do was put my arms around her. "I'm sorry, Mama," I said. "I'm so sorry." I wanted to promise her that I would never do it again, but I couldn't. I'd just seen a good part of the world outside our compound walls, and I wanted to see more. As I tried to comfort Mama, I decided that the best thing to do, for both of us, was simply to never get caught again.

Of course, I went back to The Boom, many times, with Rose. It was wonderful. The music. The dancing. Hutu kids, who wouldn't speak to me if I was by myself, accepted me when I was with Rose.

They were even nice to me, like I was a normal girl, not "that dirty Tutsi."

I started spending a lot of time with Rose. She took me to other clubs and restaurants and shops. Being with Rose was fun, and I felt safe with her. All she had to do was mention her papa, and suddenly no one would give us any trouble.

It felt like, with Rose, I could go anywhere. We would spend whole afternoons exploring the streets and alleyways of Kigali. Except for a few times when my brothers and sisters and I used them to walk from our house to our uncle's house in Nyamirambo, the Muslim neighborhood of Kigali, I never really went into the alleyways before I met Rose. They always seemed a little scary to me, the way they twisted and turned, with no clear plan to them, creating these mazes in the spaces between all of the major roads in Kigali. If you didn't know the alleys well, you could quickly get lost and have trouble finding your way out.

But when I was with Rose, I realized that the alleys were kind of a world of their own. There were all sorts of interesting things to see as you walked through them. I loved the way the walls on both sides of you kept changing as you walked. They would go from a high red brick compound wall, straight into the white stucco wall of a house, with windows set into it. I remember one that was painted purple and white, and it was set into the wall at an angle, making it look like a diamond.

As you kept going down the alley, a wall could turn into the front of a tiny shop made of mud bricks and thatch, with just enough room inside for the three or four children standing at the narrow counter buying candy. The shop might run into a bamboo fence with a courtyard behind it where a woman might be sitting on her back steps, washing sweet potatoes in a plastic basin.

The fence could turn into a hedge of light green milk bush, grown so thick you could barely see through it. The hedge would run right into the gray cinderblock front wall of another house, with windows and a door that opened right on to the alley. Across from that might be another high red brick compound wall with grass growing along the bottom edge and moss growing in the shady parts. And there would be flowers growing here and there along the tops of walls, and bright green grass in the little triangle where one alley forked off into two.

And it wasn't just the buildings and the walls. The people you'd see in the alleys and the things you'd see them doing were fascinating. There were men using bicycles like carts, with so many sacks and plastic jugs hanging off of them, there was no way anybody could ride them. You'd see people bunching up, as they negotiated a fissure, cut in the red earth during heavy rains, that ran right down the middle of an alley. You'd see people carrying massive loads on their heads: huge clay pots or two full sacks of wheat.

When I came home after spending time with Rose, Mama never asked about it. I just made sure that I never got caught staying out late, and I made sure that Rose and I spent plenty of time at my house. Mama had always liked Rose, and I thought that the two of us spending time together in front of her would put Mama's mind at ease. I often asked if Rose could stay for dinner, and Mama would always say yes.

Chapter Six: Fred

Fred Rwigema and Paul Kagame grew up in a Tutsi refugee camp in Uganda, the country just north of Rwanda. Their parents were among tens of thousands of Tutsis who had fled there from Rwanda over the decades.

Fred (that's what everybody called him) became the military leader of the Rwandan Patriotic Front, a political party and a rebel army set up by the Tutsis from the refugee camp. Paul Kagame became the RPF's head of intelligence. Their aim was to return all of the Tutsi refugees to Rwanda one day.

Most Tutsis loved Fred and thought he would be president of Rwanda some day, but Hutus just hated him. Sometimes you would hear them talking openly on the street about how they hoped that they would get the chance to kill him personally, and describing the ways they would like to do it.

TVs were pretty rare in Rwanda when I was growing up, but radios were everywhere. Even though Mama didn't allow them on in the house, as soon as you left our compound, you'd hear them everywhere: in other people's houses, and in all the shops and the stalls in the market. So, whenever something big happened, you'd hear about it on the radio.

Every time Fred made a speech, they'd broadcast it on the radio and then talk about what a threat he and all the other Tutsis were. When the RPF invaded Rwanda from Uganda in October of 1990, everybody heard the reports on the radio. And later on, when reports of Fred being killed during that attack came out, everyone heard that on the radio, too, and the streets of Kigali went wild.

It was during a school vacation week. Mama and Robert had gone off to work. The rest of us were told to stay inside the compound all day.

We were all playing tag in the garden when we started to hear the oddest combination of sounds. There were shouts of celebration, yelling and cheering, like when your team has just won a football match, but there were also gunshots, screams of horror, and shrieks of pain. We all froze in our tracks to listen.

"What is that, Claudine?" I asked.

"I don't know," she said, as she walked cautiously toward the compound gate. We all followed behind her. The sounds got louder and louder as we approached the gate. We pushed it open, just a tiny bit, and through the crack, we saw the strangest things. An army truck was driving by very slowly, with soldiers in the back, shooting their guns in the air and handing out cups of beer to everyone. Hutus were dancing, and singing, and drumming, and blowing whistles. One group of Hutus was pushing a wheelbarrow with a dummy in it stuffed with straw. The dummy had black X's for eyes and a sign around its neck that read

"RWIGEMA." People were hacking at the dummy with machetes as it went by and calling out things like: "Fred is dead! Let's kill the rest of the Tutsis!"

Off in the distance I heard a man yelling, "No, no, please, no!" and then a bunch of men shouting, and then horrible, horrible screams.

Very, very quietly, we closed the gate, locked it, and backed away from it.

"What's happening?" Alice asked. She was too small to have seen over the rest of us.

"Uh, nothing," Claudine said. "Don't worry about it. We'll just play inside the compound today. No one opens the gate! Understand?"

We all nodded.

"Will Mama be okay?" Patrick asked.

"Mama will be fine," I said, without thinking and smiled at Patrick. I was shocked by how easily I said this. I certainly didn't know that it was true. Inside, I was terribly worried about Mama, and Robert as well.

"Alice," Claudine was saying, with a big, playful smile on her face, and her hands out like monster claws. "I'm gonna get you!" Alice squealed with joy and ran off, into the back yard.

"Patrick," I said, seeing what Claudine was doing, and copying her, "I'm gonna get you!" Patrick laughed too and ran off in the same direction as Alice. "Gabriel. Gabriel!" I caught his attention. He was still looking toward the gate.

"What?"

"Come on," I said. "Help with the children."

We stayed inside the compound and played, as we would have normally. Claudine and I did our best to keep the younger kids focused on the games, hoping that they wouldn't notice the noises that kept coming from beyond the compound walls.

Mama came home late that night. We had all been so worried. We all hugged her tight as soon as she got inside.

She hugged us back saying, "Oh, my lovely children! I'm so glad to see you all, and that you're all alright!"

"We're just glad you're home, Mama," I said.

"Mama, can we go see what's happening outside?" Gabriel asked.

"Go outside, only if you want to die!" Mama burst out.

We all backed away from her. She put her hands up to her face, and then out in front of her like she was motioning for us to stop. Then she walked quickly into her bedroom. None of us knew what to do for a long moment.

Then Claudine said, "Children, it's time for bed." She took them out to the back yard, and I followed. We helped them wash and brought them back inside to get them into their pajamas. Then we tucked them all into bed. It was good to have something to do.

It was days before Mama let any of us even peek outside the compound. When we did, as I looked around, I couldn't believe my eyes. The neighborhood looked like it had been attacked. And there, in the drainage ditch, was a dead man!

"Mana we!" Mama said, then she quickly moved us all back inside the compound and locked the gate.

A little later as Claudine, Gabriel, and I were playing with the younger kids to keep them busy, we heard a large truck pull up in front of our compound. I peeked through a hole in the gate to see what was happening. It was an army truck. Two soldiers jumped out, picked up the dead man, and threw him into the back of the truck. Then they drove off.

Robert still hadn't come home. I could tell everybody was horribly worried about him, even though no one said a word.

Then, four nights after Mama's return, Robert finally came home. We were all so relieved and happy to see him that we hugged and kissed him.

Later that evening, after Mama had sent us to bed, Claudine and I opened our door a crack so we could listen to Mama and Robert talking at the dining room table.

"…And when everything was going crazy," Mama said, "we turned on the radio to find out what was happening-"

"You must have heard that Fred was killed leading an RPF attack on Rwanda."

"Yes, of course. And there was just *insanity* going on in the streets! We had to just lock the door and stay there inside the factory.

There was nothing else we could do. We didn't even turn on the lights when it got dark. We just sat down on the floor behind our desks, waiting for things to calm down outside. We were hiding in there for hours! And then there was a banging on the office door, and I could hear Francis screaming for someone to let him in."

"Francis?"

"You know, Papa's Tutsi friend. My Tutsi friend! He was screaming for someone to help him. So, I got up, and opened the door, and there he was, with a bunch of Hutus right behind him! And Robert, just as I was opening the door, choo! They chopped him! Right across the back with a machete! And I slammed the door and locked it! Mana we! I feel so horrible! If I had been just a little bit quicker!"

"If you had been a bit slower in slamming the door, you would probably be dead now, too," Robert said, "just like Fred."

"I don't know. I don't know!" Mama said and wept a little.

"Fred's death is a huge loss for the RPF," Robert said. "And then, on top of that, the Rwandan army was backed up by French special forces and artillery. Cut the RPF to ribbons and pushed them back to the Tanzanian border. But Kagame…"

"Kagame wasn't with them?"

"Oh no. He was at a military training in America, thank God. But he'll bring the RPF back together, get them in shape."

"I don't want to know about those things, Robert. I don't want to know how you know them. It's too…"

"Alright, Mama," he said. "Alright."

Claudine and I closed the door softly, crept back into our beds and eventually fell into a troubled sleep.

It was another week before Mama thought it was safe for us to leave the compound. When we finally went back to school, it was tense. The teacher kept going on and on about how great it was that Fred had been killed, and about how the Tutsis wanted "…to re-enslave the Hutus just like the Belgians had before them!" I didn't know what she was talking about. I didn't know a single Tutsi that had any interest in enslaving anybody.

When I came home for lunch that day, as usual, Robert helped me get lunch ready for Alice and Patrick, but Claudine wasn't there. *That's odd*, I thought.

"Where's Claudine?" Robert asked.

"I don't know," I said. "Maybe she got hung up at school."

I made sure to get home right after school that day. I wanted to find out what had held Claudine up at lunch. Mama was working as many hours as she could to pay the bills. So, usually Claudine and I would come home right after school and help the younger kids start their homework. Then we'd do our own homework and start cooking dinner. But that day, Claudine wasn't there. I was starting to get a little concerned. *I'm sure she's fine*, I told myself, hoping it was true. But it was getting late.

"Elise!" I heard Mama calling though the house. I was sitting in the washing area out behind the house, taking a little time to myself.

"Elise, where is Claudine?" Mama demanded, as she opened the back door.

"I don't know, Mama," I said.

"It's past seven o'clock!"

"I know, Mama, but I don't-"

"You know I have always told you girls that you have to be inside by six o'clock!"

"Yes, Mama. I know."

"I've always told you that there are all sorts of horrible, horrible things that can happen to you out there!" Mama seemed panicked. That scared me.

"Yes, Mama-" I said.

"You could get mugged by bandits!"

"Yes, Mama-"

"You could get raped! You could get killed! It was bad enough with Robert not coming home for days at a time, and now Claudine?"

I followed Mama inside. She practically collapsed into one of the dining room chairs, crying. Then she wiped away her tears, rested her chin in her hands, and stared off into space. I wanted to comfort her, but I didn't know what to say or what to do.

Claudine didn't come home that night, or the next night, or the next. None of us knew what had happened to her. We didn't know if she was dead or alive. I couldn't stop thinking about the dead man we had seen just outside the house, in the drainage ditch.

One night, after about a week of this awful uncertainty, Mama came home from work and stormed up to me, as I was doing my homework at the dining room table. *Oh no!* I thought. She *has some horrible news about Claudine!*

"Did you know about this?" Mama demanded.

"About what, Mama?"

"About Claudine."

"What about Claudine? Is she okay?"

"She called me today, at work." We didn't have a phone in the house.

"Where is she?" I asked.

"She is in Burundi at your Uncle Hakizimana's house!"

"What?" I said, amazed.

"She's been there for a week!" Mama said. "She didn't tell you anything about this?"

"No, Mama," I said.

"She said that she is not coming back. She said she is going to find a way to go to Brussels, and that that's where she is going to live!"

"Well, isn't that a good thing?" I asked. "Everybody wants to go to there." Since Rwanda used to be a Belgian colony, Brussels was the easiest place in Europe for Rwandans to enter. "I mean, what kind of life can a Tutsi girl look forward to here?" I said.

Mama slapped me across the face. "*I* am a Tutsi girl!" she said. "So are you! This is our country too, Elise! We have just as much right to be here and make a life for ourselves as anybody else!"

I held my face where Mama had slapped me.

"Come help me make dinner," Mama said.

I did.

Much later that night, as I was finishing my homework, I heard a key turning in the front door.

"Hello?" I called. I heard footsteps in the hall, and then Robert appeared in the doorway. "Robert!" I said, running to him and throwing my arms around him. I pulled back a bit and looked at him. He had a bruise over his right eye. "What happened to you?"

"Sometimes Tutsis fight back," he said.

"What?"

"It's nothing," he said, smiling. "How is Mama?"

"Did you know that Claudine went to Burundi?" I asked. "She didn't even say anything to me or Mama before she left."

"What do you think Mama would have done if Claudine had told her that she was leaving?"

"I guess she would have tried to stop her."

"You bet," he said. "Well, I'm going to get some sleep." He started walking off toward his room. Then he backed up, and he pointed at me. "You're next," he said, as he went off to bed.

Rose came over a few days later. She seemed upset. "What's wrong, Rose?" I asked.

"Elise, Papa saw us together on the street yesterday and…." She started crying.

"What is it, Rose?" I asked.

"He says I can't see you anymore."

"Why not?"

"He says because you are a Tutsi, you are evil and dirty! He's saying that the Tutsis want to become our slave masters again, and that you are foreigners, that you don't belong here!"

"That's crazy!"

"I know, I know, Elise! Of course it's crazy! But he's my papa!"

"What about your mama?"

"Oh, she's always hated Tutsis, deep down."

"Really? I had no idea. She's always so nice when I come over."

"She just *seems* that way. But then, after you leave, she always throws away all the dishes you touched."

"***Really***?" I said. "Well, I guess I don't want to go over to *your* house anymore."

"Seriously, Elise," she said. "You can't."

"Wait, did you come over to tell me that we aren't going to hang out anymore?"

"No, Elise! Of course not! But I think when we get together, it would be best if we didn't tell anyone about it."

"Oh. So you're going to make it *seem* like you're doing what your parents are telling you to do," I said.

"Of course I am!" she said.

We laughed.

"All kidding aside though," she said. "You should probably just avoid my parents. They certainly want *me* to avoid *you*."

"I think you're right," I said. "I'm so glad I have you as a friend," I said, hugging her. I was crying a little.

"We'll work all this out," she said.

And we did. We continued spending time together, but we decided it was best if we didn't tell anybody about it and if we didn't let anybody see us together in public. More and more, when Mama was out at work, Rose and I would meet in our secret spot, under the avocado tree in the far corner of our compound, hidden away from the rest of the world.

It turned out that Robert had been right about Paul Kagame. In the beginning of 1991, there were reports on the radio about him leading the RPF in an attack on the northern town of Ruhengeri, and then more reports about him leading raids on Rwandan army bases, capturing arms and supplies. Then there were reports about him recruiting and training Tutsis from all over Rwanda and growing the RPF.

And, I guessed, in response, there were more and more rallies against the RPF, and Kagame, and all Tutsis. There were people on the radio talking about how Kagame just wanted to be the king of Rwanda, like the Tutsi rulers a hundred years ago.

It seemed Kagame's attacks were having an effect, though. Because months later, everyone on the radio was talking about changing the government so that there would be Tutsis in it again, and then there were reports about Kagame and the Rwandan army declaring a cease fire.

Chapter Seven: The Boy

It used to be that wherever you went in Kigali, you would see groups of mayibobo (homeless boys). They would set up make-shift stands, by putting boards across two stacks of bricks, or they would spread out a large sheet of plastic, or a torn, ratty bed sheet on the ground, by the side of the road, where they would lay out sunglasses, razor blades, pencils, cigarettes, and other little things they would try to sell. The boys would call out to you as you walked by. They would smile, trying to charm you into buying something.

Though you might expect them to be miserable, being homeless and filthy, the mayibobo always seemed friendly and playful. When they weren't manning their makeshift stalls, you'd see them playing with a football they had found in the garbage, or sometimes even with a ball they had made out of rags. Or you would see them laughing as they ran between people in the streets, playing tag.

One morning, as I was walking to school, I saw a group of mayibobo on the side of the street. I didn't know any of them by name, but I had seen most of them before, laughing and playing. That day, though, there was something different about them.

There was an older Hutu boy with them, a teenager. Like the younger boys, he was unwashed, but the older boy was shirtless, and he stared at me with an unsettling look in his eyes, a look that seemed to say, "I can do whatever I want, and there's nothing you can do about it." He seemed to be the new leader of the younger boys. They all copied him: just staring at me, smiling, not making a sound.

Right after I passed him, the teenage boy called out, "Hey, *Rucumu! Rucuuuuu-muuuuu!" That's an odd thing for him to call out*, I thought. I had grown used to inyenzi and inzoka. But *Rucumu*? It's Kinyarwanda for "spear." I guessed he was commenting on how long and thin I was, how much like a Tutsi I looked. I didn't want to do anything to encourage attention from any Hutu. So, I didn't look back. As I kept walking, I could hear the other boys in the gang laughing.

Before she left, I would have asked Claudine about how to handle something like this. Even though I knew she would have said something dismissive, it would have been something. With Mama working so much ever since Papa died, we all used to look to Claudine. But now she was gone, and I was the oldest.

"It's like he's… into you, or something." Rose said, when I told her about the "Hey Rucumu" boy and his gang. "Like he thinks he's flirting with you," she said, laughing.

"I know," I said. I was laughing too. "It's like he's not very good with girls, and this is the best he can do." As I thought about it, though, I stopped laughing.

"I'm sorry to laugh," Rose said, stopping, too.

"No, hey," I said. "Either you laugh, or you cry, right?"

The next day, as I was leaving for school, there they were again, across the street from the compound gate, the same teenage boy with his gang. Just like the day before, they all just stared at me silently. And then, just after I passed them, the older boy called out, "Hey, Rucumu! Rucuuuuu-muuuuu!"

Again, I made sure not to look back. I didn't want to give them an excuse to… well, I didn't want to give them an excuse to do anything.

The next day, as I was walking into the market down the street from my house, a reporter on a radio that was in one of the stalls there caught my attention. She was saying that due to the massive increase in violence against Tutsis, which Paul Kagame claims has been sanctioned by the Rwandan government, he will be suspending negotiations and resuming the RPF's military offensive against Rwanda.

"You happy about that, inyenzi?" the Hutu-looking man in the stall asked.

I didn't want to start anything. So, I just walked away.

A few days later, as Rose and I were headed downtown, we emerged from an alley to find a crowd of Hutus lining one of the main roads, cheering. There was a military truck driving very slowly with a man in the back on a bullhorn calling out, "KORA KAZE KAWE!" over and over. It made me shudder.

Behind the truck was a group of teenage boys, who looked very much like the boy who kept calling, "Hey, Rucumu." They were all about the same age, teenagers, some of them might have been young men. They looked unwashed. Some were shirtless, some had shirts on, but all of their clothes were ratty.

They were all running in time with a military man, who was running next to them. He would call out, and they would respond.

"Inyenzi! Inyenzi!" the military man called.

"We're gonna find you!" The boys responded.

The man: "We're gonna step on you!"

The boys: "We're gonna kill you!"

And they continued like that as they ran down the road. There were three groups like that, running in formation, and in the last group, near the back, I saw the teenage boy, the "Hey, Rucumu!" boy! He gave me that same unsettling look, and then he winked at me.

I grabbed Rose's arm.

"What?" she said.

"Did you see that boy in the last group, the one who winked at me?"

"Yeah."

"That's the one, the one who's been calling out, 'Hey Rucumu!' to me.

"…Oh…" Rose said.

"What?"

"Well, you've got a real problem on your hands."

"Why?"

"Because he's part of the *Interahamwe*!"

"How can those boys be part of the Interahamwe?" I asked.

I had heard of the Interahamwe. It's Kinyarwanda for "those who work together." It was a sort of public service program the government used sometimes when they had a really big project to do, like building a road or a bridge. Everyone was supposed to do it, but usually homeless kids were the only ones who actually showed up. The government fed them while they were working on a project. But I had never heard of the Interahamwe being trained by the military or standing around harassing Tutsi girls.

"The army is turning the Interahamwe into something new," Rose said. "They're training mayibobo the way they train soldiers."

"Why?"

"Wait just a minute until we get up there where there aren't so many people," Rose said in a low voice. "And no matter what I tell you, remember to smile. It throws people off."

"Okay," I said, nervously putting on a smile.

"Bad things are coming, Elise," she said.

"What do you mean?"

"I think they're training those boys…" she trailed off.

"To do what, Rose?" I said, still forcing myself to smile.

"I think it's so they'll have more people to kill the Tutsis."

"What do you mean?" I said. "They can't just …"

"They can!" Rose insisted. "They definitely can. They're planning for it. They're training those boys for it! You know that Tutsi girl who got raped last week?"

"Oh, yes! Suzanne."

"Well, that was the Interahamwe. And that Tutsi man, whose body they found in the drainage ditch, just past the church, last month?"

"Marianne's father."

"Yeah, the Interahamwe did that too!"

"How do you know all of this?" I asked.

As we continued walking Rose subtly looked around to make sure that no one was listening. Then, in a voice just above a whisper she said, "I could get killed if anybody found out I was telling you this."

"Rose," I said, stopping. "You're scaring me."

"Keep your voice down!" she hissed. "And keep walking. And smile. Pretend that we're talking about something else, something…fun."

"Okay," I said, but I felt cold inside.

"Papa held a meeting at our house a few days ago," she said, "a meeting of the Interahamwe. I was in the kitchen, and I could hear what they were saying. And those boys we just saw? I saw some of them at that meeting, Elise! And one of them was talking about how he and his gang raped Suzanne! The whole gang! And they were all laughing and joking about it!"

"Mana we!" I said.

"And there were police there at that meeting, Elise! And men from the military, laughing right along with everyone else!"

I just stopped talking after that.

"I know, Elise," Rose said. "I know it's hard to hear these things, but I had to tell you. Just keep walking with me. And keep smiling."

We kept walking. I kept the fake smile on my face, but I felt like I was going to vomit.

The next morning, as I was leaving for school, I saw the same boy with his gang across the street from my compound. I saw them in a totally differently way, now. I couldn't think of them as mayibobo anymore. They were Interahamwe. That word was different, too. Now it meant something scary, very scary: mayibobo trained to harass, rape, and murder.

They seemed to be talking among themselves, joking, and laughing, but as soon as they saw me, they all fell silent and just stared at me. I kept walking toward my school, and then I heard the teenage boy call out: "Hey, Rucumu!" I could hear the younger boys in the gang laughing. Before this had just been annoying. Now it was scary. I looked straight ahead and kept walking. From behind me, the teenage boy called out again, "Ru-cuuu-muuuu!" and his gang all laughed.

I fought the urge to look back. I fought the urge to run. I had asked Rose about rape. Now I knew what it was, exactly, but I didn't know how to keep it from happening to me. I pretended to ignore the boy and his gang. It was the only thing I could think of to do.

When I left school that day, there was the teenage boy with his Interahamwe gang again, across the street from the front gate to the school. *Have they been standing there, waiting for me all day?* I wondered.

"Hey, Rucumu!" the teenage boy called out. The other boys in the gang laughed. Again, I tried to act like I wasn't paying attention to them, but I could feel myself shaking. So far, I had been thinking of this as something I would just have to deal with in the morning, but if they had been waiting for me, that meant that, to this Interahamwe boy and his gang, I wasn't just some random Tutsi girl that they saw walking by. They were seeking me out! Again, all I could think to do was to look ahead, toward home, pretend that nothing was wrong, and just keep walking. I didn't hear them following me. Even so, I didn't look back the whole way home.

The next day was a Saturday. Mama asked me to go to the market to do the shopping. Before I opened the gate to our compound, I looked out through the small gap between the two gate doors, checking to see if the boy and his gang were waiting for me across the street. "Whew," I said out loud when I saw that they weren't. *Maybe the Interahamwe doesn't work on the weekends*, I thought. *Or maybe I just got lucky today.*

As I was entering the market, I heard a reporter on a radio speaking about how Paul Kagame and the RPF were continuing to have victory after victory in battles with the Rwandan army, and how the RPF now controlled much of northern Rwanda.

I kept walking toward one of the stalls where a man sold the chili peppers and curry powder Mama wanted. And then, as I came around the end of a row of stalls, there they were: the teenage boy and his Interahamwe gang, walking toward me.

As soon as he saw me, the older boy broke into a big creepy smile. The rest of the gang looked to him and then copied his look. I immediately turned into another aisle to try to get away from them, but as soon as I did, the boy called out, "Hey, Rucumu! I see you, Rucumu! What, you don't want to talk to me? Rucumu! Rucuuuuumuuuuuu!" I looked back and saw that they were following me, from stall to stall, calling, "Rucumu! Rucuuuuumuuuuuu!" over and over again.

Some of the vendors in the stalls started joining in. Soon, "Hey, Rucumu!" was coming from all around me. I had to get out of there, but I knew I couldn't show them that I was panicking. I walked home as quickly as I could and locked the compound gate behind me. Mama yelled at me for not getting everything on her list. I didn't even bother trying to explain.

The next morning the boy and his gang were there again, in the same spot, as I was leaving for school.

As I passed them, the boy flashed his horrible smile and called out, "Hey Rucumu! Rucumu!"

I could hear the teenage boy calling out to me again, and again, and again, as he and his gang followed me all the way to school. And when I left to go home for lunch that day, there they were: the boy and his gang, waiting for me, across the street from the school.

They followed me all the way home, and then, when I came out of my compound to go back to school for my afternoon classes, there they were again. They followed me back to school. And now the teenage boy was trying something new: Adding to his usual "Rucumu" chant, he really creeped me out by getting closer and closer as he said it, until it felt like he was inches from the back of my neck, whispering it. To the rest of the gang, it was like he was doing a comedy routine. They laughed harder than I had ever heard them laugh before.

Mana we! I thought. *Have the Hutu Power bosses, men like Rose's father, told him to find one Tutsi girl and just drive her crazy?*

From then on, it was like this every day. When I left for school in the morning, there they were. When I left school to go home for lunch, they were waiting for me. They followed me all the way home and all the way back to school. They would follow me on the way home at the end of the day. They would follow me to the market, every time I went. It even got to the point where the Hutu vendors would call out, "Hey, Rucumu!" every time they saw me, even before they saw the boy and his Interahamwe gang.

I was starting to get used to the teenage boy and his gang always being there, whenever I left the compound. But I never felt calm about it. I was always afraid that things would get worse, especially with all the stories I was hearing:

"This Tutsi boy got mugged and badly beaten by an Interahamwe gang!"

"Another Tutsi girl got raped last week by a gang of Interahamwe!"

"What had they done to bring on the attack?"

"He looked one of the Interahamwe in the eye."

"She got scared when the Interahamwe gang started harassing her, and she started to run!"

It seemed like anything could set them off. And it always seemed like I was hearing stories like these more and more often.

The whole thing was a nightmare. I was terrified. I was furious. But there was nothing I could do. I didn't even want to go to Mama. I knew that she would just try to deny that anything bad was happening, or tell me that I was imagining it, or that it was my fault somehow. Anyway, she had enough to worry about by then. There was simply no point in going to the police. There was really nothing anyone, myself included, could do.

I did talk to Rose about it, a little, but all she could do was tell me that she was worried about me being a Tutsi girl and to be careful. I didn't know how to be any more careful with a gang following me, except to keep ignoring them.

Even when the teenage boy started adding new lines like, "Hey, Tutsi girl! Too good for a Hutu boy?" I didn't look back at him. But I could hear him. It sounded like he was getting ready to spit.

And then, one day, I felt this wet, warm thing hit the back of my neck. I instinctively put my hand up and wiped it away. He had spat on me. But still, I didn't turn around. I didn't speed up. I used all my powers of self-control not to let the rage and fear I was feeling make me tremble. I just kept walking at the same speed. *Please just let it not get any worse*, I prayed. *Just don't let it get any worse!*

The boy and his gang didn't spit on me every day from then on, but it became part of their repertoire. Whenever one of them did it, just like before, I kept walking, not looking at them and saying to myself, "Just, please, don't let it get any worse than this!"

But it did. One day one of them threw a piece of garbage at me. And then that got added to their bag of tricks.

I did my best to just keep ignoring them, but all of that ignoring was taking a toll. I thought about the boy and his gang all the time. It kept me up nights. It made it hard to concentrate at school. I kept asking myself if there was anything I could do. I wished I could just lock myself inside our compound and never come out.

One afternoon, as I was doing my homework at the dining room table, I heard a frantic knocking at our compound gate. As I ran to the gate, I could hear Rose whispering, as though she wanted to yell, but she was afraid of being found out, "Elise, Elise! It's me, Rose! Let me in!"

"Yes, yes. Of course!" I said. As I was opening the gate just enough for Rose to come inside, I could see the teenage boy and his Interahamwe gang waiting for me across the street.

Rose hurried inside the compound.

"What's wrong?" I said, latching the gate.

"Come on!" she said, taking my hand.

We ran to the secret spot we had in the shade of the avocado tree, at the far corner of the compound.

"I came over here as fast as I could. I had to wait for Mama to go to the market." She looked down.

I took her hands in mine. "What is it?" I said.

When she looked up, there were tears in her eyes. "Papa had another one of his meetings."

"What happened?"

"Oh, Elise, it's sooooo awful! A whole bunch of men came over and they talked about these lists."

"Lists? What lists?" I was beginning to feel cold and sick to my stomach.

"They're using the ethnic identity cards," she was whispering now. "They're making a list of all the Tutsis and where they live. In every neighborhood in Kigali, and in every city and town in the whole country! My papa is in charge of Biryogo."

"What are the lists for?" I asked.

"They're going to use them to…" she looked away.

"To what?"

She grabbed my hands and looked right into my eyes. "Wipe all of the Tutsis out!" she said.

"Oh, that's just talk," I said without thinking, like a reflex, the sort of thing I had seen Mama do a thousand times.

"No, Elise! I wish it *was* just talk, but … your name is on his list, Elise, you, and your whole family! I saw it! I snuck into Papa's office last night after the meeting was over."

"Mana we!" I said.

After a moment, Rose said, "Elise?"

I was staring into space. "I don't know what to do with that information," I said. "I mean, if I tell Mama, she'll just try to deny it, or act like I don't know what I'm talking about. All that would do is end up in a big argument."

"But you could… you know, leave."

"I wish I could, Rose. But…I'd have to go by myself. Mama would never leave. She won't even admit that there's anything bad going on."

The teenage boy and his Interahamwe gang continued to harass me for months after I had that talk with Rose. I kept praying for things not to get any worse. And for a while, they didn't, until this one day when I was walking home from school.

It started with the usual, "Hey, Rucumu! Rucumu!"

I did my best to ignore it. And then a rock whizzed right by my ear.

"Hey, Rucumu!" the teenage boy called out again.

Please don't let this get any worse! I prayed. I forced myself to keep looking ahead and to keep walking.

"Rucumu!" The boy and his gang were following me now.

Still, I said nothing and kept walking.

"Hey Rucumu! I'm talking to you! Rucumu! I know you can hear me!" Another stone whizzed by my head. "Tutsi girl too good to speak to a Hutu boy?" he asked. "Tutsi inyenzi!"

I fought to keep my walk the same, my gaze the same, my breathing the same, even though my heart was beating very, very fast. I was fighting a growing urge to turn around and yell at him. I was fighting an urge to run. I have always been a good runner, but I had seen these boys running every morning, as part of their Interahamwe training, when I was on my way to church. If I ran, and these boys caught me, this bad situation could suddenly get much, much worse. I stared straight ahead and kept walking.

Again, I heard, from behind me, "Hey, Rucumu!" and I felt a pain in my back that hurt so much I had to stop walking. I turned around to see a rock about the size of a papaya on the ground not far from me. Most of the younger boys in the gang were laughing, but not the teenage boy. He was giving me that same look, the look that said, "I can do whatever I want, and there's nothing you can do to stop me."

And suddenly I realized: *No. This is going to stop, right now!*

There was another rock, about the size of an avocado. I picked it up. It fit perfectly in the palm of my hand. By this point the boy and his gang had all turned and were walking away, still laughing. I threw the rock. I wasn't really trying to hurt anyone. But the rock was sharp on one side, and it hit the teenage boy right in the back of his head.

There was an explosion of blood. The boy fell to the ground screaming.

I had an intense feeling of satisfaction. But that only lasted until the boys in the gang started making the induru call. A crowd gathered almost instantaneously. It occurred to me that in a world that wasn't crazy, *I* would be the one making the alarm call, and everyone would be running to *my* defense, but that thought was replaced by people calling out, "She's the one! She did it! Tutsi! Inyenzi! Inzoka! She tried to kill our boy!" The crowd was turning into an angry mob.

And so then, for the first time, I ran from the Interahamwe gang and the mob that was forming around them. I ran as fast as I could, and the mob ran after me. I knew that if they caught me, they were going to beat me to death.

I ducked into the maze of back alleys, and the mob followed me. As I made turn after turn, trying to lose them, I thought about the execution lists. *Will I be the first one from my family to be crossed off?* I wondered.

I ran as fast as I could, looking at the high brick walls on either side of me. *Too high to climb*, I thought. *And even if they weren't, they all have sharp, jagged, broken glass set into the concrete along the top.*

My heart was pounding. In my panic, I stumbled over a tree root. I tried to regain my stride, but I fell against a wall and scraped my arm on the rough bricks. I cried out in pain and then slapped my hands over my mouth as soon as I did. I looked behind me. Did I give myself away?

"Over here!" one of the Hutus yelled. I could see him at the other end of the alley, motioning to the others. I ran even faster, but then I saw the Hutu mob is closing in from both sides. Some of them were blowing whistles over and over again like this was some kind of insane party.

Oh no! I thought. *But wait.* I had become a little lost, but I thought maybe I recognized this alley. *If I go just a little further this way.* I ran toward the part of the mob that was in front of me, and then I saw what

I was looking for. *Yes!* I thought, as I saw, to my right was another alley that ran up toward one of the main roads. I turned and sprinted up it, getting some distance between myself and the mob.

Once I got to the road, I knew I could run even faster, and I did. I left the mob behind me and then turned into another alley that I knew would eventually lead to our compound.

I knew the mob could still see me, though. *Maybe if I go inside our compound and hide,* I thought.

I kept sprinting, down the alley, around a corner, down that alley, and around another corner that led to the street that ran in front of my house. I ran down our street and inside our compound, not even stopping long enough to lock the gate. As I ran inside the house, I locked the front door, but I kept running, through the house and out the back door, into the small cornfield in our back yard. I crouched down and hid among the stalks.

I heard the mob smash open the compound gate, and then I heard them gathering in front of my house. I heard them yelling and pounding on the door. Then I could hear them throwing rocks and smashing windows!

Thoughts were racing through my head. *What should I do? That door can't hold forever. And once they break through it, they'll look through the house. And when they don't find me in there, they'll come out here, and then they'll find me!*

I should run! I thought. *I should run as fast as I can and climb over the back wall of the compound!* But then I imagined them catching me, pulling me down, and raping me, while others beat my head in with rocks. I realized: *This is it. I am going to die! I AM GOING TO DIE! I AM GOING TO DIE! - **I AM GOING TO DIE!!***

I waited. And listened. And as I did, the sound of the mob died down. And I thought I could hear Mama's voice! *But how could that be?* I wondered. *Mama doesn't come home from work for another three hours!*

But, like a miracle, I heard it again. It really was Mama's voice!

I couldn't make out her words, but the tone was unmistakable. Soft, and steady. And I could clearly hear some people yelling in response: "Elise was trying to kill our boy! We need money to take him to the hospital!"

I don't know how she did it. It didn't seem possible, but somehow Mama used her soft kind of power to soothe the mob back into being a crowd. She spoke calmly, never raising her voice.

I heard the chink of coins. I realized that she was giving them money. And to person after person, I could make out Mama saying, "Eeeeyyyyy," here meaning "Yes, I understand. You are right. I agree completely."

One by one, I could hear Mama talking to each person, making him or her feel better, saying that it was okay, and right, for them to just calm down. And they did. It took about an hour, but as I stayed there hiding in the cornfield, Mama convinced every single person in what had been a mob, gathered to find me and beat me to death, to just go home.

After not hearing anything for a while, I left my hiding place and walked inside the house. Mama was standing in the living room. There was broken glass everywhere.

I thought that Mama would be furious, but she didn't seem angry at all. She was just staring toward the floor, almost like she was staring through it.

I went to her. She put her arms around me. I could feel her breathing deeply several times as I hugged her. Then she took a small step back and looked into my eyes.

"Elise," she said. "Those people have gone, for now, but they'll be back. And if they find you here, they will want to kill you. And even if that somehow didn't happen, if you got up tomorrow and started walking to school, those same boys would see you, and then they would kill you."

"You have to go," she said, very plainly. "And you can't come back here, for… I don't know how long. You have to go to your Uncle Hakizimana's house in Nyamirambo. Don't change out of your uniform. Don't pack. Just go, right now."

She hugged me again, for a long time. Then she kissed me on the forehead. There were no tears. "Now go," she said.

And so, I did. I walked out the back door, past the corn. I climbed the avocado tree in the corner of the compound, dropped into the alley below, and set off for Nyamirambo.

Chapter Eight: Nyamirambo

I could feel my heart pounding as my feet hit the ground of the small alley that ran between our compound and our neighbor's. This alley ran into a main alley, where there were two streams of people, one moving up the hill, the other moving down it. My instinct was to rush into the main alley and run as fast as I could, down the hill, toward my uncle's house in Nyamirambo. But then I realized, *Most of those people in that alley are Hutus. I was just almost killed by Hutus. Running into a river of them, drawing attention to yourself, is not a good idea. None of these people know what you've done. Just walk over there and disappear into the crowd.*

I did, thinking, *That's it. Good. Look like everything's fine. As far as these people know, you're just another girl on her way home from school.* Of course, with the speed at which news travels by word of mouth in Rwanda, if I had tried to make this same walk even a few hours later, without a doubt, lots of these people would have known who I was and what I did. Someone would have raised the induru call and then… well, then I would have been right back in the same situation I had been in just an hour or so ago. *I just can't believe I'm still alive!* I thought.

I remembered running down this alley on the way to Uncle Hakizimana's house, when I was a much younger girl, with Robert and Claudine, all of us racing each other. As I remembered Robert and

Claudine laughing, it struck me: *Mana we! I don't know if I'll ever see them again! Or Mama, or Gabriel and Alice, or Rose or anybody!*

I actually had to stop walking because of the stabbing pain I was feeling in my heart. I wanted to cry out. But *No!* I thought. *You can't draw attention to yourself! You need to relax! Focus on something else.*

I started taking some deep breaths, relaxing the muscles in my neck and back. I noticed a corrugated metal door I was passing, painted a powdery blue.

Pretty, I thought. I was starting to feel better.

A deep THUNK made me jump, as I turned to see a woman chopping off a chicken's head with a machete. Through the gaps in her bamboo fence, I could see her holding the chicken's body as its wings flapped, blood squirting out from where its head used to be. Suddenly, in my mind, I was watching the rock I had thrown hit the back of the teenage boy's head and the explosion of blood.

The loud ping of sledgehammer against cinderblock made me jerk to my left. A man was knocking a hole in the wall of a house. He turned toward the inside of the building and yelled, "How big does the hole for this window need to be?"

As I kept walking, I passed a wrought-iron fence, and through it I could see a yard with a small field of corn. I flashed to hiding in our cornfield and listening to the mob smashing all the windows in the front of our house. I watched my memory of it, like I was outside of it, like I was watching a film of it. I watched myself hiding, and I couldn't help thinking, *That girl is going to die! There is no way that girl isn't going to die!*

But then, as I came around another corner, I saw something that, just like me, shouldn't have been alive. Ahead of me, there was a hibiscus bush. It had a few broken branches around the edges, but there it was, in the middle of the path, with nothing to protect it from the hundreds of people who walked by it every day. By all logic, it should have been trampled long ago, but it was big and healthy, and it had beautiful, bright red flowers blooming all over it. I walked up to the bush, knelt down, and smelled one of the flowers. It smelled sweet and wonderful, and alive!

A loud voice on a radio yelling, "*Igitegoooooooooo!*" ("Goooooooooal!") made me turn my head to see several men listening to a football game at a table by a double window that opened onto the alley. They were holding their hands over their heads, yelling along with the announcer, in celebration. I kept walking.

The blare of a truck's horn jolted me back to my senses. I had reached the main road at the bottom of the hill. I was about a third of the way to Uncle Hakizimana's house.

I crossed the road, weaving between cars, trucks, and mopeds that were stuck in the slow-moving traffic, heading toward the center of Kigali. Once I made it to the far side, a short trip down a steep dirt path brought me into the valley between Biryogo and Nyamirambo, Uncle Hakizimana's old neighborhood. The valley had a stream running through the middle of it, where women and children were filling jerrycans with water for drinking and cooking. A lot of the valley floor was farmland where people grew crops. On the parts that were too boggy to farm, high grasses grew.

I was taking a path I knew well that went deep into the high grasses. I had always loved this part of the trip to Uncle Hakizimana's house because it was so peaceful, but the feeling I had now was much deeper. It seemed as if, by crossing the main road, I had left my old life behind.

Now it was just me, and the high grass, and the wonderful, peaceful sound of the wind blowing through it. The sound inspired me to take deep breaths, and then let them out soooo slowly, like the wind was blowing over the valley, through the high grass, and right through me.

I tilted my face up and felt the warm sun on my face. I was grateful to be alive, but I suddenly found myself very aware of the fact that I really had no idea what I was walking into. I had always loved going to Uncle Hakizimana's house to see him, but he wasn't living there anymore. He hadn't lived there in years.

I remembered hearing Mama talking to somebody about how Uncle Hakizimana was afraid of being attacked by Hutus. That's why he had moved to Nyamirambo. Even though most of the people who lived there were Hutus, they were also mostly Muslims. And, as Muslims, they didn't want to have anything to do with killing Tutsis, harassing them, or even looking down on them.

But when the anti-Tutsi rallies started in Rwanda, Uncle Hakizimana moved to the Muslim part of Bujumbura in Burundi. Burundi was a lot like Rwanda. In fact, Burundi and Rwanda used to be one country. So, they had the same mix of Hutus and Tutsis in Burundi, and from what I'd heard Tutsis there often got some of the same kind of treatment from Hutus as they did in Rwanda. But I knew that Tutsis ran the military there. I knew that I'd feel a lot safer if Tutsis ran the military in Rwanda. I wondered why we didn't all move to Burundi.

Uncle Hakizimana still owned his house in Nyamirambo, though. A friend of his son named Eugene was renting it. I knew Eugene mainly because he had been interested in Claudine. For a few years he came over to our house a lot, trying to court her. I had talked with him here and there. But when Claudine went to Burundi to live with Uncle Hakizimana, Eugene stopped coming by. So, though Eugene wasn't a stranger, I wouldn't exactly call him a friend.

I wondered how he'd react when I showed up at his door and asked if I could stay with him. *It's a big thing to ask,* I thought. *If he says "No"... I really don't know what I'm going to do. But even so. He knows me. It's kind of a life-or-death situation. Yeah. Of course he'll let me stay.*

I walked up, out of the valley floor, crossed the main road on the edge of Nyamirambo, and began making my way through its back alleys, climbing up the hill, toward my uncle's house.

At that time, only the very rich people in Rwanda had telephones in their houses, but if you were Tutsi, no matter how much money you had, getting one was almost impossible. So, there was no way for Mama to let Eugene know I was coming.

Thinking through all of that, I was starting to feel afraid again.

I finally made it to Uncle Hakizimana's house. *Here we go*, I thought, as I walked up to the door and knocked. The door opened, and there was Eugene.

"Elise," he said. "What are you...doing here?"

"Who is it, Sweetheart?" I heard a woman's voice say from inside.

"It's Elise, Sonia's daughter," Eugene said over his shoulder.

"What does she want?" the woman asked.

"I don't know," he said. Then he turned to me.

"Can I come in?" I asked.

The woman came to the door and looked me up and down. "Hello," she said in a not-so-friendly voice.

"Oh, Elise," Eugene said. "This is my girlfriend, Betty."

"Hello," I said.

"Well, don't just let her stand there," Betty said. "Invite her in!"

"Oh, yes. Yes of course," Eugene said. "Come in, come in."

I did.

It was a small house, smaller than ours, but comfortable. It hadn't changed at all since Uncle Hakizimana had lived there. They even had the same tablecloth. We all went in and sat down in the living room.

"So," Eugene said. "Did your Mama send you with a message, something about Claudine?" Betty looked at him sharply. He realized that he had said the wrong thing as soon as it passed his lips. "Or...?" he tried to recover, but not very successfully. Betty was looking at me now. She didn't look happy.

"No," I said.

"Oh. So... why are you here?" Eugene asked.

"Well," I said. "It's not so easy to talk about, but… There was this boy…"

I told them the whole story of what had happened with the Interahamwe boy, and how he had been harassing me for years, and "Rucumu," and the rock he had thrown at me, and the rock I had thrown at him, and the blood, and the mob that had chased me into my house, and broken all the windows and how they wanted to kill me, and how Mama had told me to leave, because if anyone from the mob found me, they would bring the rest of the mob, and they would beat me to death. "So," I concluded. "Mama sent me here. To Nyamirambo. For safety."

"That's quite a story," Eugene said. "So, you want to… to stay? Here?"

"Well…" I said. "I think the Hutus know where most of Mama's friends and family are in Biryogo. I think that's why she told me to come here. Because it's far enough away from our house, and this is a mostly Muslim neighborhood. And…well… I just really don't have any place else to go."

"Hmmm…" Eugene said, staring at me.

"The thing is, Sweetie," Betty said, "You know that we have another house? Did you know that?"

"Um… no…," I said. "I thought this was my uncle's house,"

"Well, we have another house, and the thing is, we're trying to rent this one."

"Okay…" I said, wondering where this was going.

"So, the thing is…"

"Yes?"

"We'd really prefer it if you found someplace… else to go," she said.

I sat there, staring at her. I couldn't believe that this was happening.

"Right?" she said, turning to Eugene.

"Uh… yes," he said. "Yes. That's right. I'm sorry."

"We're sorry," Betty said.

I stared at Eugene for a moment. "Didn't you hear what I just told you?" I asked. "I don't have any place else to go, and you're basically kicking me out of my uncle's house, to… die?"

Eugene sighed and rubbed his eyes in frustration. "Well…" he started to say.

"Sweetheart?" Betty said, standing up. "Can I speak to you in the other room for a moment, please?"

"Uh…Sure," he said, and followed her into the other room.

Oh boy, I thought as I listened to them arguing in whispers. *This woman's actually crazy enough to think I've got some interest in stealing Eugene away from her. He's looking at me in that way that men do, but it is sooooo not mutual. But if I told Betty that, I'm sure it would just start an argument about that, so… I'll just sit here and… wait until they're done arguing.*

I could hear a few words and phrases here and there, her whispering things like, "I don't want her in this house! We're trying to rent it!" I wondered what gave them the right to rent a house that my uncle owned, but…

I caught Eugene whispering, "She's just a girl. She doesn't have any place else to go. Her mother's a good friend of mine."

And then Betty saying, "Oh, a good friend? How good? Better than me?"

And then him saying, "What? We're just going to put the daughter of a friend of mine out in the street to die?"

Then I heard Betty say something that seemed very strange to me at the time: "They'll all be dead soon anyway!"

Well, I thought. *I guess Betty's a Hutu. Maybe Eugene is, too.* A lot of the time you can't tell just by people's looks.

The "private" conversation ended with Eugene saying, "That is enough of that! I'm going to tell her that she can stay. For a few days."

"But-"

"It's *my* friend's house!" he said, and then they both started walking back to me in the living room with fake smiles on their faces.

"Okay," Betty said. "You can stay for a few nights, but we really need you to find someplace else as soon as you can."

I sighed and decided to just be glad about the fact that I had a safe place to stay, even if it was just for a few days. I made myself smile and say, "Thank you," to both of them.

Eugene went to hug me, but I didn't want to give his girlfriend any more reason to be jealous of me. So, I dodged him as subtly as I could, and walked around him to Betty.

"I always slept in the room at the end of the hall when I would come to visit Uncle Hakizimana," I said to her. "Is that where I'll be sleeping tonight?"

"Oh," she said. "All right. I guess that's fine. Just try to keep it clean."

"Yes, Auntie," I said (this is a term of respect we use in Rwanda, even sometimes for people who aren't actually related to us), following her down the hall.

Mama came to visit that weekend. She brought me some clothes and my schoolbooks, as well as my toothbrush and some lotion.

"I'm sorry I couldn't bring more," she said. "But I didn't want anybody to see me bringing a suitcase of clothes anywhere. I had to take a very roundabout route to make sure no one was following me. There are a lot of Hutus in Biryogo that still want to know… well… It's just… It's not… safe."

"I understand, Mama," I said. "Thank you so much for bringing what you could. And for everything. I… I'm sorry for all the trouble I've caused you. I'm sorry about the broken glass, and the stress, and…"

"Elise, I don't care about the broken glass. I just care that you're safe."

We hugged.

Mama talked to Eugene and Betty about the situation with the boy, and the rock, and the mob. They agreed to let me stay there for a while, but they weren't happy about it. I think Mama gave them some money. I don't know where she got it from. Then she gave me some money, too.

"It's for the bus," she said. "There's a bus that comes right by here that will take you to your school. So, here's some money for that, and here's some money for you to pay for school for the next few months."

Oh no, I thought. *She's not thinking about this rationally! Going back to that same school, or anywhere in Biryogo for me would be suicide!*

"Sweetheart?" Mama said.

As I looked into her eyes, I was suddenly very conscious of just how much stress Mama had been under, and how many years she had been under it. Not only would arguing with her have been senseless, it would have also been intensely disrespectful. Mama was doing everything she could to keep me alive and to keep herself from falling apart. So, I just took the money, put my arms around her, and said, "Thank you, Mama. I love you so much."

"I love you, too," she said.

We hugged for a long time, and then she said she had to go.

That night, alone in my room, I cried, and cried, and cried.

It was nice not have to go to school and not to have to put up with all of the abuse. But after about a week of just sitting around the house, I started to feel a little restless.

One morning I saw Betty getting ready to go out to do the shopping.

"Auntie?" I said. "How about if I do the shopping for you?"

"What a good idea," she said. She gave me a list.

"I can chip in some," I said. "But I'll need some money."

"Oh, yes. Of course," she said with that same fake smile on her face. Then she said, "Stay safe," but it didn't feel like she meant it.

In the market I noticed a girl, who seemed to be about my age, looking at me. I looked back at her and gave her a little wave.

"Hello," I said.

"You're new around here," she said.

"Oh, yes," I said. "I'm, uh, staying with a friend of the family for…a little while."

"You don't sound so sure," she said, smiling.

"It's a long story," I said.

"Here," she said. "I'll walk with you, and you can tell it to me, if you like. I've got time. Besides, you probably need someone to show you around."

"Actually," I said, smiling for the first time in days and days, "I… Yeah. That would be great."

"Okay," she said, putting out her hand. "My name's Raissa."

"I'm Elise," I said, taking her hand and shaking it. I have to say that Raissa was the coolest looking girl I had ever seen. She was wearing jean shorts and a tee shirt. She had earrings on and a necklace. And she seemed to take everything in stride, smiling all the time.

I already knew my way around Nyamirambo a little from when I used to visit Uncle Hakizimana. But Raissa seemed to know everything. As we walked, she showed me all the different stalls in the market, where to get the best chili peppers to make a pilipili sauce, who had the freshest vegetables, who always had the sweet plantains that were just becoming ripe.

The whole time Raissa was showing me around, we were talking. She was so open and friendly, and just so easy to talk to that I quickly found out that she lived only two houses away from Eugene's house, that she was a Hutu, and a Muslim.

She was being so open with me, I was tempted to tell her everything. I told her about how the teenage boy and his Interahamwe gang had been harassing me, and that the boy was the reason I had left my old neighborhood, and why I was living with Eugene. I didn't tell her about the rock or the mob because I didn't really know her, and because she was a Hutu.

I did tell her about Betty and how I thought she seemed to be jealous of me.

Raissa looked me up and down and said, "She *should* feel jealous. Look at you!"

We both laughed.

I should explain something here. Jealousy between women certainly isn't limited to Africa, but it can be intense there, very intense. It's not common, but I have certainly heard of African women plotting to kill, or in some cases even actually killing other women because of it. So, Betty wanting me out of Uncle Hakizimana's house because she was jealous of me wasn't an unheard-of reaction to my being there.

When I told Raissa that I wasn't going back to my old school, she immediately said, "Oh, Elise, you should come to *my* school!"

"Really?" I said.

"Oh yes. It's right here in the neighborhood. It's called the *École Zaïroise*."

"Is it run by Zairians?" I asked. Zaire was the country just to the west of Rwanda.

"Oh yes," she said. "And most of the students are Zairians or the children of Zairians. And everyone is so nice!"

I stopped myself from asking the question that was burning in my brain.

"What?" she said. Then she gave a knowing smile. "Oh. You're wondering if they're nice to Tutsis, right?"

I nodded. I felt embarrassed.

"Well Elise, you know, in Zaire no one really cares if you are Tutsi or Hutu."

I smiled. "Really?"

"Really," she said. "You should come to my school."

"What about paying?" I said. I still had some money from Mama. But it wasn't much, and I didn't know when or if I'd ever get any more of it.

"Well, when I started there, they let me go for a few weeks to see if I liked it before I had to pay. Why don't you come to school with me tomorrow and talk to the people in the office."

"Well…" I said.

"Do you have something better to do?"

I thought about how happy Betty would be that I was getting out of the house. "No," I said, breaking into a smile.

"Can you meet me here tomorrow morning?"

"I don't see why not," I said.

"Okay," Raissa said, as she turned to walk away. Then she stopped and turned back. "Elise?"

"Yes?"

"You're going to love it!"

The next morning, I met Raissa in the market, and she took me to her school. We went to the office and talked to the woman who was in charge of admissions. It turned out that everyone who worked at the school was Zairian, so they only spoke French and Swahili, not Kinyarwanda. I had learned a little French at my old school, but I really only knew enough French to carry on a very basic conversation. And I only knew a few words in Swahili. So Raissa stayed with me in the office and translated.

We told the admissions officer that I wanted to attend the *École Zaïroise*. She said they had a space. She gave me some tests to see what classes I should be in, but they were all in French. I answered the questions I could, which weren't very many, and then Raissa showed me around the school.

It was very basic, much more basic than my old school. Instead of cement, it had dirt floors. Instead of red bricks and cinder blocks, the walls were made of mud bricks and thatch. But everyone I saw looked happy, the students, the teachers, even the janitor. Linda had smiled when the teacher told her to oversee my punishments, but I don't remember her, or anyone else at my old school, ever seeming truly happy.

The next day Raissa took me back to the *École Zaïroise*, to a bulletin board where test scores and class assignments were posted, and there were the results of my placement tests and the classes that I was assigned to. Raissa was jumping up and down with excitement.

"Elise! Elise! We have three of the same classes together!"

"That's amazing!" I said. It really was. I couldn't believe it. I didn't see how I could have possibly passed any of those tests. I guessed that they must have been a formality. The only thing that made sense was that they placed me in First Year French.

Raissa was right. I absolutely loved her school! Everyone was so nice, the students, the teachers, the office staff. The language barrier was a bit overwhelming at first, but it turned out that I had a good ear for French, and the good thing about being in a situation where you have to learn a language is that you do learn it, quickly. It wasn't long before I could understand most of what was being said around me.

Raissa and I became even closer, and for the first time in my life I started making lots of friends in school. I even found a completely unexpected friend outside of school. I was walking home one day when I saw a girl walking toward me who looked familiar. I guess she must have recognized me too, because she was looking at me the same way I was looking at her, with her head tilted a little to one side.

As we got closer to each other, I pointed at her and said, "I…know you from somewhere…"

"I know you too…" she said.

"Your name's…Schiphra…?"

"You're…Elise?"

"Yes. But where…?"

"Mana we!"

"The Boom!" we both said together.

"So, what are you doing here?" I asked.

"Oh, I live here with my auntie and my grandmamma," she said. "My parents were…killed. What about you? What are you doing here?"

"I'm…staying with a… family friend…" I decided to keep it as simple as possible.

"Oh," Schiphra said. "So, you haven't always lived here?"

"No, I just got here about a month ago. I live right over here."

"No!" she said, amazed. "I live right here!"

It turned out that Schiphra's house was three houses down from Uncle Hakizimana's.

"I can't believe that! It's so amazing!"

"So, do you have any plans tonight?" she asked.

"No," I said. "I wish I could say 'I'll meet you at The Boom,' but it's so far away." We could have walked there, but I didn't really feel safe leaving Nyamirambo. In the rest of Kigali, because of the way everyone talks to everyone else, if I was seen by one person, word might get back to the Hutus in Biryogo. I started having visions of a line of Hutus snaking their way across the valley, at night, with torches, marching toward Nyamirambo to kill me.

"What do you mean?" Schiphra asked. "There's a Boom three blocks away from here. You know there's more than one Boom, right?"

"Oh…" I said. "That's great! Well, then. What time do you want to meet?"

We met at The Boom in Nyamirambo that night. I brought Raissa. We all danced and flirted with boys and drank soda. It was loud and exciting. There was a mirror ball and flashing lights, and lots of big speakers that put out so much bass you could feel it all through your body as you danced.

The good side of being a teenager living with adults who don't particularly like you, is that you can come and go as you please, and no one really cares. But the bad side of living with adults who don't particularly like you is that you can come and go as you please, and no one really cares. I honestly think I could have died, and the only thing Eugene and Betty would have felt was relief. That didn't feel so good, but it did mean that I could basically do whatever I wanted, which was…nice.

I started doing well in school. It's much easier when you are treated like a student, not like some "dirty, stupid Tutsi" that everyone has to put up with. I loved how I was listened to in class, and how I could ask questions without being afraid that the teacher would use it as an excuse to insult me or "punish" me. I remember thinking to myself, again and again: *So, this is what it's like to be in a real school.*

I realized, as I was walking home with Raissa one day, that I was actually, for the first time in a long time… happy.

But there was a shadow. I knew that Eugene and Betty wanted me gone. And, though I had paid for my first trimester at the *École Zaïroise*, I hadn't paid for the second one yet, even though we were well into it. So, I knew that eventually all of this would have to end. And when it did, I didn't know where else I could go or what else I could do.

As much as I could, I tried to just think about what was going on right in front of me, and not about anything else. That wasn't always easy, though, especially with the disturbing signals that were floating around in the air.

There was a new radio station that I started hearing right around that time called RTLM (*Radio Télévision Libre des Mille Collines*). Betty had it on all the time. That and sometimes the BBC. RTLM played a lot of popular music, and a lot of interviews with Hutus from the government. They talked a lot about how horrible Tutsis were. They would say things like "…and to all of the Tutsis out there: a day will come when the people will want no more of you! Where will you escape to then?"

They seemed to especially hate the RPF. That might have been because every time you heard news reports about them, the RPF was winning another battle with the Rwandan Army, and they seemed to keep taking and holding on to more and more of northern Rwanda.

That was right around the time there were reports about something called the Arusha Accords. On the BBC they said it was basically a peace treaty between the RPF and the Rwandan government, and that it meant that the RPF was going to be included in the Rwandan parliament.

Part of the agreement was that the U.N. sent troops called UNAMIR into Rwanda. They were from all over the world: Canada, Australia, Cameroon, and a whole bunch of other countries. You'd see them walking around in their blue army helmets and driving around in their white trucks. Nobody was quite sure what to make of them. They were supposed to keep the peace. But soon there were stories going around about Hutus beating and, in a few cases, even killing Tutsis right in front of them, and the UNAMIR soldiers not doing anything to stop it.

Mama came to visit a few more times, often with important news. One time when she came, she told me that Uncle Hakizimana's daughters, Carene and Michelle, who had been living in Brussels for quite some time, had brought Claudine there to live with them.

"That's so nice," I said.

"Mmm," Mama said. "I hope it works out for her. I'm still working on forgiving her for just running off the way she did."

"How are things at home?" I asked.

"Gabriel is having some trouble."

"What's going on?"

"Oh it's-"

"-nothing? Mama, come on. Please. Tell me. I can take it."

"Well, you know that gang. The one that was… the one with that boy that was giving you trouble?"

"Of course," I said. "It's the whole reason I'm here."

"Well, they're… they're giving Gabriel trouble. A lot of trouble."

"Oh," I said. "That's not good."

"No. It's not. Oh, Claudine found a job in a hospital in Brussels."

"What kind of job?"

"It sounds like she helps the nurses. She's sending some money home."

"That's wonderful, Mama."

"It helps," she said.

The next time she came to visit, Mama told me that things with the gang had made it too dangerous for Gabriel to stay in Kigali.

"So, what did you do?"

"I've sent him to Bujumbura to live with your Uncle Hakizimana."

"Oh," I said. *Shouldn't I be going to stay with him too?* was burning in my head, but, ever since Mama's first visit, I was extremely conscious of not doing or saying anything that would add to the stress she was already under. What I chose to say was, "Well, that must be a relief."

"Some," Mama said.

One night, a couple of weeks after Mama's visit, Schiphra and Raissa and I all went back to my house (well, really Eugene and Betty's house) after an evening of dancing at The Boom. We were just hanging out in my room when I suddenly started crying.

"What's wrong, Elise?" Schiphra asked.

"I just keep thinking, you know, what kind of life can I have here? I don't really have any place to live. Eugene and Betty made it very clear to me, again today, that I have to leave. So, I can't stay here. And I… I can't go back to live with my mama."

"Because of the gang that was harassing you?" Raissa asked.

"Oh, you too?" Schiphra said. "Those boys on the street, and the awful things they say if you're a Tutsi girl! That happens to me every time I go anywhere outside of Nyamirambo."

"It's not just that," I said. "There's more. A lot more."

"What haven't you told us?" Raissa said.

I wasn't sure that I should, but I ended up telling them the whole story about the rock and the mob that wanted to kill me.

Raissa gasped when I was done. "Elise, that's horrible!" she said. Schiphra cried.

"And today they called me into the office at school because I haven't paid the tuition yet!" I said.

"Oh, Elise!" Raissa said.

"I never know when my mama is going to come to see me next, and sometimes she brings me money to help pay for school, and sometimes she doesn't, and I never want to ask her about it, because I know that even when she does bring money, it's money she doesn't have. And I... I just don't know what I'm going to do!"

"Well," Raissa said, "I'm going to Bujumbura this weekend to see my boyfriend. You should both come with me! We'll have a great time!"

"Burundi?" I said. "I've never been to Burundi, but I've heard that Bujumbura is a fun place to go."

"I've heard that too," Schiphra said.

"Oh, it's the best!" Raissa said.

"You know," Schiphra said, "I'm in the same kind of situation as Elise. I mean, it's not like I have a mob waiting to kill me, but I can't look forward to having any kind of life here in Rwanda, either. Are things better for Tutsis in Burundi?"

"I mean, they're definitely better," Raissa said. "Things still happen to Tutsis there sometimes, but… not the way they do here."

"Would it be okay with you if I came too?" Schiphra asked.

"Of course!" Raissa said.

"It would be great!" I said.

"And Elise, you can go see your uncle while you're there," Raissa said.

I had told both Raissa and Schiphra about how Uncle Hakizimana had moved to Bujumbura. "Well, Claudine stayed with him for a while, and now Gabriel is staying with him. So, I guess I could go there. I'd love to see him. If I knew where he lived. But I guess I could call Claudine once I get there."

"I have an uncle in Bujumbura, too," Schiphra said. "And I guess I could do the same thing."

"Why would Claudine know where your uncle lives?" Raissa said.

"Oh, shut up!" Schiphra said, throwing a pillow at Raissa. "You know what I mean."

In Rwandan culture, if something's uncomfortable to talk about, we'll often talk around it or make a joke instead of talking about it directly. We didn't talk about how Schiphra or I were probably going to Burundi for good, or how gigantic of a move that was, but I'm pretty sure we all knew that that's what we were about to do.

I started packing everything that I had, which wasn't much: some clothes, a toothbrush, and some lotion.

"You know," I said, smiling. "I've never been out of Rwanda before."

"Neither have I!" Schiphra said. "This is exciting!"

We all sort of squealed, and laughed, letting ourselves be taken over by the moment.

"Oh, I can't believe I'm going to do this!" I said. "I'm just going to go!" I suddenly stopped.

"What is it, Elise?" Raissa said.

"I just don't know," I said. "I just don't know."

"Know what?" Schiphra asked.

"I feel like I should tell my mama," I said.

"But you said it wasn't safe for you to go back to Biryogo," Raissa said.

"No. It's not. But still…"

"Elise," Raissa said. "It's late. So, let's all pack our bags-"

"I'm already packed," I said.

"But you can sleep on it," Raissa said. "And then tomorrow-"

"No," I told her. "I've got to decide this right now."

"Okay," Raissa said.

Raissa and Schiphra stayed quiet and let me think.

After a minute I said, "I'm kind of scared, but I think have to do this. So, that's it. Let's go!"

Raissa already had her bag with her. Schiphra already had some clothes in my room from sleeping over before. She decided that there wasn't anything at her house that she couldn't live without. Like me, Schiphra felt that she couldn't tell anybody else that she was going. So, we all hugged and went to sleep for a few hours.

We woke up very early the next morning. And, while it was still dark, clutching our bags, we snuck out of the house and made our way to the bus station to take a bus from Kigali to Butare, a town in the far south of Rwanda. Then from there we would take a bus to Bujumbura.

Chapter Nine: Burundi

It was still dark, as the three of us stood in line to board the bus to Butare. I had taken city buses before, but I had never taken one that went from one city to another. So, I was relying on Raissa's experience. She did this trip all the time, whenever she went to see her boyfriend in Bujumbura.

"Now, when the doors open," she told Schiphra and me, "everybody's going to rush to get the real seats."

"Real seats?" Schiphra said.

"There are these horrible seats that fold out into the aisle from underneath the real seats. They just hang off the side like a flimsy beach chair. We want to make sure that we get real seats, okay? So, rush in, with everybody else."

The driver pushed past everyone in line, went inside the bus and closed the doors to hold back the crowd while he was writing on a clipboard.

"Okay," Raissa said. "Here we go."

The driver opened the doors and, just like Raissa had said, everyone rushed onto the small, cramped bus, scrambling for the "real" seats. The only light came from a dim bulb on the ceiling. Raissa and I ended up next to each other in two of the "real" seats, but Schiphra had to sit on the fold-out one next to us. She didn't look very happy as she sat down. Who could blame her?

"It's a really long ride," Raissa told Schiphra. "Sorry."

Schiphra grimaced.

"Don't worry," I said. "We can switch seats from time to time."

Luckily, no one wanted to talk much. I say "luckily" because I was still a little afraid of what I had chosen to do. I was leaving everything that I had ever known, and I wasn't sure I'd ever be coming back. I had a plan, kind of, but it was a thin plan at best. And who knew if it was going to work out or not. I couldn't help thinking about it, but I was glad that no one wanted to talk.

Of course, Schiphra was pretty much in the same situation I was. More so, actually. She had even less of a plan than I did. And I would guess that Raissa was just doing her best trying to help out two friends. So, we got as comfortable as we could and tried to get some sleep.

The bus lurched out of the station and onto the main road out of Kigali. As we slowly made our way down the long hill, onto the valley floor, I thought, *Well, there's no going back now*, and drifted back to sleep.

I was shaken awake by a huge bump in the road and the strong smell of petrol fumes. The morning mist, mixed with the cinnamon-red dust kicked up by the truck in front of us made for a beautiful sunrise. The bus was making a long, winding climb out of the valley, into the hills. I saw a woman walking along the side of the road with a bundle of firewood on her head and a sleeping baby wrapped tightly against her back in a blanket.

Raissa was shaking my arm. "Look, Elise!" she said. "Have you ever seen this before?" Three men on bikes were holding onto the back of the truck in front of us, getting a free ride up the hill.

I looked at Raissa and smiled. "First time," I said.

As the truck reached the hilltop, the men on bikes peeled off and sped down the hill past the truck. Our driver honked the horn twice and pulled out blind into the left lane, where another bus was heading straight at us! People on our bus were gasping, crossing themselves, and calling out "Mana we!" as our driver swerved back into the right lane, just in time.

We were going much faster now, which meant we were being constantly jostled by the bumps and potholes in the dirt road. Just keeping ourselves from slamming into each other became tiring work.

"So, what's Bujumbura like?" I asked Raissa.

"It's a nice place. It'll probably remind you a bit of Kigali. You know, Hutus, Tutsis."

"Is it, you know…"

"Safe for Tutsis?"

"Well, I mean, yeah."

"Buyenzi *definitely* is. That's the Muslim neighborhood in Bujumbura."

"Oh."

"Men from the neighborhood patrol the entrance with guns. 'You don't mess with Buyenzi.' That's what people there say. If you're looking to start trouble, you should go someplace else."

"That sounds good."

"With all the craziness that's been going on in Rwanda for the past few years, I'd say your uncle made the right move."

"Why do you think Muslim Hutus are so much less interested in doing bad things to Tutsis?"

"I think it has to do with that the Muslims are more concerned with being Muslims than they are about being Hutus or Tutsis. You know?"

"I guess that makes sense."

For the moment, I didn't want to think any more about Hutus and Tutsis, so I looked out the window and watched beautiful, gentle hills roll by, covered with an ever-changing quilt of greens: fields of corn, and wheat, and sorghum, and banana trees, with tea plantations running through the valleys.

There were small herds of long-horned cattle and goats grazing in fields covered with grass. Thick milk bush hedges separated fields and walled compounds containing little square farmhouses, some made of cinderblocks, with cement over them, some made of red bricks, or plastered mud bricks, or combinations of all three, where people had added on to or improved a house over the years. Here and there were little round houses made entirely of grass, with a floor up off the ground, where people stored their hay or sacks of grain.

People walking with bundles or baskets on their heads, riding bicycles, or herding cattle were using these roads as much as the cars, trucks, and buses, so our driver was constantly speeding toward crowds of people, or herds of cattle, honking his horn, and expecting all the people and animals to move out of the way. He would only slow down or stop when he absolutely had to.

At one point we came to a stop behind a long line of cars, trucks, and other buses.

"What's going on?" I asked Raissa.

"Oh, looks like a checkpoint. Get out your identity card."

"Why is there a checkpoint?"

"Oh, the Interahamwe has them all over the place."

"The Interahamwe? Mana we!"

"Elise, Elise. Shhhhh, shhhhh. You've got to calm down."

I lowered my voice. "But I told you about what happened with the Interahamwe gang back in Biryogo."

"Elise, look. I've done this a hundred times before. First of all, these guys aren't from Biryogo. They don't know you. And it's not like they're organized. Mostly they only start something when someone seems nervous, like they have something to hide. If you act like there's no problem, then they act like there's no problem."

"Really?"

"Really. Just get your identity card ready. Schiphra, you too, and let me do the talking. Do each of you have… mmm, like a couple of francs?"

"I'm getting close to the last of my money," I said.

"That's another thing. In a situation like this, a little money goes a long way. You know? And when they come on the bus, maybe sink down a little in your seat so they can't tell how tall you are. And remember: there's no problem."

"No problem?" Schiphra asked.

"No problem," Raissa confirmed.

"Okay," Schiphra and I said.

We got out our identity cards. I did my best to put on a smile, even though my heart was pounding.

Two Interahamwe guys came on the bus. I was amazed at how much they looked like the "Hey Rucumu" guy: similar age, similar dirtiness. One was shirtless. The other was wearing a shirt, but it looked pretty ratty. They both carried machetes, and they both seemed a little drunk.

"Smile," Raissa reminded me under her breath.

"I'm smiling," I said.

"Remember: no problem."

"No problem," I repeated.

"No problem," Schiphra repeated.

The Interahamwe guys made their way down the aisle, checking people's identity cards. The people in the fake seats were folding them in, standing, and letting the Interahamwe guys by. Right before they got to our row, Raissa motioned Schiphra and me to come closer to her. "Pretend I just made a funny joke," she said. We all started laughing. Raissa looked the two Interahamwe guys right in the eyes. "Hi guys," she said. "Here you go." She handed them her identity card.

They smiled back at her.

"How you guys doing?" she asked.

"Oh, fine," one said.

"Yeah, fine," the other said.

"Would either of you like a bottle of water?" Schiphra asked, taking one out of her bag and offering it to them.

"Oh, that would be great," the first one said. "You know, our bosses, they keep saying that they're going to bring us water. But they never do."

"Shut up!" the other one said. "We'll share it. Thank you so much." And with that, they had moved on to the rows behind us, without ever asking to see Schiphra or my identity cards.

Raissa motioned us in again. "See?" she whispered. "Act like there's no problem and there's no problem."

"You're good at this," Schiphra said.

"I've got my moments," Raissa said.

We were stopped at two more checkpoints, and the three of us did the same sort of routine: "no problem."

The next time we started slowing down, Raissa told Schiphra and me, "Okay. We're pulling into Butare. We're changing buses here. So, make sure you've got all your stuff."

We did, and we followed Raissa to the ticket window. We talked and joked a little as we waited in line.

"I was kind of expecting this to be, I don't know, more dangerous," I said to Raissa, lowering my voice.

"Oh, Elise. I didn't want to alarm you or anything, but, for you and Schiphra, that was incredibly dangerous. If you looked worried around those Interahamwe guys, they really might have pulled you off the bus."

"What do they do then?" Schiphra asked.

"Whatever they want," Raissa said.

"Oh!" Schiphra and I said, together.

"But you guys are doing great. Just remember: No problem."

"No problem," we both repeated. Then all three of us laughed. It relieved the tension a little. But we weren't out of Rwanda yet.

Schiphra and I gave Raissa money so she could buy our tickets to Bujumbura. We found the bus, gave the driver our tickets, and this time we all got real seats! Schiphra was really happy.

"It's just a seat," Raissa said.

Schiphra folded out the fake seat into the aisle. "Please," she told Raissa. "Be my guest."

"No, I'm good here." We all laughed as a woman we didn't know took the fake seat.

The bus filled up, and then we left for Bujumbura. The road there wasn't bumpy, it was muddy. We got stuck in mud a couple of times. All the men had to get out and push.

When we got to the border, Burundian soldiers came on the bus.

"Those guys look like Tutsis!" I whispered to Raissa. "Are they?"

"Oh, yes," she said. "Most of the military in Burundi is Tutsi."

"I don't think I've never seen a Tutsi in a military uniform before," I said. "Not in the flesh, anyway." I had seen pictures of Fred and the RPF.

The soldiers were clean and professional. They seemed polite and friendly. "Here you are," I said, handing my identity card to one of the soldiers when he got to my seat.

"Thank you, Mademoiselle," he replied. "Okay. Everything seems to be in order here," he said, handing back my identity card. "Enjoy your stay in Burundi."

"…Thank you," I said, a little amazed.

The terrain changed after we crossed the border. We started climbing up twisting roads into mountains that were covered with forests of eucalyptus and pine. When we got to the highest point, we could see water off in the distance.

"That's Lake Tanganyika," Raissa said. "And that," she said, pointing to a city down in the valley, next to the lake, "is Bujumbura."

I looked down into the valley and at the lake. It was beautiful, and huge! Raissa was right. Bujumbura did look a lot like Kigali, except with a lot fewer hills.

Well, I thought. *Here we go.*

We drove down, down, down, the side of the valley, and then all the way down, into Bujumbura. Raissa, Schiphra, and I were all tired. Raissa got us a cab and told us that we were going to her Uncle

Ibrahim's. When I think back on this time, I'm always amazed by how I just went along with everything. I had no real plan.

I knew I wanted to go to Uncle Hakizimana's, but there hadn't been any way for me to contact him. I didn't know his address. I didn't even know whether or not he had a phone. Even if he had, I realized, I didn't know the number. The only way I could think of to get Uncle Hakizimana's address was to call Claudine. But she was in Brussels, and I wasn't exactly sure how to get in touch with her. I had her number, but I had never made an international call before. In fact, I had hardly ever used a phone. The only things I knew about the whole process were that it was complicated and very expensive. The idea of calling Claudine in Brussels made me anxious. I tried to just put it out of my mind. I tried to let myself feel the excitement of being someplace new and leaving someplace that was stacked with troubles. Being with Raissa really helped. She was so positive and confident, I guess I just kind of let that carry me along.

It took us over an hour to get from the bus station to Raissa's uncle's house. The streets were clogged with cars, trucks, and people. Some were walking. Some were biking. Some were pushing homemade wagons.

"It looks so much like Kigali," I said.

"Well," Raissa said. "Same people: Hutus and Tutsis, same language. You know Rwanda and Burundi used to be one country."

"Yeah, I think we learned that in school. But I think I must have been out of school when they talked about them becoming two countries."

We entered a neighborhood that reminded me a lot of Nyamirambo. There were little mosques here and there. Some of the buildings had brightly colored patterns painted on their walls.

"Uncle Ibrahim!" Raissa called out to a man walking along the side of the road.

"Raissa!" the man called back, walking toward the cab, as it slowed to a stop, in front of what I guessed was Ibrahim's house. We all got out. Raissa and Ibrahim hugged.

"What good timing," Ibrahim said. "I was just coming home for dinner."

"Uncle, these are my friends, Elise and Schiphra."

"Hello," Schiphra and I said, shaking his hand.

"Welcome to my house," Ibrahim said. "Please, come inside."

Ibrahim had a small compound. But when he opened the gate, I could see that there was a lot inside of it. There were seven little houses and children running everywhere. Some of the younger ones ran up to Raissa. She picked each of them up and hugged them.

Ibrahim brought us inside the largest of the small houses. The only room held a big table with chairs around it. A woman came in through the back door.

"Raissa! Good to see you!" she said. They hugged. Then she hugged Ibrahim.

"Ladies, this is Naaima, one of my wives." Ibrahim said. "Naaima, this is Elise and Schiphra. They are friends of Raissa's."

"Hi," Schiphra said.

"Nice to meet you," I said, as Naaima hugged us, too.

"Would you bring us some tea?" Ibrahim asked Naaima.

"Of course!" she said with a smile and left.

"How many wives do you have?"

"Three," he said, smiling.

"Well, that explains all of the children," I said.

"Yes, well, I'm a very busy man," he said.

We all laughed.

"Seventeen kids all together. Each of my wives has her own house. Then, as you can see there's this house for family meals, there's the kitchen out back, the laundry, my house. Anyway, you will join us for dinner, of course."

"…Oh, yes. Thank you," I said, while Schiphra nodded in agreement. Back then, men having more than one wife wasn't exactly common in Rwanda, but it happened. I assumed it was the same in Burundi.

"Uncle," Raissa said. "Elise and Schiphra both have uncles here in Bujumbura who they will be staying with, but they need a few days to contact them and-"

"And work out the details. Of course."

Just then, Naaima returned with tea for all of us. In that part of Africa, we take our tea with lots of a powdered milk called Nido and lots of sugar. It's very rich, kind of like a dessert.

"Yes, yes," Ibrahim continued. "Any friend of Raissa's is a friend of ours. Of course. You can stay as long as you want."

"Oh, well, thank you!" I said.

"Yes, thank you very much," Schiphra said.

"Now, Naaima, is supper coming? I have to get back to work!"

"Padida and Aaleyah!" Naaima called. "Ibrahim is waiting for his dinner while I am feeding him tea!"

Two other women hurried in, carrying trays of food.

"Oh, we have guests," one of the women said, smiling and putting down her tray of goat. It smelled wonderful, and we hadn't eaten all day.

"Yes," Ibrahim said. "These are Raissa's friends, Elise and Schiphra. They'll be staying with us for a while." Then, to us, he said, "These are my other two wives, Padida and Aaleyah."

"We have plenty of food," Aaleyah said. "We cook for over twenty every day."

"Thank you for letting us stay in your home." Schiphra and I said at the same time.

"Yes, yes, yes. Now everyone, please, sit," Ibrahim said again. "I have to get back to work."

We all sat. Everyone except Schiphra and I chanted Muslim grace. I had heard it a few times before when I had eaten at Raissa's house back in Rwanda. Schiphra and I folded our hands and prayed silently.

We ate. The meal was delicious. The mood was light. Everyone was talking and joking as they ate.

"You look happy," Raissa said. "Are you having a good time?"

"I am," I said. "Everyone's so nice. But it's more than that. I'm just realizing something."

"What's that?"

"Well, it suddenly just sort of dawned on me: I'm out of Rwanda. I can do things here. I can have a life! Thank you so much, Raissa!" I hugged her.

Ibrahim stood up from the table and said, "Well, back to work. Ladies, I will see you later." And he was gone.

"He works very hard," Raissa said.

"And all the time!" Naaima said.

"We get lonely without him," Aaleyah said, putting her arm around Padida's neck and pouting.

"Well, speaking of that," Raissa said. "I'm off to see my boyfriend. Thank you, Aunties. Dinner was delicious!" She gave each of them a hug and a kiss, and then, continued on to Schiphra and me, saying, "I'll see you two later." And then she was gone.

"Here, I'll help you clear," I said to Naaima.

"Clear?" she said to Aaleyah and Padida, laughing.

"Second shift," Aaleyah said.

"What?" I asked, as I looked past her to the back door of the little house. There were children waiting at the door.

"Come on," Padida said, beckoning Schiphra and me toward the outdoor kitchen. "There's still lots of work left to do."

She put us to work, taking more food from the kitchen into the dining house.

Once we had laid out the food on the table, Naaima called out to the children, "Okay, dinner time."

The children rushed in and sat on mats on the floor. The table was for adults only. They all bowed their heads and prayed in unison. Then they began to eat.

Schiphra and I stood there watching the children until Naaima commanded: "Come on, come on, the both of you. There's work to do."

We must have looked a little surprised because Naaima glared at us and said, "What? Did you think you were just going to come and live here and eat our food for free?"

"No, of course not," I said.

"What can we do to help?" Schiphra asked.

"Well," Naaima said. "Come on."

We followed her to the kitchen where she and Aaleyah and Padida put us to work washing and cleaning the pots and pans and plate, after plate, after plate.

"Maybe we can actually have a night off for once," Padida said to Aaleyah.

Late that night, when we had finished scrubbing the last pots, Naaima took us to a very little room in one of the small houses and showed us a bed.

"You two can share this," she said, and left without saying another word.

"Thank you," Schiphra and I both called after her.

"Well, I don't know about you," I said, "but I'm exhausted."

"Me too."

The next morning Naaima woke us up early and put us to work helping them make breakfast for the family. Ibrahim invited us to eat with him and his wives, which we did, but just as I was about to ask him about my calling Claudine, he was standing up and saying, "Well, off to work." And he was gone. Then the wives put us back to work cleaning, and after that, preparing for the next meal.

Ibrahim didn't have a phone in his house. So, I knew that to call Claudine I would have to use a public phone. And to do this, I would have to get to a public phone. When I had a chance, I asked Naaima about how I could do this. She said the only place with public phones was in the middle of town, and the only way to get there was by car.

"Or, you could go out in the street and hail a cab," she said.

How am I going to make this happen? I wondered. I knew that calling Brussels cost a lot of money, and I would have to call at the right time of day. I didn't want to call and have Claudine not be at home. I realized that would have to get some money, too. I had used the last of what I had to buy my bus ticket to Bujumbura.

Ibrahim didn't come home for lunch that day. Instead, the wives and the children sat down at the table together. Schiphra and I sat down too.

Naaima, Aaleyah, and Padida stared at us. "What are you doing?" Aaleyah asked.

I thought she was joking, so I smiled and said, "Eating lunch?"

Naaima, Aaleyah, and Padida all rolled their eyes.

"Oh, the two little Tutsi princesses are sitting down to eat lunch," Padida said.

Aaleyah shook her head and clucked her tongue.

"Do you want me to make a list of all of the things I've told you two to do today that you still haven't done?" Naaima asked, folding her arms.

"I'm happy to…"

"We're hungry," Aaleyah said. "Go bring us in our lunch."

"We're waiting…" Padida said.

So, Schiphra and I left the table and got back to work.

For a week I tried to get into town, but Ibrahim's wives were always putting Schiphra and me to work, cooking and cleaning, and watching the children.

We didn't mind. They were letting us stay there, but staying there wasn't why either of us came to Burundi. I kept wondering where Raissa was and when she was coming back. The most important thing to me was calling Claudine. I thought that asking Ibrahim for help would probably be the smartest thing to do, but I almost never saw him. He seemed to almost always come home after I had fallen asleep. And every morning, as soon as he rushed through his breakfast, he'd leave before I could ask him anything.

One morning I finally managed to talk to him about it, and he said, "Oh, you'll need some money for that. Here," and he gave me some money.

"Thank you!" I said. "That's very nice of you, but about getting to the phone, I-"

But he was already up and walking out the door, saying, "Well, back to work," and he was gone. And as soon as he was, Ibrahim's wives put Schiphra and me back to work.

"Raissa!" I said when she finally returned. We hugged. "Where have you been?"

"I had to go back to Kigali for school. Now it's the weekend again, so, here I am to see Jerome. And you guys."

"Who?"

"Jerome?" she called. A man came inside.

"My boyfriend, Jerome."

"Oh. Hello," I said, shaking his hand. He was good looking and tall, but it was hard to tell if he was Hutu or Tutsi. "Nice to meet you," I said.

"You must be Elise. Raissa's told me a lot about you."

"Raissa!" Schiphra said, coming in from the kitchen and hugging her. "You're still alive!"

"I am! I am."

"She's been with Jerome."

"Me," Jerome said.

"Oh, nice to finally meet you," Schiphra said, shaking his hand.

"I need to get to a phone," I said, not wanting to let any more opportunities slip by.

"Oh. You haven't called your sister yet?" Raissa said.

"I haven't had a way to get to the center of town."

"Right," she said. "Well, why don't we go now? You can make your phone call, and Schiphra, Jerome and I can do some shopping, and then all of us can go out for lunch."

After a week of making so little progress on this, finally here it was. "Okay," I said. "Let's go!"

We drove to the middle of town. Raissa pointed me to the public phones and said that they'd be back to pick me up in a little while. I jumped out of the jeep and went into the call center. I asked the woman at the desk how much it was to call Brussels. She pointed to a chart. I found Bujumbura to Brussels: 45 centimes per minute! Ibrahim had given me a five-franc note, which was a lot of money then, but still... I would have to be quick on the phone and not waste any centimes, as I only had enough money for a few minutes.

I got some change from the woman at the counter, went to a phone, and dug in my pocket for the crumpled-up piece of paper that Mama had written Claudine's number on many months ago.

I put in some coins in the phone, dialed the number, and waited nervously as the phone rang. I was hoping desperately that Claudine would answer. If someone other than Claudine picked up, and she wasn't there, the call would be a waste. There was no way she could call me back, and my money would be gone. The phone kept ringing. My heart beat fast. "Please pick up, Claudine!" I said to myself. It rang a few more times.

No one answered. I quickly hung up. I couldn't risk a wasted call.

I got my coins back from the phone. But now, here I was, sitting by the phone, still without my Uncle Hakizimana's address. I heard a car horn beeping outside. I didn't want to hold them up. I gathered my things and walked out into the street, looking for Jerome's car. It wasn't there.

Just then I heard the horn of another car. This time it was Jerome. Raissa was motioning for me to come quickly. I could see that they were blocking traffic.

"How'd it go?" Raissa asked.

"No luck," I said.

"Did you leave a message?"

"I hung up after it rang a few times. I hope I did the right thing."

"Well, we can try another time," she said.

"Sure."

"How about some lunch?" Schiphra said.

I tried to remember the last time I had eaten lunch. It had been back in Rwanda. "Lunch would be great!" I said, and we drove on.

Lunch was great. I always loved spending time with Raissa, and it was a break from our chores back at Ibrahim's house. But eventually the afternoon came to an end, and Raissa and her boyfriend brought Schiphra and me back to Ibrahim's house.

"Are you coming in?" I asked Raissa. I didn't want her to go. It was so much fun to be with her.

"I'm sorry," Raissa said. "My boyfriend and I want to, you know, be alone."

"Oh, pleeeeeease?" I said.

"I guess we could come in for a little while."

"Great," I said.

She and Jerome came in. Ibrahim's wives joined us, and we all started talking and joking, and really having a great time. Eventually Ibrahim came home and joined us all. It got to be quite late. So, Ibrahim invited Raissa and Jerome to spend the night.

*   *   *

"Elise! Schiphra! Wake up!" Raissa hissed. It was dark.

Outside the compound I could hear people running, and shouting, and screaming, and there were gunshots.

"What's going on?" I asked, still groggy.

"Shhhhhhh!" Raissa said. "Quick," she whispered desperately. "Come with me, and stay down! Don't let yourself be seen through the windows!"

Schiphra and I crawled in the dark, feeling our way out of the room we had been sleeping in, into the hall. The only light was from the dim moonlight filtering in through the windows. I crawled up to whisper in Raissa's ear.

"What's happening?" I asked.

"I don't know exactly," she whispered back. "But people are saying President Ndadaye has been shot by a couple of Tutsis, and now Hutus are killing Tutsis! I'll tell you more when I can, but right now we need to hide you and Schiphra! Come on, this way."

We crawled on the floor behind Raissa as she led us into her uncle's bedroom.

"This is the only place that's big enough to hide the two of you," she whispered. "Come on. We have to get both of you under the bed. The Hutus are going house to house, looking for Tutsis!"

I tried to crawl under the double bed, but I bumped into something. "Raissa!" I hissed.

"What?" she hissed back.

"There's something in my way!"

"Oh, yes," she said. "My uncle stores things under here."

"Like what?" I asked, feeling around in the dark trying to find out what was between me and a safe hiding place.

"Pots," she said. "Here, let's move them."

We started shifting them, but it wasn't easy in the dark and without being able to get up off the floor. Finally, we had cleared enough of them away to crawl under the bed. Then I ran my knee into something that cracked.

"Anything else?" I asked.

"Plates," she said, and we cleared them away as well.

As Schiphra and I crawled under the bed, Raissa started packing the pots and plates around us so that no one could tell we were in there. Clever, but not exactly comfortable, especially on a cement floor.

"Raissa?" I whispered.

"Yes?" she whispered back.

"How long do you think we'll have to stay here?"

"I don't know."

"Um…" Schiphra whispered.

"Yes?" I said.

"I have to go to the bathroom."

Raissa sighed, and whispered, "I think you have to hold it."

"How long?" she said.

"Until it's safe for you to come out."

A few hours later, Raissa snuck Schiphra into a corner of the room and had her go into a pot. She told us that with what was still going on outside, they couldn't risk a trip to the toilet, which was a separate building, behind the main house.

It turned out that Schiphra and I had to stay under the bed all night and all the next day. After dark, when no one was around outside, Raissa came and told us we could come out, but that we still had to stay down and out of sight of the windows. We didn't turn on any lights. We had to stay low and sneak our way to the toilet. Raissa kept watch the whole time. Then she took us into the dining house.

Ibrahim invited us to sit down at the table with him and his wives. All of the windows in the dining house faced into the courtyard, and there was a back door that would allow us to sneak back into our hiding place if someone came into the compound looking for Tutsis.

"So, I guess Raissa told you that some Tutsi soldiers killed President Ndadaye," Ibrahim said. "He was a good man. The first president we ever elected here in Burundi. He was a Hutu, and he was trying to bring more Hutus into the government. He was trying to bring everyone in Burundi together. But you see, the army here is almost all Tutsi and they're involved in a lot of the businesses here."

"They profit from it. And I think the thing that got him killed was that he was questioning a lot of those contracts, you know, maybe interfering with people in the army making money, and so, they killed him."

"And so, now, apparently Hutus are killing Tutsis all over the country. And I am so sorry, Elise and Schiphra, it is not safe here at all for Tutsis. If they saw you in the street, or if they found you here inside our house, they would surely kill you, too. I think that under the bed is the best place for you to stay until this is over."

"I'm sorry you lost your president," Schiphra said.

"Yes," I added. "And thank you so much for… well for hiding us and putting yourselves at risk."

"Well," Ibrahim said. "I think all of this hatred that's been going on between Hutus and Tutsis, that's been going on for as long as anyone can remember, has got to stop. That's just… that's what I believe. In any case, let's just concentrate on keeping you hidden for right now. We'll see about getting you back into town once things have calmed down."

"When will that be?" Schiphra asked.

"I don't know," he said. "Maybe a day, maybe a month. We will see. Until it is over, both of you will have to stay under the bed during the day. You will only be able to come out at night. That's when you will have to eat and bathe and use the toilet. It's the only way that's safe. I don't think anyone outside this room, other than Jerome, knows that you're here, and we want to keep it that way."

We knew he was right. It was the only way. So that's what we did. Every day Schiphra and I hid underneath the bed. We slept off and on, but it was very uncomfortable. Lying on our backs, on a concrete floor, with the bottom of the bed right in front our faces, it felt very closed in, very confined. I kept fighting the thought that it was like being in a coffin.

Each night, at dinner, the only time it was safe enough for us to come out from under the bed, Ibrahim would tell us some version of: "It's still not safe. Hutus are still killing Tutsis whenever they find them." He would tell us about how Hutus who were hiding Tutsis or helping them in other ways were being killed as "Tutsi collaborators."

He would explain how "…right now, it's still very dangerous, for all of us. So far, our plan is working. But we need to keep it that way. Not just for your safety, but for our own as well."

And so, Schiphra and I would crawl back into our hiding place for
another night and another day without knowing when, or if, this would
ever end.

On the sixth day under the bed, with Schiphra, I began crying.

"Shhhhh," Schiphra whispered. "It's not safe to make noise, even
here, under the bed. What's wrong?"

"It's just… when we were coming here, I really thought that
Burundi was going to be better, that it was going to be someplace
where we could make a new life for ourselves, and now here we are,
and I'm just thinking, I left my family, my home, my country for…" I
couldn't keep myself from sobbing, "for this?!"

"Shhhhhh," she whispered again. "This can't go on forever, Elise.
Soon, everything will calm down, and we'll be able to go outside, and
find our families. You'll be able to call your sister and get your uncle's
address. And things will be so much better there." She rubbed my back
and then put her arms around me. "Shhhhhh," she whispered again.
"Shhhhhhhh."

The longer we spent under that bed, the more slowly time seemed to
go. I thank God that I had Schiphra there with me. Without her, I think
I might have just lost my mind. I might have just pushed the pots aside
one day, walked outside, and waited for some mob of Hutus to find me,
beat me, and kill me while I yelled, "Just hurry up and get it over
with!"

About two weeks later, Ibrahim said, "I think we've finally reached a point where it's just safe enough to try something, if you're willing. Elise, we'll get you out first, and then, Schiphra, we'll come up with a plan for you. Maybe the same one if it goes well with Elise."

"What do you have in mind?" I asked.

"Well, I think it's worth attempting a trip to the call center, so you can call your sister, get your uncle's number, and get out of here."

"Isn't it still dangerous?"

"They're still killing Tutsis. But they haven't killed any here in this neighborhood in a couple of days. I think, if we consider everything, this plan is our best hope."

"Here's how it's going to work," Raissa said. "Jerome has agreed to drive you into town, very early in the morning. And we think, if you wear a disguise, we might just be able to pull it off."

"What kind of disguise?"

"We'll dress you up like an old woman, in sunglasses and a scarf. And we'll give you a cane. You'll walk bent over, leaning on it…"

"…which will hide my height!"

"Now you're catching on."

"Alright," I said. "Thank you, so much! Let's do it!"

The next morning, when it was early enough that most people would still be in bed, I woke up, and gave Schiphra a big hug. "You're next, right?" I said.

"You're not coming back?"

"I don't know. Jerome says the fewer trips we have to make with me outside, the safer it will be, so…"

"Well then, good luck, Elise."

"You too," I said.

Just as we had planned, Jerome and I set out for the call center. I had my head covered with a scarf. I had sunglasses on, and I was bent over, pretending to limp, as I leaned on the cane. If the situation hadn't been so deadly serious, I think it might have been kind of funny. I had the coins I would need clutched in my hand. I had memorized the number. I wanted the whole thing to be over as quickly as possible.

"Slow down," Jerome said, as we walked. "Remember, you're an old woman."

"Right," I said.

When we got to the call center, I dropped the coins into the phone and dialed Claudine's number. The phone rang. Once. Twice. Three times. "Please, God," I whispered. "Let her be there. Let her pick up." The phone rang a fifth time. "Oh no," I said to myself. My stomach began to sink. "No, no, no, no!"

"Hello?" a woman said, on the other end of the line.

"Hello, is Claudine there?" I asked, trying not to sound desperate.

"It's very early in the morning," the voice said. "You woke us all up with your phone call."

I didn't know who it was, and I didn't remember the names of Uncle Hakizimana's daughters, so I just said, "Can I speak with Claudine, please?"

The woman on the other end sighed. "I think she's still asleep."

"Please, wake her up. It's Elise."

"Who?"

"Her sister! From Rwanda! Would you please just get her? I don't have much time!"

There was another sigh. "Fine," the woman said. "Hold on."

"Hurry-hurry-hurry-hurry!" I was saying to myself. I was afraid that my money would run out.

"Do you have any more coins?" I asked Jerome.

"I think so," he said, looking in his pockets.

"Elise?" Claudine said, picking up the phone.

"Claudine!" I said. "It's so good to speak with you!"

"Where are you?" she demanded. "Mama said you just left? Without saying goodbye? What's wrong with you, Elise?!"

"Claudine? Claudine!" I said. "I don't have much time!" I said. "I'm in Burundi!"

"Burundi?" she said. "What are you doing in Burundi? You should be back in Rwanda with Mama. She's worried sick! Why haven't you at least called her to let her know you're okay?! Do you know there have been killings in Burundi? Hutus killing Tutsis!"

"Claudine? Claudine!" I was trying to get her to stop talking. "Of course I know! I don't have time to explain. I need Uncle Hakizimana's address!"

"What do you need his address for? He-"

"Claudine! I'm in trouble! It's dangerous for me to be here! I need Uncle Hakizimana's address so I can go there!"

Claudine didn't say anything.

"Please, Claudine!" I was on the verge of tears. With everything that had happened so far, it was hard not to break down.

"Alright," she said. "Hold on."

"Please hurry," I said. "I'm on a pay phone."

I had a pen ready to write on my hand. "Hurry, Claudine," I whispered.

Finally, she came back to the phone. "Do you have something to write wi-"

"Yes, I have something to write with!" I cut her off. "Please, Claudine!"

She gave me the address.

"Thank you! Thank you, Claudine! I, I…" I knew we were going to get cut off any second. I didn't know what to say, so I just said, "I love you."

"I-" There was a click on the line, and then two more, and I knew Claudine was gone.

I sighed. Then I turned to Jerome. Showing him the address I had written on my hand, I asked, "Do you know where this is?"

"I can't believe this," he said. "This is like a five-minute drive from Ibrahim's."

"What?"

"Don't worry," he said, smiling. "This is good. This is lucky. I can take you there right now, and that will get you out of sight again."

We made it to Uncle Hakizimana's block in almost no time.

"Is that the house?" Jerome asked.

"I don't know," I said. "I've never been here before."

"Stay in the car," he said, pulling up to the house. "I'll go check."

There was a high brick wall around the compound, with a metal gate where you could drive a car inside. Jerome got out of the car and knocked on the gate. I couldn't hear what was going on, but then Jerome turned to look at me with a huge smile on his face. He walked quickly back to the car. "This is it!" he said excitedly. "Mission accomplished!" He smiled and put a thumb up. "Come on," he said.

I was still nervous, expecting something to go wrong. I was still doing my old woman act as I got slowly out of the car and walked, hunched over, and using the cane to support me as I went to the gate.

Chapter Ten: Uncle Hakizimana's House

"Here she is," Jerome said through the gate, "your niece, Elise."

"Elise?" I heard the voice of an old man, much older than I remembered, say though the gate. "Is that you?"

"Yes, Uncle Hakizimana," I called. "It's me. I'm in disguise," I said, lowering my voice.

"Come in, come in!" he said opening the gate, and then closing it quickly behind us.

I took off my disguise.

"Elise, how are you?" Uncle Hakizimana said, throwing his arms around me. "I haven't seen you since you were a little girl! Do you remember me?"

"Of course!" I said, hugging him back.

"What are you doing here?" he asked. "Come inside the house, and you can tell me in there."

"Excuse me, Sir," Jerome said. "I think it would be best for me to go."

"Yes, all right," Uncle Hakizimana said. "Thank you so much for bringing Elise here."

"Yes. Thank you, so much," I said hugging him. "And tell Ibrahim, and Raissa, and the whole family, 'Thank you, so much' for everything they did."

"I will," Jerome said, "I should go. The car's still running."

"Thank you again," I said, hugging Jerome one last time.

"We'll bring you your things," he said. "Good luck." And he was gone.

"Well," Uncle Hakizimana said. "Come on inside, and let's get you some breakfast. It's so good to see you!" He hugged me again.

"It's good to see you too," I said, hugging him back. "I'm sorry we couldn't let you know I was coming."

"Oh, no, no. That's fine," he said. "I know how hard things can be for a Tutsi in Rwanda, especially now."

"I had some trouble with some Hutus back home in Biryogo."

"Yes, Gabriel told me."

"Where is Gabriel?"

"He's probably in his room," Uncle Hakizimana said.

"Elise!" I heard Gabriel say. I turned to see him standing in the hallway.

"Gabriel!" I said, opening my arms, ready to run to him and hug him. He had changed since I had last seen him. He was so much taller! He looked so grown-up for a sixteen-year-old. I was smiling at him, but his face was dark and angry.

"What are you doing here?" he said in an accusing tone.

"Gabriel," I said. "I have so much to tell you…"

He stared at me coldly.

"Gabriel, aren't you happy to see me?"

"I can't believe you," he said. "You were supposed to stay with Mama." He turned and walked back down the hallway, away from me.

"Gabriel? Gabriel…" I said. I looked at Uncle Hakizimana.

He shrugged.

"Gabriel. Gabriel!" I called after him.

Gabriel stopped and stood, with his back to me.

"I had to come here, Gabriel! I couldn't stay in Kigali. I would have been killed!"

Gabriel turned toward me with his head down. Then he looked at me, and then he started shaking his head slowly, back and forth. "You don't understand, Elise," he said. "You just don't understand." He turned away again, walked into the room at the end of the hallway, and slammed the door.

I didn't know what to say. I didn't know what to do. I didn't know what Gabriel was talking about. *I should have stayed with Mama?* I didn't understand that. I just felt confused and rejected by the last person I would ever expect to reject me. That, on top of everything that I had been pushing down since leaving Nyamirambo, rose up and started spilling over its banks. I began to cry.

Uncle Hakizimana hugged me and said, "Give him time. Give him time." Then he brought me over to the couch. We sat down. I stopped crying. I could hear someone in the kitchen.

"Who's that?" I asked.

"Oh, Olive? Come meet my niece, Elise."

A woman came out of the kitchen and put out her hand. "I'm Olive."

"Elise," I said, wiping my tears, standing, and shaking her hand. "Nice to meet you."

"Olive is my cook," Uncle Hakizimana said.

"Whatever you're making smells good!" I said.

"Oh, thank you. So, you're Gabriel's sister?"

"That's right."

"Well, it's very nice to meet you, too. I've got some things on the stove I need to get back to, but I'll see you later." She turned and went back into the kitchen.

"She seems nice," I said.

"She is. Great cook, too. So, where did you just come from?" Uncle Hakizimana asked.

I told him everything, all the things that had happened to bring me there. I told him about school, and Linda. I told him about the "Hey Rucumu" boy and the rock. Eventually I got to Nyamirambo and Eugene and Schiphra.

"I'm going to have to talk to my son about that," Uncle Hakizimana said. "It's my house, not my son's, and certainly not Eugene's. And I don't want him treating it as though it's his! And treating you the way he did! Disgraceful! I'm so sorry."

"Well, it took some convincing, but they did let me stay there."

"Telling you the whole time that you had to leave as soon as possible!"

"I made it through, though. And now I'm here."

"You did, and you are. And it's wonderful to see you. That I'm happy about."

Then I told him about coming to Burundi, thinking I was escaping all of the danger and madness in Rwanda, only to end up having to hide under the bed. I told him about having to get in a disguise to call

Claudine. "…and I think one of your daughters answered. I'm sorry, I don't remember their names."

"Carene and Michelle," he said.

"That's right."

"Do you remember them? You were all young girls the last time you all saw each other."

"A little," I said. "Do they ever come to visit? Do you think I'll get to see them while I'm here?"

"They visit… every once in a while. They seem to be busy with… their boyfriends in Brussels, and, I don't know, shopping or something."

"Oh, I'm sorry," I said. I felt like I had stumbled on a sore subject for him. "Let's talk about something else."

"No," he said. "It's fine. It's just that… I'm their father and… well, to begin with, I would feel a lot better if they were married, instead of… I don't know, whatever kind of… arrangement they've got. But, they're in Brussels, and somehow, they're sending me money. So, I assume they're doing okay, you know, as far as money goes."

"Claudine has been staying with them for a while. That was nice of them, to take her with them."

"Well…" he said.

"What?"

"Well, I think they might have had another reason why they took her in. I think they saw an opportunity to have a house girl they didn't have to pay, a servant."

"Oh," I said.

"I wish I had nicer things to say about my own daughters, but… there it is. Louise is nice though. Do you remember her?"

"Is she about my age?"

"That's right. She lives in Remera now."

"Oh. She's still back in Rwanda."

"Mm. She's married. Good guy. She has two kids. I haven't seen them in the longest time. It's tough for them. They don't have a lot of money."

"Mm."

"So, you're not going to believe this: When I talked to Claudine and got your address, it turned out that the whole time I had been in Burundi at Raissa's uncle's house, I was just a few blocks away!"

"Amazing," he said. "Your whole tale. You're lucky to be alive."

"Oh, I know," I said. "I know."

We kept talking until Olive told us it was time for lunch. She called to Gabriel, too. He came and sat down at the table with Uncle Hakizimana and me. He ate, but he didn't speak. He wouldn't even look at me. As Uncle Hakizimana and I talked and joked with each other, I kept looking over at Gabriel, waiting for him to say something, anything. I tried to make him laugh. But he gave me nothing. He just finished eating, got up, and went to his room.

Again, I looked at Uncle Hakizimana. Again, he shrugged.

It really bothered me that Gabriel wasn't talking to me. I was concerned, too. But what could I do? I changed the subject. "You have a beautiful house," I said. "Tile floors, high ceilings, an indoor kitchen, indoor bathroom."

"Two," he said. "Even so, Carene and Michelle always complain that both bathrooms have squat toilets."

"Well, I'm fine with them. I've been using squat toilets all my life. I don't understand why they care. I mean, it's your house."

"Actually, Carene and Michelle pay the rent on it. Well, their rich boyfriends do. It's not the ideal situation, but…" he looked around the house. "It could be worse."

"It could be worse," I agreed. I looked down the hall, toward Gabriel's room.

"You're still thinking about Gabriel," Uncle Hakizimana said. "I know. He's going through a lot. I mean, clearly both of you are. But, you should know."

"Tell me."

"First of all, he won't talk about it, but I can tell that he's intensely sad about having to leave home and having to leave your mama. I know he looks all grown up, but I can tell he's very, very homesick. And he probably feels like he's too old to feel homesick, so he's embarrassed. And, from the way he talks about it, I get the feeling he has an idea in his head that he should have stood up to the gang back in Biryogo. But I also think everybody, him included, knows what happens to people that stand up to the Interahamwe. So, he's probably, you know, torn inside."

"Mmm."

"And so, he's angry. You know, he feels that he's gotten a raw deal. And he has. All Tutsis have. I'm not quite sure what this whole 'you should have stayed with Mama' thing is. I think he probably feels like he should have stayed with your mama. He's very concerned about her. With good reason, I'm afraid. Things in Rwanda keep getting worse. More dangerous."

"It's not exactly safe for Tutsis *here*, now." I said.

"Mm. It's different here, though. You know, with Tutsis controlling the military here."

"Mm."

"So, I don't think the killings that have been going on here are going to continue for long. In Rwanda, though…"

"Mm."

"But back to Gabriel. Your Mama and I talk from time to time. I call her sometimes when she's at work."

"You have a phone?"

"The woman who lives next door, Marie. She has one. She lets me use it."

"I thought only Hutus could have phones. Is Marie a Hutu?"

"No, she's a Tutsi. But she's very rich."

"Wow. So, this is how you keep in touch with Carene and Michelle?"

"Mm."

"Well, that's awfully nice of Marie."

"It is. I've got great neighbors here. Anyway, your mom's told me she's concerned about Gabriel, and that she has been for a while. She said that sometimes he acts … without thinking."

"Oh. Yeah," I said. "That's true. Not all the time, but…"

"Well, I hadn't really seen any of that, until he started this with you. I have to say, it does seem a little… you know, irrational."

"Mm. I could see Mama being afraid that, with a gang giving him trouble, he'd do something without thinking, something that would end up getting him hurt, or killed."

"The same way his sister almost got *her*self killed?"

"It had to stop, Uncle! It had been going on for years, and it was getting worse. More dangerous."

"Oh, Elise, I'm sorry! I shouldn't make light of that, at all. I'm sure it was horrible. I'm amazed that you didn't do something like throwing that rock much earlier. Sounds like the little punk had it coming."

"Well…" I said.

"He did!"

"So, how's Gabriel doing here, in Burundi?"

"Oh, very well. He's getting good grades in school, and he has turned out to be an incredible football player!".

"Oh yes? He's always been good at football. Papa was very good too."

"Well, since he came here, Gabriel has really gone to another level!"

"Really?"

"Oh yes. It almost seems unfair for him to play against boys his own age. You really must come watch him play!"

"I'd love to," I said. Then I yawned.

"You're tired."

"You'd think, all that time, under a bed…"

"Afraid that a band of Hutus could burst in at any moment and kill you? I'm sure that was stressful."

"It was."

"I'd certainly understand if you wanted to take a nap. Follow me."

"I get to sleep here?" I said. "By myself?"

"Well, no, actually this is my room. That's my bed there, and then I have this extra one over here. I think you should sleep in here for now. I only have two bedrooms, and I don't think putting you in Gabriel's room is a good idea. Definitely not right now, anyway. I hope you don't mind sharing the room with me. Is it okay?"

"Oh, Uncle," I said. "Just a bed of my own, and I get to sleep on *top* of it?"

"If you're used to sleeping under the bed, on the floor, you could sleep there, I suppose," he said grinning. "But seriously, lie down and take a nap. I can tell you've already had a long day."

"A long couple of weeks!" I said. "Thank you so much, Uncle." I gave him a hug and then sat down on the bed.

"I'll close the door," he said, "and give you some privacy."

I let out a long sigh. You really appreciate privacy when you haven't had it. I sat on the bed, and suddenly, I was even more tired. *I just need to lay down for a minute or two*, I thought. I did.

When I woke up, I was still in my clothes. I still had my shoes on! As I sat up and stretched, I realized that I hadn't felt relaxed or rested in weeks. The whole time I had been hiding under the bed at Ibrahim's house I hadn't really slept. I would close my eyes, and maybe get fifteen minutes here or an hour there, but I can tell you, it's very hard to relax when you're worried that you're about to be killed by a roving band of Hutus.

Having slept, though, I felt good: calm and well rested. I was already dressed, and since I didn't have any other clothes to change into, I got up and went into the kitchen.

"Good afternoon," Uncle Hakizimana said. "Would you like some early dinner?"

"Dinner? How long was I asleep?" I asked.

"Most of the day," he said, smiling warmly.

"Where's Gabriel?" I asked.

"I think he's in his room, reading."

I went to Gabriel's room. The door was closed. I knocked. "Gabriel?" I called. There was no answer. I opened the door slowly. "Gabriel?"

He was lying on his bed, by the window, reading. He didn't look up.

"Gabriel? Won't you speak to me?"

He kept reading.

"Please, Gabriel. I haven't seen you in all this time, and now you won't speak with me?"

He sighed and turned away from me.

For a whole week it was like that. I would ask Gabriel a question, and he would ignore me, pretending I wasn't there, or he would just stare at me with an angry, angry expression on his face.

Well, I thought, *he can't stay mad at me forever*. So, I kept trying.

But he *did* stay mad at me, for days and days. I tried everything. I would even walk down the street beside him, sometimes in silence, sometimes saying things to him, trying to get him to say something back.

One day, as I was doing this, we passed a girl who looked like she was about my age, walking toward us. She smiled and waved. I smiled and waved back.

After we passed her, Gabriel said, "You see that girl?"

"Yes," I said, a little shocked that he was actually talking to me.

"She's been getting raped by the *Sans Échec*, and if you don't be careful, if you go out at night too much, they'll rape you too."

"What is the Sans Échec?" I asked, thinking, *It's French for without check. Maybe it meant something like: no one keeps them in check?*

Gabriel scoffed, as though I had asked a stupid question. "Well, you know the Interahamwe, back in Rwanda?"

"Yes."

"Well, they're all Hutus. But this is a Tutsi neighborhood. You've seen the men with guns at the borders of it?"

"Yes."

"Well, they're Sans Échec. It's like the Interahamwe, but for Tutsis. Because of them, Hutus know that if they came into this neighborhood looking for trouble, the Tutsis are going to give them a fight."

"Oh," I said. The girl Gabriel was talking about looked like she might have been a Tutsi. I wondered why a gang that was trying to be the Tutsi version of the Interahamwe would rape a Tutsi girl. It kind of seemed like Gabriel was making it up. I had known Gabriel to make up stories before. I thought maybe he was concerned about my safety when I went out at night, but he was angry, so this was the only way he could express it. "How do you know about the Sans Échec?" I asked.

"Oh, they all like me," he said. "They're all big fans. They come watch me play football. I'm friends with some of them. There are some of them over there. Jean! Alan!" he called to a group of boys across the street.

"Gabriel!" they yelled back.

Gabriel smiled and waved to them. "This is my sister, Elise," he yelled.

They all waved.

I waved back, a little hesitantly. I really wasn't sure how I felt about this, any of this. I was glad that Gabriel had some new…friends? But looking at the group of boys I could see what Gabriel meant. They looked a lot like the Interahamwe boys who had harassed me back home. They didn't seem any better, just Tutsi instead of Hutu.

I thought that, in its own strange way, this had been some kind of break-through with Gabriel, that he had started talking to me again. But after that talk we had about Sans Échec, every time I would try to strike up a conversation with Gabriel, all I got in return was an angry look and him shaking his head at me. Luckily, that was right around that time I started making new friends in the neighborhood.

A few days after the Sans Échec conversation, as Uncle Hakizimana and I were having tea in his living room, there was a knock at the door.

"Let's see who that is," Uncle Hakizimana said, struggling to get up from his chair, and walking slowly to the door.

He's really getting old, I thought, watching him, and worrying.

"Doreen!" Uncle Hakizimana said, answering the door.

"Hakizimana!" the girl at the door said. They hugged, as I was getting up from the couch.

"You're the girl from the street," I said.

"What?" Uncle Hakizimana asked.

"We passed each other on the street the other day," Doreen explained. "She was walking with Gabriel, and I decided to come meet the new girl in the neighborhood."

"Oh. Well, this is my niece, Elise. Elise, this is Doreen. She lives two doors down from us."

"Nice to meet you, officially," I said. I shook Doreen's hand.

"Come in, and join us for tea," Uncle Hakizimana said.

"Oh, I would love to. Thank you."

The three of us sat down and began to talk. Doreen and I really hit it off, right from the start. I found out that she was my age, that she was living with her auntie, who it turned out was her actual aunt, and that she had fled the troubles in Rwanda, just like me.

When Uncle Hakizimana decided that he was going to take a nap, Doreen stayed, and we kept talking. She told me that she had found some good clubs and a fun group of people to hang out with in Bujumbura.

Raissa came to visit every once in a while. It was always good to see her. One time when she came, she told me that Schiphra had found her family and was living with them. It was good to hear about someone having a happy ending.

It wasn't long before Doreen started showing me the good places to go in Bujumbura and introducing me to her friends. We always had a great time when we went out together. Doreen had a boyfriend named Samuel.

His best friend was a man named Benjamin. He was a very tall, very handsome man, in his thirties, with very Tutsi looks. I guess he liked the way I looked, too, because he walked right over to me, shook my hand, smiled, and started talking to me. He stayed with me for the whole night. We danced, we talked, we drank, we joked. It was wonderful.

I started seeing Benjamin a lot, and soon we were deeply in love. He was my first. Back when I was living with Mama, she would have a neighbor who was a nurse come by twice a month and check to see that Claudine and I were still virgins. This wasn't that uncommon. It was embarrassing, and I didn't have any say in the matter. Here in Burundi, though, it was different. Uncle Hakizimana basically treated me like I was an adult. I could make my own decisions, and I did.

Being in love with Benjamin was wonderful and exciting. We spent a lot of time going out with Doreen and Samuel. It was fun having a boyfriend and a group of friends to go out with. At the same time, I was always worried about what was going on in Rwanda. I would hear things on the radio. I felt guilty having fun, while Mama, Robert, Alice, and Patrick were in danger. I wished there was something I could do to help them.

Benjamin owned several hotels, houses, and apartment buildings. We would get together at one of his hotels a few times a week. Sometimes I would wonder why he never took me to his house, but things between us were so intense that a question like that never stayed in my head for too long.

Until one day, as I was walking home from the market, one of the Sans Échec boys Gabriel had called out to that day we were talking came up and started walking beside me. I flashed back to the Interahamwe gang. I was working to control my fear.

"Elise," he said in a low voice.

"Yes?"

"We just wanted you to know, Benjamin's wife? She paid us to kill you."

I stopped breathing, but I kept walking. We weren't far from Uncle Hakizimana's door.

"But we're not going to do that," the boy continued.

Then I stopped walking and turned to him. "What? Benjamin… Wait, but… why are you telling me this? Why aren't you going to kill me? Not that I'm complaining."

"You're Gabriel's sister. We love him! He's our boy! We would never do anything to hurt him, or his family."

"Oh," I said. "Well, uh… Thanks for not killing me. And, I guess… thanks for letting me know?"

"Tell Gabriel about this, will you? That we were supposed to kill you, and we didn't?" the boy asked.

"Well, that could be hard," I said. "He doesn't really speak to me."

"Oh. Well, then, we'll tell him." The boy said. And then he was gone.

Benjamin's wife!? I thought. ***That's*** *why he never took me to his house!* I had never considered that, by being with him, I might be doing something bad. But now… I wondered about his wife.

Obviously, she knew. I wondered if he had kids. I felt terrible. I never thought of myself as the type of person who would help someone cheat or lie to his wife. I told myself to end it.

The next time I saw Benjamin, I told him I knew about his wife.

"But I love you, Elise!" he assured me. "I don't love her anymore. I love *you*!"

I told myself not to give in, but I kept seeing him. I had all sorts of reasons in my head why I shouldn't: It was wrong. He was married. His wife knew about me and wanted to kill me! He wasn't talking about leaving her and marrying me. I wondered what kind of future we could have together. But I was young, and I was in love. All I really knew then was that I loved being with him.

I kept trying to get Gabriel to speak to me. Every night I was at Uncle Hakizimana's house for dinner, which was most nights, I went to Gabriel's room to tell him it was time for dinner. Usually when I got to his room, I'd find him lying on his bed, reading. I would tell him that dinner was ready, and he'd pretend to ignore me. I would turn to go, and Gabriel would eventually come to the table.

I did this for weeks, with the same result. Until one night, when I told him, as I was turning to go, he said, "You were supposed to stay with Mama!"

I turned back to him. He was glaring at me.

"Why do you say that, Gabriel? You know what happened. My life was in danger. I had to-"

"I don't want to hear it!" he said.

"Mama *sent* me away!"

"To Nyamirambo!" he yelled. "Not to Burundi! Not here! Mama was worried sick about you!"

"Eugene and Betty didn't want me in Nyamirambo!" I said. "They kept asking when I was going to leave so that they could rent the house! And if any of the Hutus from Biryogo found out where I was-"

"You have to go back!" he said, cutting me off.

"To die?"

"You have to go back!" he persisted.

"Well, I'm not going back," I said.

He sighed and said, "Someone has to be with Mama."

"What are you talking about? Patrick's there, and Alice."

"They can't defend her!"

"Neither can I! Neither can you! This is… this doesn't make sense! Robert is there!"

"You have to go back!"

"Well, I'm not going back," I said folding my arms.

"No?" he said.

"No," I said. "You go back."

Then Gabriel went under his bed and took out a suitcase.

"What are you doing?" I said.

"I told you: you don't understand," he said, taking clothes out of his dresser and putting them into the suitcase.

"Understand what?"

"Someone has to be with Mama," he said, continuing to pack.

"Gabriel…"

"I was doing well here, Elise! There were scouts from professional football teams that were coming to watch me play! I could have finished school and gone on to university!"

"Gabriel, what are you doing?" I pleaded.

"You know what I'm doing, Elise. You know very well!" he said. "If you are not going to go back, then I have to!"

"Gabriel, what are you talking about? When I said, 'You go back,' I was kidding."

He looked through his books, chose three, and put them in his suitcase. Then he closed it, picked it up, and walked out of the room.

Walking behind him, I called, "Gabriel. Gabriel!"

He continued walking, through the house and out the front door.

"Gabriel…" I yelled.

He kept walking, out to the front gate.

"Gabriel!" I called. "It's not safe! It's gotten worse since you left, much worse!"

He didn't look back. He was walking down the road now.

"Gabriel!" I called again.

But he didn't stop.

I watched him until he disappeared around the corner.

I walked back inside the house, fell to my knees, and began to cry.

Uncle Hakizimana kneeled down and put his arm around me.

When I had stopped sobbing, Uncle Hakizimana said, "I just want you to know: you didn't make him go."

"I'm not so sure," I said.

"No-no, Elise. This was something in him, a number of things. Like I told you when you first arrived: he was so intensely homesick, I think part of him wanted to go back, but then another part of him knew that he was being a little childish, and he was embarrassed. And it's much easier to get angry at someone than it is, especially for a boy his age, to admit that he… misses his mama. You just happened to be here. Anybody could see that you going home would be…" he stopped himself.

"…suicide."

"We don't know what will happen. Hopefully this is just a kind of… tantrum and he'll be back later on tonight, or tomorrow."

"What if he doesn't come back?" I asked.

I went to bed in Gabriel's room that night. I lay there, re-playing the argument in my head, wondering if there was anything I could have done or said that would have kept him from leaving.

Days turned into weeks. Still there was no word about Gabriel. Uncle had a radio that we listened to all the time. I was always hoping I'd hear news about what was happening back in Rwanda but dreading it at the same time. The news from there was never good. Uncle Hakizimana had a radio that he listened to a lot.

There kept being more and more reports about "ethnic tensions between Hutus and Tutsis," and "continued violence and killings," and how anti-Tutsi rallies were becoming more and more common.

It was worried about my family. I hoped everyone was alright. I prayed that Gabriel had made it back to Rwanda somehow, but I didn't know for sure.

Until one day, when Marie came over and told us that Uncle's daughters had called.

"Olive," Uncle Hakizimana called. "Elise and I are going next door to Marie's house to call my daughters."

"Okay," she called back.

As we started to walk over to Marie's house, Uncle Hakizimana asked, "When I call Carene and Michelle, if you'd like, we can see if Claudine is still there. And if she's available to talk with you."

"That would be great," I said. "Maybe I can get some news from home."

"Maybe."

"How could you leave Mama alone like that without even telling her?" Claudine demanded.

"What? Mama's not alone!"

"Well, not anymore. Gabriel had to go back to Rwanda to be with her!"

"Gabriel actually made it back home?" I said. "Oh, thank God!"

"Of course he did," Claudine said. "You know Gabriel. Once he gets an idea in his head, there's no stopping him."

"Uncle Hakizimana said he thinks Gabriel was just homesick and he missed Mama."

"That's not what *he* says."

"Well, of course that's not what he says. But you know how he is. Sometimes he does and says things that are kind of… you know, without thinking. What else is going on back there? Is everybody okay?"

"Everyone's fine."

"Is Gabriel still having trouble with that gang?"

"Mama didn't mention it."

"Is everyone safe?"

"Safe? As safe as they've ever been in Rwanda."

"It's so strange," I said to Uncle Hakizimana, as we were walking back to his house.

"What's that?"

"That talking to someone in Brussels, thousands of kilometers away, is the best way to find out about what's happening in Kigali, just a few hundred kilometers away."

"It's certainly the safest way."

"Mmm. Uncle, you've said you've talked to my mama on the phone, right?"

"Oh, yes."

"Well, do you think I could be there the next time you call? Or do you think maybe I could ask Marie if I could call her?"

"I do, but you know, it's her phone, and it's… expensive. So maybe space it out? Give it some time before you ask?"

"Okay, Uncle," I said. "I will."

I gave it about a week. Then I asked. Marie was very gracious. "Of course," she said.

I was careful to pick a time when I knew Mama would be at work at the soap factory. The phone rang. A woman answered. I asked if I could speak to my mama, including: "Please tell her it's her daughter, Elise."

I waited.

The same woman came back. "I'm afraid she can't come to the phone right now."

"Did you tell her it was her daughter, Elise?"

"I did. I'm sorry."

I couldn't understand why she didn't take my call. *Maybe she was just really busy*, I told myself, but I was afraid it was something else, something bad.

I tried again, about a week later. Mama was the one who picked up the phone this time.

"Hello?"

"Mama, it's Elise!" The line went dead.

"What happened?" Uncle Hakizimana asked when I got back to his house.

"I think she hung up on me!" I said. "I don't understand it. What do you think is going on?"

"I honestly don't know," he said. "The best I can do is guess."

"What's your guess?"

"I think your mama is very stressed."

"But, Uncle Hakizimana, I'm her daughter!"

"I know. But when people are very stressed, sometimes they do things that don't make sense. I'm sure she's afraid for you and Gabriel and all of her children. And it's easier to feel angry than it is to feel afraid."

"What can I do, Uncle?"

"Oh, Elise," he said. "I'm so sorry. I don't think there's anything you *can* do."

I tried calling Mama two more times. Both times she wouldn't talk with me. I was crushed, but Uncle was right. There was nothing I could do.

Whenever Carene and Michelle called, I always went with Uncle Hakizimana to call them back. I always asked to talk with Claudine. I wanted to know how she was, but I was also trying to find out about what was happening with everyone else back home.

Claudine always seemed to speed through all of that and start talking about her life. She told me that there was a man she had met at the hospital where she worked, and that he was a Tutsi who grew up in the refugee camps in Uganda. She said she couldn't tell me why he had come to the hospital in Brussels to get treated, because it was a secret. She did say that he was very nice and very handsome, and that they had started dating.

I was glad to hear that she was happy, but I always wished that she told me more about our family in Rwanda. It's not that I didn't care about Claudine, but Brussels was safe. There were no Hutus killing Tutsis there.

I would try to ask Claudine more detailed questions about what was going on in Rwanda, but then she would always ask me when I was going to go back home, or when I was going to enroll in school. As far as going back to Rwanda, Claudine seemed to be totally disregarding the fact that there was still a gang there who wanted to kill me. But I didn't bother arguing. *What's the point?* I would think.

I had started thinking about my future, though. I thought about how I *did* need to get back to school. I wasn't getting any younger. But who was going to pay for it? Mama wouldn't even talk to me.

I thought about maybe trying to find a job, but at that time, as a single woman, there were almost no opportunities for work. Basically, there were nurses and schoolteachers, and you needed to go to university for both of those. The way most girls left their fathers' houses was by getting married, or some girls found a boyfriend who would pay for their expenses.

I was still seeing Benjamin, which felt wonderful. I was having fun being with him and going out with my friends, but it felt like, at least, in part, I was having fun to distract myself from the anxiety I was feeling about everything else. I knew Benjamin was cheating on his wife. So, our relationship had no future. And with things getting worse and worse back in Rwanda, where most of my family still was, I was worried that there might not be a much of a future to anything.

Chapter Eleven: It Begins

I'm inside our house in Biryogo. I've just locked the front door to keep the Hutu mob that's chasing me from getting in. Backing away from the door, I trip over something and fall to the floor. I try to get back to my feet, but I find that I'm slipping in a puddle of blood, and that I've tripped over a body that's covered in machete wounds! I have to use my hands and feet to push myself away from it.

Then the body starts to move! It turns its head toward me until I can see its face. It's a woman I don't know. She reaches out to me. "Elise…" she says, but she's saying it in Mama's voice!

I need to wake up, but I can't! I can't move! I try to scream, but nothing is coming out of my mouth! I struggle to pull myself out of this. I feel like if I can't, I'll drown!

I woke up screaming. I didn't know where I was. Uncle Hakizimana burst into my room.

"Elise!" he said, out of breath. "What's wrong?"

"Oh, Uncle!" I said. "I was having a nightmare. I'm sorry. I didn't mean to frighten you."

"You don't have to be sorry, Elise," he said. "I was afraid something had happened to you. Do you want to tell me about the dream?"

"I was being chased by the Hutu mob. They wanted to kill me. There was blood everywhere. There was a dead body that turned out to be Mama! Or, well, she was using Mama's voice."

"Terrible," he said. "I'm sorry. Do you want me to stay with you?"

"I'm okay now," I said. "It's just…"

"What?"

"Well, do you think dreams… mean anything?"

"What do you mean?"

"Do you think they can be more than … just dreams? Like warnings or, I don't know, some sort of like… communication or… predicting the future maybe?"

"Hm," he said. "Well, yes. I think that they can. I've seen it happen. But I think most of the time dreams are just your mind trying to work out whatever it is you're concerned about. And even the times when they *are* something else, they're all going through your mind, so it's very hard to tell what's what."

"It's just that I keep having horrible nightmares about Hutus chasing Mama and me. And I'm worried that something horrible might be about to happen to her and the rest of my family back in Rwanda. And the reports we keep hearing on the radio about what's going on there make me worry even more."

"I know," Uncle Hakizimana said. "I know. I'm concerned, too. I just don't want you to take a nightmare for something more than it is and then use that as a reason to do something foolish like running back to Rwanda. I think one of the hardest things about what's going on there for us is the fact that there really isn't anything we can do. I mean, even if you did make it back to Rwanda, what could you actually do, except probably get killed?"

"I guess you're right, Uncle," I said.

"Now, do you want me to stay here with you until you fall asleep?"

"Oh, thank you, Uncle," I said. "But I think I'll be okay."

"Alright," he said, groaning as he got up from the bed and shuffling a bit as he walked out of the room.

The way he did things like that made me worried about Uncle Hakizimana's age. He was in his seventies, and he had had a hard life. I was worried that he might fall, or that something worse might happen to him.

One night, after supper, Uncle Hakizimana said, "Elise, you haven't touched your food. And you don't look so good. Are you feeling all right?"

"I'm not sure," I told him. "I feel weak and dizzy."

"Why don't you go to bed," he suggested, "and see if a good night's sleep doesn't take care of it."

"Okay Uncle," I said. I started to get up from the table, but the next thing I knew I was on the floor with Uncle Hakizimana and Olive were kneeling over me, saying, "Elise, Elise!"

"What happened?" I asked. "How did I get on the floor?"

"You fell!" Uncle Hakizimana said. "It's a good thing you didn't hit your head on the way down! If we help you, do you think you can stand?"

"I'll try," I said. As they got me to my feet, I cautioned them, "Oh, slowly. Slowly. I'm very, very dizzy. And I really don't feel very good."

"Are you going to vomit?" Uncle Hakizimana asked.

"I don't know," I said.

"Olive, could you give us a bowl from the kitchen?"

"Of course," she said, as Uncle Hakizimana helped me to my room.

"This is really strange, Uncle," I said, lying down on my bed. "I almost never get sick. And this doesn't feel like anything I've had before."

Uncle Hakizimana put his hand on my forehead. "You're not warm," he said. "That *is* odd."

A lot of Rwandans believe that there are many things that can make you sick. There are germs, of course. But we also know that sometimes when a person gets sick, especially if it's a strange kind of sickness, that it may be a warning that something very bad is happening or is about to happen to someone they care about. I was worried that this was what was happening to me. Thinking that is the last thing I remember for the next several days.

When I woke up, I still felt very sick, and I had the same feeling of dread. I slowly got out of bed and unsteadily made my way to the kitchen table, where Uncle Hakizimana was listening to his portable radio.

"Good morning, Uncle," I said.

"Just a minute," he said. "I want to hear this." He turned up the volume. I was having trouble sitting up, so I sat and put my head down on the table.

"And so," a voice on the radio was saying, "these Tutsi snakes, these invaders, if they are not stopped, will put us back into slavery! And that is why, in our own defense, we Hutus must send them back up the Nyabarongo River to Abyssinia where they came from! This is RTLM, the voice of freedom in Rwanda."

A bright, happy-sounding song was playing, as I worked to lift my head and prop it up on my hands. "It's just talk, right, Uncle?" I said.

"I'm not so sure," he replied. "Are you feeling any better?"

"About the same. I still feel so dizzy and weak."

"Why don't you stay in bed today? Do you want Olive to make some soup and bring it in to you?"

"Thank you, no, Uncle," I said. "I don't really feel like eating. I'm afraid it's not a normal sickness, that it's a warning."

"Well," he said. "That may be. Or maybe you're just sick. You've been under so much stress for so long. That can make you sick all by itself. Try not to worry. Get some rest. Drink some water. Have some warm soup when you feel you can handle it. It will probably make you feel better."

"I hope you're right," I said.

"In any case, sleep is the best thing for it. Just call if you need anything, and I'll be right there."

"Okay, Uncle. Thank you." I said. "I will." I made my way back to my room and into bed.

When I woke up the next day, I felt even worse. I didn't even get out of bed. Eventually Uncle Hakizimana knocked on the door. "Elise?" He called. "May I come in?"

"Yes," I said in a croak.

"Still sick?"

"I think I'm getting worse, Uncle." I tried sitting up a little, but as soon as I did the room started to spin. "Oh!" I said, and immediately laid back down again. "Definitely worse!"

"Same symptoms?" he asked.

"I feel hot and achy, and dizzy when I try to sit up," I said. "Oooh, and my head hurts!"

Uncle Hakizimana felt my forehead. "Huh," he said. "You still don't feel like you have a fever. That *is* strange."

"I talked to my doctor friend. He thinks you might have a flu, or malaria. If it is either of those, it's a pretty weird case, though. I've had malaria, and I've seen it in other people. I've never seen a case where the person didn't have a fever and chills. Sorry to ask, any diarrhea?"

"No."

"Hm. Of course, you haven't eaten anything. I'm going to have Olive bring you some soup. Will you try to eat a bit of it, for me?"

"I'll try, Uncle," I said. "Thank you, for everything."

A few days later I woke up feeling a little bit better, like maybe I was starting to get over whatever I had. I tried sitting up. I still felt dizzy, but the room didn't start spinning. I tried standing. I still felt a little unsteady, but I kept going. I headed toward the kitchen, bracing myself on the wall as I went.

"Uncle," I said, walking fast into the kitchen. "Good news!"

"Shhhh!" he said, holding a hand out. He was listening to the radio. His face was dark and wrinkled with concern.

I made my way to the table, sat down, and listened with him. "We are calling on all Hutus to do their duty, to retaliate against the Tutsis for this unforgivable act! The time has come to exterminate the inyenzi! To not leave one alive!"

"What happened, Uncle?" I finally had to ask.

"Oh, Elise," he said. "It's started."

"What's started?"

"They shot down President Habyarimana's plane. And Ntaryamira, the new president of Burundi, was on the plane too. They're saying the Tutsis did it, of course."

"Who do you think did it?"

"I think it must have been the Rwandan Army. The plane was shot down by a missile. I've been listening for hours. And ever since they announced that the plane was shot down, they haven't just been telling Hutus to kill all the Tutsis, they're actually directing them! They're telling Hutus where the Tutsis are, like they've got some kind of list!"

The death lists Rose told me about! I thought. *My whole family's on one of those lists!* "Oh, Uncle!" I said.

"Wait," he said. "There's another report. We have to hear if there's any mention of Remera, where my daughter is, or of Biryogo!"

We listened for hours and hours, as the announcers reported on "a nest of Tutsis" hiding out in this town and that town and in this neighborhood, on this street and that street in Kigali. In between, they would say things like, "The time has come to cut down the tall trees!"

Then, as though they were narrating a football match, they started gleefully announcing the killings. Town by town, neighborhood by neighborhood, street by street, they were celebrating the Rwandan army and the Interahamwe "wiping the Tutsis out!" boasting about how many Tutsi "cockroaches" had been killed here and how many had been killed there.

What we were hearing was making me feel sicker and sicker. I rested one side of my head on the table, sometimes closing my eyes, sometimes looking over at Uncle Hakizimana. He looked so tired. It was horrible to watch the tension in his face building, as he kept listening. But neither of us could stop. What if they mentioned Biryogo or Remera while we were doing something else?

The reports of Tutsis being killed went on and on and on. And in between the reports they were playing music! There was one song that sounded like a traditional song or a song you might hear in church, except the words were:

Come and rejoice friends Cockroaches have been exterminated!

Let us rejoice friends!

God is never wrong.

There was also speaker after speaker saying things like: "The Tutsis are a dirty race. We have to exterminate them. All of them. It is the only way." There were pop songs in English, and songs in Kinyarwanda. There was one called "I Hate Hutus", about the singer's hatred for any Hutus who help out Tutsis. They were reminding people that if a Tutsi woman is pregnant, there's another Tutsi inside her too, and to make sure that you kill both. It was like some crazy kind of instruction manual! There was praise for the Interahamwe and the army, boasting about the hundreds and thousands of Tutsis they had killed in Ruhengeri, and Kigarama, and Butare. In Kigali, in the neighborhoods of Kicukiro, Nyamirambo, and Kanombe.

I shouldn't have left! I told myself, even though I knew it wasn't logical. It felt like my grief, my guilt, and my mysterious illness were churning around inside me, making my head spin, and intensifying my nausea. *Please don't let any of it mean that any of my family's in trouble,* I prayed. *And please don't let them mention Biryogo or Remera!* I was terrified that if I stopped listening or praying, even for a minute, that somehow it might cause our family there to be killed.

It was the craziest, most horrible thing I had ever listened to. As it got dark outside, the announcers started telling people that there were places that had been set up in different towns and neighborhoods where the people doing the killing (which sounded like it was basically everybody) could go to rest for a few hours and get food and water.

They reminded people, "If you are tired you can cut the Tutsis'
Achilles tendons. Then you can come finish them off later."

The announcers went on, telling Hutus where to look for Tutsis
that might have gotten away, or where they might still be hiding,
encouraging the Hutus who were manning the checkpoints on the
roads, finding the Tutsis who were trying to escape in cars. "You are all
doing good work," they said. "Keep doing your work." The "work"
was killing Tutsis. And every time they announced a new number of
how many Tutsis had been killed in this town or that neighborhood,
you could hear the glee in their voices.

We listened all night. We didn't speak. I was so sick, I kept losing
consciousness. Every time I woke up, Uncle Hakizimana was still
there, with his radio tuned to RTLM, helping me raise my head to drink
from a glass of water or a bowl of broth. At some point, I must have
passed out.

I woke up in my bed. I couldn't remember how I had gotten there.

I tried to sit up, but I just couldn't. I was too dizzy and too weak. I
just lay there, with the room spinning, moving in and out of
consciousness. I don't know how long I was in bed. I think it was
several days. Every time I woke up, I would hear Uncle Hakizimana's
radio, tuned to RTLM, playing in the kitchen.

One time when I woke up to find Olive helping me sit up a little to drink some water and have a few sips of soup, I asked her what was happening.

"I'm so worried about your uncle," she said. "He just keeps listening to that radio. He always has it with him. I don't think he's slept since the killing started."

I tried to say something, but I just passed out again.

One morning I managed to sit up, and then, bracing myself on the bed to stand, steadying myself on the wall as I went, I made it all the way to the kitchen table. There was Uncle Hakizimana, still listening to his radio. They were playing this strange happy-sounding song about getting rid of the Tutsi invaders. I was afraid to ask him anything. I just sat, put my head down on the table, and listened.

There were more reports of Tutsis killed here and there, more music, more encouraging of the killers.

Then a female announcer came on. "Some new reports have just come in!" she said. "It turns out that our Hutu brothers and sisters have been working hard all day and they have killed nine hundred and sixty-three Tutsi in…" (it was like she was announcing the winner of a contest) "Remera! Yes, it appears that, yes, yes, we have someone on the telephone from there now, and they are telling us that, like cockroaches will, a few of the Tutsi tried to scamper away and hide in the bushes. But they've finally all been found, every last one, and we are happy to report that all of the Tutsi in Remera have been wiped out! That's right! Remera is finally free of our Tutsi oppressors! And we would like to say to all the people there that did such fine work today, good job, and thank you from all of your Hutu brothers and sisters!"

Uncle Hakizimana clicked off the radio and sat back in his seat. He stared into space for several minutes. Then suddenly he said, "I have to go to the bathroom." He got up and walked to the toilet.

I stayed in my seat, with my head still down on the table. I didn't know what to do. Part of me wanted to turn the radio back on to hear if there were any reports from Biryogo. But another part of me was afraid to. What if there were? Plus, I was so sick that turning the radio back on seemed like a giant task that would take more energy than I had. I knew that if I put my head up, I would get dizzy again and I might fall over. While I was thinking this through, I passed out.

I don't know what time it was when I woke up, but it was dark out. I think I had been unconscious for a long time, several hours. Uncle Hakizimana wasn't back at the table. I called out to him, "Uncle?"

There was no response.

"Uncle?" I called out again, this time louder. Still nothing.

I sat up, and the increased dizziness hit me immediately. It was hard to stand, but I had to find out if Uncle Hakizimana was okay.

"Uncle!" I called out again. The dizziness was making it very hard to walk, and I was starting to feel even more sick to my stomach. "Uncle?" I called again outside the bathroom door.

There was no response.

I opened the door, and I caught a glimpse of him squatting with his pants down. I quickly turned away. "Oh, Uncle!" I said. "I'm sorry! I didn't…"

But still, he didn't say anything. I opened the door again. I saw that he wasn't squatting. He was just propped up against the wall, leaning into the corner of the bathroom. I rushed over to him. His eyes were open. He wasn't blinking. He wasn't moving. He wasn't breathing. I took him by the shoulders. "Uncle? Uncle!" I called. But there was no one there. He was gone. He was cold to the touch. I rushed out of the bathroom and ran outside, making the *induru* call.

All the neighbors came running. They asked me what was wrong, and I told them, "Inside! Uncle Hakizimana!" That was all I could get out through my sobs.

Some of the neighbors helped me back inside the house. Others went into the bathroom to see what had happened to Uncle. I wished that I had been able to pull up his pants or put a sheet over him, or something, but I hadn't been able to think straight. All I had the strength to do was let my neighbors lay me down on the couch and continue to sob until I lost consciousness.

When I woke up, Marie was sitting next to me on the couch. "I'm so sorry for your loss," she said, laying a hand on my shoulder. "We've called the hospital," she continued. "And we've called Hakizimana's daughters in Brussels. They say they'll be here in a few days."

"Is Claudine coming with them?" I asked.

"…They didn't mention anything about Claudine," she said.

"…Oh. Have you been listening… to the radio? Have you heard anything about Biryogo?"

"I'm sorry," she said. "I haven't."

"Uncle had just heard about Remera, where his daughter lives. Lived," I corrected myself.

"Oh no!" Marie said, putting her hands to her mouth.

"And I'm so scared for my family in Biryogo!"

"Of course you are," she said. "I'm sorry."

Soon a truck came from the morgue to take Uncle Hakizimana's body away.

Chapter Twelve: The "Aunties"

Mama and I are lying together in her bed. She is holding me in her arms, singing softly to me, the way she did when I was little. It's so wonderful to feel her arms around me, to feel her warmth, and hear her soft, loving voice.

But then, from a radio next to the bed, "This just in: Our work is continuing today in…Biryogo! As I am speaking to you now, our Hutu brothers are wiping out the inyenzi there! Keep listening for updates!"

In the distance, on a bullhorn a man is yelling "KORA KAZE KAWE!"

"Mama!" I say. "We have to hide!"

"Elise," she says, with a smile so calm it makes me feel cold inside, "If we're going to live, we're going to live. If we're going to die, we're going to die. Either way, there's nothing we can do."

"No, Mama!" I yell, dragging her up by her arm. "We have to go! We have to find a place to hide!"

I pull her to her bedroom door. I open it. When I pull her through, we are in our church. It is packed with other Tutsis. Some are sitting on the benches. Some are standing in the aisles. The doors are all locked. Everyone is silent, terrified, waiting.

All at once the stained-glass window in one of the doors is smashed in by a booted foot. The door shakes, as it is kicked again and again.

I stand with Mama next to the ramp that spirals down to the classrooms where I used to take catechism classes. I pull on Mama's hand. "Come, Mama, we can hide downstairs!" I whisper urgently.

"It's in God's hands," Mama says. "Stay with me, Elise," she pleads.

"Mama, we have to go!" I insist. I try to pull her with me as I start down the ramp, but I lose my grip on her. Even so, I keep going.

"Elise," she calls after me. "Elise…"

"Elise? Eli-ise!" a woman's voice was calling in a sing- songy voice from out in the front room, pulling me out of a deep, deep sleep. "Come say hello to your aunties! Elise!"

My aunties? I thought, as I was struggling my way into being fully awake.

"Elise is still very, very sick," I heard Marie say. "And she's heartbroken over Hakizimana's death. She really shouldn't be getting out of bed."

"Oh nonsense," the other woman said. "Too sick to come say hello to her aunties? Elise!"

I dragged myself out of bed, pulled on a robe, and staggered into the living room. There were two women there I didn't think I knew, one shorter and one taller, standing with Marie.

"You look horrible!" one of women I didn't think I knew, the shorter one, said.

"I'm very sick," I replied.

"Oh nonsense," the woman said. "If you were really sick, then you'd be in a hospital."

"Well, no, actually, Uncle said-"

"Elise," the taller one said. "You know it's not polite to contradict your Auntie Michelle."

Carene and Michelle? I thought. *Uncle Hakizimana's daughters?* This was not good. As a child in Rwanda, you are taught to honor and respect an auntie, whether they're related to you or not. The thing is, this would never apply to your cousins, which Carene and Michelle were. I was concerned that by referring to themselves as my "aunties," Carene and Michelle were trying to force a relationship in which they were the adults and I was the child, in which they had higher status and more power than I did.

This whole situation was very odd, and I was so weak and dizzy from being sick. I didn't really know what else to say, so I just said, "Sorry, Auntie."

"Well, you've just forgotten your manners, yes?"

Again, I didn't know what to say. I was starting to feel even more dizzy; in fact, I was starting to have a very hard time standing up. I had to sit down.

"Your parents did teach you manners, didn't they, Dear?" Carene demanded.

"Yes. Yes, of course, Auntie," I said.

"Elise!" Michelle said. "Stop sitting down! Go fix us some tea!"

"Elise is still quite sick," Marie protested. "I really think she needs to be in bed!"

"You know," Carene said, "you have been awfully nice, taking care of Elise the way that you have." Then she put on the fakest smile I had ever seen. "But she's among family now. And I think we know what's best for her. Elise…"

"You know," Marie said. "Olive, your father's cook, is still here. She's in the kitchen right now. She can make you some tea."

"Yes, well," Michelle said putting an arm on Marie's shoulder and guiding her to the door, "thank you again, ever so much for all you've done, but we'll take it from here."

"Thanks for coming," Carene said, practically pushing Marie out the door and closing it behind her.

"Now, Elise, that tea…"

"Uh, yes, yes, Auntie," I said, getting unsteadily to my feet. I had to brace myself against the wall as I made my way into the kitchen.

Olive must have overheard the conversation in the living room, because once I made it into the kitchen, I could see that she was already heating the water and laying out everything for tea on a tray.

"You just have a seat here," she whispered, guiding me to a chair. "While I get everything ready."

When the water had boiled, she poured it into the kettle, helped me to my feet, and handed me the tray. "Once you've served them this, you go straight back to bed. I'll take care of anything else your aunties need."

"Thank you, Olive," I whispered back to her. "They're not even really my aunties. They're just my cousins. Oh, has there been any more news about Rwanda? About Biryogo?"

"More of the same: more killing." Olive said. "I haven't heard anything specifically about Biryogo."

I tried my best to carry the loaded tray into the living room, but with each step I became more and more dizzy, until finally I collapsed, spilling everything from the tea tray all over the floor.

"Oh, Elise!" Carene said. "Look at the mess you've made!"

"You'll have to make sure that you clean all that up," Michelle said.

That was the last thing I remember before I passed out.

*   *   *

Just like when Papa died, the ikiriyo for Uncle Hakizimana lasted many, many days. Friends and family members, some of whom lived very far away, came to pay their respects. No one could come from Rwanda with the killings going on.

The neighbor women all took care of Carene, Michelle, and me, cooking and cleaning for us, making things easy for us during our time of mourning. The neighbors were treating me like I was one of Uncle Hakizimana's daughters, but the "aunties" were going out of their way to make it clear that they saw me as a house girl. Every morning one of them would wake me up with a demand.

"Elise, get me some tea!"

"Elise, cook us some food!"

"Elise, this bathroom is so dirty! Come clean it, right now!"

When I told them how sick I was, that I felt dizzy and like I was going to vomit almost all of the time I was standing up, how I had no energy, and how I was also sick with worry about my family, they acted as though I was just making excuses.

Everyone that had come for the ikiriyo was talking about the killings that were still raging in Rwanda. I kept asking people if they had heard anything about Biryogo. I asked Carene and Michelle. "How should I know?" Michelle said.

"Maybe I should call Claudine," I said.

"Well, if you do, don't bother wasting your time calling our apartment," Carene said. "She's gone to stay with our brother, George."

"Oh. Well, what's his number?"

"I don't know," she said. "I'm not very good with numbers. Ask me when I have my address book in my hand."

"In the meantime, we could use some more tea," Michelle said.

If Carene and Michelle were sad about their father's death, they didn't seem to be showing it. The only emotion I saw in them was resentment; resentment that they had to be there in Burundi. They obviously couldn't wait to leave and get back to their rich lives in Brussels. I was worried, though. When they went back to Brussels, where was I going to go?

One day, as the ikiriyo was coming to an end, I suddenly stopped feeling sick. I wondered if that meant something. The whole sickness had been so odd. If it had been because my family had been suffering, did it mean that they were safe? Did it mean that their suffering was over because were dead? Did it mean anything? I had just finished boiling water for tea when I heard Michelle whispering to Carene in the next room, "We're going to have to do something with Elise."

I heard Michelle clicking her tongue.

The next day, as I was walking down the street, a white van pulled up beside me. Two large men got out and stood beside me. Inside was Michelle.

"Elise," she said. "Come, get in. I need to speak with you."

I was wondering what was going on.

"Elise, come on! Now!" Michelle insisted.

I got into the van, and before I could even finish sitting down, we were racing away from the curb.

"Where are we going?" I asked.

"Well," she said. "You know that your auntie and I have to be getting back to Brussels…"

"Yes…" I said. "But-"

"Well," she cut me off, "your auntie and I have been talking, and since your uncle Hakizimana's house has already been rented-"

"What? When did-"

"Elise!" she said, looking at me with a shocked expression. "It's not polite to interrupt your auntie!"

"Well, I need to go get my things," I said.

"Oh, no. We'll send them along to you."

"Send them along? Are you sending me somewhere?" I asked.

"You have relatives in Tanzania," Michelle said.

"I do?"

"Yes, yes!" she said. "They can't wait to meet you!"

"Where are they?" I asked.

"What?"

"Where do these relatives of mine live?" I asked.

"Oh, in, uh, why in Dar es Salaam, of course," she said.

"Oh."

"Yes, and since your auntie and I need to be on a plane tonight, we need to make sure that you're on your way, so we've arranged for a driver to take you there. He's… well, I'm sure he's a very nice man."

"But Auntie," I said, "I don't have anything. I just have the clothes on my back. I'll need something for the trip, won't I?"

"Oh, so many questions, Elise! Don't worry. We've taken care of everything. Remember, we're not charging you anything for the trip to Dar es Salaam."

"But Auntie-"

"Look. Here we are," she said, with a strange smile on her face.

"Where?" I asked. We just seemed to be pulling up to another street corner.

"Now," Michelle said in an excited voice. "You just get out here on this corner, and the driver should be along in no time." We came to a quick stop, and then Michelle practically shoved me out of the van.

"But Auntie-" I tried to argue as she slammed the door shut and the van sped off.

So, there I was on a street corner I had never been to, with nothing but the clothes on my back.

I stood there on that street corner for a long time. *This is bad,* I thought, as the sun started going down. I didn't know this part of Bujumbura at all, but it definitely didn't look like a good neighborhood. *Is there really someone coming to pick me up?* I wondered. *Should I just start walking somewhere, or should I stay here and keep waiting?*

Chapter Thirteen: Jean-Jacques

It was dark. A slightly beat-up white sports car slowed to a stop next to me. A man inside leaned over and rolled down the window.

"Please let this be the guy who's supposed to pick me up, not a man who thinks I'm a prostitute," I said to myself.

The man looked up at me and smiled. "Elise?" he asked.

Well, he knows my name, I thought. *I guess that's ... good. If any of this can be considered ... good.*

"Are you Elise?" he asked again, smiling at me like he had just won a prize. He was older. He looked like he was somewhere in his thirties. He looked strong, but oafish. He had a kind of desperate air about him.

Even so, he was a ride out of this scary-looking neighborhood. *If I don't go with this man, now*, I thought, *I'm really not sure I'll be alive tomorrow morning.* So: "Yes," I told the man. "I'm Elise."

"Good. I'm Jean-Jacques. Come on," he said, opening the door and motioning me into the car. "Get in."

I did.

"No one told me I'd be driving such a beautiful girl!" Jean-Jacques said, still smiling, as we drove away.

I didn't really know what to say. Thank you, came to mind.

But before I could say anything, he said, "Oh, you're a shy girl. That's okay." He was still smiling. "We'll only drive for a few hours tonight. If you get too far out of Bujumbura after dark, you're likely to run into bandits on the road. But don't worry. I know a place where we'll be safe."

"Okay," I said.

"That is," he said, "as long as you can control yourself around me. I know it might be hard, but please, try. I'm a very sensitive man!" He reached over and put his hand on my knee.

Oh no! I thought, stiffening.

Then he laughed like we were sharing a funny joke and took his hand away. "Ah-ha! And you're a sensitive girl! So, we're a good match!"

"This is going to be a good trip!" he continued. "I usually have to do it alone!" He turned on some happy-sounding music and then turned it up very loud.

What have I gotten myself into? I thought.

*   *   *

"We're here!" Jean-Jacques said, waking me up.

It was dark. We were stopped outside a roadhouse, the sort of place where truck drivers stop for the night.

"Where are we?" I asked.

"We're still in Burundi," he said. "Let's get something to eat!"

"I don't have any money," I said. I wondered if admitting this was a good idea.

"I'll pay, my darling."

"Thank you," I said. But *My darling?* I thought. *We don't even know each other!*

We walked inside. It wasn't clean, and I was more nervous than hungry. Besides the waitress, I was the only woman in the room, and it seemed like every man there was either leering at me or making catcalls, or both. One man even reached out to grab my behind.

"Hey!" Jean-Jacques said, shoving a finger in the man's face, "Keep your hands off my girlfriend!" His face looked very serious. It was the first time I had seen him not smiling.

Everyone in the room froze, waiting to see what would happen next.

Girlfriend? I thought.

The man who had reached for me suddenly smiled and put his hands up, like he was surrendering, saying, "Ohhh, I'm so sorry. I didn't know. You're a lucky, lucky bastard. Jean-Jacques! Ha-ha!" The man opened his arms wide and the two of them hugged. I guessed that they knew each other.

Jean-Jacques wiped two cockroaches off the table at one of the booths Then he stepped on them as we sat down. He ordered for us.

I decided that this whole thing might be a bit more comfortable if I talked with Jean-Jacques. Also, I was thinking, *Maybe I can get some information about what exactly is going on.* I was still trying to puzzle out the whole thing with me being picked up in a van and rushed off to the spot where Jean-Jacques had picked me up. "So," I said. "You're a driver? I mean, professionally?"

"You want us to get to know each other," Jean-Jacques said. "That's good. Yes, I'm a professional driver."

"And my 'aunties' are paying you to drive me to Dar es Salaam?"

"What? Oh, no, no, no! You're just along for the ride. I'm- Do you know Erik?"

"Who?"

"I guess not. Erik. He's my boss. I drive cars for him from Bujumbura to Dar es Salaam."

"Why?"

"Why? To make money!" he said. He was smiling again. "And I do aaallll right. You can sell a car there for much, much more than you can get for it in Bujumbura."

"Oh," I said.

"And then I take a bus back and do it all over again. I think Erik is friends with your aunties. I think he sees them sometimes when he travels to Brussels."

"Does he travel a lot?"

"Oh yes. He's a very rich man."

"From selling one car at a time?"

"No-no. This is just a little side business he has. And he has a lot of drivers like me. But mainly he's into racing."

"Car racing?"

"Oh yes. He sets up races all over Africa. I'm surprised you've never heard of him."

"Have you heard anything about the killings?" I knew that this was a risk. I actually really couldn't tell whether Jean-Jacques was a Hutu or a Tutsi.

"Just what's on the BBC," he said. "And RTLM." He motioned me in closer. "You know there are a lot of Hutus here in Burundi who are secretly cheering the killings on. And there are still a lot of Tutsis being killed by Hutus here. I think the only reason the killings aren't spreading here is because the military here is controlled by the Tutsis."

"I have family in Kigali," I told him.

"Oh," he said. "I'm sorry."

"Have you heard any mention of Biryogo on the radio? I'm going out of my mind with worry."

"About Biryogo? No," he said. "Not that I recall."

The food came, brochettes, thin strips of grilled beef and liver with wooden sticks through them. Jean-Jacques smiled and rubbed his hands together before he started eating them, one after the other.

Even though I hadn't eaten since breakfast that morning, I didn't have much of an appetite. I made myself eat a little, though. I didn't want to be rude, and, with no money, I figured I should eat when I could.

"Not so hungry, Elise?" Jean-Jacques asked.

"I've got a lot on my mind," I said.

"The killings," he said.

"That, and my uncle just died. I had been staying with him. We had gotten really close. I was the one who found him."

"Oh, that's awful," Jean-Jacques said, between bites. "Do you want any more?"

"I'll just finish this one," I said. "I don't feel that great. I was sick for a long time. I've been feeling better, but I'm afraid it's coming back."

"Oh, well, I'm done," Jean-Jacques said, wiping his hands. "It's bedtime, anyway."

We went upstairs, where there were a few big rooms filled with beds. I guessed that things were set up that way because, if you're a truck driver, you probably don't want to pay for a whole hotel room every night you're on the road.

But even so, these rooms were really gross! They looked like they had never been cleaned, and there were cockroaches crawling everywhere. I was seriously thinking about asking if I could go sleep in the car. But I was exhausted, and I didn't want to offend Jean-Jacques or make him mad.

"Here we are," he said. We had arrived at a bed. Jean-Jacques wiped some cockroaches off of it. "There you go," he said.

"No…sheets?" I said.

"Elise! Come on. This isn't a fancy hotel."

"I just thought I'd ask," I said. The mattress looked absolutely filthy. I was sure it had other bugs in it besides the cockroaches. But I was exhausted. I lay down, and Jean-Jacques laid down next to me. He tried to put his arm around me, which made me even more sick to my stomach. I sat up. "I think I'm going to be sick!" I said. I was breathing deeply, trying to steady myself.

Jean-Jacques huffed, turned away from me, and, I guess, went to sleep.

After a long time, exhausted, I finally lay back down and fell asleep.

The next morning, we got up, and I followed Jean-Jacques. I thought that he was going to the cafeteria. When I turned a corner after him, it turned out I had followed him to the washroom, a big cement stall with one side open, the side I was looking at. It was full of big, soapy, naked guys taking bucket baths. Luckily, none of them noticed me. I turned around and went the other way.

I came upon the toilets. They were filthy, but I didn't know when I'd find another, so I used one. Then I found a plastic basin, some water, and a corner, away from everyone else, I washed my face and hands. But I was not going to take off any clothes in that situation.

I guessed that Jean-Jacques would end up in the cafeteria, so I went there to wait for him. Eventually he came in. He bought me breakfast: bread and margarine with tea. I found that I was actually hungry, so I ate.

"Aaah," he said, "I see you got your appetite back. That's good!" That same unnerving smile was back.

I did my best to smile back.

After breakfast, we got back on the road. I tried to concentrate on the scenery we were driving through, which was mostly beautiful rolling green hills of farmland with bright blue skies above. I was trying not to think about anything. I was trying not to think about the killings that were still going on back in Rwanda. I was trying not to think about the future. I could only guess at where Jean-Jacques was taking me, or why he was taking me there.

Jean-Jacques had the radio on, playing that bright, happy-sounding music. He was playing it pretty loud. I didn't care for it much, but it saved me from having to speak with him. The only problem was, if I didn't talk to him, then I was basically alone with my dark thoughts.

Finally, I couldn't stand it anymore, so I turned to him and said, "Jean-Jacques?"

"Yes, my princess?" he said, turning down the music.

I really didn't know how to respond to the "princess" part, so I ignored it and asked him, "Where are you taking me?"

"To Dar es Salaam, of course."

"Did my 'aunties' tell you to take me to a particular place?"

"Oh, we'll work all of that out when we get there," Jean-Jacques said, smiling.

I hadn't really believed Michelle when she told me she was sending me to stay with relatives in Dar es Salaam. *Mana we*, it suddenly hit me: *Is it possible that Carene and Michelle just...**gave** me to this man?*

Trying to fight my rising panic, I forced myself to just stare out the window. I did this for hours and hours, until we pulled up to another roadhouse.

Jean-Jacques turned off the car, and turned to me, smiling, and touching my knee, saying, "Lunch time!"

I made myself smile. "Okay," I said. I was realizing that, from then on, I would have to do whatever I had to, in order to survive.

The cafeteria in this place was just as dirty and disgusting as the last one. There seemed to be more cockroaches. Lunch was the same as dinner the night before: brochettes. And again, even though I was sick with anxiety, I made myself eat. I wasn't going to starve to death.

"You're feeling better!" Jean-Jacques said with a smile. "Good!"

We got back on the road and drove more, until it was time for dinner. We pulled into another roadhouse. We ate. Brochettes again.

As we ate, I was getting more and more nervous thinking about what might be coming next.

Jean-Jacques pretended to yawn and stretch, saying, "Long day of driving."

I followed him out to the front desk. He spoke to the man there and then turned back to me, smiling. "Come on," he said. "Time for bed."

I started climbing the stairs. He followed behind me.

The dingy second-floor hallway was lit with a dim flickering fluorescent light.

"To the right," Jean-Jacques said.

I turned right and entered a smaller room than the one we had been in the night before.

"Over here," Jean-Jacques said. I could see his hand coming from behind me, pointing to a bed on our left. "This one is ours."

"You first," I said, forcing a smile. "I may have to go to the toilet."

He lay down on the bed, then I got in facing away from him. He pushed his body right up against mine. I could feel his hot moist breath on the back of my neck. He put an arm around me. I could feel his manhood, hard beneath his clothes, against my bottom.

"Please, no!" I cried. I pushed him away and pulled myself as far as I could, right over to the edge of the bed.

Had he stopped? I hoped he had. I waited. I didn't speak. I didn't move. I barely breathed. After a long time, I was pretty sure he had fallen asleep. I let myself do the same.

I am in one of the classrooms in the lower level of our church in Biryogo. I can hear screams coming from the sanctuary upstairs, awful, awful screams. I hear Mama's voice calling out: "Elise!..."

Mama is up there! I'm thinking. *What should I do?* I know it won't be long before the killers realize that there might be people down here!

"Elise…" I hear someone whisper.

When I look, I see Albert, the cute boy from school, in a closet, waving me toward him.

"Elise!" he whispers again. "In here. Hide!"

I feel like I should go back upstairs. Maybe there is something I can to do save Mama!

One of the panes of colored glass set into the metal door that leads outside is smashed in. The door flexes inward again and again. Someone outside is trying to kick it open!

"Elise! Quickly!" Albert is insisting.

I rush into the closet and close the door behind me. It is stuffed full of people. The air is thick with sweat and fear. Through the door we can hear the smashing of metal and glass and then the footsteps of the killers on the concrete floor. We can hear them yelling and overturning desks and chairs. Just as I am thinking that the closet was not a good place to hide, the door is ripped open. All of us are trying to push further inside, as though that will save us. The killers reach in and grab us. I try to push their hands away, but it is no use.

I awoke to find Jean-Jacques' hands on me. I tried to push him away so I could get up, out of the bed, but he was too strong.

"No, no!" I kept protesting.

He grabbed me and forced me down onto the bed.

"No! Stop! Please! Stop!" I cried as I tried to push him off, but he straddled me and pinned my hands.

"Be quiet! BE QUIET!" he demanded, slapping me across the face, hard.

I can't stop this from happening, I realized. *He's really going to do this! If I keep fighting, he's just going to beat me.* I thought about Papa's face the night of the beating when I was five.

"Okay – okay – okay – okay – **OKAY!**" I said, finally catching Jean-Jacques' eyes.

He stopped for a moment, looking at me.

"I will let you have sex with me," I said. "Just don't rape me."

It was awful, but it was over quickly. Then he turned on his side and fell asleep. I stayed awake the rest of night. I was worried about getting pregnant, and about HIV, and any of the other diseases Jean-Jacques might have just given me. On top of that, I was trying to think of some way I could escape this nightmare! But even if I could, I realized, there was no place I could escape to, and there was no one who could help me.

The next day was very much like the one before. We drove for most of the day, with Jean-Jacques blasting his music, and without talking much. We stopped for lunch, then we got back on the road.

That night we stopped at another dirty roadhouse, ate dinner, then went to bed. He started to force himself on me again, and again I stopped him and told him that I wouldn't resist him, if he'd promise not to be violent.

It went on like that for about a week, which, I knew, was longer than it took to get to Dar es Salam. I realized that Jean-Jacques was stretching out the trip.

On RTLM, either in the roadhouses or sometimes in the car with Jean-Jacques, they kept broadcasting reports about the killings, how the Hutus were "stamping out the inyenzi" and "sending the Tutsis up the river, back to Abyssinia." I couldn't believe it was still going on. And it seemed like the rest of the world was just letting it happen.

The whole time I was thinking horrible thoughts. *What if I just walked out into the road and let a truck run me over? Or maybe I could find some way to make it back to Rwanda, so I can be with my family. At least that way we'd be together when we died.*

But eventually I realized that I wanted to live. So, I decided that I would stay on the lookout for any way to get away from Jean- Jacques, but that, until then, he was a source of food, and shelter, and protection from other men. I wasn't going to lie to him or anybody else by telling him I loved him, or even that I liked him. But I decided that, for the time being, I was going to stop fighting him.

After ten days, we finally reached Dar es Salaam. Jean-Jacques got us a real hotel room. It was clean and had a real bathroom with a shower. He took me out to eat. He bought me things: clothes, lotion, perfume. And every night I would let him have sex with me, and every time it was awful.

After a few days, I heard Jean-Jacques on the phone:

"No, no, Erik, Erik, Erik!" he said. "I don't know how long."

"No, no, it's not like that. I love her, and she loves me!"

This man really has lost his mind, I thought.

"Well, I know," Jean-Jacques continued. "I mean, I will, eventually. Yes. I don't know when I'll sell the car. I can't keep talking to you now. I'm taking her out to lunch."

We kept going out, eating, shopping. I almost never said more than about three words to him at a time. Erik kept calling, wanting to know where his money was. Jean-Jacques would say things like, "Well, what am I going to do, just drop her off on a street corner? That's what Carene and Michelle told me to do. No. No. She has nothing and nobody."

And the days went on like this. I was thinking that if he usually drove a car from Bujumbura to Dar es Salaam, sold it, and took the bus back, all in about four or five days, him staying here with me in this hotel room must be costing him and Erik a lot of money.

One day, after about a month of this, I heard Jean-Jacques on the phone with Erik saying, "No, no. Because we love each other and we're going to get married!"

My eyes almost popped out of my head.

"What? Why?" Jean-Jacques continued. "But…Fine. Fine!" He walked up to me and handed me the phone. "My boss, Erik wants to talk with you."

“What?”

“He told me to give you the phone.”

I took it. “Hello?” I said.

“Do you have dark skin, or light skin?” The man on the phone said.

“What?” I asked.

“Do you have dark skin or light skin?”

“Um… I have dark skin,” I said.

“That’s good,” he said. “I have dark skin too. This just might work.”

“What might work?”

“My plan. Sorry. I’m Erik. I’m Jean-Jacques’s boss.” His voice was kind and warm. “I’m sorry. I’m sort of starting in the middle of things. I know your cousins, Carene and Michelle.”

“You do?” I asked.

“Yes, and your sister, Claudine.”

“Oh,” I said. “How is she?”

“She’s fine. I think. The last time I talked with her, it wasn’t for very long. I mainly talked with Carene and Michelle. They told me that you’d have people to stay with in Dar es Salaam, and that Jean-Jacques was going to take you to them. But I think they were lying. Now I think they must have told Jean-Jacques something horrible, like that they were giving you to him to do with as he pleased.”

“I was starting to think the same thing,” I said.

“Well, I’m terribly sorry about all this, but I have an idea.”

“What is it?” I asked.

"Well, here's the thing," he said. "Jean-Jacques has been there with you for a month, and clearly he has lost his mind."

"Yes…" I said, looking at Jean-Jacques, trying to sound like Erik and I were talking about something else.

"And clearly, you need to get out of there."

"Yes…"

"And every day Jean-Jacques and you stay there, it's costing me money."

"Okay."

"So, I think I know how to fix things for both of us."

"Okay…"

"I have a wife named Amanda who lives in Dar."

"Okay…"

"I'm going to call her and tell her to come pick you up at the hotel."

"Yes…"

"But here's the thing: she is insanely jealous. I'm going to tell her that you are my sister."

"Okay…"

"And you must make her believe that you *are* my sister. Do you speak Swahili?"

"Not really," I said.

"Good. She doesn't speak Kinyarwanda. That means you have an excuse not to talk to her. The less you two talk, the less chance there is that she will find out that you're not my sister."

"Okay…"

"Because if she did, and I'm not exaggerating, she would kill you."

"…Oh," I said.

"So, when we're done, you're going to give the phone back to Jean-Jacques. I'm going to tell him that you're going to leave, and that he's going to get on a bus back to Bujumbura. And then I'm going to call Amanda. So, gather your things, go down to the lobby of the hotel, and wait for her. I will get there as soon as I can, and we'll figure out what to do with you, okay?"

"Okay," I said. "Thank you." I held the phone out for Jean-Jacques. "He wants to talk to you again."

Jean-Jacques took the phone. As he was yelling things like, "No, no! How could you? But we're in love! We're going to get married!"

I was thinking, *Thank you, God! This is unbelievable! This is wonderful!* I looked around the hotel room. I didn't want any of the things that Jean-Jacques had given me. So, I just stood up, walked out the door, and went down to the lobby. I couldn't keep from smiling.

Chapter Fourteen: Amanda

I had been sitting in the hotel lobby for about half an hour, partially thrilled with the possibility of freedom, partially scared that something could still go wrong, when a very beautiful woman, maybe in her late thirties or early forties, walked in, took off her sunglasses, and scanned the room. Her eyes landed on me. She smiled and said, "Elise?"

"Amanda!"

A river of Swahili started flowing out of Amanda's mouth as she ran over and threw her arms around me.

I knew only a few words in Swahili from my days at École Zaïroise. "Amanda, Amanda, Amanda. Uh..." I struggled to remember the words. Basically, I told her in broken Swahili that I didn't speak Swahili. Then she told me in broken Kinyarwanda that she didn't speak Kinyarwanda.

But even with the language barrier between us, I could tell from her tone of voice, how much she was smiling, and her body language that she was being extremely friendly toward me. It was odd, though, because this was based on something that wasn't true. Of course, even if I could have told her the truth, it would have put me back in a very bad situation, and, with the language barrier, there was no way I could have explained what was really going on to her.

Amanda took me to her car, a really nice Mercedes, and drove us away.

We pulled up to a huge compound. There was a high black metal fence surrounding it. Behind that was a milkbush hedge that had been sculpted into a wall, too high to see over and too thick to see through.

Inside the gate was the most beautiful, most elegant compound I had ever seen. There was a large, green lawn being mowed by a gardener. Lining the lawn were beds of gorgeous flowering bushes. There were mango and avocado trees that were being pruned by two other gardeners. Amanda waved and greeted them in Swahili as we drove up the driveway, toward her house. The house was beautiful, and huge! It had white plaster walls, a red tile roof, and it was maybe four times the size of Uncle Hakizimana's house.

The inside of the house was just as beautiful as the outside. As we walked through room after room, Amanda kept talking and motioning to this and that, big, comfortable-looking leather couches and chairs, lamps, a coffee table, paintings. I didn't know what she was saying, but it seemed like she was very proud of her house. I would have been, too.

Then she led me out to the back yard where there was a swimming pool. I had never seen a swimming pool in someone's house before. The water was so clear and beautiful. I leaned down and put my hand in it.

"It's warm!" I said.

Amanda kept nodding and talking enthusiastically. I had no idea what she was saying, but I smiled at her and nodded.

When we went back inside, Amanda introduced me to three women. One of them, who I thought must have been the nanny, was holding a boy who looked like he was about five-years old.

"Mama!" he shouted and threw his arms wide when he saw Amanda.

"Philbert!" Amanda said, taking him in her arms. She gave him a big kiss, and then gave him back to the nanny.

Another of the women, who I guessed must have been the cook, guided us into the most modern kitchen I had ever seen. Then the third woman, who I thought must have been the maid, led me down a long hall with a high ceiling to a bedroom. She and Amanda were both going on and on in Swahili, pointing to things here and there, but from the few words I understood, it seemed that she was showing me not just my own bed, but my own room.

I burst into tears and hugged them both. I thanked them in Swahili.

They hugged me back, as though they were my family. It felt so good to have human contact like that. It made me cry.

Then we all went back into the living room where the cook had laid out tea for us. That made me cry even more. The last time I had seen tea being served, I had been the one serving it, right after Uncle Hakizimana died.

Amanda guided me onto the couch and hugged me. She and the other three women were all focused on me, talking in soothing mothering tones. I didn't understand anything that these women were saying, but one thing was clear: they were all being so wonderful to me.

I hadn't known kindness like this since Uncle Hakizimana was alive. Remembering him and his kindness made me cry even harder.

Amanda and the other three women went on comforting me. I wasn't sure why they were doing it. They didn't know me. But, especially after what I had gone through with Jean-Jacques I was thinking, *Who cares why they're being so kind to me? There's no danger here. Well, at least not as long as Amanda doesn't find out that I'm not really Erik's sister. But with my Swahili and her Kinyarwanda being as bad as they are, I don't think there's too much danger of that happening.* So, I let them be kind to me and comfort me. I gave in to it, and I cried for a long, long time.

The next day I woke up alone, in my own beautiful room. I stretched. I smiled.

I was amazed at how much things had changed in such a short time. Just a day before I was basically being held captive, and now here I was in the most beautiful house I had ever seen. I was safe, at least as long as Amanda didn't find out that I wasn't really Erik's sister. Lying to her felt wrong. She was being so nice to me.

But obviously Erik knew Amanda better than I did. If he said I had to lie to her, I wasn't going to question that. I wanted to live.

Just then, Philbert, came into my room, got onto my bed, and curled up with me. I let him, but it didn't make me feel any better.

I took Philbert by the hand and we walked out to the dining room. Amanda was already there eating breakfast: croissants, sliced mango and guava, and coffee.

"Elise! Philbert!" She waved us over, clearly very happy to see us both. She gave Philbert a big hug and a kiss, and then she did the same to me. Just like the day before, there was a river of Swahili flowing out of her mouth, as she picked up a framed photograph and seemed to be talking about it very excitedly.

Is this a picture of Erik? I wondered.

Amanda went on, pointing to it, talking, and smiling. I came around behind her thinking, *Maybe I'll finally get a chance to see what Erik looks like!* It turned out to be a picture of a boy.

Amanda had stopped talking. She was looking up at me. I nodded and smiled.

She said more things that I didn't understand. Then the smile dropped from her face.

I took a risk. "Erik?" I asked, pointing to the photo, and putting a huge smile on my face.

She was smiling again. I had said the right thing, thank God! Her tone of voice was back to being happy. She was talking excitedly again. There were so many words I didn't understand, but every once in a while, she would say the word "Erik" again. Every time she did, she would look at me, and I would put on my big smile and again say, "Erik!"

I wonder how long I can keep this up, I thought.

Even though Amanda was around the house most of the time, she didn't spend very much time with Philbert. So, he started spending a lot of time with me. He would keep coming to me. We would play games together. We would go in the pool together. He would talk to me in Swahili while he played with his toys.

Being with him reminded me of playing with Alice and Patrick back home. I liked spending time with Philbert, but underneath, it didn't feel right. He was interacting with me as though I was part of his family, but that wasn't true. I didn't even know how long I'd be there. But it wasn't like I could push him away. I had to keep up the lie that I was part of his family.

Amanda had a TV, a big one. I had never really spent any time watching TV before. They were still pretty rare in Rwanda back then. And there I was, sitting on the most comfortable, luxurious, couch I had ever sat on, watching BBC news reports about the killings that were still happening back in Rwanda, on the biggest television I had ever seen, while a cook kept serving me tea because she thought that I was the sister of the master of the house.

What is happening to Mama and Robert, and Gabriel, and Patrick, and Alice? I wondered. *Are they in danger? Are they even still alive?* Even though Amanda had a phone, I was afraid to ask her if I could use it. I didn't want to do anything that would put questions in Amanda's head.

Finally, one day, I heard Amanda on the phone saying, "Erik? Erik!!" She went on for a few minutes in Swahili, and then Amanda handed the phone to me, smiling and saying, "Erik!"

I smiled back and took the phone. "Hello?"

"Elise, thank God! I'm sorry it took me so long to contact you. Things have been crazy with the killings going on."

"Yes, about the killings. Have you heard anything about my family, or Biryogo?"

"I'm sorry, Elise. I haven't. I only have a few minutes, and I have some very important things to tell you."

"Okay," I said.

Amanda was still looking at me, smiling and nodding. I smiled and nodded back.

"I'll be there in a few days," Erik said.

"Oh, great," I said.

"Well, here's the thing. You and Amanda are meeting me at the airport."

"Okay... Oooooh," I said. "And you and I have never actually met before."

"Exactly. Has Amanda shown you any pictures of me?"

"A lot," I said. "But only from when you were a boy."

"Oh. Yes," he said. "Is she looking at you?"

"Yes."

"Are you looking back at her?"

"Yes."

"Are you smiling and nodding a lot?"

"I am!" I said, trying to look like we were talking about something else, something I was excited about.

"Good. You keep that up! You remember what I told you?"

"Oh yes. Yes, of course!"

"Well, you're just going to have to do the best you can to keep playing along. She doesn't seem to suspect anything so far."

"That's very good news, Erik!" I said, keeping up the act.

A few days later, Amanda and I went to pick up Erik at the airport. Amanda was clearly very happy and very excited. We made our way to the gate, and we waited. Then we waited some more.

Amanda went to one of the airline counters, I guessed, to ask what was going on.

Mana we! I was thinking. *I still don't know what Erik looks like!*

Amanda came back to me, saying something in Swahili. She seemed to be getting more and more nervous the longer she talked. Finally, she pointed to her watch, and then to the monitor that had the flights on it. I realized that she was saying that Erik's flight was late.

I nodded.

She kept talking. From the bits of Swahili, I could understand, and her gestures, I could tell that she wanted us to split up, so that we wouldn't miss Erik. She directed me to go close to the door where the passengers would be coming through, and she indicated that she would go further away, just in case I missed him.

We waited like that for about ten minutes, and then the passengers started coming through the gate. I was looking at all of the men, trying to pick out one who looked anything like the childhood photos I had seen of Erik.

Amanda called to me from where she was standing.

I looked at her, smiled, and waved, but she kept waving, and she was saying something.

I didn't understand until she said, "Erik!"

I looked back at her, shrugging.

She was pointing wildly and saying, "Erik! Erik!" She was pointing to a man who had already walked past me.

I walked up to the man and tapped him on the shoulder. "Erik?" I asked.

The man turned around. "Elise?"

We hugged tentatively. It was a little weird.

Amanda came running over to us. She and Erik hugged and kissed.

Then Erik turned to me. "Elise!" he said and gave me another big hug. "Sister! It's so good to see you!" he said in Kinyarwanda.

"Erik!" I put on a smile and hugged him back. "It's good to see you too!"

Amanda was going on and on about something.

"What's she saying?" I asked Erik.

"Oh, just that she's happy to see me." He said something to her in Swahili.

Amanda said something else.

"What's she saying now?" I asked.

"She's saying, 'How could you two have missed each other? You walked right by her!'"

"Tell her it's the beard," I said, still smiling.

"What?" Erik said, also still smiling.

"And the sunglasses. Tell her I didn't recognize you with the beard and the sunglasses."

Erik gave me a concerned look.

"Hey, if you can think of something better…"

Erik turned to Amanda and said something in Swahili. She said something back to him, and then he said it again, pointing to his beard and his sunglasses, laughing and hugging and kissing her again.

She looked at us both a little sideways for a moment.

Mana we, I thought. *Does she know?* Erik and I both stood frozen for a moment.

And then, just like the moment in the cafeteria between Jean-Jacques and the man who turned out to be his friend, Amanda's eyes widened, and she pointed at both of us and said something in Swahili.

Then she and Erik were laughing and hugging again.

Over Amanda's shoulder, I said to Erik, "What did she say?"

"She said she was playing with us," he said. "Pretending that she didn't believe us."

"Oh," I said. "Well…"

Amanda turned toward me. I hoped that the relief I was feeling would look to her like I was enjoying her joke. I hugged Erik again, turned to Amanda, and put on a smile.

As we walked to the car, I asked Erik, "Have you heard anything about Biryogo? That's where my family is. Or the killings?"

"Nothing about Biryogo, no." he said. "I'm sorry. I've been hearing on the radio that the RPF has taken Gitarama."

"Oh, yes?"

"That's where the Rwandan government was in exile. The BBC says that they had to move to Gisenyi. The RPF's definitely winning."

"But they haven't taken anyplace in Kigali?"

"Part of the Arusha Accords was that the RPF was given a small base within the parliament building in Kigali. Even though they keep being attacked by the Rwandan military, they've held on. But as far as I know they haven't broken out into any of the neighborhoods."

"Could we listen to the radio now?" I asked. We were at the car.

"Of course," Erik replied as we all got in. He tuned the radio to a report about the killings going on in Rwanda. It sounded a lot like other reports I'd heard, but they were using a word I had never heard before: "Genocide."

Erik explained what it meant.

"Mana we!" I said.

"Well, it's pretty clear that's what they're trying to do. They're trying to wipe us all out."

That night, as we ate a welcome home dinner of roasted goat, matoke, and ugali, Amanda was smiling and talking very fast and with great excitement to Erik.

He smiled and said things back to her. It was all in Swahili, so I only understood a word or two here and there, but I smiled and nodded, trying to match their mood.

Then Amanda gestured to me. Her sentence in Swahili ended with "Elise."

"She wants me to translate for her," Erik said.

"Oh," I said. "All right."

Amanda said something in Swahili.

"She says she wants to know about you and me growing up together in Rwanda," Erik said.

I looked at her and smiled. Then I looked at Erik and said, "Oh…"

Erik smiled back at Amanda. Then, still smiling, he turned to me and said, "The longer we're both here, the more often this sort of thing is going to happen."

I nodded, still smiling.

"We need to get you out of here as soon as possible!" Erik said.

"Yes, we do!" I agreed, still smiling, acting like we were talking about something else. "Yes, we do!"

Chapter Fifteen: Back to Bujumbura

Amanda left to check on the dessert. Erik pulled a cell phone out of his pocket.

"You have a cell phone?" I said. They were very expensive and rare back then.

"Yes, I'm just going to check my messages."

"And then can we call Carene and Michelle? I need to get in touch with Claudine to see if she knows anything about what's happened to our family back in Rwanda."

"Didn't she move out?"

"I think so. Carene and Michelle said that she moved in with their brother, George. Unless you have his number."

"I don't. Let's try Carene and Michelle. I think Claudine and George still spend a lot of time there, so… Here, I'll put it on speaker phone."

"Hello?" Claudine said.

"Oh, Claudine. Hello. It's Erik. I didn't expect you to answer."

"It's still my habit from when I used to live here," she explained. "How are you?"

"I'm good. I'm here in Dar with Elise."

"Elise? Mana we! How are you? What are you doing in Dar es Salaam?"

"I'm fine," I said. "Carene and Michelle sent me here."

"What? Why?"

"They told Elise and me that they were sending her to live with relatives here," Erik explained, "but I don't think that's true."

"We don't have any relatives in Dar es Salaam! Carene! Michelle! What is this? My brothers are dead! My mother is dead! And now I find out you were sending my sister to Dar es Salaam to die?!"

"What?" I asked, panicked. "What do you mean 'my brothers are dead; my mother is dead'?"

But all I could hear on the other end of the phone was Claudine arguing with Carene and Michelle.

"Claudine! Claudine!" I said into the phone.

They hung up.

"Can you call them back?" I asked Erik.

"I'll try." He did, but it just rang and rang. Nobody picked up.

"What did she mean?" I asked Erik, crying. "Why won't they pick up the phone?"

"I don't know, Elise. I wish… Well, look. We really don't know…"

I was sobbing.

Erik put a hand on my shoulder.

Amanda came back in. She and Erik talked in Swahili. "I'm just telling her that you got some bad news about a friend in Rwanda."

Amanda gave me a hug.

I kept crying. *Please, God!* I prayed in my head. *Please let her be wrong!*

I cried myself to sleep that night.

The next morning Erik and I went for a walk. We tried calling Carene and Michelle again. But no one picked up.

"Damn it!" I said.

"I'm sorry," Erik said, "about everything. I hope Claudine is wrong. I'll keep trying them. But in the meantime, there's something else we need to talk about. As I told you, your life is in danger here. So's mine, actually."

"But Amanda seems so nice."

"She is. But like I told you, she's also an extremely jealous woman."

"To the point where she'd kill someone?"

"Elise, young and beautiful as you are, this can't be the first time you've run into this sort of thing."

I thought about Betty, Benjamin's wife, and maybe even Carene and Michelle? "No," I said. "I guess it's not."

"She almost poisoned an au pair I hired to look after Philbert. I had to get her out of town. And we need to do the same with you, as soon as possible. Is Bujumbura the best place for you to go right now? Do you have anyone you can stay with there?"

"I do."

"Do you need to make any calls?" He offered me his phone.

"I don't have anybody's numbers. Could we call Carene and Michelle again? I need to talk to Claudine and see what she knows about our family.

"Of course." He dialed the number and put it on speakerphone. It rang. All we got was an answering machine. Erik hung up. "I'm sorry," he said.

"Can we try them later?"

"Well, actually, I've made some other calls and there's another driver coming to pick you up. So, this will probably be the last time we see each other."

"Another driver?" I said. My stomach tightened again.

"Don't worry," Erik said. "He's a nice older gentleman."

"Okay," I said. "I guess that's good."

"Really, Elise. He's a good man. He'll be coming by to pick you up."

"Oh."

"In about an hour," he said.

"Oh! And where…is he taking me? Not back to Rwanda?"

"What? No, no! Of course not! No. That's why I was asking you about Bujumbura."

"Oh. Well, I have a friend there named Doreen."

"Doreen. Okay. Good. Oh, uh, here," Erik said, handing me a bunch of Burundian francs."

"Oh, I don't-"

"Elise. Please. Considering everything you've been through. I feel responsible, at least in part. When your aunties asked me to have you brought to Tanzania, I didn't understand. Please."

"Okay," I said. "Thank you."

"Now, we'd better get back inside. You need to pack."

"I don't have much. Amanda took me shopping a couple of times. She bought me some clothes. She's been so nice. I felt so bad lying to her."

"Yes, she's a very nice person. As long as you don't cross her. Or make her jealous. But I think we're okay so far on that front."

"So, you don't think she suspects anything?"

"As far as I can tell, she doesn't. Not a thing."

"Well, I guess that's good. I'd like to wake up tomorrow morning."

"Me too," Erik said.

A car pulled up to the house about an hour later. The driver got out and came inside. He looked like a kindly uncle or a youngish grandfather. He and Erik greeted one another and hugged.

"George," Erik said. "This is Elise, your passenger."

"Very pleased to meet you," George replied in Kinyarwanda.

"So good to meet you, too," I said. Already I felt safe with him.

"Well, can I help you with any bags?" George asked.

"I just have this," I said, pointing to my backpack.

"Oh. Well then, let's go."

"You make sure to take extra special care of her. Okay? Take her anyplace she needs to go," Erik said, smiling and putting his hand on my shoulder.

"You've got it, Boss," George replied.

"Elise, you don't have to worry," Erik said. "I trust George completely."

Amanda came up and gave me a big hug. Philbert did, too.

And then we were off.

"So," George said, as we pulled away. "Where are we going?"

"Oh. Right," I said. "Bujumbura. To my friend Doreen's house?"

"Like the boss said, wherever you need to go."

"Okay. Great. Thank you."

"No problem. So, you're a Tutsi? From Rwanda?"

"Yes," I nodded, cautiously.

"It's all right," he said. "I am too. Well, sort of. I grew up outside of Bujumbura, but my parents are from Gisenyi."

"Oh, yes?" I said. "Have you heard anything about Biryogo?"

"No, nothing about Biryogo. I heard on the radio, on the way here, that Kagame has surrounded Kigali."

"My mama, my brothers, and my sister are still there, I think. I hope. I'm praying that they're still alive."

"Well," he said. "You don't know anything like that until you know it for sure."

"I guess that's true. Do you have a phone? Could we try calling my sister in Brussels? Well, actually, it's Carene and Michelle, my cousins. Claudine, my sister used to live with them, but now she lives with another cousin of mine."

"Do you have the number?"

"I think so," I said, rummaging in my bag for the little notebook I had Carene and Michelle's number in, while I told George about the conversation with Claudine when she had said that all of my family who were still in Rwanda were dead.

"And then she just hung up, without explaining anything to you?"

"I don't know," I said. "Maybe we lost the connection."

We tried calling Carene and Michelle, but there was no answer. "Damn it!" I said. "Can we try again later?"

"Once we're out of the city there really isn't any signal available for the phone. Maybe we could try again once we make it to Bujumbura."

"I'm sorry," I said. "Is this costing you a lot of money?"

"It's fine. Erik told me to take care of you, so…"

"Well, thank you, again," I said. I looked out at the pretty landscape going by for a moment. Then I said, "So, you said you're from Gisenyi?"

"Yes. That's right."

"Beautiful country," I said.

"You've been?"

"My brothers and sisters and I used to stay with an uncle of ours there sometimes in the summer when I was a kid," I said. "Do still go back there?"

"Of course," he said. "We still have family there. Well, that is, I hope they're still there. Or… I hope they're not there. I mean… I hope they're…"

"Safe," I said.

"Mmm," he said. "It's insane."

"The genocide," I agreed. "I know."

"Everything," George was shaking his head. "Erik told me a little bit about what happened with you, your troubles with Jean-Jacques. I'm sorry about that."

"It's not your fault," I said.

"No, I know. But that sort of thing really shouldn't happen to a nice young lady like you. It shouldn't happen to anyone!"

"Well, I'm still alive, thank God."

"Heeeyy." George said.

After driving for a few hours, we pulled into a roadhouse, and somehow it didn't seem quite as bad as the ones I had been to with Jean-Jacques. I was hungry, so I ate. Brochettes and tea, but this time it all tasted good.

When we were finished with dinner, George said, "About the sleeping arrangements…"

My stomach tightened. I couldn't help it.

"I won't be able to get you your own room, but I'll get you a bed next to mine so that no one will bother you."

"So, I'll have my own bed?" I said.

"Well yes, of course," George said. "You don't have to worry about that kind of thing with me. If anybody tries to give you any trouble, any of the truckers, or anyone else, you just let me know."

"All right," I said. "Again, thank you."

"No need," George replied. "No need."

As we were getting into bed, George handed me a sheet and then put one on his own bed.

"This isn't for sleeping under," he said. It's to keep whatever's in the bed from getting on you. Just remember what side you put down, and you can use it for the whole trip."

"Thank you so much," I said. "That's good thinking." I slept well that night.

The next morning George and I got up, washed, had breakfast, and got on the road. On the radio in George's car, and on the radio in the roadhouses we stopped at, reports kept going on and on about the genocide. But there were also reports of how the RPF was doing raids behind enemy lines, into Kigali, to rescue pockets of Tutsis who were still hiding out and bring them out of the city. I started crying.

"What's wrong, Elise?" George asked.

"I just hope that Claudine was wrong about everyone in my family being dead, and that… that the RPF got them out. But they could all be dead, or they could be alive and in trouble. And there's nothing I can do, except just sit here listening to the radio!"

"I'm so sorry, Elise. I wish there was something I could do."

"You're doing a lot," I said.

On the third day of our trip, as George and I were having breakfast, he said to me, "Well, today is our last day on the road."

"Thank you so much," I said. "For everything."

"Well, you're welcome, but I'm really just doing my job. In any case, the weather's good, and we don't have too many miles to go. We should have an easy, relaxing drive today."

"That would be nice," I said.

We listened to the radio. They were reporting that the RPF had begun the attack on Kigali.

"Well, that's good news," George said. "It's amazing, though. The whole world knows that this genocide is going on, and it really seems like Kagame is the only one who's willing to do anything to stop it!"

"I know," I said. "It's just crazy."

As the sun was getting low on the horizon, we were coming around a curve in the road. "Just a few more kilometers to Bujumbura," George said. Just then, we saw two men standing in the road ahead. George slowed down. As we got closer, we could see that they had rifles and that they were wearing masks.

"George!" I said.

"Stay calm," George said. "Stay calm," as we came to a stop about twenty yards from them.

The two men pointed their guns at us. One of them ordered, "Get out of the car!"

George stared at them.

"I said get out of the car!" the man said.

"Oh no - Oh no - Oh no!" I was whispering.

George looked at me, said, "Don't worry," and winked.

"What? But the guns!"

"I said, don't worry," he smiled.

"Out of the car or we'll shoot!" the man said, raising his gun.

"George?"

"We'll be fine," George said as he stomped on the gas pedal and sped toward the two men.

"GEOOOOOOOORGE!" I screamed.

At the last minute, both men jumped out of the way.

We just kept going.

"You did it, George!" I screamed. "You did it!! They didn't even shoot at us!"

"Of course not!" George said. "They're highway bandits. They probably couldn't even afford to buy bullets!"

"But how did you know?"

"Elise, you don't get to be my age, doing this job, without learning the way things work on the road."

"You are amazing!" I said.

"Just doing my job."

About an hour later we drove into Bujumbura. I had to direct George, turn by turn, to get to Doreen's house. A few of them were wrong turns. There were only street signs on a few of the main streets, and, back then, a lot of the smaller streets didn't even have names. But eventually we made it there.

"Elise!" Doreen said throwing her arms around me.

"So, you must be Doreen," George said, stepping in to shake her hand.

"Oh, yes. Doreen, this is George, my…well, angel?"

"All I did was give her a ride here from Dar es Salaam," George said.

"All the way from Dar? Wow! You guys must have some stories to tell," Doreen said. "Well, thank you so much for delivering her here."

"It's no problem. No problem at all," George said. "In fact, I enjoyed getting to know Elise."

"So, Doreen," I said. "I need a place to stay…"

"Elise!" she said, shocked. "Of course you can stay! As long as you need to. You know you don't have to ask."

"It's just… been a very confusing time," I said, starting to cry.

Doreen put her arms around me. "We'll be fine," she told George. "Again, thank you."

"Yes, George," I said, throwing my arms around him. "Thank you so much! You've been so kind and so… just great!"

"You're welcome," he said, hugging me back. And then he let me go. "Take care of yourself," he said, and then he drove away.

George really made me feel like maybe there were still some good people in the world.

"Have you heard anything about Biryogo?" I asked Doreen.

"Just what's on the news," she said. "Nothing specifically about Biryogo."

I told her about the conversation with Claudine that had been cut short.

"Elise," Doreen said. "I'm so sorry! Maybe she's just assuming."

"I hope you're right," I said. "Have you heard anything about *your* family?"

"No. I'm going out of my mind with worry about them, too. Oh, but did you hear about the RPF?"

"I heard on the radio in the car that they were attacking Kigali. Has there been more?"

"Just that they seem to be winning."

"Wow!"

"So, what happened to you? I mean, you just…disappeared!"

"Well, you know my 'aunties?'" I said.

"The nasty ones?" she said smiling. That was how we always referred to them.

"They kidnapped me!"

"What?"

"I was just walking down the street one day," I said. "And one of my 'aunties' pulled up in a van and told me that they were sending me to live with some aunt and uncle of mine in Dar es Salaam."

"I didn't know you had an aunt and uncle who lived in Dar es Salaam."

"That's what *I* said. And when I asked who they were, Carene got very vague, all of a sudden."

"That's not good."

"And that was just the beginning." I told Doreen all about Jean-Jacques.

"Mana we, Elise!" she said, again and again, as I went through the story.

Then I told her about Erik, and then about Amanda. "I told you George was my angel? Well, Erik…"

"He saved you, Elise! Like he was sent from God."

"Yeah. I mean, it wasn't totally selfless on his part. Jean-Jacques was costing him money, staying in that hotel room with me. And getting me out of Dar definitely kept an incident with Amanda from happening, but Erik really did do right by me."

"And how was the ride here?"

"Oh, that's a whole story all on its own." I told her about George and the bandits. By the end, she was just staring at me, barely blinking.

"Mana we, Elise! I'm amazed that you're alive! God must be looking out for you!"

"I know," I said. "I can't believe I'm alive either. It's strange."

"Well, you're safe here, Elise."

"Thank you," I said, hugging her. "Thank you so much!"

"You know," she said, "Benjamin comes by here all the time to ask if I've heard anything about you. He's been going out of his mind!"

"I should get in touch with him," I said.

"Well, why don't we go out tonight? We'll find him." Doreen said. "It'll be like old times."

I wasn't really in the mood to go out. I was still out of my mind with worry about my family and the genocide, but once we were out, there were so many distractions right in front of me. There was the music, and the dancing, and the alcohol, and then there was Benjamin!

He picked me up and spun me around. I was so happy to see him again. I told him about some of the things that happened to me. I didn't tell him about Jean-Jacques. I was sure that if Benjamin found out about that, he would run off to hunt Jean-Jacques down and kill him. I actually considered that, but even with all of the horrible things that Jean-Jacques did to me, I didn't want to be responsible for a man's death. I also didn't want Benjamin to leave me.

The next day Doreen and I went to the phone center. I finally got through to Carene, but she told me that Claudine wasn't there. I asked for Claudine's number. She gave it to me. "What was Claudine saying about 'My mother is dead; my brothers and sister are dead?'"

"Oh, I don't know. It's something she heard, I think."

"You *think*? It's important! This is my family we're talking about! I need to know if they're alive or dead!"

"Well, call Claudine." She said and hung up.

I called Claudine. There was no answer.

Doreen and I spent a lot of time listening to the radio. We listened to the BBC. We listened to RTLM. There were ongoing reports about all of the killings and the dead bodies. It was incredibly stressful. Just like when I was sitting with Uncle Hakizimana, listening to the same sorts of things, part of me was hoping to hear some news about Biryogo. But another part of me was pretty sure that anything I did hear about Biryogo would be awful. It was possible that Claudine had been wrong and that my family was still alive. Unlikely as it was, *I* was still alive. I prayed for them every day.

Mixed in with the news about the killing and the dead bodies, there was news about the RPF, too. They kept winning and taking more and more of Kigali.

I called Claudine again, and she finally picked up.

"Claudine, why did you say that Mama and Robert and Gabriel and Patrick and Alice were dead the last time we talked?"

"Well, because of the genocide."

"So do you know that they're dead?"

"No, I was just assuming. I was emotional. And then the way that Carene and Michelle treated you? Just giving you to that man?"

"So, you don't know that anyone from our family is dead?"

"No."

"So, they could be alive?"

"I guess. I mean, it's not *im*possible."

"Oh, thank God!"

"But, I mean, Elise. I think you should prepare yourself for the worst. Where are you? Are you in Dar?"

"No," I said. "I'm staying with my friend Doreen in Bujumbura."

"So, Elise," she said, as though she hadn't heard me. "You know that guy I told you about, that I had started dating?"

I was a little bit amazed that she was talking about romance when there was so much killing going on in our country, but I didn't want to spend the little time I had with her on the phone arguing. So, I said, "Uh, yeah."

"Well, his name's David, and," she whispered, "and he's an officer in the RPF! He was horribly wounded during one of their battles to re-take Rwanda. He got reconstructive surgery."

"Why are you whispering? I can barely hear you. It's not a great connection."

"Well, he's here under a false name. For security. But we've been dating, and he finally told me his real name! Isn't that wonderful? Aren't you happy for me?"

"Yes, Claudine." I said. "I'm very happy for you. Congratulations." I heard the tones on the line that indicated that the time I had paid for was coming to an end, and I had put in all my coins. "Well, I have to go, Claudine."

"What? Why?"

"I'm out of money and I'm out of--"

There was a loud click on the line. The call was over.

So, for about a month Doreen and I just waited and listened to the BBC, and sometimes RTLM. And then, most nights we went out to clubs. Benjamin and Doreen's boyfriend would usually meet us wherever we went. It was a good distraction from the stress and the horror of what had sort of become our day jobs: listening to the reports of so many tens of thousands of Tutsis hacked to death in this village, churches filled with bodies, the overwhelming stench of death.

The RPF kept winning, though. They already controlled most of Rwanda, and day after day they took more and more of Kigali.

On July 4th, Kagame declared victory and said that the RPF controlled all of Rwanda except Gisenyi, where what was left of the Rwandan government was still holding out.

"Well," Doreen said. "I guess it's time to go back to Rwanda."

"I guess so," I said.

I told Benjamin that I needed to go back to Rwanda.

"It's still dangerous!" he protested.

"I have to go find out what happened to my mama and my family!" I told him. "Benjamin, I have to go."

He realized that there was nothing he was going to say that was going to change my mind. "Here," he said. "You're going to need some money."

I found Doreen and told her that Benjamin had given me the money I needed. Doreen and I hugged each other. We were going home.

279

Chapter Sixteen: Going Home

It was still dark when Doreen and I got up the next morning. At first, the streets were empty. But as we kept walking, we kept seeing others who were, like us, carrying suitcases and backpacks.

At first there were just a few small groups, but the closer we got to the bus station, the more the streets became like rivers, feeding into a sea of people.

"I don't think I've ever seen so many Tutsis," I said.

"I don't think I've ever seen so many people," Doreen replied.

"It feels good to be surrounded by so many of... you know, us."

"And it feels good to be going home."

Neither of us said it, but along with our happiness about the genocide being over and the fact that we were going home, I think Doreen and I were also both very worried about what we were going to find once we got there.

It took hours and hours of waiting in a line to get to the door of a bus. The buses were lined up, one after the other. As soon as the bus in the front of the line was full, it would leave, and the whole line of buses would move up one place. No one was bothering with tickets. Everyone was just paying the drivers directly. But even with all of the people pressed into that one area, there was no pushing or shoving. Everyone seemed to be feeling the same mix of feelings that Doreen and I were: happy on the outside, but underneath, very, very worried.

Our bus was packed. Some people were sitting on other people's laps. Others were happy to stand in the aisles, even though they knew they were going to be standing for the whole day. Some people even begged and pleaded with the driver to ride on top of the bus, saying they'd be happy to pay the full fare. With no space left inside, the driver closed the door, and we were off.

As our overloaded bus made it to the top of the first rise coming out of Bujumbura, I saw a sight like nothing I had seen before.

"Doreen," I said. "Look!"

In front of us, filling the entire road, as far as the eye could see, was a stream of buses, and trucks, and cars, packed with Tutsis. Even the sides of the road were packed with people walking, with children on their backs, and baskets and gourds on their heads. Some people were pushing bicycles loaded down with their possessions.

Like a flow of lava, we were all slowly streaming back toward Rwanda.

"Mana we, Elise!" Doreen said.

Doreen and I were both exhausted from getting up so early. We tried to sleep. I drifted in and out. But I was drifting in and out of other of things too. The slow speed we were moving at was excruciating. On one hand I felt like I was dying inside with wanting to get home and find out what had happened. But on the other I was afraid I would find out that everyone had been slaughtered. I kept imagining horrible scenes of walking into my house and finding blood on the walls, and the corpses of Mama, Robert, Gabriel, Patrick, and Alice. I kept trying to put these images out of my head, praying, *Please let everyone be alright. Please let everyone be alright*, as I eventually fell asleep.

"What is that smell?" I said, waking up. I had to put my hand over my nose and mouth. Doreen and everyone else on the bus was doing the same thing.

As we came around a bend in the road, we saw the Rwandan border checkpoint. Just over the border, there were dead bodies everywhere, littering the streets. Some had been shot, but it looked like most of them had been hacked to death with machetes. I noticed one body bent over in the frame of a window that had had the glass smashed out of it.

Everything was stained with blood, the ground, the sides of buildings, even the drainage trenches on the sides of the road were flowing with it. The buildings were all riddled with bullet holes.

Big black *sabaka*, scavenger birds, were circling in the sky, dropping to the ground, and feeding on the corpses. The stench of death was overwhelming. Some people were vomiting out the windows of the bus. Some people didn't make it to the windows.

Some people were crying.

RPF soldiers were manning the border gate, but they weren't stopping the busses to check papers. They couldn't. Too many people were flowing back home, into what was left of Rwanda.

As our bus drove on, past the border, we could see that the dead bodies and blood weren't limited to the checkpoint. They were everywhere. For hours, we swerved around the dead bodies that were littering the streets and through the stream of the living. Eventually we pulled into Butare. Some people got off the bus. Some others got on. Then our bus continued slowly on to Kigali.

Just like the station in Bujumbura, the central bus station in Kigali was a sea of people. But here, instead of moving toward the station, everyone was moving outward, going in different directions. Some were being met by people who were waiting for them, but most people, like Doreen and me, were going off to find out what had happened to their people and to their country.

As Doreen and I were getting off the bus, I was shocked to hear someone calling my name. I searched the crowd and saw that it was an old friend of mine from Biryogo. He looked so different from the last time I had seen him. He looked so grown up. He was wearing an RPF uniform and driving an army truck. He pulled over, jumped down from the cab, and walked over to me. We hugged.

"Bernard!" I said. "It's so good to see you!"

"It's good to see that you're alive!" he said.

"You too. And you're a soldier!"

"I'm more than that."

"Doreen, this is Bernard, a friend of mine from Biryogo..." I turned to introduce her, but she wasn't there. "Oh, I guess she's gone to find her family, if any of them are still alive. I need to do the same thing. What do you mean, you're more than a soldier?"

"You know about David, right?"

"Claudine's David?"

"Mm-hm. I'm his driver," he said with pride. "So, I know Claudine. She said that she told you about David on the phone."

"A little," I said. "She said he was an officer in the RPF?"

"He's a hero!"

"Oh," I said. "So, are they... here?"

"No, no," Bernard said. "I mean, David is, of course! But Claudine? No-no. She's still in Belgium making wedding plans."

"Oh…" I said. "They're getting married?"

"Oh yes."

"Do you know anything about the rest of my family?"

"Oh, I'm sorry," he said, "but I think maybe they have all been killed."

His words hit me with brutal force. It felt like a dam inside me broke. I had been holding on to the hope that maybe everyone was still alive. But now, to hear this from an RPF soldier made me feel like everything had just been pulled out of me. My knees buckled. I fell to the ground, sobbing.

Just then Bernard got a call on the radio.

"Yes, sir," he responded.

"I'm sorry, Elise," he said, still standing above me, clearly uncomfortable about what he should do. "I'm so sorry, but I have to go. To pick up David. I'll…"

I was sobbing so hard I couldn't speak. I could barely breathe. It was like the hurt was being wrung out of me, but with each breath, there was just more hurt there to replace it.

As Bernard was walking to his truck, I barely managed to get out, "Bernard, can you give me a ride to Biryogo? Please? I need to..."

"No," he said. "I'm... I'm so sorry, Elise. I really have to go!" He got back in his truck and drove away, leaving me alone, on the ground, sobbing.

But just then, I heard someone else calling to me. "Elise? Elise!"

"Rose?" I said, looking up. It *was* Rose!

She kept calling, "Elise! Elise!" and waving to me from the window of a white truck that was driving toward me with the letters "UN" stenciled on the door. The truck stopped. Rose got out. We ran to each other, and we hugged for a long time.

"Elise! It's so good to see you, to see that you're alive!"

"It's good to see you too, Rose! It's been so long."

"I know. Months and months since you left for Burundi. Oh, this is my boyfriend," she said. "Issa."

By the way he said, "Nice to meet you," in Kinyarwanda, as he shook my hand, I could tell he wasn't a native speaker.

I shook his hand, saying, "Nice to meet you, too."

"He's from Ghana," Rose said. "He's an officer in UNAMIR."

"Oh," I nodded.

"Did you just get back?" she asked.

"Just now," I said.

"So, you haven't been to your house yet?"

"No. I…" I started crying again.

"What's wrong?" Rose asked.

"I just heard from an RPF soldier that he thinks my whole family is probably…dead!"

"Does he know for sure?"

"I don't know," I said through my sobs. "He was called away before I could ask him any questions."

"Well, we can take you to your house to see if you can find out anything else there. We can take her there, can't we, Issa?"

They talked a little bit in English, which, at that time, I didn't speak at all.

"Yes. Come on. Get in. We'll take you to your house," Issa said.

"Okay," I said, hesitantly. I needed to go there, but I was almost shaking with fear over what I might find.

The drive to Biryogo was slow. There were even more dead bodies littering the streets than there had been on the way into Kigali, so the smell was even worse. I kept seeing places I recognized, but now they were riddled with bullet holes and stained with blood.

"Have you been there since the genocide?" I asked.

"I've driven by it," Rose answered.

"I think the Rwandan army was using it as a hospital," Issa added. "If it's the place I think it is."

"I'm afraid about what I'm going to find inside," I said.

As soon as we pulled up outside my compound, I jumped out of the truck and ran to the gate.

"Wait!" Issa yelled.

"Elise!" Rose called. "Wait!"

I found the gate was unlocked and swung it open, revealing the house. It was a corpse of its former self. The walls were riddled with bullet holes. It looked like everything that could be taken, had been taken. Even the door and window frames were gone, leaving empty holes where they used to be. The fields had been stripped.

I ran into the compound and then into the house. There was nothing inside but bloody bandages and bullet shells littering the floor. As I walked through each room, I found the same thing. Every piece of furniture, every carpet, every wall hanging, everything that had been my family's, was gone.

Except, in Mama's room, there was still a large drawing of Papa that had hung over her bed. It was the only thing left in the house. I took it off the wall and looked at the image of Papa. Tears spilled down my face as I kept looking at the drawing. Then I drifted out into the living room, kneeled down on the floor, and wept.

"Elise! Do you want to die?" A man was yelling at me. It made me look up. Silhouetted in the doorway, was a soldier. "You've got to get out of there!" he yelled. "It's not safe!"

I got to my feet and ran toward the man. Once I was outside, I could see that the man was my cousin, Theo. He was wearing an RPF uniform. He put his arm around me and pulled me away from the house.

"Theo!" I said, amazed. "What are you doing here?"

"My squad's been patrolling this area," he said. "I saw that the gate to your compound was open. It's a good thing I was coming by when I was, or you might have been killed!"

"What do you mean?" I asked. "I thought everything was over."

"As the Hutus were pulling out, they booby-trapped a lot of the Tutsis' houses!"

"What?"

"Oh yes, Elise. I've seen it! I've seen what's left of people. They go back to their house. They think everything is fine. Then they go to open a cabinet or a drawer, and BOOM! That's it! Because it was booby-trapped with a grenade!"

"Oh!" I said. "That's horrible!"

"They even buried mines in people's gardens with the onions or the potatoes! So, you think since you're back in Rwanda everything's safe, then you go to dig a yam out of your garden, and BOOM! That's it for you! There are teams from the RPF that are going house to house to clear them of all the booby traps, so DO NOT go back inside until one of those teams has been through your house! Got it?"

"Yes," I said. "I've got it."

"All right," Theo said. "I have to go check other houses."

"Wait," I said. "Do you know anything about the rest of my family?"

"I haven't heard anything, but I have to tell you, Elise. This is Biryogo. You know, the center of Hutu Power."

"I know."

"And the center of the Interahamwe. I'm sorry to tell you Elise, but I just don't see how there could be any Tutsis still alive in Biryogo."

I started sobbing again. I realized I still had the drawing of Papa in my hands.

"I'm so sorry to leave you like this, but if I don't get to as many houses as I can, more people might die. I'm sorry. I have to go," Theo said, and then he was gone.

I walked out into the street and fell down next to Issa's truck, I was crying so hard.

"Why are you crying?" I heard a woman yelling at me.

I looked up to see Nadine, a Tutsi neighbor of ours, walking toward me. I couldn't speak.

"I said, 'Why are you crying?'" she demanded, walking up to me. "My whole family is dead! My husband! All of my children! Every one of them! They are all DEAD! I had to pretend *I* was dead! I laid there, inside the church, with the dead bodies, including your mama."

I started bawling, shaking with sobs.

"For a whole day," she continued, "until it was dark, and I could sneak out and find another place to hide!" She was kneeling down in front of me by this point. She grabbed my arms and started shaking me. "What do you have to cry about? Some of your family are still alive!"

"What?" I said, wiping the tears from my face.

"Patrick is with a Hutu family in Kicukiro, and Alice is in Zaire with a friend of your Mama."

"Thank you!" I said, standing up and throwing my arms around her. "Thank you so much! What about Robert and Gabriel? Do you know anything about them?"

"I'm sorry," she said. "I don't."

I hugged her again, saying, "Thank you! I'm so sorry about your family."

"Well, don't just stand here hugging me," she said. "Go get your brother!"

I rushed into Issa's truck, yelling, "Patrick and Alice are alive!"

"What?" Rose said. She was crouched down in front of her seat. "Issa, can we drive on?"

"Sure," he said, starting the truck.

"What are you doing down there?" I asked Rose.

"Well," she explained. "The RPF's still looking for my father. I figure, if they find me, they might arrest me to try to get information about him."

"Do you know what happened to him?"

"I think he and my mama are probably in Gisenyi, but I don't know. I just couldn't stay with them. But what were you saying about Alice and Patrick?"

"They're alive!" I said. "Nadine, our neighbor, just told me that Alice and Patrick are alive!"

"Well, that's wonderful!" Rose said.

"But my mama is almost certainly dead." I was sobbing again. "Nadine told me she saw her body inside the church."

"Elise. I'm so sorry," Rose said, climbing between the two front seats, into the back seat, with me. She hugged me.

"I'm so sorry, Elise," Issa said, from the front of the truck.

"Did she say anything about Robert or Gabriel?" Rose asked.

"She said she doesn't know about them."

We all sat in silence for a moment.

"So, can I ask you for another favor?" I said.

"Go ahead," Issa said.

"Well, do you think it would be possible to go get Patrick and Alice?"

"Issa?" Rose asked. "Can we go and pick up Elise's brother and sister?"

"Where are they?" he asked.

"Alice is in Zaire," I said.

"Oh," Issa said. "There's still a lot of Rwandan army and Interahamwe activity going on there, and even if there wasn't, we're assigned to Rwanda. I'm really not allowed to go to another country. What about Patrick?"

"He's in Kicukiro."

"Let's find out where."

Issa and I spoke to Nadine. She told us exactly where Patrick was.

I thanked Nadine and hugged her again. Then we got back into Issa's truck and drove away.

I cried for a long time as we drove, until I was left staring into space, feeling numb. "I almost died again," I said, realizing it as I was saying it.

"What?" Rose asked.

"An RPF soldier came into my house, when I was in there, and told me that the house was probably booby-trapped!" I explained.

"I was worried about that," Issa said. "That's why we were yelling at you."

"But just then, we saw an RPF patrol coming toward us," Rose added. "And, like I told you, there's a good chance they're looking for me. So, I had to stay out of sight."

"And I didn't want to draw any attention to us, so I stopped yelling at you and stayed in the truck. And then you came out pretty much right after the soldier went in. I'm sorry. It just wasn't safe for me to go in after you. I mean, it wasn't safe for you to go into your compound either, but…"

"Well, I'm still alive," I said. "… Again."

As we drove toward Kicukiro, weaving around the dead bodies in the street, Issa turned on the radio. There were reports of Rwandan refugees streaming into Gisenyi, and spilling over the border, into Zaire.

"How did you end up, you know, not with your parents?" I asked Rose.

"Oh. Well, I mean, I just kept watching the unspeakable things that Papa was organizing. And I met Issa, I guess, right around the time you left for Burundi. And I started spending more and more time with him."

"And when her parents were talking to her about leaving," Issa explained. "I told her that if she went with them to Gisenyi, there was a good chance that they were all going to end up on trial at The Hague, or, with all the revenge killings going on, dead. And, as for the people who carry them out… I can't say I blame them. I mean, you come back to Rwanda to find out that your family has been killed by your Hutu neighbors? You know, people you thought were your friends?"

"So, Issa and I got a room at Le Méridien, and after a while I just … stopped going home."

"Didn't your father try to find you?" I asked.

"Oh, of course! I even heard through the grapevine that he was using the Interahamwe to try and find me, but I guess eventually they all had to, you know, leave?"

"That's who almost all of those refugees they were just talking about on the radio are," Issa explained. "Most of them are Hutus who took part in the killings during the genocide, and they're afraid they're going to be killed in retribution by the Tutsis that are still alive."

"My mama and papa included," Rose said.

"Mana we, Rose! That must be hard."

"It's not easy, but when you look at what my papa is involved with…" she gestured to a body we were driving around, that looked like it had been hacked to death.

When we got to the house Nadine had told us about, the three of us walked up to the door and knocked on it.

A man answered, "Yes?"

Patrick ducked under the man's arm, bolted outside, threw his arms around me, and wouldn't let go. I was amazed at how much bigger he was than the last time I had seen him. He was almost as tall as me. *He must be, what? eleven now*, I realized.

"Oh, Patrick! It's so good to see you!" I said, hugging him and crying. "How are you?"

Patrick didn't say anything. He just kept hugging me really tightly.

"Who are you?" the man demanded, coming out of his house.

"I'm Elise, Patrick's sister."

"You're not Claudine."

"No," I said. "Claudine is our sister."

"Give him back," the man demanded, moving toward me.

"Hold on," Issa said, getting in between the man and me.

"You can't just take him!" the man said.

"What?" I said. "Of course I can! I told you, I'm his sister!"

"I'm waiting for Claudine to come take him!" the man said.

"What's the difference?" I asked.

"I'm a Hutu! Do you have any idea of the risk I took in hiding your…Tutsi brother?"

"Well, thank you for doing that. Really. But-"

"You can't just take him!" the man insisted.

"Elise," Rose cut in. "He wants money. Somehow, he knows about Claudine getting married to David, and he thinks that she'll pay him a lot of money for Patrick."

"That's disgusting!" I said. "He can't just … keep him!"

"Elise," Issa said. "I'm sorry to say, I've seen this kind of thing before."

"Issa," Rose suggested. "Talk to him. Man to man. I'm sure you can work something out."

"Okay," Issa sighed. "Okay." He took the Hutu man aside and spoke to him quietly.

"Patrick, are you okay?" I asked.

But Patrick still wasn't saying anything. He just held on to me like he was drowning, and I was something that floated. As I kept hugging him, I suddenly realized that, being in Rwanda during the genocide, he must have seen some truly horrific things. "It's okay," I re-assured him. "I've got you." I saw Issa take out a roll of a kind of money I had never seen before. "What kind of money is that?" I whispered to Rose.

"It's American. That's what the guys from UNAMIR get paid in.

"Why?"

"I don't know. I think because the USA feels guilty that it didn't do anything to stop or end the genocide, so now they're trying to make up for it by giving money to the UN."

Just then, Issa came back over to us, walking fast. "Come on," he said. "Let's go!"

"You worked it out?" Rose asked.

"We can take Patrick?" I asked.

"Yes, we can take Patrick. Come on! Get in the truck!"

Patrick held on to me, even as we were climbing into Issa's truck. "It's okay," I repeated, still hugging him. "It's okay."

"Well," Issa said, as we were driving away, "that… human pile of garbage is set for the next…year!"

"How much did you give him?" Rose asked.

"Two hundred dollars, American," he said, rubbing his forehead in frustration.

"That's a huge amount of money!" Rose said.

"Well, it was that, or shoot him! And we're not supposed to be shooting anyone, regardless of what they do, or what they did! GOD DAMN IT!!" He started slamming his hand against the steering wheel.

Patrick tightened his grip on me.

"Issa!" Rose said, seeing Patrick's reaction.

"I'm sorry. I'm sorry," Issa said, pulling the truck over to the side of the road. "It's just that … that's all we did. That's what they ordered us to do. Even when they were killing people right in front of us! Even when the genocide was going on! And then, when everything's supposed to be over, we still have to deal with people like that guy?!" He paused. I could see he was working to get himself under control.

Rose was rubbing his back with one hand and holding his shoulder with the other.

"I'm sorry," Issa said. "I'm sorry."

"No, I…" I didn't know how to finish. "It's just, Patrick…" I looked Patrick in the face. His eyes were wide. I hugged him again and kept holding him.

"Of course," Issa said. "Again, I'm sorry. Let's go get a drink."

"Good idea," Rose said. She hugged Issa's neck, kissed his cheek, and said, "You're a good man."

He didn't reply.

"Gabriel is dead," Patrick said, seemingly out of nowhere.

"What?" I asked. I looked at his face again.

He had that same wide-eyed stare, and a lack of expression on his face. "I was there," he said.

"Mana we, Patrick!" I hugged him especially tight. Tears were rolling down my cheek. I looked at him again. "Can you … Can you tell me … what happened?"

"We were hiding at a neighbor's," he began. "And an Interahamwe gang burst into the house. And one of the guys in the gang grabbed Gabriel by the collar and said, 'Okay, cockroach! Now we're going to kill you and your little Tutsi brother!'"

"And Gabriel said, 'He's not my brother. He's my servant. And he's not Tutsi. He's Hutu.'"

"Then the leader of the gang said, 'Well, let's see if that's true.' And he put his machete up to Gabriel's throat, and he said, 'Is that true? That he's not your brother?' Then he looked at me and said, 'Is it true, that you're a servant? A Hutu? Huh? Well then you won't mind if I do this!' And Elise, he cut off Gabriel's ear! And Gabriel was screaming, 'Look, you see? Nothing! He doesn't care about me at all!' And I knew that if I said anything, or if I cried, or if I made any kind of face, then they would kill us both, right there."

"Mana we, Patrick!" I said, hugging him again. "What did you do?"

"I couldn't *do* anything! So, I just stood there. I didn't cry. I didn't even show anything on my face! But I think that made the leader of the gang even more angry, because he said, 'No? Nothing? How about if I do this?' and he cut off Gabriel's nose! And still I just stood there, which made him even more angry, so he cut off Gabriel's other ear, which made Gabriel scream even more. But I just stood there, watching. And then they cut off Gabriel's fingers and then his feet, and they just kept, cutting … parts of him off, until finally he was dead. And they took so long to do it, Elise! And finally, they just left."

"And they just left you there?"

"Yes. Until the Hutu man that was keeping me found me."

"Patrick!" I said. "I'm so sorry that you had to go through that!" I didn't know what else to do, so I just kept hugging him. He hugged me back. He didn't say anything else for a long time.

We drove to Le Méridien, the hotel in Kigali where Rose and Issa were staying and went to the restaurant there. I hadn't eaten a real meal since I'd left Bujumbura. I wasn't hungry after hearing Patrick's story, but I made myself eat. I encouraged Patrick to do the same.

The whole scene was so strange. Right outside there were still bodies littering the streets. And here I was, at a table in a restaurant, looking at a menu, and being asked by a waiter what I wanted to order.

"Um…I don't know," I said.

"Why don't you get the steak?" Rose said. "It's delicious!"

"Okay," I said. Patrick was back to not speaking.

"The same for him," Rose said.

Then Issa raised his glass, and Rose and I raised ours. "To the end of the genocide," he said.

After we ate, we all went back up to Issa and Rose's room. I took Rose aside and spoke quietly to her: "Uh, Rose, you know our house in Biryogo is booby-trapped…"

"Oh, yes."

"So…Patrick and I don't have any place to sleep tonight," I said. "Or tomorrow night. Or at all. I don't know when the house will be cleared."

"From what I've heard it could be tomorrow, or it could be months from now."

"I'm sorry to ask, but…"

"Issa, sweetheart? Elise and her brother don't have any place to stay."

"Yes," Issa said. "I've been thinking about that. Let me call a friend of mine. He's staying here in the hotel, too." He picked up the phone and made a call. I couldn't really hear what he was saying. He hung up and said, "Well, Elise. There's someone I'd like you to meet."

Then there was a knock at the door. Issa answered it. In the hall was another man in a UNAMIR uniform, a fat, ugly man. My stomach sank.

"Sekou!" Issa said.

"Issa!" the man replied.

The men hugged, slapped each other on the back, and began speaking in French. *It's amazing how quickly you lose a language when you don't use it,* I thought, frustrated that I couldn't understand them.

They were looking at me and talking and smiling. Suddenly I felt like I was a cow that one man was selling to another.

When they gestured to Patrick, there seemed to be some disagreement between the two of them, but then clearly Issa was bringing the conversation back to me. There were smiles, and wide eyes, and then a handshake. And Issa brought the other man over to me.

"Elise," he said. "I'd like you to meet a friend of mine. Sekou, this is Elise. Elise, Sekou."

"Hello," I said. I shook his hand, but I was afraid. The look in his eyes reminded me of Jean-Jacques.

"Why don't you two go back to his room and … get to know each other?" Issa said. "And take Patrick with you. Rose and I are…tired."

I looked to Rose.

She took me aside. "It will be fine, Elise. Don't worry. And it's…important that I keep Issa…happy."

I looked over at Patrick who was sitting in the corner of the room, staring into space. "But…"

"Elise, you know who my father is. How do you think I've stayed alive this long? It will be fine. Go with Sekou. He's a good man."

Neither Patrick nor I wanted to go with Sekou, but we didn't have any place else to go. We didn't have anything.

"Well, Elise. Here we are," Sekou said, as we entered his room. He put his arms out and stretched. "I'm tired," he said. "Let's go to bed." There was only one double bed. "Patrick can sleep…"

I took Patrick and got into bed with him. We both stayed in our clothes.

"Oh…" Sekou said. "Well…" He got undressed, turned off the lights, and climbed into the bed next to us. I wished that I could have slept, but I had known this sort of feeling before. It was the same way things felt with Jean-Jacques. With my arms around Patrick, I stared into the darkness. *I can't go through that again*, I thought. *I don't know what I'll do, but I just can't!*

I don't know how long I lay there, but eventually I could hear and feel Sekou moving, moving toward me and Patrick. Then he was still and silent for a while. I relaxed, just a little, but then I could feel his hand trying to snake its way to one of my breasts, and immediately I started shrieking at him, "**WHAT DO YOU THINK YOU'RE DOING? WHAT KIND OF MAN ARE YOU? MY ELEVEN-YEAR-OLD BROTHER AND I HAVE JUST SURVIVED A GENOCIDE, AND YOU WANT TO TRY TO MAKE ME HAVE SEX WITH YOU?!**"

Patrick started wailing, making such a racket, I think Sekou didn't know what to do, other than turn on the lights and try to calm us down.

"Elise! Hey, hey! It's okay. It's okay!" He tried to put his arms around me, but I threw him off, pulled myself and Patrick away, and ran to the nearest corner of the room, yelling, "**IT IS *NOT* OKAY! THERE'S NOTHING OKAY ABOUT IT! IT'S DISGUSTING WHAT YOU'RE DOING!**"

He put his hands up in front of him in a surrendering motion. "Okay. Okay. Okay. It's… I'm not… I won't try to touch you. I…" He sat down on the bed. "I'm sorry. I'm very, very sorry. I really… I didn't understand." He sighed. "But now I do. I'm…I won't try to touch you."

I didn't know if I could trust him or not.

"Please," he said. "Come get some sleep. I'll… I'll sleep on the floor." He backed away from us.

I decided to trust him. It was that or find someplace else for Patrick and me to stay that night. I took Patrick back to the bed and got into it. We lay there for a minute. I thought about Sekou. I really didn't know if it was a good idea or not, but I said, "You don't have to sleep on the floor."

"What?" he asked.

"It's okay, if you sleep in the bed."

"Oh, well, okay!" he said.

"It's just…you can't…try to touch me. Can you…can you understand that? Can you do that? Please?"

"Okay," he said. "I understand." He sat on the bed. "I'm…I'm very sorry." He got under the covers, on the other side of the bed from where Patrick and I were.

Even though I was exhausted, physically and emotionally, I lay there for hours holding on to Patrick, staring into the darkness. I wondered about what had happened to Robert. *He could still be alive*, I thought. *Is it possible Nadine was wrong about Mama? That maybe she saw the body of someone who looked like Mama? Maybe Patrick knows something about Mama or Robert.* He seemed to be sleeping. I didn't want to wake him up. Eventually I fell asleep, too.

The next morning, I woke up feeling rested and refreshed. I actually stretched and yawned. I felt good. Then I remembered Sekou and felt tense again. I wondered, *Am I going to have to keep convincing him not to try to touch me?* He was coming out of the bathroom with the steam from his shower.

"Good morning, Elise," he said. "I was thinking we could go get some breakfast. You and Patrick can take showers before we go, if you like. And if it would make you more comfortable, I could go down to the restaurant and wait for you and Patrick. Okay?"

"Okay…" I said.

"Oh, and…here," he took a key out of a table next to the bed. "This is for you. Go ahead and take it. It's a key to the room."

"…Thank you," I said, cautiously.

"Well, I'll see you down at breakfast."

"Wait," I said.

"Yes?"

"Why are you being so nice to us?"

"Ah. I…during the genocide. We were ordered to stand by and watch while…terrible, inhuman things were happening to the Tutsis here, sometimes right in front of us. And…I … I feel like now I have the chance to…to actually do something for you and your brother. For me it's…a second chance maybe. Again, I'm sorry for last night. I'll… I'll give you some time alone," he said and left.

I locked the door behind him.

I hadn't showered in days. It was wonderful to feel clean. I washed the clothes I had on. I had two changes of clothes in the bag I had brought with me from Bujumbura.

Patrick was very quick when he took his shower. He still wasn't speaking much, but when I looked at him and smiled, and said, "It's really good to see you, Patrick," he smiled back at me.

It was the first time I had seen him smile since we picked him up. It made me breathe a little bit easier. "It's been so long since the last time I saw you. You've gotten so much bigger!"

He smiled again.

"Elise! Patrick! Come join us!" Sekou said as we entered the hotel dining room.

"Good morning," I called out to them as we walked over to their table.

"Good morning," Rose said giving me a hug. Then, lowering her voice she said in my ear, "Was your night… okay?"

"Not at first," I said. "But when I explained everything that had happened to me, he left me alone."

"Oh," she said. "Well, good." She seemed a little surprised.

As we were finishing breakfast, Sekou looked at Patrick. "Those are the same clothes you wore yesterday."

Patrick shrugged.

"He was hiding with a Hutu family during the genocide, and I have to say, the man who met us at the door when we went to get him was…not very nice," I said. "I wasn't about to ask him for Patrick's things. If he even had any."

"She is being much nicer to that man than he deserves!" Rose said. "He wanted money for Patrick!"

"And I didn't shoot him!" Issa said.

"Well, you know what?" Sekou said. "How about the three of us go shopping and get the two of you some clothes?"

"I would say, 'No, no, we couldn't,'" I said, "but…we really could use some new clothes."

"I insist," he said. "I'll pay."

"Well, thank you again," I replied. I was wondering if that would put me more in debt to him. I had been able to hold him off up until then, but I kept wondering if he was waiting for something else, later on.

Patrick looked at him and smiled. "Thank you," he said in a small voice.

"Look at that!" Sekou said, grinning. "The silent boy is speaking!"

"The silent boy is speaking," we all said, raising our glasses and drinking.

I put a hand on his back and rubbed it a little. Then I said softly in his ear, "Do you know anything about Robert?"

"The last time I saw him was before the genocide started. I don't know what happened to him, but…"

"I know," I said. "I'm worried about him, too."

Sekou continued to be kind to us. He bought us food and more clothes. When we thanked him, he would say things like, "Hey, what the hell else am I going to do with all of this money?"

But after we had been living with him for a week, I started to think about the future. He was being very nice to us, but I really wasn't interested in him romantically, and I knew that whatever we were doing, it couldn't go on forever.

It turned out that a lot of the UNAMIR soldiers were staying at Le Méridien. Every night there was at least one party going on in one of the UNAMIR soldiers' rooms. I was surprised at how many girls I saw at these parties that I recognized from school, or from The Boom, the club Rose and I used to go to.

One afternoon, as I was walking through downtown Kigali with Patrick and Sekou, Bernard pulled up to us in his RPF pick-up truck.

"Elise," he said. "David has had me looking for you and Patrick."

"Really?" I said. "Why?"

"Claudine is coming here tomorrow."

"I thought Claudine was staying in Brussels."

"Oh no," Bernard said. "She insisted that David give her a proper Rwandan wedding, right here in Rwanda."

"Oh," I said.

"And she wants me to bring you and Patrick to David's house tomorrow."

"Not today?" I asked. "Not right now?" I was a little surprised that she hadn't had us brought to David's house weeks earlier.

Bernard shrugged. "Orders," he said.

"Uh, well, okay," I said.

"So, could the two of you meet me here tomorrow, maybe around ten?" he said.

"And you're going to take us to David's?" I asked.

"That's the plan," he said.

"Well, okay," I said. "I guess we'll see you tomorrow."

I told Sekou that Patrick and I were going to be leaving for Claudine and David's house the next day.

"That's great that you're getting back with your family," he said.

I thanked him for everything he had done for us and gave him a hug. I went to Rose and Issa's room and told them too.

"I'm so happy for you," Rose said. We hugged.

"Thank you, Issa," I said. "I don't know what we would have done without you."

"Well, I told you, it felt good to be able to actually help. Good luck, you two."

The next morning Bernard picked Patrick and me up, as planned. As we were driving to David and Claudine's house, I was surprised to see that most of the bodies had been removed from the roads. In a lot of places, though, they still hadn't been buried. The RPF, and some civilians too, were burying people all the time, but there were just so many bodies everywhere.

I also noticed that some people were starting to patch the bullet holes and rebuild buildings.

On the radio they were talking about how the whole government had to be re-done, and how what was left of the Rwandan army and the Interahamwe were using the refugee camps in Zaire as bases to hide out in during the day and then come back into Rwanda at night to try to keep killing Tutsis.

When we arrived at David and Claudine's compound, Claudine came out of the house, and as soon as she saw us, she started crying.

"Don't just stand there!" she yelled at the soldiers. "Bring them in!"

We went inside and there were hugs and tears all around. I let out a long sigh. I had gotten Patrick and myself to safety. We literally couldn't have been safer. We were staying with our family. Soldiers were guarding the house, the house of a major in the RPF, which had just won the war.

"Do you know about Alice?" I asked Claudine. "That she's in Zaire?"

"Of course we do," she said. "David's my husband! We're just trying to find out exactly where she is. And when we do, David will take a team of soldiers to go get her."

"Do you know anything about Mama, or Robert?"

Claudine started crying. "I do," she said. "I do. And I am so angry, still!"

"Tell me," I said.

"Oh, Elise. Mama was… Mama was killed."

"You're sure?" I asked. "Who told you?"

"David. His intelligence people found out the whole story. I just found out a few days ago."

"So, what happened?"

"Well, during the Genocide there were actually a bunch of times when Mama was stopped by the army and the Interahamwe. And each time they were about to kill her, a Hutu who knew Mama would see what was going on, come over, and say, 'No-no. We shouldn't kill her. She's been so good to us. She fed us when we were hungry,' or 'She gave me a job when I needed one,' or 'She lent me money and let me pay it back whenever I could. No, leave her alone.'"

"And they wouldn't kill her?"

"That's what David's intelligence guys told me. They said that that happened a few times, until Rose's mama found out about it."

"Then what happened?"

"Well, it sounds like Rose's mama got frustrated with how many Hutus seemed to love Mama, and how they kept saving her. So once Rose's mama found out who was hiding our mama, she took a bunch of soldiers, burst into the house, and dragged Mama out onto the street, yelling, 'You think everybody loves you? Well, they don't! Get out of this house!' And I don't understand why she didn't have her killed right then. Maybe she was afraid that there were Hutus in the crowd that would speak out against her. Maybe it was because she didn't want witnesses. I really don't know. I can only guess. But she didn't kill Mama. She just told her to go."

"But the Rwandan army was already using our house as a hospital, so there was really only one place Mama could go: the church. The thing is, I'm pretty sure Rose's mama knew that the army and the Interahamwe were planning to kill everybody in the church on that day."

"Mana we!" I said.

"So, the army came into the church, and started checking everyone's IDs, and telling the few Hutus who were there to leave. And then the Interahamwe came in, and they slaughtered everyone who was left, all the Tutsis, including Mama," Claudine said, crying.

"Oh Claudine!" I said. I was crying, too. "That's horrible!"

"I know," she said.

We hugged for a moment, sobbing.

"And what about Robert?"

"He was hiding in another church with a bunch of other Tutsis. And when the Rwandan army got there, they threw a grenade into the church. I was told that Robert caught the grenade, ran into the group of soldiers that threw it, and killed a whole bunch of them when the grenade went off."

"And he..?" I asked.

"He was still holding the grenade."

"Mana we!" I said. I was overwhelmed by the pain of hearing this and imagining it. Claudine and I hugged again.

Like the house that Claudine and I grew up in, Claudine and David's house was high up on a hill. I looked out over the hills going off into the distance, realizing that there must have been thousands and thousands of Tutsis hearing stories about what had happened to their families that were just as horrible as the ones I had just heard about what had happened to mine.

Patrick and I met David that night, when he came home. He seemed like a genuinely nice man. I could understand why he was an officer. He had a smile and a way about him that put you at ease and gave you the sense that everything was going to be okay.

We had a feast that night to celebrate our family getting back together. There was goat, with peanut and tomato sauce, and matoke, and ugali. We even had beer and urwagwa, everyone except Patrick.

The food was delicious, and it felt good to be together as a family, especially since we had just lost almost half of it.

David told us stories about how, mainly on foot, and with just machine guns and a few RPGs (Rocket Propelled Grenades), he and his RPF soldiers kept winning battle after battle against the much larger, much better equipped, Rwandan army, which was being backed up by French commandoes, artillery, and even armored cars that David said were basically small tanks.

He told us about one time when he ambushed one of these armored cars by rushing out from his hiding place, throwing a grenade down the barrel of its gun, and blowing it up.

I was so thankful that Patrick was safe, and so was I, physically. But I almost never slept through the night. I would wake up screaming from nightmares about things I had seen, things I had survived, things I had heard about, and things I imagined, like Mama and my brothers being killed during the genocide.

Also, there was trouble between Claudine and David and me. I had been mostly on my own, taking care of myself for almost a year. I was nineteen, almost twenty, but whenever I would be on my way out to see Benjamin, or Rose, or any of my other friends, Claudine and David would tell me that I had to be in by dark, like I was a child. The three of us argued about it all the time.

As the months went by, we re-found and re-connected with a lot of our extended family: cousins, uncles, and aunts. The aunt I had always been the closest to was my Aunt Irène. She lived not far from Claudine and David's house. I would often go there to sit with her and talk.

Aunt Irène was very soft and loving. She really seemed to understand the things I had been through, and she treated me like I was an adult.

I told her about the fights I got into with Claudine and David, and she said, "Well, it sounds to me like it would be a good thing if you found someplace else to live."

"But I don't have any money," I said. "And there are no jobs, especially for women."

"No, no, Elise," she said. "You can come live with me."

"Really?" I said, hugging her. "That would be wonderful!"

"Well," she said smiling, "I just don't think anybody should have to put up with treatment like that if they don't need to."

Soon after that, I moved in with Aunt Irène. Patrick stayed with Claudine and David. Everything was so much better, except my nightmares. They kept happening. Also, I found myself crying all the time.

One day as Aunt Irène and I were sitting out in her back yard, snapping the ends off some beans we had just picked, I told her, "Aunt Irène, I have nightmares almost every night! And I cry all the time!"

"I know, sweetheart. I can hear you when you wake up screaming, and I've seen you crying. But don't worry about any of it."

"Don't worry about it?" I said. "What do you mean don't worry about it? How can you say that?"

"Well," she said. "I think it just means that you're finally safe."

"What? That doesn't make sense. Shouldn't you have more nightmares and cry when you're stressed?"

"Not for someone as strong as you," she said, smiling.

"Strong?" I said, surprised. "I don't think I'm strong."

"Of course you are! You've told me about some of the things you've been through. You probably haven't even told me all of them.

Those are things that would have killed a lot of people, or driven them crazy, or made them want to die! But not you."

"But I have nightmares every night! I cry every day!"

"Well, I've found that your mind stores things up when you're surviving something. It's like you can't afford to have the nightmares. But then, when you feel safe, that's when your mind feels that it's okay to deal with it all. You've been through so much, and in such a short time. It just means that you're starting to… hm, digest it all? Don't worry. In its way, it's a good thing. Even if it does wake up your poor old auntie every night."

"I'm so sorry, Auntie."

"No, no, my dear," she said. "I'm just playing with you. You just keep doing what you need to do."

One morning Claudine called me at Aunt Irène's.

"You need to come home," she said.

"What do you mean?" I asked.

"I mean you have to come home."

"Why?"

"David's intelligence people have located Alice!"

"Really?"

"Yes. He left early, early this morning. He took a whole platoon of soldiers into Zaire to get her. They should be back this afternoon."

"That's wonderful, Claudine! I'll be right over!" I told Aunt Irène's what had happened and rushed over to Claudine's house.

Claudine, Patrick, and I waited. Finally, David pulled into the compound in a jeep with Alice! She had grown so much since the last time I had seen her, about a year before. *She must be, what? ten now?* I thought.

Claudine, Patrick, and I rushed out into the courtyard and threw our arms around her. We were all crying.

What was left of our family was finally back together. It felt good.

I spent a lot of time at Claudine and David's house with Patrick and Alice. We'd play games. We'd spend time in the garden. Sometimes we'd play tag on the lawn. Part of me wanted to ask them about the things they'd seen during the genocide. I was sure they must have seen and experienced things far worse things than I had, and they were just little kids.

But I didn't want to push anything. I decided to just be there and to listen when they wanted to talk. Patrick stayed pretty quiet. I thought maybe that was a carryover from when Gabriel had been killed, and he had to stay silent and not show any emotion. Sometimes I would hug him or Alice, just to let them know that they were loved.

Chapter Seventeen: Sam

I had made some new friends since returning to Rwanda: Bridgette, Gigi, Suzanne, and Eloise. They all lived near Aunt Irène's house. We were all in similar situations: Tutsi girls who had lost family members in the genocide, living with aunties or sisters.

We went out dancing some nights, not because we were celebrating anything. It was more to distract ourselves from the memories of what we had been through and the stress of having no idea of what we were going to do with the rest of our lives in a country that was in ruins.

One afternoon, as we were all sitting out in back of Auntie Irène's house, we began talking.

"How's your new job going, Gigi?" Bridgette asked.

"It's not easy being a *domestique*," (a maid) she said. "But at least it's a job."

"You're lucky!" Eloise said. "Jobs are so hard to find these days in Rwanda?"

"Especially if you're a girl," Suzanne added.

"And if you haven't gone to university," I said.

"We have to get back to school," Eloise said, sighing. We all sighed and looked down and away.

"What's the point?" Suzanne asked. "The only way to support yourself is to find a man to take care of you!" Suzanne had a boyfriend who was married.

"He's going to open a shop for me," she said, smiling. This was what a lot of girls in Kigali were hoping for at that time, that a man with some money would set them up in an apartment and open a shop for them. The apartment part happened a lot. The shop part? Not so much. I smiled and didn't say anything.

"And how's your man, Elise?" Bridgette asked.

"Benjamin?" I said. "He's… good. Things are… good."

"When is he going to open a shop for you?" Suzanne asked. "Or at least get you an apartment?" Eloise added.

"Oh, he's asked," I said. "But I like living here with Aunt Irène."

"We all love your auntie, Elise."

"She's the coolest."

"But you can't live with her forever."

"I know," I said. "I know. At some point we'll all have to do … something else." Everyone looked kind of uncomfortable for a moment.

Then it hit me: "You know what we need, right now?" I said.

"What?" Bridgette asked. "What do we need?"

"We need to stop sitting around, being stressed," I said. "We need a vacation!"

"Eeeeeeeyyyyy," everyone said, nodding in agreement.

"We should go to Lake Kivu," I said.

"Eeeeeeyyyyyyy," everyone agreed.

"But all the hotels there in Gisenyi are so expensive!" Gigi protested. Though it had been the last spot where the old Rwandan government held out against the RPF, before that, Gisenyi had been a resort town a lot of Rwandans went to when they vacationed at Lake Kivu. Now that the genocide was over, people were vacationing there again.

"Well," Bridgette reasoned, "now, let's think about this. We've all, at some time in our lives, slept two or even three people to a bed, right?"

"Eeeeyyyyyy," we all agreed.

"And the thing to do there," Eloise added, "is to just get the cheapest hotel room you can find, because who cares about where you're sleeping, and then just go and hang out by the pool at The Serena." The Serena is the nicest hotel in Gisenyi.

"And," Bridgette went on, "if we all split the price of one room…"

Then we all spoke, kind of on top of each other: "That sounds like a good idea!"

"Of course! Why didn't I think of that?"

"One room! That's a really good idea! We'll split the cost four ways!"

"And we could just go for two or three days," Gigi said.

"So then," I announced, "it's decided. We're taking a vacation at Lake Kivu!"

We all cheered.

All of Rwanda is beautiful, but Lake Kivu is beautiful even for

Rwanda. It runs along the whole western edge of of the country. It's so

big that in most places you can't see one side from the other. It has

beautiful beaches, palm trees dotting the shores, and little islands that

look like they should be on a postcard or in a coffee table book.

The bus to Gisenyi was crowded, but being with friends made the trip

fun. We talked, and joked, and laughed the entire way there.

We did everything we could to make the little money we had go as

far as possible. We walked from the bus stop instead of taking a cab,

and we checked into the cheapest hotel in Gisenyi. The room wasn't

very nice. But none of us cared about the room. We cared about going

to The Serena. So, after changing into our bathing suits, that's exactly

what we did.

We walked into the pool area at there and looked around. We each got

a drink at the bar (one each was all we could afford). Then we sat down

at one of the tables and talked.

"That handsome *muzungu* sitting over there is looking at you,"

Suzanne said, giggling. Muzungu is Kinyarwanda for white person.

"I know," I said. I was looking right back at him. The muzungu

smiled.

I smiled back. I felt warm inside. Since the end of the genocide

there had been a lot of white people in Rwanda who had come in with

international aid organizations or the NGOs (short for Non-

Governmental Organizations). I had never flirted with a muzungu

320

before. But I was really interested in this one. And he seemed to be interested in me too.

"Let's go into the pool!" Gigi said. Gigi was the only one of us who really knew how to swim. The rest of us went in with her, but we stayed in the shallow end, standing on the bottom. I tried to pay attention to my friends, as we were laughing and splashing each other, but I found myself looking over at the muzungu again and again. I was trying not to be obvious, looking out of the corners of my eyes. He was really good looking.

The muzungu stood up. He was tall! He dove into the deep end of the pool. I moved toward him, as he swam under water. Then came to the surface near me. He was looking straight at me, smiling. I smiled back at him and used a hand motion to show that I liked that he was tall, and that so was I. He swam closer and stood next to me in the shallow end of the pool.

"*Amakuru?*" I asked him, which is Kinyarwanda for 'How's it going?'

He replied, "*Ni meza,*" which means "Very well." But then he added, *"Je ne parle pas vraiment Kinyarwanda. Parlez-vous français?"* which meant, or, at least was supposed to mean, "I don't really speak Kinyarwanda. Do you speak French?"

I hadn't spoken French since I was in school, almost a year before, so, it wasn't great. "*Uh, un peu,*" I said. (A little.)

As we talked, I realized that his French wasn't so great either. But I really wanted to talk to him, and it seemed that he really wanted to talk to me, too. So, we struggled our way through a conversation that included a lot of smiling, and laughing, hand gestures, and sometimes acting things out.

He communicated to me that his name was Sam. I communicated to him I was Elise. He repeated it back to me. I liked the way he pronounced my name. I liked the way he spoke French in general. He didn't even try to do a proper French accent. It was kind of funny and kind of cocky at the same time. It was very attractive.

As we kept talking, I found out that Sam was doing the same thing we were: staying in the cheap hotel but spending most of his time here at the pool at the Serena. *Smart*, I thought. I even found out, to my delight, that he and I were staying on the same floor!

My friends had been watching Sam and me the whole time, talking among themselves, and giggling. I did my best to ignore them. Eventually they called to me and convinced me that it was time for us to go back to our room. I wanted to keep talking to Sam, but my friends were all leaving.

"Always leave them wanting more," Gigi said.

I considered that, and decided she might be right. So, I went with my friends.

Later on that evening I crept down the hall of our hotel, to Sam's door, and knocked.

He opened his door, smiled, and said, "Oh, hello." He must have just gotten out of the shower; he still had wet hair. He had on shorts and a tight-fitting tee shirt. He looked good.

"Uh…nous avons une" *What's the word?* I thought. "Uuhhh…" I made a drinking motion with my hand. "…de notre chambre. Voulez-vous venir?" I said, gesturing to our room. I was trying to say (We're having a party in our room. Would you like to come?)

"Uh, okay…" he said hesitantly.

We walked back to my room, where my three friends were all lying on the bed. Sam came in. We had a bottle of gin. I poured Sam a glass, gave it to him, and sat on the edge of the bed.

"He's even cute with all of his clothes on!" Gigi said, and everyone giggled, everyone except Sam that is, because she said it in Kinyarwanda. He looked confused.

"Donc, c'est tout?" Sam said, which means, 'So, is this everyone?'

"Oui," I said, shrugging and smiling.

My friends kept on saying things to each other in Kinyarwanda and giggling.

I guess after a while this wasn't very much fun for Sam, because eventually he started yawning and stretching and saying, "Bien, je suis très fatigue." (Well, I'm really tired.) "Merci. Je vais partir." (Thank you. I'm going to go.) He got up and left.

I closed the door behind him. I was a little frustrated by my unsuccessful attempt to get to know him, and a little frustrated with my friends. *Maybe one-on-one would be better*, I thought.

The next day, as our group was arriving at The Serena, I saw Sam heading for the beach. I followed him.

"Sam," I called.

"Ah, Elise. Bonjour. Comment ça va?"

"Ah, ça va bien, merci. Et tu?"

"Ah, ça va bien. Ça va bien." (I'm good. I'm good.) "La plage et le lac, c'est beau, no?" (The beach and the lake are beautiful.)

"Oh, oui, oui," I agreed. We started walking along the beach and kept talking.

It took some time, and a few conversational missteps, but eventually I found out that Sam was from America, and that he was working for an NGO. I told him a little bit of my story, that half my family had been killed, and that I was living with my aunt. I felt my throat get tight, but I kept myself from crying.

We walked for about an hour along the shore. I was happy that I was talking to him and getting to know him. I hoped that he was feeling the same.

The next morning, I found Sam at the pool again. He was swimming laps. I wished I could swim like he could. I sat on the edge of the pool waiting for him to finish. His head emerged from the water, at my feet. He was smiling. He got out of the pool and toweled off. I watched. We sat and talked some more.

I was amazed at how much Sam and I were communicating, considering how little language we had in common. It took some work. But we were working together, suggesting a word when the other didn't know it, or finding a different way to say something, or a hand motion we could both understand.

Sam said that he lived in Kigali.

I got excited that I might be able to see him again.

The next day, as my friends and I were leaving our hotel to get the bus back to Kigali, Sam saw me and waved me over to his truck. It was a Land Cruiser. I liked it a lot. Sam said that he and his friends were heading back to Kigali, and he asked me if I would like to ride back with them. He introduced me to them. There was Giselle, a Rwandan woman, and her boyfriend, Adil. Adil was a Moroccan man who worked with Sam. There was also Jean-Pierre, a Rwandan friend of Sam's.

I told Sam I had to talk to my friends. As I walked back to them, the girls were all joking and rolling their eyes. I was a little bit nervous, but I was also excited.

"He wants to give me a ride back to Kigali," I said. "Oooooooohhhhh," they all said.

"So, I think I'm going to go with him."

"Be careful," Bridgette said. "Are you sure you know what you're doing?"

It was a good question. I barely knew this guy. But I had a good feeling about him. "I think so," I said and walked back over to Sam.

I felt a little tense during the ride back to Kigali. I hoped that with everyone talking, and joking, and laughing, Sam wouldn't notice. I did my best to be part of the conversation, even though most of it was in English. Giselle and Jean-Pierre did what they could to translate into Kinyarwanda for me. And Sam did what he could to translate into French.

I like Sam's friends, I thought. *I like Sam, too.*

We got to Kigali, and Sam started dropping people off.

Finally, it was just Sam and me, and we were headed for my aunt's house. I was thinking, *I like Sam, but I barely know him. I'm not so sure I want him to know where I live.* So, as we got close to Aunt Irène's house, I told Sam, "Uh, c'est ça! C'est ça!" (This is it! This is it!) I had picked a house about half a block away from Aunt Irène's.

Sam stopped his truck.

I pulled my bag out of the back, hugged him, and said, "Merci pour le…Qu'est-ce que le mot?" (Thanks for the …. What's the word?)

"Ride?" he said, in English.

"Ride!" I said. "Oui. Merci." I knew a few words in English.

"C'est rien," he said. (It's nothing.) "Oh, est-ce que tu connais The Piano Bar?" (Do you know The Piano Bar?) "Ici, en Kigali?" (Here in Kigali?)

"Oui."

"Si tu veaux me trouver, je vais souvent. Le band la? C'est magnifique!" (If you want to find me, I go there a lot. The band that plays there is great!)

"D'accord." (Okay) I said. I got out and slammed the door of his Land Cruiser. "Oh, pardon!" I said. (Sorry!)

"C'est rien," he said. "C'est rien."

I waved goodbye. But Sam didn't leave. I waved again. He waved back.

"J'attend pour tu d'aller dans votre maison," he said. (I'm waiting for you to go inside your house.)

"Oh non," I said. 'C'est bien." (That's okay.)

"Non-non," he said. "J'attendrai." (I'll wait.)

Damn it! I thought. *This isn't working!* Then I smiled and said, "Bon, d'accord…Encore, merci, pour le…ride." (Well, okay. Again, thank you for the… ride.)

We both laughed.

I kept smiling. Sam still wasn't leaving. *He's really going to wait until I go inside!* I thought. *Well …*

I went up to the door of the house that wasn't my Aunt Irène's, got out my keys, and pretended to unlock the door, thinking *I hope no one hears me and comes to the door!* I turned back to look at Sam, smiled and said, "C'est bon!" (I got it.)

"Okay," he called. "A bientôt." (See you later.) He drove off, finally, and I relaxed.

A woman opened the door. "Can I help you?" she asked.

I pretended to look at the house. "I'm sorry," I said. "I'm at the wrong house." I turned and started walking toward Aunt Irène's.

That night, as I was lying in bed, I couldn't stop thinking about Sam. I thought about every conversation we had had. I tried to remember everything he had said. I knew he came from America, but did he say where? Some of what he said in French I hadn't understood. What had he wanted to tell me, or were these conversations just small talk? I was a little obsessed.

A couple of days later I worked up the courage to go to The Piano Bar. As soon as I got inside, I started scanning the place for Sam, but I didn't see him. I was disappointed, but I was a little relieved at the same time. *Be realistic*, I told myself. *Just because you worked up the courage to come here doesn't mean that Sam's magically going to be here on the same night, at the same time.*

And you know what? It's early, and I'm in a bar. I might as well- Oh... I realized I didn't have any money to buy a drink.

So, I just sat at the bar. I kept scanning the room, but still, there was no Sam.

He was right about the band, though. They were great. The people in the bar were a combination of muzungus from the NGOs and locals. There was a lot of mixing going on as people were talking and drinking. A few people were dancing. Even those who weren't couldn't help swaying to the beat of the music.

Eventually it got to be late. I did a scan of the bar. *Still no Sam. It's fine.* I told myself. *I guess, for tonight, at least, it's not meant to be.* Still, I felt a little like I had failed, or had been stood up.

I was looking down on the way out of the club, and I banged my head right into the chest of a man who was on his way in. I looked up to see that it was... a guy I didn't know. He had a very annoyed look on his face.

"I'm sorry," I said. "I'm really sorry."

I kept trying to apologize. "I'm sorry," I was saying to the man's back, and so I wasn't looking where I was going. Then, when I turned around, I was face to face with...

"Sam!"

"Elise!" he said, smiling.

"Comment ça va?" (How's it going?) I asked.

"Ça va bien," he said. (I'm doing well.) "Actually, très bien." (Actually, very well.) I loved the way he combined English and French.

I wanted to say, "I'm surprised to see you here," but I had no idea how to say it in French, so instead I said, "Je ne savais pas tu serais ici." (I didn't know you would be here.) At least I think that's what I said.

But Sam said. "Pourquoi? Je vous ai dit que je viens ici." (Why? I told you that I come here.) He was smiling. I liked his smile.

I was smiling too, "Eh bien. Je suis très content… voir…tu." (I'm very happy to see you) or something like that.

"Bien, je suis très heureux… de… vous voir… aussi. Voulez- vous prendre une boisson?" (I'm very happy to see you, too. Would you like to have a drink?)

"D'accord." (Okay.)

I knew I had had enough to drink, and I had been feeling tired and ready to go home. But now I felt excited. I had butterflies in my stomach.

Sam and I got a table. We listened to the band. We joked. We had a few drinks. We even danced. I had heard that muzungus couldn't dance, but Sam was actually pretty good.

We had a really good time. I liked having his arms around me. He pulled me close. I put my head on his shoulder. I felt like I was floating. Sam felt so strong but gentle at the same time, very different from Benjamin, very nice.

Sam and I started dating after that. Each evening was better than the one before.

And then, one night, I went home with Sam. We slept together. It was so much different than anything I'd known before. Sam was kind, gentle and loving but also strong. Being with him was wonderful. I started getting a lot less sleep, but I had never felt so awake and alive.

The more time I spent with Sam, the less I spent with Benjamin. Benjamin was a jealous man. When he found out about Sam, he told me, "You tell me who Sam is! You point him out to me!"

"Why?" I said. "So you can hurt him? No, I don't think so." After that happened a third time, I didn't really feel like being around Benjamin anymore. I still had feelings for him, but Sam was really winning my heart.

I was spending a lot of nights at Sam's. When I would wake up screaming from my nightmares, he would hold me and comfort me. I would cry, and shake, as I told him about my dreams. But in his arms, as he spoke to me in his soothing voice, I would eventually relax and fall back to sleep.

Sam eventually asked me to move in with him. It felt like a big step. But I loved him. So, I did.

I started arranging things in the house the way that I liked, now that I was living there. But Sam had a maid named Margaret, who kept putting things back the way they had been. There was a bit of a power struggle between us. It wasn't easy, and I wasn't completely sure it was safe. But eventually, I had to put my foot down and establish that I was the lady of the house. I was thinking about asking Sam if he would fire her, but it was a complicated situation.

At that time, it was so inexpensive for NGO workers to hire people to work in their houses, and there was such a need for jobs, it was kind of expected for NGO workers to hire as many Rwandans as they could. So, even though Sam told me that he didn't make a lot of money, like a lot of NGO workers, he had a maid, and a cook, and a gardener. To Sam, it was a good thing that he was providing these people with jobs.

But Sam and I had very different views of the people who worked for him. Margaret was a Hutu. The gardener had been in the

Interahamwe and, for all I knew, still was. Every time I saw him with a machete, I wanted to walk the other way.

Sam had a guard for his compound, too, but his presence didn't give me any feelings of security. Just like Sam's gardener, the guard had been Interahamwe. I would find myself thinking, *Is this what we have to do now, to get on with our lives, just forget? Just accept those who killed our friends and family?* The killers were everywhere. When I'd bring it up with Claudine or any other Tutsi, the most common way for these conversations ended was, "Hey, what are you going to do?"

*   *   *

After I had been living with Sam for a while, I started both hoping and fearing that Sam was going to ask me to marry him. I definitely wanted him to. I loved him, and I knew he loved me. I often found myself imagining building a life with him and having children. But, at the same time, I wasn't sure that it was the time was right to marry him, or anybody, for that matter.

Sam was almost ten years older than me. He had been to university. He even had his master's degree. He had started his career. I, on the other hand, was 20, about to turn 21 and I had not gone to university. I still liked going out at night, staying out until two or three in the morning. Sam often couldn't do that. "I've got to get up for work tomorrow," he would say.

Sam told me that people in his kind of work didn't usually stay in the same place or even the same country for all that long. I had just gotten what was left of my family back. For the first time in my life, it felt like Rwanda might be turning into something new. I wanted to be there to see what it was going to become. But, I really loved Sam.

One night Sam and I were having dinner at a restaurant. He had been looking at me for the entire meal, and I had the feeling he was going to ask me something. Eventually, he put down his fork, took my hand, and said, "How about we get married?"

Part of me really, really wanted to just say "Yes!" and throw my arms around him, kiss him, and marry him, right then. But another part of me was really concerned that, if I married Sam, I would be defined from then on as Sam's wife and probably the mother of his children, that I would end up living in some foreign country, not able to see my family or my friends. I was concerned about the difference in our ages. I honestly wasn't sure which way I should go. Sam was still holding my hand.

I looked at him, and I was sure of one thing: that I loved him. "Well, okay," I said. "I guess so." It wasn't very romantic, but it was honest. I was happy, but I was also very nervous about the whole idea. "Oh, and Sam," I said. "You really need to talk with David about this!"

"I do?"

"Well, if my father was still alive, you'd need to ask him for his blessing. It's tradition."

"Oh, David is the, what, the ranking man in your family?"

"That's right," I said.

"Well, if that's what I've got to do, that's what I'll do."

Sam went to see David the next day.

"How did it go?" I asked Sam when he got back.

"Oh, fine," Sam said.

"Sam...?"

"Mm?" He was smiling.

I shoved him playfully, laughing. "Tell me!"

Sam's smile widened. His eyes lit up. "David has given his blessing."

"Oh, Sam!" I said, throwing my arms around him. We hugged.

This is really happening! I thought. I was so excited.

"So..." Sam began, "they gave me some... cultural training at CARE about Rwandan customs. And from what I understand, the marriage process here in Rwanda is... a little different than it is in America?"

"Yes," I said. "Now we do the dote."

"The dote," he said. "Right. And there's something having to do with cows, right?"

"Yes. You have to give my family cows."

"I have to give you cows. Right. How many?"

"Well, you have to work that out with the family."

"How much does a cow cost?"

"Maybe..." I told him the amount in Rwandan francs. He did the conversion.

"Huh," Sam said. "About two hundred American dollars." He was making a face like he was pulling off a bandage. "'Cause you know, Elise, I'm not a rich muzungu. I really don't make very much money."

"I know, sweetheart," I said.

"Okay. Good. Now, I understand I have to get an old man to... speak for me or something like that?"

"Yes. You have to find someone who speaks Old Rwandese."

"Is that different from Kinyarwanda?"

"A little," I said. "It's much more… distinguished."

"And he has to...speak for me at the dote?"

"Yes. He has to convince my family that you would make a good husband for me. And he has to negotiate the number of cows you're going to pay my family for me."

"Okay," Sam said. "So, this should be a man who knows me."

"Oh, yes. Of course."

"So, this needs to be an old Rwandan man who knows Old Rwandese, and who knows me."

"Yes."

"I think I know someone who can do that," Sam said. "And there are... three parts to getting married here, right?"

"Oh, very good, Sam!"

Sam just looked at me.

"What?"

Sam kept looking at me.

"It's good," I said. "It's good that you know this. Not a lot of muzungus know this stuff."

Sam smiled. "So, the first part is the dote. The second part is the... like the civil ceremony?"

"That's right," I said. "It takes place at City Hall."

"And that's the legal ceremony where you actually sign the wedding contract?"

"Seriously, Sam. I'm impressed that you know this."

"Well, I'm marrying into this culture, so I feel it's my business to know about it. And the marriage contract gives the woman certain...legal rights?"

"Yes. Well, you know that here in Rwanda sometimes a man will take more than one wife? I'm not trying to put any ideas in your head, by the way."

"I have no plans to have a second wife," Sam said. "I have no interest in a second wife. I have you. That's plenty." He hugged me and gave me a kiss.

"Well, good," I said. "But in Rwanda the dote is really the big deal. The marriage contract makes sure that if anything happens to the man, then the woman he legally married inherits everything. It keeps a second, or third wife, or any other woman, from trying to make a claim on any of the money or property. As long as the first wife, the legal wife, can produce the marriage contract, any dispute is over."

"Has it always been like that here?" Sam asked.

"Oh, yes," I said. "Since way, way back."

"And what about the actual wedding?"

"Well, you know. It's a wedding. We do it in a church."

"Well, sounds a little public, but if that's the custom here in Rwanda…"

"What sounds a little … Oh, ha, ha, ha, Sam. Mister Joker. No, the wedding, Sam. The wedding is what we do in the church."

"So, the dote is the biggest deal. Like a big party?"

"Biiiig party!" I said. "Yes. But it's much more than that!"

"There's like… some …theater to it, right?"

"What do you mean?" I asked.

"Doesn't like, doesn't someone from your family have to bring out other marriageable young women and say something like, 'Elise is our loveliest daughter. We couldn't possibly part with her for the number of cows you propose. Wouldn't you rather marry one of these girls?'"

"You have really done your homework on this, Sam," I said.

He smiled and shrugged. "And then I guess… David and I, right? have to pretend to haggle on the number of cows even though the number has already been set beforehand."

"Sam," I said. "You haven't gotten married here in Rwanda before, have you?" I pretended to pull away.

He pulled me close. "Pretty smart for a muzungu, huh?" he said, grinning. "I've…well, I've been asking around. I know other Rwandans, you know."

Then, suddenly I realized something else: "Mana we! Are your parents coming?"

"I actually think we should tell my mom *after* the wedding is over."

"Why?" I asked. I wanted to meet them. I wanted to know the people this wonderful man came from.

"Well, I've told you that my mom's in a wheelchair."

"Yes."

"Well, even so, she's a very determined woman. Like you."

"Oh, yes?" I said, smiling.

"Well," Sam continued, "even though she's in a wheelchair, I think if we told her before the wedding and the dote…"

"Yes…"

"I think she would try to make it here. And you know, it would be wonderful to have her here for the wedding, but there would be some major problems. I mean, most of the streets here are still, you know… dirt, and when it rains, this really isn't a place you can get around in a wheelchair, especially hers. It's a three-wheeled scooter, with little wheels. And she needs special bathrooms and… I just think it would be better to tell her… that it will be happening, but not when, and then tell her that it's happened after it's happened."

"I get it," I said. "Okay. Then that's what we'll do."

The next day Claudine called and asked me to lunch in one of the best restaurants in downtown Kigali.

"Sure," I said, but I thought I knew what this was. Claudine had never asked me out to lunch before. She and David must have talked. And as soon as I walked into the restaurant and saw that Claudine was sitting at a table with my Uncle Alexandre, and several other uncles and aunts, I knew that this was not just a lunch. It was a planning meeting, which was fine, great actually.

I had been thinking that Sam and I would plan and organize the wedding, but there really is a tremendous amount that goes into putting a Rwandan wedding together. And it really was nice that Claudine had stepped into the role of wedding planner.

"Elise!" Claudine called, in a sing-songy voice, with a big smile on her face. I walked over to their table and sat down.

"Well," she said. "Do you have something to tell us?"

"Like what?" I said.

"Something special? Having to do with Sam?"

"Um, he made me a really nice breakfast this morning. You know, he's a really good cook."

"Elise!"

"I'm getting there. And last night he asked me to marry him, and I said yes!"

"Everyone at the table acted surprised and congratulated me. Then it was right into: "Where are we going to have the dote? Who are we going to get as dancing girls?" and all of the other hundreds of other details that go into planning a dote.

"Sooooo, a rich muzungu!" Claudine said. "Well, I'm sure that we can count on him for say... ten cows." This was what I was *not* looking forward to.

"No, Claudine," I said. "He's really *not* a rich muzungu. You know he works for CARE. He's sort of like a priest. He really doesn't make very much money."

"Well," Claudine said, "how many cows do you think he could afford?"

"I don't know," I said. "Maybe… one cow?"

"One cow?" Claudine yelled. "One cow?! That would just be embarrassing! One cow! I'm not sure we should allow this marriage!"

"All right, all right," Uncle Alexandre said. "Let's just calm down." Uncle Alexandre was my oldest male relative, so, by Rwandan custom, he had the last word. "How about, Elise, do you think he could do… two cows?" he asked.

"Yes, Uncle Alexandre," I said. "I think he could do two cows."

"Two cows?" Claudine said.

"Look, Claudine," Uncle Alexandre said, "if a man, an educated man, an American, wants to marry Elise, and loves Elise. Elise, does he love you?"

"He does, Uncle Alexandre."

"And do you love him?"

"I do. I really do."

"There. You see? This Sam is a young man. He may not make much money now, but one day I'm sure he will. No, no, this is a good thing. Tell him two cows."

"Oh, thank you, Uncle Alexandre!" I said. "Thank you, Claudine! Thank you all, so much!" I hugged everyone, and we ate lunch, and continued planning the dote, and the civil ceremony, and the wedding.

We decided that the dote would be at Uncle Alexandre's house, both because he was my oldest living family member, and because he had the biggest house. When lunch was over, I went back to Sam's house to tell him the good news about the cows.

We called Sam's parents in America soon after that. I had never talked with them before. Sam had just started teaching me English. I was learning quickly, but I'd only been at it for about a month. I think any woman who was about to talk to her future mother and father-in-law for the first time would be nervous. The fact that I would only be able to speak to them in a language that I was very new to didn't make things any easier.

We called. Sam's mama and papa picked up. We told them that we were engaged. But, as we had planned, we didn't tell them that we were planning the wedding.

I tried to talk with them the best I could. There was a lot of starting and stopping and Sam translating. But even so, I could tell that Sam's mama and papa were really nice people. I was happy to have met them, even if it was just over the phone.

After talking with Mama Sam and Papa Sam (that's how we refer to people's parents in Rwanda, Mama or Papa and then the first name of the eldest son), I missed my mama and papa. I knew that the dote and wedding would be fun and meaningful, but without them there, it wouldn't be the same event that I had dreamed about as a young girl.

Keeping with Rwandan tradition, Sam went to meet with Uncle Alexandre. Afterward, Sam told me that it had gone well.

"And did you two talk about the details of the haggling at the dote?" I asked.

"We did," Sam said. "The old man who's gonna speak for me and I will offer two cows. And then we agree, and I give Uncle Alexandre the fake envelope that stands for the cash for the two cows, even though I gave him the cash today."

"Oh. Good. Yes. Right."

"And after we do that, then you and I are basically married. And then we party. Right?"

"Pretty much," I said.

"And does he actually buy cows with that money that I gave him?"

"Oh yes. And those cows and any babies that they have are mine."

"We don't have to keep them here in the house, do we?"

"No, Sam, all of my family's cows are out in a town outside of Kigali."

"Could we go visit them?"

"Sure."

"What if I wanted to sell one?"

"They're not yours to sell. They're mine."

"Oh," Sam said. "Okay."

When I got to Uncle Alexandre's house, on the morning of the dote, the workmen who had already put up a giant tent over most of the back yard were busy setting up couches and chairs for the three parts of the wedding party: my family, Sam's people, and the family elders, which, in this case, were Uncle Alexandre, Aunt Immaculée, Claudine, and

David. Other workmen were busy setting up folding chairs for all of the guests.

Claudine, Alice, and I, and the rest of the women and girls in the wedding party, lots of cousins and aunts and nieces, got our hair and makeup done. Then we all got dressed in our *mushanans*. The mushanan is the traditional Rwandan wedding dress: a silk wrap-around skirt with a matching sash that goes over one of your shoulders. Underneath we all wore leotards.

The tradition in Rwanda is that the bride doesn't appear until almost the end of the dote. Keeping to this, I stayed inside Uncle Alexandre's house, but there was a window that allowed me to look out and watch everything that was going on in the back yard. Aunt Immaculée left the back door open so that I could hear what was going on, too. I watched all of my family members and all of the guests arrive. I was starting to get nervous about where Sam was.

Just as the dote was supposed to begin, Sam finally arrived with his friends from work and an old man. They were all dressed in suits. Sam had a smile on his face. He did seem to be sweating a little.

Maybe he's just nervous. I told myself. I knew the old man Sam told me he was getting to speak for him, but the old man Sam had brought with him was someone I had never seen before.

The dote began, and the old man Sam had brought, who seemed to be a little drunk, began to speak, saying things about Sam that were good…but very general. "This muzungu is a good man. This muzungu is a strong man. This muzungu is a highly intelligent man." Strangely he never used Sam's name. He just kept referring to Sam as "this muzungu." And he went on like that for about fifteen minutes, naming all of the reasons why Sam and I should get married. Then Uncle Alexandre did the same for me.

Then Sam and Uncle Alexandre shared a ceremonial sorghum drink from a ceremonial gourd. And then it was time for the bridal procession. A line of girls danced ahead of me as I walked down the back steps of Uncle Alexandre's house and under the tent, up to where Sam and Uncle Alexandre were. Sam and I exchanged gifts, and then it was time for the dowry negotiation.

Uncle Alexandre stood and asked Sam how many cows he would offer for me.

Sam offered one cow.

"Elise is very beautiful," Uncle Alexandre said. "But there are other girls from our family we could offer you," and then several of my young female relatives of marriageable age in Rwandan wedding dresses came out and stood around Uncle Alexandre.

"You could have one of these, but Elise is our best daughter. If you want her then you should give us more cows." Again, this was just part of the show.

Sam offered two cows.

Uncle Alexandre pretended to consider this and then told Sam, "Two cows it is."

Then Sam gave the old man he brought an envelope, which the old man gave to Uncle Alexandre. And then, by Rwandan tradition, we were married. Legally, we still had to do the civil ceremony, and we still had to have the church service. Some people in Rwanda do all three in one day, but we decided to do them separately.

Then came the biiiig party. There was a lot of music and dancing, and wonderful food.

Later on, as Sam and I were dancing, I said, "Sam?"

"Yes?"

"The man who spoke for you, that wasn't the old man you know from CARE."

"No," Sam said. "He couldn't make it."

"What do you mean?" I said. "Where is he?"

"He was on his way here from Bugesera this morning, but there was a bridge that got washed out, and there was no other way to get from there to here."

"So," I said, pointing to the old Rwandan man Sam had brought, "who is that?"

"Oh. Well, since I found out about the bridge kind of at the last minute-"

"Yes..?"

"Well, Seth and I" (Seth was a friend Sam's) "started going into bars looking for old Rwandan guys, and every time we found one, we asked him if he spoke Old Rwandese. In the third bar we went into, we finally found one. Seth told him about the situation, and our... new friend, was only too happy to help. Especially when we told him that he would be our guest at the dote, and that there would be lots of free urwagwa there."

"So, you had no idea who he was?"

"Nope," Sam said, grinning. "I never even caught his name. And I'm pretty sure he never got mine."

"And that's why he kept referring to you as 'this muzungu' instead of 'Sam!'"

"That's right," Sam said.

We laughed, as we kept dancing, long into the night.

A few days later, Sam and I had our civil ceremony at the Kigali city hall. We had a little reception at Claudine and David's house afterward.

Sam was going to take his month of annual leave that May. He said we should spend it at his parents' house in America.

"That way you'll all get a chance to meet each other," he said.

We gave them a call to talk about it. Mama Sam suggested that we do the church wedding in America, in Sam's home town. We hadn't done our church wedding yet, and both Sam and I thought it was a great idea.

I was excited to be going to America and meeting Sam's family, but also, I was a little scared. I had never been out of Africa. I'd never been on a plane before. I didn't like the idea at all. It scared me.

But soon, there I was, on a big plane, at Kigali airport, ready to take off for Brussels. From there, Sam told me, we would get on a plane to Zurich, and there we would get on a plane to America. I was incredibly nervous. My heart was racing. I was sweating, and I think I might have been cutting off the circulation in Sam's hand, I was holding it so tight.

Every time the plane bumped or jiggled, as we rolled down the runway, I had to stifle myself to keep from screaming. Then the plane sped up. I was sure that going that fast was dangerous, and that we were going to crash before we even got off the runway.

"Mana we! Sam!" I said, trying not to scream.

"It's fine, Elise. It's fine," Sam reassured me. Then the whole plane tipped back.

"Sam!"

"It's fine, Elise. It's fine."

We kept going up and up and up and up. I couldn't believe we were going so high! I kept sneaking a look out the window, which would again make me say, "Sam!"

To which Sam would reply, "It's fine, Elise. It's fine."

I didn't want to make a scene. So, I just closed my eyes. I wished that I could fall asleep, but I just couldn't relax.

From time to time, Sam would say, "Elise, you've got to see this. It's beautiful!"

I would open my eyes just a bit and look at what he was trying to show me: Lake Kivu, or a large patch of forest or desert. What he was showing me was always beautiful, but still, the height we were at would make me say, "Oh, Sam!"

To which he would reply, "It's fine, Elise. It's fine."

I didn't know anything about America. I just knew that it was very far away, and very big, and that it was full of rich, happy muzungus.

Mama Sam and Papa Sam were wonderful. The wedding was wonderful, too.

We stayed with Sam's parents for a couple of weeks. Then Sam and I went back to Rwanda. Sam still had another seven months on his assignment there.

Our family's house eventually got un-booby-trapped, but I never went back there. There was no reason to, really. With no doors or windows and damaged as it was, no one could live there. Everybody in our family already had a place to live, so there was no real pressure for anyone to spend the money it would take to fix it. So, it just sat empty for a while.

I never went back to our old church during that time, either I just couldn't. Well, except in my nightmares.

Sam's next assignment was in Kenya, so we moved to Nairobi.

Over time, Sam's jobs took us all over the world. We had Paul and Imani, four years apart. Sam eventually got a job with the UN that paid well and continued taking us all over the world. We lived in a lot of beautiful places. Paul and Imani went to great schools. Eventually Sam got assigned to Washington, D.C. We bought a house near-by and lived there for a few years.

If you looked at my life from the outside, you would say things were going really well for me. And they were.

But I was still having horrible nightmares.

Chapter Eighteen: Going Home Again

I'm crouched down in our corn field, hiding from the mob that wants to kill me, thinking, *I AM GOING TO DIE! I AM GOING TO DIE! - **I AM GOING TO DIE!!*** I can hear the mob yelling and smashing the windows in our house.

But then those sounds start to die down, and I think I can hear Mama's voice! *But how could that be?* I wonder. *Mama doesn't come home from work for another three hours!*

And then, like a miracle, I hear it again. It really is Mama's voice! I can't quite make out her words, but her tone is unmistakable, soft, and steady.

"Eeeeyyyyy," I hear her saying again and again, using her soft kind of power to soothe the mob back into being a crowd, and then back into just our neighbors. I can tell by the tones, that Mama is talking to each person, making them feel better.

And then I don't hear anything, for what seems like a long time.

Finally, I decide to risk going into the house. I'm trying to be quiet, but there's broken glass everywhere and it crunches under each of my steps.

"Mama? Mama!" I call out in whispers. But there's no one there.

I open the front door as quietly as I can and walk outside. I can see that the compound gate is open a crack. I walk up to it and peek outside, terrified that someone from the mob will see me and start making the induru. But just like the house, the street is empty.

A fog has rolled in, covering everything. As I walk out into it, the fog gets thicker. *Where could Mama be?* I wonder. I keep moving forward.

The fog has gotten so thick now, I can barely see in front of me. I stumble over something. I look down, to see that it's the still-bleeding body of someone who looks like they've been hacked to death with a machete!

When I look up, the fog has cleared just enough so that I can see more bodies lying in the road in front of me. Gruesome, but I need to find Mama. So, I keep moving forward, through the fog.

Eventually I come to the large metal gate of another compound. *This is the gate to our church*, I recognize. It's been left open a crack.

I try to make as little noise as possible, as I push the gate open just enough for me to slip inside. And when I do, I see the church in front of me. The walls are pockmarked with bullet holes! There are bleeding bodies on the ground reaching toward it!

As I walk toward the doors to the lower level of the church, I remember overhearing Mama once saying that during killings in the past, Tutsis had taken refuge in churches and survived.

So, maybe Mama's inside, I think. I pull one of the doors open, and step inside. But I find that I'm stepping into a puddle of blood! I can see blood flowing from under the double doors that lead up into the sanctuary. *Is Mama up there?* I wonder. *Where the blood's coming from?* I'm scared, but I have to know!

I pull the doors open, and I'm hit by a wave of blood! I feel like I'm drowning in it!

I woke up screaming into my pillow, making almost impossible to breathe in. I turned over and took breath after breath, thankful to be alive. I found that I was drenched in sweat, that I was at home, in bed, in America, and that I was safe. "Oh, thank God!" I said.

I was alone, though. Sam was traveling for work.

As quietly as I could, I crept out of bed and down the hall, to Imani's room. *Still asleep,* I assured myself, looking in on her. *Good.*

Then I checked on Paul. He was still asleep, too. *Good,* I thought.

I tip-toed back to my room, closed the door, and sat on the bed, just like I had so many nights like this before.

I checked the time. *3:15 a.m.,* I thought. *Six hours later in Rwanda. Aunt Irène should be awake.*

"You would think that the further you get away from something in time, the more it would… I don't know, get better," I said, "or at least start to fade. But it's been, years, and years, Auntie, and I'm still having these nightmares all the time! And I think they might be getting worse!"

"Maybe you're not done with them yet," Aunt Irène said. "Or maybe *they're* not done with *you.*"

"What does that mean?" I asked her.

"I'm not sure, exactly," she said. "That's just what… I'm getting."

Aunt Irene was a little bit psychic. But psychics often speak in riddles. And I needed answers.

"Are *you* still having nightmares?" I asked Claudine.

"Sometimes," she said. "Not like you, though, I don't think. But I didn't go through all the things you did, Elise. I got out pretty early."

I had talked with Claudine on the phone a lot over the years since the genocide. I had told her just about everything.

"I don't know what to do," I said. "I mean, these nightmares are driving me kind of crazy. And when I wake up screaming, which is most of the time, it wakes up the kids. And I can tell that they're really scared. And then they ask me what's going on, and I do that same thing that Mama used to do to us. I tell them, 'Everything's fine' and send them back to bed."

"Well, they're little kids, Elise. What are else are you going to do, tell them that you're having nightmares about people who have been hacked to death with machetes, and worse, that you've actually seen things like that? I mean, if you're worried about screwing up your kids…"

"No. I know. I know. But doesn't it bother you that Mama and Papa are gone, and that we don't really know anything about their lives, or their… stories, because they never told us anything?"

"Of course it does. But, like I said, what are you going to do? It sounds like, right now, your biggest problem is those nightmares."

"Sam had me try therapy," I said.

"Hah!" Claudine laughed. "Therapy only works on muzungus."

"That's what *I* said. So, then he suggested that I write a book to, you know, 'get it all out of me' or something."

"Well, I don't know," Claudine said.

"What?" I said.

"Well, maybe you *should* write a book."

"Me? Write a book? I mean, Claudine. Come on. You've seen my writing. Even in Kinyarwanda it's not great. At all. In English?"

"Well, get someone else to write it for you."

"Huh," I said. "Actually, that's what Sam said, too. His brother's a writer. He's thinking about maybe asking him to write it."

"Okay. So…"

"You think?"

"Elise, you're in America now. Isn't that what people in America do? Something horrible happens to them, and then they write a book about it. And then the book gets turned into a movie, and the person becomes rich and famous by talking about the horrible things that happened to them?"

I imagined myself on a red carpet, in a sparkling dress, with all of the camera flashes from the paparazzi. That made me smile.

But then I imagined doing a reading from a book about my life, and I suddenly realized: *Then re-living the most horrible things that ever happened to me would be my job! Yeah. I'm pretty sure I don't I want to do **that**!*

But I kept having nightmares. And I kept waking up my kids with my screams. And I kept lying to them. And I kept not knowing what else to do.

I am in our church in Biryogo, slipping on the blood flowing down the ramp that spirals up into the sanctuary. I make it to where I can see into the sanctuary. Bodies are covering the benches and the floor, and everything is soaked with blood. In some places there are bodies piled on top of each other. I hear a muffled cry coming from underneath one of these piles. I rush over to it and start pushing corpses aside. And underneath is Nadine, our neighbor!

She reaches out to me and looks into my eyes. "Elise…" she says, but she's saying it in Mama's voice!

"No! **NO!!**" I am screaming, terrified. I feel like I will drown if I can't pull myself out of this. I'm struggling to wake up, afraid that I will die if I can't!

"Mommy, **MOMMY!**" I can hear Imani calling.

"**MOM!**" Paul is saying.

Paul was shaking me awake.

I got out of bed and hugged them. "I'm sorry," I said, over and over. "It's okay," I told them. "Everything's fine. Go back to bed."

But as Imani was turning to go back to her room, she turned and gave me a look that reminded me of something. Her look really stuck in my head. I couldn't stop thinking about it, and I didn't know why.

For hours, I tried to get back to sleep, but I just couldn't. Eventually I tried going to the bathroom and splashing cold water on my face, because that always relaxes me. Then, as I was toweling off, I caught a reflection of myself in the bathroom window.

I am five years old, lying in my bed. We have just saved Papa from being beaten to death. After we dressed Papa's wounds, Mama told us, "Everything's fine" and sent us back to bed.

I'm looking at my reflection in my bedroom window, thinking, *W... wait a minute. 'Everything's fine'? Well, that's... that's clearly not true. But Mama's saying it. So that means that... Wait, Mama is ... **lying** to me? So, I... can't... **trust** that what Mama says is true?*

And I realized: *That expression of... losing trust! In the person that you should be able to trust the most: your mama. I had on my face! That's the same expression Imani had on **her** face!*

Then I realized, *I'm doing that exact same thing to Paul and Imani that Mama did to me! And now they must be wondering if they can trust **me**! That's why Imani gave me that look!*

And she's... she's right! She shouldn't trust me. Because I'm lying to her! I'm lying to both of them! Just like Mama did to me! And it's led me... here. Miserable. Afraid to go to sleep. Lying to my kids, and right at the brink of having them feel like they can't trust me!

I don't want to pass that on to them! I can't! I want something different for them.

Then I thought about Mama. *She probably thought- Yes, of course, she **must** have thought that she **had** to lie to us, because we were in a time and a place where everything was about surviving. Surviving the next day, sometimes surviving the next **moment**! And in that place, at that time, that was the best she could do.*

Come to think of it, that's probably what her mama did with her. Maybe her mama, too. Who knows how far back? Well, yeah. That's the thing. That's exactly it! No one knows, because they all kept so many things from their kids! They kept silent about so many things that... I thought about Mama's life, about the story I had of her life. And I realized that because of her silence, I had so little that I could pass on to Imani and Paul! And that I had even less about Mama's mama! I had almost nothing to pass on, almost nothing that they could learn from. And I understood their silence … for them.

Then I realized, *But that's not the situation here…. and now. I don't have to worry about surviving the next day. We're safe. Well, saf**er**, anyway. So, I've been not telling Paul and Imani the truth... why? Out of habit? Or just because I don't want to deal with... well, all of... this? My God! By doing what Mama did to keep us safe, I'm actually hurting Paul and Imani!*

And I don't want to keep doing that, or what Mama did to me, or what her mama did to her! The problem is … silence. It's not... speaking.

*Claudine's right, though. I can't just sit them down and tell them everything, young as they are. But I guess, maybe there is... well, something I **can** do.*

I called Sam.

"I think we should call your brother," I told him.

"Really?" he said.

"I've got to do… *something*, Sam," I said. "And this seems like… what there is… to do. You know?"

"Okay," Sam said. "Good. When I get back, we'll call Philip."

"Okay," I said. "Well, I guess I'll let you try to get back to sleep."

"What about you?" Sam asked.

"Well, I guess I need to remember things, the stuff I've been avoiding. Actually, I've been finding myself doing that lately. The past couple of weeks. Especially at night. It's just … happening. All by itself. But now that I've decided to write a book, like that I'm not going to be battling myself to keep my past away," I said. "Who knows, maybe remembering things will actually help me get back to sleep."

"Okay," Sam said. "Elise?"

"Yeah."

"This is the right thing to do."

"Let's hope," I said.

The next day, when Sam got back, we called Philip.

"Hey," Sam said to Philip. "So, you know that Elise survived the Genocide, right?"

"Well yeah," Philip said. "Of course."

"And did you know that she had to leave her home before the genocide because there was this Hutu gang in her neighborhood that was harassing her?"

"I didn't know that," Philip said. "Tell me about that."

"See?" Sam said to me.

Then we told him all about the "Hey Rucumu" boy and the rock.

"Wow," Philip said. That's quite a-"

"And did you know that she had to flee to Burundi?" Sam went on.

"I didn't know that either," Philip said.

So, we told him about my going to Burundi and how I had to hide under a bed while a massacre was going on outside.

"This is fascinating," Philip said. "But, uh, why are you telling me all of this?"

"Oh, right," Sam said. "Well, Elise wants to do a book."

"Oh yeah?" Philip said. "That's great,"

"And we want you to write it," I said.

"Oh. Wait. Really?"

"Really," Sam said.

"Oh wow! I'm… w- I'm… I'd be honored to write that book."

So, a few days later, Philip started interviewing me.

It felt good to be doing something with my past other than trying to block it out. And it felt good to be getting my story down so that it would be there for Paul and Imani.

I never really looked forward to doing the interviews, though. It's not that I didn't like talking to Philip. I liked talking to him a lot. He turned out to be a really good interviewer. He was good at making it feel like we were just talking. And he had definitely done his research. There were many times when I would be telling him about something I'd been through, and he'd say something like: "Oh, that must have been when…" this or that "…happened," mixing my experience with his knowledge of historical events. That was all great.

What I didn't like was remembering all of the awful things I had been through and then the nightmares I would have every night after we did an interview.

One time, when Philip was interviewing me, he said, "You know, Elise, I can ask you all of these questions, and you can tell me what Rwanda looks like, and I can imagine it. But you know, what we really should do, if we can swing it, is we should go to Rwanda for a research trip, so I can see everything, and so you can show it to me."

"Oh." I said. "Yeah. No. That's a good idea. That's a really good idea. We should, um… we should do that." But thinking about going back to Rwanda caused this horrible feeling of dread, right in the pit of my stomach. I hadn't expected that.

Rwanda *was* home. I hadn't been back since I had left with Sam. But so many horrible things had happened to me there. Rwanda was the setting for all of my nightmares.

Even so, Philip *was* right. We really did need to go so that he could write the book. So, I agreed, and we booked our tickets.

It turned out that we were going to be in Rwanda during Christmas. In Rwanda, Christmas is mostly a religious holiday, we don't do the whole thing with the tree and the presents like people do in America. Usually, you just go to church and have a nice meal with your family.

I wasn't crazy about being away from Sam and the kids for Christmas, but my nightmares were getting worse, and I was getting less and less sleep. I had a feeling that there might be some sort of answer to all of this for me in Rwanda, and that if there was, I needed to find it as soon as possible.

*   *   *

As Philip and I drove through the streets of Kigali, during the first few days we were in Rwanda, I was amazed to see how much the country had changed for the better. Everywhere you looked you could see that things were improving. You could feel it.

It seemed like all of the roads were either paved or being paved. People had cell phones and computers. And everywhere you looked, people were smiling.

"So, Philip," I asked. "What do you think of Rwanda?"

"It's beautiful!" he said. "It's amazing! I didn't really know what to expect, but..."

"Grass huts?" I joked.

"Well," Philip smiled. "I don't know about that... but it definitely wasn't this. I mean, it's so... modern! Look at this. There are skyscrapers going up all over the place here in Kigali. Oh, and David" (David was a general in the RPF now. He was showing Philip around the country.) "took me on this trip to some place up north, and I saw this construction site on the side of the road. So, I asked him, 'What's going on there?' And he said, 'Oh, we're running fiber optic cable all over the country. We're building an internet hub here in Rwanda that's going to service all of Central and East Africa.' I mean, that's just mind- blowing! And do you know that they're building this station on Lake Kivu that's going to pump the methane up from the bottom of the lake that will run a generating station that's going to power most of the country, and that they're actually going to sell power to the surrounding countries?"

"I heard about the power station," I said. "It's really amazing."

"And, I mean, when I look around here, it just… it really kind of reminds me of Europe, the south of France, maybe."

"Really?"

"Oh, yeah. I mean, look at this highway we're on: That stonework those construction workers are doing on the drainage channels? That's going to last for, what? … a hundred years, probably. And look at all the cars and trucks. It's just… well, like I said. It's not what I expected."

Philip kept asking when we were going to go to Biryogo. Every time he brought it up, I was struck by that same horrible feeling of dread. Biryogo was where so many horrible things had happened to me. It was where all of my nightmares took place.

But I knew that seeing those places in Biryogo where the horrible things had happened to me was the main reason that Philip had come to Rwanda. So, after putting him off a number of times, we finally went.

I decided that the first place we should go was our old house. My family still owned it. We had been renting it out.

As we drove through my old neighborhood, the feeling of dread was back. My heart was beating fast. I could feel myself sweating. I felt like I needed to get out of the car.

"Are you okay?" Philip asked.

"I'm fine," I said, kind of automatically, I suppose out of habit, a habit formed in this place, of controlling my fear.

We drove up to the compound gate. I got out and knocked. I thought getting out of the car would make me feel better, but it didn't.

One of the tenants answered. I told her that I used to live there and asked if Philip and I could look around. She said it was fine.

I honestly wondered if this was going to be too much for me. I didn't know what was going to happen. The last time I had been here was right after the genocide, when the whole place had been shot and looted and boobytrapped.

Was I going to find myself in one of my nightmares, but with no place to wake up to because I was already awake? *Why are you doing this?* I wondered. But then, I found myself answering: *Hey, what else are you going to do? Turn around and go home?*

I drove the car inside the compound and parked.

"Did you grow stuff out here?" Philip was asking.

"What?" I said.

"When you lived here. You know, vegetables and stuff."

"Oh. Yes," I said. "We had some out here, in front of the house. We had some over there, beside the house." Now it was all just lawn. It felt kind of weird. "But we grew most of our crops out behind the house."

"Can you show me?"

"Uh… sure," I said.

As we started walking around the house, I kept walking, even though I wasn't feeling well, the same way I had kept walking when the teenage boy was walking behind me yelling, "Hey, Rucumu!" and I had to control the urge to panic that was raging inside me.

I showed Philip where we used to grow squash and yams. "And the corn?" Philip asked. "Where was that?"

Philip always does get right to the heart of things, I thought, as I felt my heart beating even faster.

"Are you alright?" Philip asked.

"I'm fine," I said, smiling, like a reflex. *Why am I smiling?* I wondered. *I'm not fine. More old habits*, I guessed, as Philip and I began walking over to where the cornfield had been, out behind the house.

"The kitchen was over there," I showed Philip as we passed the back corner of the house. My palms were sweating. The closer we got to where the cornfield had been, the worse I felt. Even so, I felt like something was drawing me on, toward it.

"Is this it?" Philip asked.

"This is it," I said. "Right here." Like the front yard, this was all just lawn now.

"This is where you hid out, from the mob?" Philip asked.

"That's right," I said. I felt like my heart was about to beat out of my chest. I had to control my breathing.

I think Philip could tell there was something wrong with me because he asked, "Do you want to leave?"

I was flashing back to crouching down, hiding from the mob, hearing their shouts and the sounds of glass breaking, convinced that I was about to be beaten to death. But even so, I found myself realizing, as I was saying it, "Actually… no. I'm … okay."

"You're sure?"

"Yes," I said. And I was. It was amazing. I was in the exact spot where one of my worst memories and one of my worst nightmares took place, and it was hard. It was stressful. But I was doing this! I was facing my past. My heart was hammering in my chest, but I wasn't losing my mind. I wasn't trapped inside one of my nightmares. And that felt… good, the way running does, where even though you're doing something hard, painful even, you're still doing it. I took a deep breath and let it out.

"Can I see the inside of the house?" Philip asked.

"Um, sure," I said, remembering my nightmare where I had come in from hiding in the corn, walking through the house with broken glass crunching under my feet, waiting to be discovered and then beaten to death.

But, after asking the tenants if it was okay if we came inside, I saw the exact opposite of my nightmares. The house actually looked fine.

"This is new," I explained as we walked through the indoor kitchen, complete with indoor running water. I walked through the dining area and into the living room. I remembered Mama hugging me and telling me that I had to go. Tears came to my eyes, but I found I was smiling, for real this time, like finally, I didn't have to guard myself against the tears and the feelings that came with them. I could feel my heart rate returning to normal.

"You seem better," Philip noticed.

"I am," I said. "I am better!" The feeling of dread seemed like it was going away.

I showed Philip all around the inside of the house. I showed him where my room used to be, and Mama and Papa's room. Then we went back outside.

I showed Philip where the outhouse used to be, and the avocado tree that Rose and I used to sit under.

"Could you show me the alleys you went down to get to Nyamirambo?" Philip asked.

"Sure," I said. "It's this way." I was feeling lighter now, after seeing that my nightmares about this place didn't actually exist here in real life.

We walked out of the front gate, then along the outside of the compound wall, to the alley that ran between our compound and our neighbor's. "This is it," I said.

"But you started by going over the back wall of the compound, right?" he asked.

"That's right," I said. "I didn't want anybody to see me."

"Well, no," Philip said. "Then you would have been right back where you were before your mother came home."

"Exactly," I said.

"So, can we go down there?"

"Sure," I said.

We walked into the alley. It was just as I remembered it, with tiny flowering plants growing from crevices between the bricks, and green moss growing on the shady parts of walls, and the roofs of the colorfully painted houses. I showed him the alley between our compound and the compound behind us. "That's where I went over the wall," I said.

"Wow, that's a really high wall!" Philip observed. "Wasn't it hard to climb over?"

"Oh, by that point I was pretty good at it," I said, smiling. I thought that going into the alleys was going to bring back that feeling of dread, but I was pleased to find I was still feeling okay. Confident even.

As we were coming out of the alley, I heard a man's voice calling, "Elise!"

I turned around to see an old neighbor of mine that I hadn't seen in years, since before the genocide.

"Gervais!" I said. I instantly felt sick to my stomach. All of the sense of relief I had been starting to feel instantly evaporated and was replaced with the feeling of dread but much worse than it had ever been before.

Gervais walked up to me and hugged me.

I wanted to vomit. Even so, I hugged him back. It would have been even more awkward not to. "Uh, Philip, this is, this is Gervais. He's … he's an old, uh…" *not a friend,* I thought. "Uh, neighbor of mine."

"Oh," Philip said, shaking his hand. "Nice to meet you."

"Uh, here," Gervais insisted, "Take our picture!" putting his arm around me.

"Okay," Philip agreed. He did.

"It's so good to see you!" Gervais said. He had the weirdest smile I've ever seen.

"It's, uh, it's good to see you, too," I said, automatically.

"Well, I've got to go," Gervais said, and left.

"Come on," I told Philip. "Let's go."

"Are you okay?" he asked. "You look… I don't know. You don't look happy."

I moved in close to Philip and lowered my voice. "He was one of the killers!"

"Oh my God!" Philip said, his eyes wide.

"And he's trying to act like everything's fine! Like everything's the same as it was before!"

"Yeah, I thought he had kind of a strange expression on his face," Philip said. "Maybe he feels guilty. I mean, he must. Right?"

"I don't know," I said. "Come on. Let's go."

"Yeah, yeah. Of course." Philip said.

As we were driving away, Philip asked, "So, Elise, your neighbor, Gervais. I mean… how do you feel about him? Do you… I dunno. Do you… hate him?"

"I don't … I don't know *how* to feel toward him." I tried to explain. "It's complicated. It's very complicated. We grew up together. We went to school together. I always considered him … a friend."

"And then... he killed people, Tutsis, that we both knew, our friends and neighbors! I mean, how could he *do* that? How could anybody do that? I don't know, Philip. I just don't know!"

"And then he wants to take a picture with me? He wants to put his arm around me? No! I don't think so! It's just..." I motioned with my hands like I was pushing him away. "No. No. He's pretending like he's a good person, but he's *not* a good person!"

On top of the intense anger I was feeling, I felt panicked, and I still felt sick to my stomach. And now I didn't know *what* to think about facing my past.

No, my nightmares hadn't come out of my memories to make me lose my mind, but just as I was starting to feel the slightest bit of confidence, a real-life person who had killed friends of mine just popped out at me. And now I was reeling into fear and anger and not being sure at all about anything. "Do you mind if we see the rest of the things in Biryogo tomorrow?" I asked.

"No, no. Not at all. Of course. That's fine," Philip said. "I can tell this has been an intense day for you."

But we didn't go back to Biryogo the next day. Or the day after that. Philip kept asking me when we could go to my old church there. I knew that he needed to see it to help him write the book, but I *really* didn't want to go.

I am in our church. Everything is drenched in blood. I'm pushing aside bodies, and underneath is Mama!

She reaches out to me and looks into my eyes. "Elise…" she says.

"No. **No!**" I screamed, fighting my way out of being paralyzed and into being awake.

"Damn it!" I said. I sat up and took my watch from the bedside table. *3:34,* I read. *Way too early to get up, but the last thing I want to do is go back to sleep!*

So, I didn't. I just lay there in bed until it was six o'clock.

Then I called Aunt Irène and told her about the situation and about my nightmares.

"So," she said, "you always wake yourself up at that point, right when your mama, or your Mama's voice, I guess, is about to say something?"

"It's like if I don't, I'll drown!" I said.

"But it's a dream, Elise. You can do anything you want in a dream. Maybe when you go to the church, in real life, you can imagine that you're in the dream and stay in it."

"But Auntie, I know what Mama's going to say! She's going to say she's so angry at me for leaving her and Gabriel to die! And I just don't think I could handle that! I think I would lose my mind!"

"Well, look at what's happening to you now, Elise. You told me that you're afraid to go to sleep? I mean, you have to sleep! Look, maybe in the dream your mama will do exactly what you're afraid she'll do, and maybe she won't. Either way, do you really want to keep going the way you are now? It just seems like… you need to do this, Elise. And you *can* do this, even though you're afraid.

"But that's… that's not what we do, Auntie!"

"That's not what your *mama* did-"

"-And now she's dead," I realized, completing Aunt Irène's thought.

"But you're not! Look, you said you want this book to be there for your kids, right?"

"Yes…"

"Well, maybe you tell Philip about this when it's all over, and maybe it ends up in the book. That would be good for your kids to read about, right?"

"I guess it would," I said.

So, the next day Philip and I went to my old church. My cousin, Justin, came, too.

As we drove into the church compound, the feeling of dread was back, and it was worse than it had ever been before. I could feel my heart pounding in my chest as we got out of the car. I could feel sweat running down the back of my neck.

"Are you okay?" Philip asked.

"I'm… sad," I told him. "I'm very, very… sad." That was true. But mostly I was terrified.

"My brother was killed right over there," Justin said, pointing to a large tree.

We all bowed our heads and were silent for a long moment.

Then, in a hushed voice, Philip asked me, "Is it okay to go inside the church?"

"Oh yes. Let's go in," I said, even though I really didn't want to.

The church had been built into the side of a hill. So, there was one entrance on the upper level that led directly into the sanctuary. And on the lower level, where we were, there was another entrance that led to two classrooms if you went straight, and a ramp that spiraled up into the sanctuary off to the left.

We were at the door to the lower level. As I put my hand on the door handle, my nightmares of having to hide in the closet inside one of the rooms were right there, in my head.

"Were there people hiding down here," Philip whispered, "during the genocide?"

"Oh yes," I whispered. "I heard they were the last ones to be killed."

Nervous and shaky, I opened the door, not knowing what would happen when I did.

We went into one of the classrooms. It was empty and quiet. There were just some tables and chairs. On the back wall, there was a door. It was the door to the closet from my nightmare. I walked up to it. I put my hand on the handle. I flashed for a moment to Albert, in my nightmare, trying to wave me into the closet which was already stuffed with people hiding from the killers outside, and the sounds of gunshots and the glass of the outer doors being smashed, and screams coming from the sanctuary upstairs.

I opened the door.

It was empty, except for a stack of chairs. *What did you think was going to be in there?* I thought. Of course, after the experience at my old house with Gervais, I didn't quite know *what* to expect.

We went back out into the foyer. There was another door. I knew that it just led to another classroom, but I couldn't help myself. I opened that door to find that there was a class going on inside.

"Sorry," I said to the teacher and closed the door. Then we turned to face the other set of doors.

"Does that go up to the sanctuary?" Philip asked.

"It does," I said, holding my hand above the door handle.

"What's wrong?" Philip asked.

"I'm…" I was so terrified of my nightmare that I was frozen. I couldn't even finish my sentence. *Nothing bad is going to happen to you*, I told myself. But I was seeing the blood and the bodies and Mama grasping my hand and looking into my eyes.

Then I remembered Aunt Irène telling me, "…you need to do this, Elise. And you *can* do this, even though you're afraid."

And so, even terrified as I was, with my heart was pounding, feeling sick to my stomach, I knew I had to do this, that there was nothing else to do. So, I put my hand on the handle, pushed the door open, and began walking shakily up the ramp.

"Elise, what's wrong?" Philip asked.

"It's just so… I'm just… so sad," I told him.

"Do you need to take my hand?" he asked.

It probably would have been a good idea, but I said, "No. I'm… I'm okay." I wasn't. At all. But I knew I had to keep going.

Each step up the ramp was harder than the one before. I was afraid I was going to vomit or pass out. Even so, I kept walking, step by hard step.

Somehow, I made it to the top of the ramp.

I was so afraid of what I was going to see when we came around the final bend. My nightmare was right there in my head: the bodies of hundreds of people who had been hacked to death, shot, and blown to pieces covering the sanctuary floor. Everything soaked with blood. Mama reaching out to me, grabbing me, and looking into my eyes and saying, "Elise…".

We rounded the bend, and…

There was no blood. There were no corpses. In fact, everything had been completely restored. It was beautiful. The colorful mosaic on the wall behind the altar was reflecting the sunlight that was flooding in through the big windows above the naive. The stained-glass windows had all been replaced.

There was a mass going on. Philip, Justin, and I filed in and watched, in silence.

"It's beautiful in here," Philip whispered in my ear.

"Mm." I agreed.

It turned out we had gotten there just as the mass was ending.

"Go in peace," the priest said.

I wish I could, I thought. But I wasn't feeling any peace. It was a huge letdown. I had been expecting that something important was going to happen here in the sanctuary. I was sure that all of my nightmares had been pointing me here. But here we were and …

nothing. Just a beautifully restored sanctuary and the end of a service.

What now? I wondered.

The doors were opened, and Philip said, "What is that?"

"What is what?" I asked, as the three of us were exiting the church with the congregation. And then I saw it. "Oh, that," I said. Across the courtyard from the church, there was a raised rectangle of grass with a knee-high cement wall around its base.

I had heard about this, but I had never seen it before, except in my nightmares. But as we walked toward it, I suddenly realized that, for me, this had been the real destination of this trip to Rwanda all along.

I broke into sobs. I was shaking. My heart was hammering in my chest. I was fighting not to hyperventilate. This was the worst yet. My body was screaming at me to drop to the ground, or turn back, or do anything not to keep going forward. But I knew in that moment that Aunt Irène had been right. This was something I had to do. I kept walking forward.

"This is the grave where the victims of the massacre are buried," Justin explained to Philip.

"This is a mass grave?" Philip asked.

"That's right," Justin said.

"And that's where Elise's mother is buried?"

"It is."

"Oh, my God!" Philip said. "Elise, I'm… I'm so sorry."

We all stared at the grave silently.

After a moment, Philip asked, "What's that written on the… well, I guess the… gravestone at the far end? Is it… French?"

Justin started to translate: "Even though I walk through the… what's the word? canyon? of the shadow…"

"Oh, yeah," Philip said. "I recognize that. It's from the Bible... It's from one of the Psalms... It's the, uh… oh, The Twenty-third Psalm. 'Though I walk through the valley of the shadow of death…'"

"Yes," Justin said. "'I… won't be afraid.'"

"'I will fear no evil... VICTIMS OF APRIL 1994'," Philip read. Then he turned to me. "That's amazing!" he said.

"What?" I said.

"Well, it's just… that's… that's you."

"What?"

"Well, that's… What's written on the tombstone. That's...That's you. I mean, that's what you did!"

"What?"

"You… you walked through the valley of the shadow of death."

"What do you mean?"

"Well, everything you went through," Philip said. "Growing up as a Tutsi in Rwanda in the years leading up to the genocide, Linda, the Interahamwe gang, the Hutu mob-"

"…When the Hutus were killing Tutsis in Burundi," I said, "and I had to hide under the bed, Amanda, the bandits on the road back to Bujumbura."

"The booby traps the Hutus left behind in Biryogo," Philip added.

I thought through all of the times I almost died, and I thought about all of the nightmares and all of the fear. Then I suddenly realized: "Oh! I walked through the valley of the shadow of death! Yes!" I said.

"That *is* what I did! And that's what I've been doing! I **have** been walking through the valley of the shadow of death! For all these years since!" And then I realized: *To get... here!*

"I don't know about 'I will fear no evil.' though," Philip said. "I mean, from what you told me-"

"Oh, I was afraid, plenty," I said. "Most of that time, actually."

"But you didn't... you know, I mean, I guess the important thing is, you didn't... let that stop you. Do you know what I mean? You kept going."

"Well," I said, "there were times, there were *so many times*, when I could have died, when, sometimes I've thought... I **should**... have died."

"Do you mean, like you're amazed that you didn't?"

"Well, that too, but... no. I mean, that..." I was crying again.

"What?"

"Well, Gabriel... died ... *for* me."

"What? No, he didn't. That's-"

"No, Philip, if I hadn't gone to my uncle's house in Burundi... Gabriel would probably be alive right now!"

"But he was-"

"That doesn't change the fact that..."

"...Oh," Philip said. "No. I guess... -Oh! Oh. Yeah."

"And Mama! I mean, why didn't I tell her I was going to Burundi, and why didn't I beg her to come with me?"

"Elise. Come on. I mean, you were a kid, You-"

"Again. Doesn't change the fact."

"Huh. That's…"

"So why should *I* be alive?"

"Oh," Philip said. "You mean, when so many other people died."

"Including Gabriel and Mama!"

"God, Elise. I'm sorry. I'm… I mean. I honestly don't know. What do you think?"

"I don't know. I don't know if there is a reason or not. I mean, Maybe I'm just lucky, you know? I mean, obviously unlucky, but lucky, like, inside of being unlucky enough to be born into a country that had a genocide, but inside of that? I mean, I'm very lucky to be alive."

"Oh yeah," Philip said. "It's amazing that you *are*."

"There were times, though, when... When I... I almost let myself die."

"What do you mean?" Philip asked.

"There were times, when I could have… you know, if I didn't do something, I would have died."

"Oh, you mean, there were times when, if you had just, sort of stood still. Like if you had stayed in Nyamirambo instead of going to Bujumbura?"

"That's right," I said.

"But you didn't."

"No," I said.

"You kept going."

"Yes."

"And now you're telling your story. You're… speaking."

"Speaking…" I said, nodding and letting it sink in. Then I said, "Claudine told me once that I couldn't keep my damned mouth shut."

"Well, maybe that's what kept you alive," Philip said. "I mean, if you had just done nothing, if you hadn't have picked up that rock-"

"The rock that almost got me killed," I said.

"Well, yeah. But it probably saved your life, too."

"Yeah," I said. "That's what's so strange!"

"I mean, if you hadn't thrown that rock, you probably wouldn't have left Rwanda."

"And now I'd probably be dead," I said. "Who knows? …" I knew I shouldn't have, but I couldn't keep a little laugh from slipping out as I motioned to the mass grave.

"Right?" Philip said. He was laughing a little too, but covering his mouth with his hand as he did it.

"I guess it's true," I said. "It's hard. But it's good. It feels good to… speak."

"It *is* good to speak," Philip said, nodding.

I looked at the mass grave stretching out in front of me, and I knew that I wasn't done. I was still very afraid, more afraid than I had ever been before. I felt like I was vibrating with fear, like I was about to leave my body. But I knew what I had to do.

I knelt down at the base of the mass grave, placed my hand on it, and closed my eyes.

My hand is in Mama's. I am terrified and crying.

She is looking into my eyes. "Elise…" she says.

"I'm sorry, Mama!" I am saying. "I'm so sorry! I'm…I know

you're angry at me, and I know you were trying to protect me by not telling me things, by staying silent. But things have changed. Now, for me, it's… It's good to speak! And-"

"Elise…" she said. "I see you. I see you all the time. I see how afraid you are of me, how you wake yourself up every time I try to talk to you. You think I'm angry at you? For, what? For being alive?"

"When I left you to die? Yes!"

But then I realize, Mama's not *grabbing* me. She's *holding* my hand, lovingly. And I realize that she isn't glaring at me with accusation. I realize that I'd never actually looked at her in any of my dreams. I was always trying to get away. But now that I am, and I can see that she's looking at me with love in her eyes.

"You didn't leave me to die!" she says. "No, no, no. Kobwa! No! When I sent you to Nyamirambo I *wanted* you to leave! I knew that there was nothing at home for you but death."

"I'm proud of you for getting yourself out of Rwanda. And I'm glad that you're alive! That's what I've been trying to tell you! And that you're right. You're completely right. Things *have* changed for you. You *have* gotten yourself to a much better place. That's what I wanted for you all along. And that you've found a husband, and had children, and that you're trying to do what's best for them. And I can tell you from experience, that sometimes it's very, very hard to know what that is. But the fact that you're trying to figure that out just … that delights me!"

"And I know that you're terrified of remembering your past. I know that there are so many horrible things in there that are hard to remember. But I want to remind you that it wasn't all just the genocide and all the horrors that went with it."

"What's that music?" Philip asked.

I opened my eyes. "It's the choir," I said. "They're practicing. That's a song we sing every Christmas."

"Oh, yeah," Philip said. "I guess with all the traveling and everything, I forgot. It's almost Christmas."

"Mm," I said.

"It's really beautiful!" Philip said.

And, as we stayed there, at the foot of the mass grave, Mama's grave, the choir sang on, and we listened. I heard the church doors opening as the last of the people were leaving. I looked inside the church, and I could hear Mama's voice again in my head. "Elise... Remember..."

We are all there, inside the church: Patrick, Robert, Alice, Gabriel, Claudine, Papa, Mama, and me. The church is flooded with sunlight.

We're all singing that song, the one we sing every Christmas. Everyone is smiling and swaying to the music. Papa, Robert, Gabriel, and all the other men in the church call out the low parts of the song, and Mama, Claudine, Patrick, Alice, me, and all of the other women and children respond with the high parts. Mama turns to me and smiles. She is glowing.

I opened my eyes and stood up. Then Justin, Patrick, and I stood there listening to the choir in the distance, singing the song that, with its depth, its beauty, and its high wailing harmonies, sounded like joy, and pain, and beauty, and love, all at the same time.

Author's Note

Before I began the research for this book, I thought I knew the story behind the Rwandan Genocide. It was the same story that most of the world had been told on the news: There were two tribes that lived in Rwanda, and, over the centuries, about once every sixty years or so, one of the tribes would go crazy and start killing the other one. Many of the news reports from the time described the Genocide using words like "chaos," "anarchy," and "insanity," and explained it with terms like "ancient tribal hatreds," "tribal warfare," and "…one more round of tribal bloodletting that has plagued this part of Africa for centuries." I think I remember one newscaster reporting from refugee camps in Zaire saying something to the effect of, "Like a plague, this madness has descended on this otherwise peaceful and beautiful country." In the news, the Genocide was mostly portrayed as being like a natural disaster: horrible, unstoppable, and incomprehensible.

But as I started doing the research, I found out that the modern history of Rwanda was almost entirely the result of African colonialism. As I learned more and more, I quickly went from seeing that the story everybody had been told about the Genocide was incomplete, oversimplified, and inaccurate, to realizing that it was actually a piece of propaganda, a cover-up, an out-and-out lie. It

383

became glaringly obvious to me that the Rwandan Genocide wasn't caused by "ancient tribal hatreds." Nothing could be further from the truth. Eventually my research revealed that, like the Holocaust in Nazi Germany, the Rwandan Genocide had been engineered by a small group of people who, in a quest for money and power, manufactured an "other" on which to focus all of their population's anger and frustration. In Rwanda, that "other" was the Tutsis.

I also found out that though the Hutus and the Tutsis have been referred to as "tribes" for well over a hundred years, it turned out that the term "tribe" isn't really appropriate to describe them.

Archeologists and anthropologists believe that the original inhabitants of Rwanda were a group of hunter-gatherers called the Twa. There are still Twa in Rwanda today, although they make up less than one percent of the population. There are two main theories about how the Hutus and the Tutsis came to Rwanda. One is that sometime over the last few thousand years the Hutus migrated there from western Africa, followed at some point by the Tutsis. Another is that both groups slowly migrated into Rwanda, little by little, over the centuries.

Traditionally the Hutus have always been farmers, and the Tutsis have raised cattle. Because cattle equals wealth in many parts of Africa, over time the Tutsis came to be the ruling class in Rwanda, even though they were, and continue to be, in the minority, making up only about 15 percent of the population, with Hutus comprising 84 percent. Some anthropologists believe that over centuries of intermarrying, sharing the same land, the same religion, and the same language, the terms Hutu and Tutsi transformed from tribal distinctions into social classes. Others theorize that Hutus and Tutsis were never actually two separate tribes, but were merely social classes that arose over time. In any case, before the arrival of white people in Rwanda, someone could be born a Hutu, accumulate cows, and eventually become a Tutsi. The inverse could happen as well.

Because it was surrounded by vast, dense rain forests, and because it is high up in the mountains, close to the center of Africa, Rwanda had never been colonized or even visited by white people before the late 1800s.

The Germans were the first non-Africans to arrive there, and when they did, they could not believe what they found: Rwanda was a complex, highly developed country. It had a government comprised of a monarchy and a complex system of chiefs and sub-chiefs at both the regional and village levels. There was even, for each village, a chief in charge of land, a chief in charge of cows (which were the main monetary system in Rwanda), and a chief in charge of the military. There was a legal and judicial system, a large, well-organized, highly trained military, and an intricate system of roads. There was a vast agricultural system, iron, pottery, textile, and basket weaving industries, an educational system, even a nation-wide bureaucracy of tax collectors. Rwandans had their own religion, philosophy, music, and poetry. And it had all been created by black people.

This simply didn't fit with the Germans' beliefs. It didn't fit with the beliefs of most Europeans or Americans at that time, either. Ever since the beginning of race-based slavery and European and American colonization of the rest of the world, the enslavers and colonizers had been trying to justify their horrific behavior.

In the early 1800s a new system of thinking referred to as "Race Science" had started to take hold in the Western World. In fact, "Race Science" was not a science at all; rather it used techniques that looked like science to "prove" something that white people wanted to be true: namely that white people were superior to all other races, and therefore their domination of other peoples was not only morally right, it was predetermined by natural law. And so, starting in the early 1800s and going right through the end of World War II, scores of white men in white lab coats were dispatched all over the world with scales, and measuring tapes, and calipers, to measure the cranial capacities, nose widths, and other physical characteristics of non-white people, to show how they were different from, and therefore inferior to, white people. This was the first in a long string of lies that would eventually lead to the Rwandan Genocide.

The Germans colonized Rwanda, but since the Rwandans were already running everything there so efficiently, they decided to rule it indirectly and support the Tutsis, since they saw them as superior to the Hutus. They kept the existing Rwandan government in place. The only changes the Germans made were that the actions of the king (or in Kinyarwanda, *mwami*), the chiefs, and the sub-chiefs had to be approved by the German colonial authorities, and that the mwami, or any of the chiefs or sub-chiefs, could be dismissed and replaced by the German colonial authorities. Whenever a Hutu group challenged the power of the Tutsis, the German government sent troops in to put that challenge down.

At the end of World War I, Belgium was given Rwanda as a war prize. The Belgians' style of ruling Rwanda was far more ruthless than that of the Germans. The Belgians continued the policy of viewing the Tutsis as superior to the Hutus and supporting them politically and militarily, but they pushed the ideas of separation between Hutus and Tutsis, and Tutsi superiority, much further, in several ways.

Historically, there had always been Hutu chiefs and sub- chiefs in Rwanda. The Belgians replaced all of them with Tutsis. They also codified who was a Hutu, who was a Tutsi, and who was a Twa. They issued ethnic identity cards and passed laws that required Rwandans to carry them at all times. Even though the Belgians began this designation process by measuring people's heights, and cranial capacities, and the widths of their noses, they soon found this too time consuming. Even with all of their supposedly scientific definitions, the Belgians often found it very difficult to determine exactly who was a Hutu and who was a Tutsi. So, it wasn't long before the Belgians started making this determination simply by the number of cows each family owned: If you had ten or more cows you were a Tutsi; if you didn't, you were a Hutu.

Much like they had done with what is now the Democratic Republic of the Congo, the Belgians essentially turned Rwanda into a giant plantation, producing mainly tea and coffee. They set up a system of forced labor for the Hutus. Like the Germans, they left the Tutsis in charge, but the Belgians put the Tutsis in a position much more like slave bosses than rulers of the Hutus. Though evil, this was a brilliant move on the Belgians' part. As the Hutus' anger about the horrible treatment they received in the plantations of Rwanda grew, they didn't blame their suffering on the Belgians. They blamed the Tutsis.

For decades after Rwandan independence, successive Hutu administrations pursued a policy of harassing, oppressing, and killing Tutsis in order to amass and cling to power, while the whole world looked on and did nothing. This was the direct legacy of Belgian colonialism in Africa. For decades, with no regard for the people they were subjugating, the Belgians were allowed to ruthlessly pursue every drop of profits they could squeeze out of their African Colonies. Here also, the world looked on and did nothing, as though there was no cost to this ruthless reaping of profits, as though there was no cost for the rest of the world's inaction. But the pain, the horrible suffering, the unfathomable loss that so many Rwandans and other Africans were forced to endure, that was the cost.

*   *   *

During my trip to Rwanda, I had a surprising experience. I went to the Kigali Genocide Memorial Museum. The first two floors are all about the Rwandan Genocide. It was intense to take in all of the images of killing and bodies, and people who were hacked to death, and people who their attackers thought had been hacked to death, but had lived. It was chilling to see actual Ethnic Identity Cards, and some of the actual weapons used during the Genocide.

But then I went to the third floor of the museum. The third floor was dedicated, not to the Rwandan Genocide, but to genocide in general. There were exhibits on the Armenian Genocide, the Genocide of the Kurds, the Nazi "Final Solution to the Jewish Problem." There was even a timeline that showed all of the recorded genocides since the late 1800s. And looking at this exhibit, I came to realize that since the late 1800s there has always been at least one genocide going on somewhere in the world.

As I read about each of the genocides, I realized that every single one of them, the Rwandan Genocide included, had in common some person or small group of people that stoked the hatred of one group for another in order to get something for themselves, whether it was land, or wealth, or power. And it was suddenly glaringly clear to me that no genocide just happens. They are not like plagues. They are not like natural disasters. They are created. They are man-made. They are intentional. They are engineered. And in almost every case the story that the person or group stoking the hatred puts out is a lie.

And all of this made me wonder when we, as a species, are going to start getting wise to this and stop falling for it.

Stories like this are difficult to take in. Even if we are only reading about it, the suffering of others is hard to stomach. And no one wants to believe that people are really capable of committing genocide, not intentionally, not deliberately. We want it to be an act of insanity, inexplicable, something that can only happen in a far-off land that we can't possibly understand.

But that's just denial, and it sets us all up for it to happen again and again. Genocide is part of who we are. This story shows how a whole country was being indoctrinated for decades in preparation for the Genocide. Tutsis were killed by their friends and neighbors. And though everyone would like to believe, "It can't happen here," wherever "here" may be, the thinking that leads to a genocide is always out there, in every country.

I'm not naïve enough to think that writing this book is going to end genocide. But maybe, someday, if enough people who have been through an atrocity tell their stories, and enough people read them, then little by little, people will see that we are capable of it and that it can happen.

Perhaps, by learning the stories of survivors, we'll be able to start seeing the warning signs of an oncoming genocide. Maybe the next time someone is stoking hatred in one group for another, we'll be able to start seeing through the lies, through the cover stories, and take a long hard look at who will benefit when the groundwork for the next genocide starts to be laid. And then, perhaps one day, we'll actually keep a genocide from happening. Then maybe we'll prevent another, and then another, until we understand that not only are we capable of committing genocide, we're also capable of preventing it, on a regular basis. What an accomplishment that would be for our species, like ending legal slavery, like landing a man on the moon.